# EYE OF THE WIND

## Jane Jackson

Published by Accent Press Ltd – 2013
ISBN 9781909335868

Printed and bound in the UK

Cover design by Madamadari

# Chapter One

Melissa looked along the gleaming mahogany table toward her father as his shaking fingers turned the crystal goblet round and round.

'The whole point of the battle was to prevent the merchant fleet reaching France. Yet though our navy captured six French ships of war and sank another, that American grain still reached Brest.' Francis Tregonning shook his head.

She wished she could find words that might comfort him.

Though there were only the three of them at table tonight he had taken particular care with his appearance. A square-tailed frock coat of dark blue brocade over a waistcoat of cream figured satin, breeches, silk stockings and buckled shoes, indicated respect for the sad occasion, but not mawkishness. She had aimed for similar effect with her own long-sleeved chemise gown of white muslin over lilac watered silk.

'Still.' He sighed, before raising his glass and swallowing deeply. 'I suppose it was a victory of sorts.'

'Indeed it was, Papa. Remember how the papers mocked the French for their poor ship-handling and gunnery?' She studied him, trying to hide her anxiety. A large man, sturdily built, his face had grown thinner of late. No longer full and firm, it had fallen into deep grooves. There were new lines around eyes sunk deep below his bushy brows. Beneath his elderly wig his cheeks were unnaturally flushed.

'Yes, but if Howe had renewed the action –'

'It still would not –' She stopped abruptly. But her father guessed.

'You're right, of course. It would not have made any

difference. Not to Adrian. The letter said he died early in the battle.'

Melissa reached across to touch her father's hand.

Glancing at her, he smiled wearily. 'I know. Talking about it won't change anything. And we have much to be thankful for. When I think of Sir John Poldyce ...' He shook his head. 'To have lost a son in battle is bad enough. But to lose another to a duel ... Such a waste. Yet life goes on. We go on.' He was silent for a moment, then raised his glass in salute. 'To Adrian.'

'To Adrian,' Melissa echoed, glancing at her mother over the rim of her glass.

Emma Tregonning's hand trembled and she barely wet her lips before setting down her glass. In her half-mourning of lavender glazed cotton worn over a quilted silk petticoat of paler hue, she looked as small and fragile as a bird. Puffed white gauze filled the low neckline of her bodice, hiding a now non-existent bosom. Her world might have collapsed with the loss of her son, but she still clung to standards. Her brown hair, beneath a small lace cap, had been carefully dressed in curls and gathered into a low chignon at the back. But over the last 12 months the silver threads at her temples had broadened into wings.

Aware of this poignant anniversary, Mrs Betts had taken special pains with the meal. Melissa was relieved to see her father eating, though she doubted he was truly aware of what passed his lips.

She felt slightly ashamed of her own robust appetite. But, having that morning ridden out to the farm to collect this quarter's rent, then later taken a long and furious gallop to try and dispel the inevitable frustration of her aunts' visit, she had come down to dinner ravenous.

Her mother was finding it harder to cope. As the butler leant down to serve her a portion of salmon in a lemon and Madeira sauce with steamed asparagus tips, Emma raised her hand in refusal.

'Lobb, please tell Mrs Betts how much I appreciate her efforts, but I find I have little appetite this evening.'

Exactly a year ago, on 1st June 1794, her firstborn son, a

second lieutenant on one of His Majesty's frigates, had been killed in action against the French.

Melissa had been shocked and saddened when the news came. It still grieved her to think she would never see him again. But, ten years her senior, Adrian had gone away to school when she was only three. George, two years younger, had followed his brother to school, then into the navy. Duty had sent them to far-flung corners of the globe, making their visits home rare and brief. So to her, growing up virtually an only child, they were strangers.

Though she loved them, for they were her brothers, her strongest feeling toward them was gratitude. Had they chosen to enter the family business instead of the navy, her life would have been far less fulfilling. She would also have been less of an embarrassment to her mother and the rest of the Tregonning family.

'Mama, I didn't get a chance to tell you earlier. I received a letter from Robert this morning.' It was nearly two months since his last. But he had warned her at the beginning that even if his duties allowed him time for writing letters, he was rarely ashore to post them, and would have to rely on a passing packet-ship.

Emma's head came up and her eyes, washed of colour by the ocean of tears she had shed, brightened briefly. 'That's nice, dear. What does he say? I don't suppose –'

'No, Mama.' Melissa was gentle, hating to disappoint. 'He didn't mention George. But as Robert is in the Mediterranean with Admiral Hotham's fleet, and George is in the West Indies with Admiral Jervis, it is very unlikely their paths would cross.'

'Has Robert been in action?' Francis asked.

Melissa nodded. 'On 14th March. He says they took two French warships.'

Francis straightened in his chair. 'That's more like it. Vice-Admiral Hood shattered the French navy in '93 when he burned Toulon dockyard and captured 15 French frigates. If our commanders will keep up the pressure, the French have no hope of building ships fast enough to replace those captured or

3

sunk.'

Though Robert's descriptions of British encounters with the French were always carefully phrased, Melissa's imagination had created its own vivid images of war at sea, fuelled by articles in the newspapers and snatches of male conversation overheard at assemblies. She visualised the chaos and carnage. Officers directing sweating men toiling at thundering guns, all about them noise and smoke, the acrid stench of gunpowder, spars falling, canvas and rigging shot away, and the deck gritty with sand strewn to give bare feet grip on a deck slippery with blood.

Robert's letters had given her an understanding of what Adrian had faced. But she could picture all too clearly how he had died. Despite the warmth of the summer evening, her skin tightened in a shiver. She gave herself a mental shake. Such thoughts achieved nothing. Yet, though Adrian had been her childhood hero, she was finding it increasingly difficult to remember his face.

This had worried her terribly. So much so that, one day, when Dr Wherry had been visiting her mother, she had drawn him aside as he was about to leave. It had taken her a moment to screw up her courage, for it seemed such a dreadful admission. But to her enormous relief he had told her it was perfectly natural and no cause either for shame or alarm.

'Please.' Emma raised her napkin to her lips then replaced it on her lap. 'Might we talk of something else?'

'Oh, Mama, I'm so sorry.' Melissa was guilt-stricken. Though Emma had tried to handle her grief with the dignity befitting a gentlewoman, her increasing ill-health was an indication of how desperately hard she had taken Adrian's death. Melissa turned again to her father.

'You must be pleased with progress on the new packet, Papa. When I was at the yard yesterday Tom was saying how well they are getting on. But he's becoming concerned about the wood store. It's –'

'Yes, all right.' He lifted a hand, fending her off with a weary gesture. 'I'll organise something. There's just been so much to think about recently.'

Unease feathered across Melissa's mind like a cat's paw of wind on still water. He was tired. He was concerned about her mother's health. With the first anniversary of Adrian's death imposing additional strain, it was not surprising he should have become vague and forgetful in recent weeks.

'Mama, what do you think we should name her?'

'Who?' Emma blinked.

'The new packet-ship.'

'I don't know.' Emma raised a nervous hand to the gauze at her throat. 'Won't the Post-Master General name her?'

'He's only responsible for naming those the post office pays to have built. Isn't that so, Papa?'

Francis nodded. 'But this one is being paid for with private money. As we hold the largest number of shares in her, then you, my dear –' he smiled down the table at his wife '– should have the honour and privilege of choosing a name for her.'

Emma covered her mouth with her fingertips. 'Goodness. What if I choose the wrong name?'

'If you choose something you like it will be perfect.'

'Melissa.' Francis Tregonning sat forward, linking his hands on the polished table. 'My dear –'

'What your father is trying to say –' Emma broke in sharply '– is that while your interest in the shipyard and estate are truly commendable, it is time you were thinking beyond them, to marriage.'

'Why, Mama? Truly, I would much prefer to go on helping Papa.'

'And you've done a wonderful job of it,' her father rumbled. 'I don't know how I'd have ... Especially after ... But there are certain things even you ... Melissa, the business needs a man at the helm.'

'It has one, Papa, you.'

'I'm not as young as I was. And the truth is it's more than I can manage.'

Melissa caught her lower lip between her teeth to stop the denials spilling out. She had guessed as much, though she had been unwilling to recognise it. If her father too had come to the realisation, then it would be both patronising and dishonest to argue with him. Though hating to see him forced to acknowledge his failing powers, she must accept the reality.

'Is there not some other way we might deal with this? Is it really necessary that I marry?'

Emma gazed at her daughter with a quizzical frown. 'I don't understand; why are you so set against marriage?'

'I'm not, Mama. But of the men who have shown interest in me, each in his different way has left me in no doubt that I should consider myself fortunate to have his attention. Nor can I feel flattered to receive an offer from an impoverished baronet who makes it plain that it is my dowry rather than my person that attracts him.'

Emma's expression was sympathetic. 'I understand, my dear. But that is the way these things are done.'

'I know, Mama. I have learnt –' how painfully she had learnt '– not to expect romantic declarations. But I do feel I deserve more than mere tolerance just because I happen to be – different. When – if – I ever meet a man who sees beyond what Sir William chooses to call my freakish height, a man who values me for myself, then I will be happy to marry. Until then, I would much rather –' She broke off, aware of how selfish she sounded. 'Is it really so urgent?' She watched her mother's struggle to find the right words.

'My dear, you are now one-and-twenty. You have been four seasons out in society. Your Aunt Louisa was saying only this afternoon that there is talk you haven't *taken*, that you will soon be considered unmarriageable.'

'Dear Aunt Louisa,' Melissa murmured. 'So kind, such sensitivity.'

'She does mean well, Melissa. She believes we have a right to know what is being said. If we are not aware, we cannot hope to quash such cruel gossip.'

'I'm sorry, Mama, truly I am. But to have to sit in silence and listen while my aunts discuss my future – and as for Aunt Sophie suggesting Lord Stratton as a possible suitor, a man I have never met, and do not wish to –' Melissa struggled against rekindled anger. 'A perfect match indeed. I cannot imagine why she should think so.'

'You did not give her a chance to tell you,' her mother pointed out.

'I certainly did not! Mama, how could she even speak his name? After what he did.'

'I agree, dear. It was quite wrong of her.'

'I know she had no high opinion of me, but to imagine I would even consider ... His father must have powerful friends indeed.'

Emma looked puzzled. 'I'm sure he has. But –'

'I would think far better of the Marquis of Lansdowne had he made his son stay and face justice instead of helping him flee the country.'

'We don't know that he helped –' Emma began.

'Oh come, Mama. With his elder son a semi-invalid and the succession at stake? Of course he helped.'

'When I was a girl –' Emma toyed restlessly with her napkin, the snowy starched linen now creased and crumpled '– duels were fought all the time. Of course, we were not supposed to know. Such matters were not considered suitable for a lady's ears, even though it was most unusual for anyone to be actually killed.'

'Someone died this time,' Melissa reminded her.

Emma sighed. 'It's such a sad business for both families. Clearly Lord Stratton would be quite unsuitable. Besides, he is the *younger* son. I only mention this in passing, my dear, but do you think you might consider the possibility of his elder brother?'

'Mama!' Suddenly, and quite inappropriately, Melissa giggled. 'Have you no heart? What would the poor frail Earl of Roscarrock make of me?'

'Mmm, perhaps not,' Emma reluctantly allowed. 'Though I must say, to see you a countess would have been truly ...' She sighed. 'Well, if it is not to be, and I am sure you are right, surely there must be someone who –'

Melissa lifted one shoulder in a tiny shrug. 'I'm too tall, Mama.'

'That's nonsense,' Emma scolded, looking to her husband for support. 'Tell her, my dear.'

'Your mother's right, Melissa. Though I admit you are somewhat above average height for a girl, that is not –'

'Papa, at six feet in my stockings I am a freak.'

'No, Melissa, I will not have you say so.'

'I *tower* over most of the men I meet.'

'But you are also a young woman of admirable qualities, as well as one of great social accomplishment.'

'I do play cards well. And so I should, for that is how I spend most of my time at assemblies.'

Francis frowned. 'But you are an excellent dancer.'

'Thank you, Papa. Though I love to dance, I rarely have an opportunity to do so. Men simply do not like partners taller than themselves. They like to feel protective.' She pulled a wry face. 'It would take more imagination than most men possess to view me as fragile or in need of protection.'

'Such men are fools, and not worthy of you,' her father said gruffly. 'No man was ever blessed with a better daughter. I don't know how I would have managed –' He broke off, looking away.

'Oh Papa.' She laid her hand briefly on his forearm. He was not a demonstrative man, but she knew he loved her, and she wanted him to know how much his love and approval meant.

'A good marriage will ensure your place in society. Melissa, your mother and I want you to be happy. You know I value your help in managing the estate and the yard. I see no reason why that should cease. Though when children start to come along … Still, that's for the future, eh? In the meantime, the way the war is going, we should be expanding the yard to meet the demand for new ships. I'm getting old, and I'm tired. Expansion means even more work. And though I have the utmost faith in your abilities, I know, and you do too, that you could not handle it on your own. Please, for my sake, and your mother's, will you think about what we've said?'

'And go to the assemblies?'

His face creased in a weary smile. 'Are they really such a bore?'

Knowing she had no choice, Melissa forced a smile as she lied, 'No, Papa, of course not. Perhaps I have been too choosy.

But you are the standard by which I judge the men I meet, and I find it difficult to settle for less.'

'Now don't think you have to rush into anything. All we want is that you keep an open mind.' He looked to his wife for confirmation.

Emma nodded her agreement. 'Truly, dear, we want you to be happy. And for a woman the greatest chance of happiness in society lies within the married state. So please do think about it.' She touched her napkin to her lips once more. 'If you'll excuse me, I think I'll retire.'

Noting the twin patches of colour high on her mother's cheekbones and the glitter in her eyes, Melissa rose immediately and went to her mother's side.

'Oh Mama, why didn't you say you were unwell? Do you think it's another cold?'

'I do feel a trifle feverish, dear. This afternoon was something of a strain. But they do have our interests at heart.'

Melissa did not believe that for a moment. Could her mother really not see what lay behind the concern of her sisters-in-law? Or was she defending their motives to spare herself more heartache? If so, who could blame her? But Melissa had no doubts whatsoever that her happiness mattered not a jot to her aunts.

They did not approve of her involvement in the shipyard or estate matters, and wanted her married off as soon as possible. Who she married was immaterial to them. In the meantime their only concern was that her activities should not in any way reflect on their families, or damage their own children's marriage prospects.

'Come, Mama, I'll take you upstairs.' Drawing the thin arm through her own, Melissa led her mother from the dining-room.

'But what will you do for the rest of the evening?'

'I shall sit and talk with Papa.'

'But he's going into Truro.'

As her mother's voice grew shrill with anxiety, Melissa realised it was important to get her settled as quickly as possible. The day had taken more out of her than any of them had realised.

'Oh Mama,' she teased, gently pressing her mother's arm; there was so little flesh on the fragile bones. 'I am not a child needing to be amused. I have plenty to keep me occupied. Now stop worrying.'

Handing her mother into the capable and comforting hands of Addey, her childhood nurse and now her personal maid, Melissa went to her own room. She had no desire to remain indoors. The cloud had cleared to reveal a beautiful evening. She would take a stroll across the fields above the woods.

From her closet she took out a light shawl fringed and embroidered in silk. Closing the door, she caught sight of her reflection in the cheval glass. Suppressed emotion from the discussion with her parents had left shadows in her green eyes. Though it had been overcast that afternoon, riding without a hat had deepened her skin's golden tint. She shrugged. What use was a porcelain complexion when you stood head and shoulders above most of your acquaintances?

Tilting her head, she surveyed her image with critical objectivity. Riding kept her figure slim and firm, though perhaps her shoulders were wider than most from controlling a succession of big hunters. Yet she would have looked, and felt, ridiculous mounted on one of the light-boned hacks favoured by her contemporaries.

For dinner she had released her hair from its confining ribbon, allowing it to cascade loose down her back: a fashion that pleased her in that it demanded little time or effort.

Raven black, glossy, and naturally curly, her hair was a source of intense envy and annoyance to her female cousins who derided their own fair colouring, claiming their delicate complexions would have shown to much greater advantage against dark hair. Why, they demanded unanswerably, had she been blessed with what would have been of far more use to them? It was so unfair.

Why indeed? With an ironic smile at her reflection, Melissa turned away. Quickly changing her satin slippers for ankle boots, she swung the shawl around her shoulders and went out.

Crossing the paved terrace, she skipped down the shallow stone steps onto the gently sloping lawn. At the bottom, she climbed over the fence with speed born of practice and a desire never to be caught in such an unladylike act.

On the far left of the field, where the fence bordered the carriage drive, several horses grazed in the long shadows cast by the avenue of slim Cornish elms. She set off at an angle across the park, passing a massive horse chestnut decorated with candle-like flower spikes. A large bough, dense with leaves, lay on the grass. It must have come down after last week's storm. It was a rare summer that didn't see at least one great branch broken off by the weight of rain in the foliage.

She hesitated, wondering if she ought to check the woods to see if any more trees had fallen. But it was too late tonight. In any case, the wet spring had produced so much new growth her light muslin gown would never survive the twigs and brambles. She would try to get down there in the next few days.

She walked on, thinking over all her parents had said. As their only daughter she had a duty to make a good marriage. Yet since entering society, she had not met one man she wished to her own fault. They had not told her how they had arrived at this conclusion, merely scolded her for her arrogance in denying what to everyone else was perfectly clear: that considering her *disadvantages*, she was fortunate to receive any gentleman's addresses. It was not just her height that told against her, her impertinence in involving herself in matters considered men's business was both unseemly and unnatural.

But the idea of marriage without love or respect, and at the very least some shared interests, was something she could not contemplate. And how could she respect men who considered intelligence in a woman a handicap? One would-be suitor had actually prefaced his proposal with this statement. Another, whose horsemanship she admired, had confided that she would suit him well for she reminded him of his favourite brood mare.

In making their declarations, neither had given even the smallest consideration to her feelings. Yet both had been startled then aggrieved by her polite but firm refusal. Why had they assumed that because, in the words of Tom Ferris, the yard foreman, she was "some 'andsome great maid", she could not feel hurt? Why should sensitivity be the prerogative of small, doll-like young women, who simpered prettily, and fluttered their eyelashes above their fans, playing the coquette as they gazed up with tilted heads?

Melissa sighed. It was impossible, unless you were an acrobat, to look coquettish when the top of your partner's head only came up to your chin.

About her feet, bees droned lazily amid purple clover. Magpies *chacked* and clattered, and high overhead a buzzard soared in effortless circles.

Her brothers had never shown the slightest interest in the estate. She, on the other hand, had since childhood followed her father about like a shadow, never happier than when riding with him over Bosvane's farm to collect the rent, or discuss yields and the new season's planting.

Down in the creek beyond the woods she glimpsed curving mud banks gilded by the lowering sun and the narrow seep-water channel winding sinuously between them. The faint mournful cry of gulls rose and fell on the breeze. The boatyard was not visible from here, but she knew every inch of it.

She loved watching progress on the bigger ships under construction, and seeing small boats leave with repairs completed, replaced by others with weather damage or rot that needed attention.

Her aunts found such interests incomprehensible, besides revealing a singular lack of decorum. In vain, Melissa protested that, having regularly accompanied her father since she was a child, the men were used to her presence and showed no sign of discomfort. She was always greeted with smiles and treated with respect.

And how else, her aunts had demanded impatiently, would the men have dared to greet their employer's daughter?

Their carping had strengthened her resistance. To her delight, her father had taken her side: his enjoyment of her company outweighing family disapproval. Then, after Adrian died, what had begun as pure enjoyment continued out of necessity.

As her father's exhaustion affected his concentration, she had found herself acting as a messenger between him and Tom

Ferris. She had delighted in her increased responsibility for it had given her a sense of purpose and reassurance of her worth, something she craved even while she despised herself for seeking it.

Born into a life of privilege, her every material need met, she had received an unusually broad education for a girl. Her intelligence, courage, and love of horses had forged a bond between father and daughter; a bond strengthened by their shared involvement in the estate and boatyard.

She walked on across a sloping hillside dotted with clumps of bright yellow gorse that smelled of melted butter, and mounds of thorny brambles. The boundary hedge was a tangle of wild roses, deep pink ragged robins, delicate froths of Queen Anne's lace, and white loops of convolvulus. On the far side of the creek, a hay field rippled in the breeze like water. Next to it, bright green ripening wheat was sprinkled with scarlet poppies.

A cloud of rustling starlings dipped and swirled across the sky, heading for a far pasture, while overhead, swallows swooped and darted, feeding on the wing.

Retracing her steps, Melissa paused on the terrace, inhaling the sweet fragrance of honeysuckle cascading over the stone balustrade as she watched the huge fiery orb of the sun sink behind distant wooded hills. Clouds edged with molten gold blushed rose, then darkened to lilac and purple in an aquamarine sky.

The wind dropped. But as the sun disappeared, Melissa felt a stirring of air against her face, like cold breath. Her skin tightened in a shiver and she felt a moment's unease. Dismissing it as reaction to a tiring and emotionally fraught day, she drew her shawl more tightly around her then turned and went into the house.

Lying in bed, the muslin curtains drawn back and wafting gently, she gazed through the open window at the half moon. She found herself thinking of Robert. They had met at an assembly. A friend of her brothers from naval college, he had been introduced to her as Lieutenant Bracey, of His Majesty's ship *Defence*.

The following week they had renewed their acquaintance at a card party. She had beaten him three times at whist. Blaming the distraction of her beauty, he had asked if he might request her father's permission to write to her when he returned to his ship. Her father, she recalled with a wry smile, had been delighted to agree.

She had found Robert pleasant, though a little stilted in his manner. But she was used to that, for people seemed to find her height intimidating. Yet she was at heart reserved, even shy, though good manners demanded she make a deliberate effort to be outgoing and put others at their ease.

Fair-haired, blue-eyed, and with a tendency to plumpness, Robert had nevertheless proved light on his feet. Dancing with him had been very enjoyable, not least because he was only a few inches shorter than her. But there had been no tug of attraction.

Though she enjoyed receiving his letters, she had to admit to a greater interest in his descriptions of life aboard a 74-gun battleship than in his increasingly frequent assertions that he missed her. These, she was sure, were occasioned more by prolonged separation from female company than by any particular attachment to herself.

No, she could not imagine marrying Robert. Or any of the other men she had met at the assemblies. Yet surely there must be someone, somewhere, who would see beyond her freakish height? A man who could command her respect and her love? A man to whom she could give her heart?

# Chapter Two

Gabriel woke with a start, his heart racing, disoriented by the darkness and the fact that he was out in the open. He lay perfectly still, only his eyes moving as he fought panic and tried to remember where he was. As looming shapes, more solid than shadows, resolved themselves into trees and broken stone walls, a wave of relief left him sweat-drenched and shaking. It was true then. Thank God. He was back in Cornwall.

Three days ago he had been chained to the wall of a French prison, too exhausted by pain even to raise his head when the gaoler's daughter arrived with food. Her hasty, whispered instructions as she released him had kindled both flaring hope and the sickening dread of another betrayal.

With his larynx crushed, the flesh of his throat raw and infected from the too-tight iron collar, speaking had been painful. But he had forced the words out, his voice a rasping croak.

'Why would you help me?' he had managed in the Breton dialect swiftly acquired to enable him to move about, barely noticed, in the dockyards of Brest and Lorient.

Swiftly binding the terrible wound with the kerchief still warm from her bosom, she had hissed, 'Zis Bonaparte is a godless butcher. 'E is as much our enemy as 'e is yours.' Bretons, she reminded him, were Celtic like the Cornish, sharing a similar language and a tradition of smuggling. Gabriel was well aware that as well as the usual cargoes of brandy, wine, and tobacco smuggled out of small Breton ports and transhipped to Cornish fishing smacks, the free traders frequently carried secret information, a compromised agent, or an escaped prisoner back to England. Indeed, he had entrusted them with his own dispatches, knowing as he did so that he was making their already risky ventures truly dangerous. The skipper of the small boat had shrugged off Gabriel's concern, saying simply that they lived in dangerous times.

No Breton had been involved in his capture, Gabriel would swear to that. But if he had not, by a careless word or action, somehow given himself away – and he was certain he had not – then how had it come about? Only one possibility remained: he had been betrayed. But by whom? No one in Brittany had known his true identity, or why he was there.

Pushing to the back of his mind the question that had gnawed at him for 52 terrible, pain-racked days, he eased himself upright. Every muscle protested as he rubbed his bearded face then raked calloused hands through the thick mane of black hair that fell in tangled curls to his shoulders. His own mother would be hard pressed to recognise him. He shook his head. Family and loyal friends believed Lord Roland Gabriel Stratton to be abroad. They were anxious he remain so. All were aware that if he returned to England he would hang. That alone was sufficient incentive to remain hidden.

However, he had another, even more pressing reason for retaining his new identity: his need to discover who had betrayed him. Not only for his own satisfaction, but also to warn those who had sent him of the possibility of treachery. Neither his family nor his friends had known of the work he was doing in France. For his instructions – from the highest government circles – had been given to him the night he left. But someone other than himself, Lord Grenville, and Sir John Poldyce, the Foreign Secretary's spokesman and aide, had known. Or had somehow found out, and then betrayed that discovery to the French.

Now he was back in Cornwall he needed a new name. "Gabriel" was virtually the only part of his old life he could safely claim. For a surname he would use Ennis, one of his grandfather's forenames. He could imagine the long-dead earl's reaction: one corner of the thin mouth quirking in dry amusement as the saturnine brows rose.

Stabbing pains in his stomach reminded him of his immediate needs. Food first. Then he must find some means of making this roofless, tumbledown ruin watertight. The gauzy halo surrounding the moon warned of a coming change in the weather.

Wrapping spare shirt and breeches in the thin blanket, a parting gift from the gaoler's daughter and his only possessions apart from the dagger on his belt, he tucked the bundle behind a tall stand of thistles in a dark corner and covered it with several large stones. Then, after making his way carefully back to the path and scooping a few handfuls of water from the small, clear spring that bubbled from the base of a steep bank, he set off through the woods.

As he followed the overgrown path upriver, he noticed several fallen trees. Some leant at crazy angles, still supported by other trees or their own broken boughs. Two had crashed to earth: snapped roots, exposed on the underside of the huge plate of earth, gleamed white like splintered bones.

To his left and far below, he glimpsed moon-silvered water and wondered if the little boat he had stolen from Falmouth was lying stranded on a mud bank, or adrift in the Carrick Roads. Though unavoidable, he still regretted the theft, and hoped boat and owner would eventually be reunited.

The trees sighed softly, their leaves whispering secrets to the gentle night breeze. Something pale and silent suddenly swooped across the path just above his head. He froze, heart hammering. Reason told him it was only an owl, but instant clammy sweat glued his shirt to his lacerated skin, and the sudden dryness of his mouth warned of nerves stretched to snapping point.

Food would build up his strength. His back itched intolerably, but it was a welcome discomfort as it indicated the welts were healing. He adjusted the grubby cloth covering his throat. That wound, and those on his wrists left by the iron manacles, would take longer.

It was almost a year since he had left Cornwall: a year during which he had lived on his wits and a knife-edge. The last six weeks he refused to think of, for that way lay madness.

He needed time and a safe haven in which to recover. Also unless he wished to starve, he had to find work: a job where, despite his imposing height, he would be just one more pair of hands.

Then, though it would not be easy, and might take considerable time, he intended to find out who had betrayed him. When he did …

A sudden rustling made him stop. Something small and furry darted across the path and into the undergrowth. Letting his breath out slowly, he walked on, his heart pounding. A short while later he became aware of a new sound. Stopping again, he listened intently, recognising the humming of the wind in ships' rigging. He couldn't be far from the boatyard he had seen from the water.

A faint trail, possibly a badger track, angled down from the main path. Gabriel followed it through the tangled undergrowth. The trees ended abruptly at the edge of a low earth cliff. Below it, the stony foreshore was strewn with débris, and a line of seaweed marked the reach of the high tide. Dropping quietly to the shingle, Gabriel stood back against the earth overhang, and peered upstream. Beyond the boatyard, a small village straggled along the side of the valley. But the dark blue of night had begun to fade to the grey that heralded dawn. He did not have much time if he wanted to avoid being seen by an early-rising fisherman or farm worker.

Threading his way between the beached boats, he moved stealthily up through the yard and on to the deserted street. He heard faintly the thin wail of a fretful baby. Further along, loud snores issued from a half-open upstairs window. In the distance, a dog barked furiously for several seconds, then yelped and fell silent. On the opposite side of the street stood an inn, separated from a terrace of cottages by the dark mouth of a narrow alley. After a swift glance in both directions, Gabriel darted across the rough road, silent as a shadow despite his size. Never in his proud, arrogant, impatient youth had he dreamt he would one day owe his life and freedom to stealth and self-effacement. But learnt swiftly and of necessity in France, both were now second nature.

Once in the alley, he felt his way along the wall and around to the rear of the inn. Avoiding a couple of empty barrels, he almost tripped over a wooden bucket lying on its side near the back door. Picking it up, he sniffed warily, relieved there was no pungent reek of slops. Setting it quietly on one of the barrels, he drew his dagger, inserted the point just below the widow catch, and slowly eased it up. Sheathing the dagger, he inched the window open, and climbed in, gritting his teeth against the dragging pain of his scars.

He stood perfectly still, listening for a nervous footstep, the creak of a floorboard or a loose stair. But the silence remained undisturbed. He was in the kitchen. The stone shelves of a walk-in larder held a joint of cold beef, several loaves, a ham, four pies, the remains of two roast chickens, a basket of eggs, and a large jug of milk.

Mouth watering, Gabriel cut himself a slice of beef and stuffed it into his mouth. He had eaten at the best tables in England, but no meat had ever been so welcome or tasted so delicious. While he chewed he cut several more slices, then moved on to the ham. Peering under a muslin cloth, he hacked off a wedge of cheese. Wiping his blade, he returned it to its scabbard and scanned every surface, hoping he wouldn't have to open cupboards or drawers. A gleam of white caught his eye and elation curved his mouth briefly. It was so long since he had smiled it felt strange and unnatural.

From the pile of linen he took two napkins and an old sheet, clean but worn and frayed: ideal for bandages. Wrapping the meat in one napkin and the cheese in another, he hesitated over the eggs then left them: too difficult to carry. Instead, he selected the smallest loaf and one of the pies. Dipping his finger into a glazed dish, he sucked. Cornish butter had a flavour all its own, but would quickly turn rancid in the June heat.

He moved on to check the contents of other pots on the shelf. To his astonishment and delight, one of the small stone jars contained a large chunk of honeycomb. He had seen honey smeared on wounds to cleanse and heal them. It would be an ideal salve for his throat and wrists. Skirting the table to the stone sink, he picked up an almost new bar of rough soap, and took a china mug from the dresser. He would have given a year of his life for a flask of brandy, but dared stay no longer.

Piling everything into the centre of the folded sheet, he tied the corners together and lowered the makeshift sack carefully out of the window. He followed, leaving the window slightly ajar. Someone would be punished for not locking up properly.

At least the missing food could be blamed on an opportunist thief. He hoped his need would not result in some poor kitchen maid being turned off without a reference. A year ago, such a thought would not have crossed his mind. But this past 12 months he had walked in another man's shoes, and lived far removed from the life he was born to.

Gathering up his harvest and the bucket, he paused at the alley entrance, then slipped across the road and down through the yard to the beach.

Back in his hideout, Gabriel unfastened the sheet and divided the food roughly into three equal portions, keeping the pie for his next meal. Drawing his dagger, he hacked thick slices off the loaf. Bread would help fill his empty stomach and make the ham and cheese go further. Leaning back against the wall, he savoured the first wholesome food he had eaten for weeks. Though he was ravenous, he forced himself to eat slowly. He'd seen starving men bolt food down only for their stomachs to reject it, or to be crippled with violent pains. He could afford neither.

Replete, he took the china mug to the spring. Draining it, he filled it again and, back within the tumbled walls, he soaked another of the napkins and wrapped it around the one containing the remainder of the food to keep it cool. After he had piled stones around the food to protect it from foraging animals he lay down, propping his head on the makeshift pillow of his spare clothes, intending to plan his next move. But within moments, weakness and exhaustion overtook him, and he fell into oblivion.

Melissa was shaken out of a deep sleep by a hand gripping her shoulder. It seemed only minutes since she had closed her eyes, for she had lain awake for a long time. But as she turned over and blinked up into Addey's face, creased with anxiety beneath a large frilled mob cap, she was immediately alert.

'What's wrong?' She raised herself on one elbow.

'You'd better come,' her mother's old nurse blurted. 'She don't look right to me.'

Throwing back the bedclothes, Melissa pushed her feet into slippers and grabbed the wrapper that lay across a tapestry chair. She was already halfway along the landing before she had finished tying the sash. Addey hurried along in her wake.

'I stayed with her till she went to sleep, then I thought I'd better get some rest myself. The poor dear soul needs looking after. If it isn't one thing 'tis another with her just now. I can't help but wonder if doctor do know what he's doing.'

Melissa didn't waste her breath arguing. Addey knew perfectly well that Dr Wherry, having lost his own son in a hunting accident, had a special sympathy for Emma Tregonning, and took particular care over her treatment. But in her anxiety for her mistress the old nurse needed someone to blame.

Looking small and lost in the huge four-poster bed, Emma Tregonning was as white as the rumpled sheet except for the hectic flush of fever across her cheekbones. Her eyes were closed, her brows puckered, and her head moved restlessly on the lace-trimmed pillow.

Melissa laid the back of her hand against her mother's forehead and was startled by the heat. 'Mama?' she spoke softly. 'Mama, are you in pain?'

Emma's eyelids quivered but did not open. 'George?' she muttered. Melissa picked up her mother's thin hand. It burned against her palms. Twin tears rolled from beneath Emma's closed eyelids. 'Where are you? Why don't you write?' Her breathing was shallow and harsh.

Melissa heard a muffled mewing sound behind her and turned to see Addey's eyes brimming in sympathy as she wrung her hands.

'If he've gone too, it'll break her heart.'

'Stop it, Addey!' Melissa whispered sharply. 'As he's so far

21

away there could be any number of reasons why his letters haven't reached us. We'll probably receive several all at once. Instead of thinking the worst, let's concentrate on making Mama more comfortable. Fetch some water and bathe her hands and face. As soon as I've dressed, I'll send John for the doctor.'

Later that morning, Melissa preceded the short, wiry figure downstairs.

'Your mother has influenza,' Dr Wherry confirmed her suspicion. 'I've seen four cases in the past two days. All are people your mother knows. If they have visited, she might have caught it from any one of them. I'll leave you some Peruvian bark and calomel, and James's Powders.'

As she glanced over her shoulder, Melissa's eyes were level with the doctor's as he paused on the stair above hers. 'She seems very restless. Is there anything else we can do to make her more comfortable?'

His shoulders moved in the faintest suggestion of a shrug. It was not lack of interest, Melissa knew, but frustration with the limitations of his weapons in the fight against illness and disease. 'A sponge bath with tepid water might help bring down the fever. Ensure she takes plenty of liquid, something bland, like lemon barley water.'

Melissa nodded quickly. 'Addey's already making some. It's always been her standby. Whenever I was poorly –'

'A rare occurrence as I remember.' The doctor's brief but kindly smile drew an answering one from her.

'Indeed. All I remember of those times is the jug of lemon barley water beside my bed. Addey will have it ready at any moment. What about food?'

'No meat. Only light and easily digested dishes. But don't worry if she declines them. She may have no interest in eating until after the fever has broken, which might not be for a day or two.'

Melissa indicated the drawing room. 'May I offer you coffee or a glass of Madeira?'

Dr Wherry shook his head. 'Most kind of you, my dear, but I have a long list of calls to make. So, much as I'd like to, I cannot stay. Please give your father my regards. I had thought to see him. But it's of no consequence.'

'I know he'll be sorry to have missed you. He had urgent business in Truro this morning, and left early.'

About to speak, the doctor changed his mind, simply nodding and giving her another brief smile as he settled his hat firmly over his eyes. Then, turning to his horse, he fastened his bag to the strap, heaved himself into the saddle, and gathered the reins. With a nod to the stable boy who released the bridle and scurried away, he looked down at Melissa.

'If he finds himself in Truro again tomorrow, ask him if he'll call and see me. Nothing to worry about,' he reassured. 'I'd just like a word.'

Raising his hat, the doctor turned his horse and trotted off down the drive.

Watching him for a moment, Melissa wondered what he had been about to say. Then she wondered if she should have mentioned her own concerns about her father's forgetfulness and preoccupation, the lost weight, and his air of exhaustion. Yet they were not exactly signs of illness, and might easily be attributed to his grief at Adrian's death: grief he had suppressed in order to support her mother.

Though lately he had relied on her to do the routine visits to the farms and boatyard, he was not sitting at home idle. Indeed, this past ten days, when he was not closeted in his study, he had ridden several times into Truro, whereas he usually went only once or twice a fortnight.

The first anniversary of Adrian's death was bound to be a difficult time. In a week or two all would be easier. Meanwhile, rather than waste precious time and energy on fruitless worry, she would be better employed attending to household matters, looking after her mother, and giving serious thought to the problem of finding a suitable husband.

Gabriel jerked awake, dry-mouthed, his heart thudding. But this time his disorientation was brief. The angle of the sunlight slanting through the trees told him it was late afternoon. He lay for a moment watching a cloud of midges dart and spiral in the golden shaft. Then he stretched, wincing, hoping his aching muscles would loosen once he got moving.

Food and rest had restored him, and there was much he must do in the few remaining hours of daylight. His main task was to roof at least one end of the shack before the rain arrived. But in order to do that he first needed to raise and level the two standing walls.

Ignoring the renewed hunger that urged him to eat again – supper must wait until it was too dark to work – he swallowed a mug of water from the spring, and set to.

He was careful to take stones from beyond the back wall, or from inside among the nettles, so that disturbance of the undergrowth in front would remain unnoticed should anyone unexpectedly come by on the path.

After his first effort collapsed he tried a different approach: layering and overlapping large stones with smaller ones, careful to ensure he maintained the slight inward slope of the lower half. Then he filled in the gaps with bits of rubble.

Heedless of cuts, grazes, and trapped fingers, he worked until the sun was low and all sounds from the yard had stopped. Washing the blood from his hands, he drank more water, sawed off another thick slice of bread, and wrapped it around the last of the cheese.

Then, chewing as he walked, he set off along the path in the direction of the village. He had no intention of showing his face there yet. There were things he needed. And the most likely place to find them was in the vicinity of the shipyard.

Passing the fallen trees again, this time in daylight, Gabriel saw that though some were casualties of recent storms, others had been down far longer. He did not understand why valuable timber was simply being allowed to rot. Judging by what he had seen already, these woods, right behind the shipyard, must be full of oaks. Who owned them? Why was such an important and much-needed resource being so shamefully neglected?

It was six years since the ordinary people of France, driven to despair by high rents, the rocketing price of food, and oppression by a nobility and clergy who cared nothing for their suffering, had vented their rage in a bloody revolution. It was now two years since King Louis, aged 39, had lost his head to the guillotine, and Bonaparte had declared war on Britain.

To defend her territories and attack the French, Britain needed a strong navy. The navy needed additional ships. Prime Minister Pitt's decision to allow private yards to build the smaller frigates had incurred the Navy Board's disapproval. But the move had released the royal yards to concentrate on building larger warships, and on repairs to those damaged in battle.

But a shortage of wood meant Britain had to import what she needed, and that meant running the gauntlet of Bonaparte's blockade; risking ships and men the country could ill afford to lose. Yet there must be enough oak here in these woods to build a dozen ships.

A short distance from the buildings and quays of the yard, Gabriel waited under cover of the trees until he was certain the men had all gone home, then dropped down onto the stony beach.

The stretch of shingle was a scavenger's paradise. Here he found torn and stained sail canvas, broken spars, an axe-head, and a filthy iron cooking pot. It was missing both handles but seemed free of holes. He pulled a tangled length of frayed rope from beneath the seaweed. Some ancient chunks of tarred oakum would burn long enough to dry out green or damp wood.

Tying everything but the cooking pot together with one of the ropes, he hoisted his hoard up into the shelter of the trees. Returning for the pot, he also scooped up several handfuls of coarse sand. In the French shipyards, lacking soap, and fearing for his health, he had discovered that sand would scour the filthiest pan clean.

The mellow light of a summer's evening filtered through the leaves as he retraced his steps up the trail to the main path and back to the small stone ruin. This, he guessed, had once been a hide either for a gamekeeper, or for preventive officers needing a secret lookout to watch for smugglers.

Fastening sail canvas around the spars, he roofed half the shack, adding branches from one of the fallen trees as additional cover. As the leaves died the camouflage effect would lessen. But at least the extra weight would stop the canvas being torn off in the event of further gales. With the roof secure, he began scouring the iron pot with sand moistened with water from spring.

Suddenly the corners of his mouth quivered. If his valet could see him now. Berryman had always taken great pride in maintaining, regardless of provocation, the aloof, slightly supercilious countenance he considered appropriate to his position. The state of his master's clothes and person after a day on the hunting field, or a night in town, had provided many a stern test. Even his legendary composure would surely crumble at the sight of his lord performing the tasks of a humble scullery maid.

As thoughts of home threatened his hard-won detachment they were ruthlessly suppressed. Gabriel's features grew bleak. After rinsing the pot thoroughly, he refilled it with water and returned to the shack.

Night had finally vanquished day. Though the summer evening wasn't totally black, it would be dark enough to hide any tell-tale drift of smoke. Anyone around to smell it would be as much a trespasser as himself. For it was only too clear these woods had not been properly managed for some time.

Needing dry wood for his fire, he ignored the twigs on the ground, and instead broke off pieces from inside an ancient and hollow oak. This would burn hotter and produce less smoke than a damp or resinous wood.

Pulling his tinder-box from the pocket of his spare breeches, he cleared a small space on the shack floor of twigs, grass, and leaf litter. Then, pushing a handful of frayed oakum into the pile of dry oak bits, he struck flint and steel, blowing very gently until the sparks erupted into a tiny flame that caught, flared, and curled hungrily around the matted fibres.

Feeding more wood onto the flames he was soon able to add a couple of thicker chunks prised from inside the log. As soon as they had begun to burn, he placed the iron pot on top. Smothering a yawn, he pushed himself to his feet, broke enough dry branches from nearby dead trees to keep the fire going for a couple of hours, then carried the bucket to the spring and filled it.

As the water began bubble in the pot, Gabriel unbuttoned his filthy shirt. His nostrils twitched. God, he stank. Pouring the boiling water into the half-full bucket, he reached for the bar of soap and, using one of the napkins as a sponge, he began to wash. Drying himself as best he could, he stripped off his breeches, drawers, stockings, and boots, and completed his makeshift bath.

The combination of cool night air and residual weakness made him shiver but it felt good to be clean again. Pulling on his breeches and spare shirt he wrestled his boots onto bare feet and returned to the spring for more water. While waiting for it to boil he ate the meat and potato pie and stared into the flames.

After washing his linen and shirt, he hung them on a branch to dry. There was only one more task to be faced: one he did not relish but dare not put off any longer.

Tying his hair back with some twisted strands of hemp fibre, he removed his shirt once more. Carefully unwrapping the wet and filthy bandages from his wrists, he dropped them into the flames where they hissed and burned.

The binding around his throat took longer to remove as the discharging wound had matted beard growth to gauze. Gritting his teeth, he pulled it free. Averting his gaze from the dark stains of blood and putrefaction, he flung it into the fire, unable to suppress a shudder.

In the firelight he examined the deep abrasions on his wrists, relieved to see new pink flesh beginning to form. He wished he could see his throat, then was immediately glad he could not.

Bathing the wounds in clean hot water, he patted them dry, then covered and bound them once more with strips torn from the stolen sheet and liberally smeared with honey. By the time he had finished his hands had begun to shake and he cursed his feebleness.

He drew up his knees and rested his head on his arms, fighting the fear and isolation that threatened to overwhelm him. He was free from prison, free from further risk of betrayal to the French, but not free to return to his home and family. He was as much a fugitive here as he had been in Brittany.

It was impossible that anyone there had known his purpose. During his torture stubborn pride and a refusal to let them win had somehow given him the strength to maintain his cover. Over and over again he had repeated the same story.

He worked at the shipyard and sometimes made a few extra francs helping the free traders. He knew nothing of secret messages: all he did was carry kegs of brandy. He was paid, he said, for his strong back and silent tongue. His inquisitors had laughed, vowing to break both his strength and his silence. They had come close, too close, to succeeding.

A soft pattering roused him as rain began to fall. The fire had burned down to red embers in a pile of ash. Stirring it into fresh life with more dry oak, he fed the flames with green logs that would burn more slowly and keep it going longer. After he had gathered his still damp linen and hung it on a twig wedged into the new wall, he wrapped himself in his blanket and settled down beneath his shelter.

As he lay listening to the rain, his shaking eased. So he could not go home. Yet had he not been as much a prisoner there as he had been in France? With his own life severely restricted by his father's insistence he remain at home as understudy to his sickly elder brother, he had been unable to follow either the family tradition that a younger son entered politics or his own deep desire to join the navy.

The shackles of duty were not visible like an iron collar and manacles, but they were equally heavy, and left even deeper scars.

It was only due to the efforts of his tutor and friend, Brenton Staveley, that for two marvellous years he had enjoyed a freedom impossible for him in England. With an eloquence that combined appeal and dire warning, Staveley had managed to convince the marquis that unless his younger son's formidable energy and intelligence were given useful direction, the likely outcome would be ruin for him and disgrace for the family.

So with the Grand Tour no longer an option since France

had become too dangerous for foreigners after the outbreak of Revolution the previous year, Staveley had taken the twenty-year-old Gabriel instead to Switzerland to study forest management. For, as he had pointed out separately to father and son, whether Gabriel inherited or remained his brother's second-in-command, what he learnt would enable him to greatly increase the estate revenues to the benefit of all concerned.

Staveley's shrewd handling of the situation had given him the two happiest years of his life. The infected bullet wound that killed him deprived Gabriel not only of a mentor, but a close and trusted friend.

The accident had occurred late one night as they were returning to their lodgings in a patrician house in the Grossmunster area of Zurich. They had been dining with Sir William Wickham, whose wife Eleanora was a distant relative of Staveley's, and inadvertently strayed into a skirmish between French and Swiss soldiers.

It wasn't until Staveley was in his last throes that Gabriel learnt the other reason for their sojourn in Switzerland, and the true measure of his tutor's trust in him. For he had told him of secret intelligence regarding the war on the Continent. Information gathered by Sir William's network of agents throughout Switzerland, of whom he, Brenton Staveley, had been one.

It was vital, Staveley had gasped through fever-cracked lips, that the latest information was taken at once to England. Gabriel had instantly volunteered. But Staveley had warned of grave difficulties. The Foreign Office had been kept in ignorance of the arrangement between Wickham and Lord Grenville, so there would be no diplomatic protection for him should he be caught. Gabriel must think very carefully before committing himself. He was only 22 years old. He had a responsibility to his family to remain alive and unharmed.

For Gabriel there was no choice. Had the information not been of immense importance Staveley would not have mentioned it Nor would he have considered entrusting Gabriel with the task had he not felt him capable of achieving it.

At least he would be spared the formidable task of gaining access to the Foreign Secretary in London. The information was to be delivered to Lord Grenville at Boconnoc, his family seat near Liskeard.

Gabriel had worn the package, wrapped in oiled silk, next to his skin for the entire journey back to England. And, like a blade at his throat, had been conscious of it every moment.

The journey had taken several weeks, and, as he travelled, he had swiftly learnt to dissemble, to pretend boredom, interest and amusement, to hide his thoughts, and to remain alert and wary even when it appeared no danger threatened.

He had left England wild, angry, frustrated, and resentful. He returned, two years later, quieter, calmer, a man whose mettle had been tested and proved.

His mission discharged, he had immersed himself in work on the estate, astonishing his father with his breadth of knowledge and the diplomatic way in which he introduced new methods and techniques. Within three years, revenue from the woods had shown a dramatic increase, and a new programme of felling and planting was under way.

He had found purpose and contentment. He had even begun to entertain his mother's suggestions that it was time he contemplate marriage.

Then accusations of cowardice forced him into a duel. He had deliberately aimed wide, intending merely a graze in order that honour might be satisfied. But something had gone wrong, a young man had died, and the marquis had ordered, then begged, him to flee abroad. He had agreed to go, but not until he had seen Sir John to offer in person his apologies and condolences.

A wrenching sigh shook him. The past could not be changed and memories were a luxury he could not afford. As long as no one discovered his identity he was free. He had a roof – of sorts. He had food and water. Tomorrow he would find work.

# Chapter Three

Waking early, Melissa looked out of her bedroom window. To the east a soft pink glow heralded the sunrise. The sky was cloudless, the air clear and cool after the overnight rain. It was too beautiful to waste. An hour alone in the fresh summer morning would prepare her for the demands of the day ahead.

Pouring water from the tall ewer into the basin, she washed quickly and put on her riding dress. Sweeping her hair back and tying it in a ribbon, she crept downstairs on stockinged feet. As she headed for the back door the quiet murmur of voices from the kitchen told her that the housemaids and footman were already about their duties. Pulling on her boots, she let herself out and quickly crossed the paved court, passing beneath the stone arch into the stable yard.

Just as she reached for the latch, one of the tall double doors swung open, revealing the tousled stable boy in mid-yawn. Eyes flying wide, he gasped.

'Dear life, miss! Gived me some shock, you did.'

'I'm sorry, John.' Melissa smiled at the boy. 'Next time I'll sing or something to let you know I'm here.'

Sucking air through his teeth, he shook his head and shot her a cheeky grin. 'Better not, miss.'

'You're probably right,' she agreed ruefully. 'I'd only frighten the horses.'

'Want Samson saddled up, do you?'

'It's all right; I'll do it. You get on with your work. I don't want you getting into trouble with Mr Hocking.'

Relief flashed across the boy's face. 'Thanks, miss.'

Melissa went past him into the big, airy building, inhaling the combined smells of sweet hay, leather, turpentine, and the not unpleasant odour of fresh dung. She passed the spacious box stalls containing the carriage horses, her father's hunters, and her mother's gentle mare. Samson was loose in the biggest stall, chewing on hay. As she approached, carrying his saddle and bridle collected from the tack-room, he turned. Lifting his great dark head over the wooden bar that kept him in his stall, he made a soft whickering sound of welcome.

'I won't be out very long,' Melissa told the boy as he returned with two buckets of oats. 'Samson can have his when he gets back.'

Letting herself into the loose box she hoisted the saddle onto his back. Accepting the bit, Samson's ears pricked and he blew down flaring nostrils, nudging his velvety muzzle against her shoulder as she fastened the throat strap. Sliding the bar to one side, Melissa led the huge horse out across the yard to the mounting block. Settling herself on the side-saddle she tightened the girth, arranged the skirts of her dress, and gathered up the reins. John had opened the gate for her. The minute they were through into the park, Samson lengthened his stride.

Melissa gave him his head, relishing the speed, the rush of cool air against her face, the sense of freedom. Though rarely ill herself, she felt genuine sympathy for her mother's suffering. Yet she couldn't avoid a sense of relief that she would not, after all, have to attend the assembly the following evening. She knew most people would find it ridiculous that what, for them, was enjoyable entertainment should be, for her, a kind of purgatory. And naturally, as soon as her mother was well again, she would comply with her parents' wishes and do her very best to find a husband acceptable to them and herself. But, in the meantime, her mother's illness provided a most welcome reprieve.

She bent low over Samson's neck as he thundered across the rolling field, only reining him in as they neared the woods. The massive fallen bough of the horse chestnut reminded her of her intention to see what damage had resulted from the storms. This was the ideal opportunity, and meant her father would be spared the effort of coming down himself. His manner over the past months, anxious and indecisive, was so unlike him. She had assumed that after a year – though Adrian's loss would remain with him always – her father's abstraction would have receded. Instead, it had increased, especially during this last eight weeks. Yet who could say how long or how deeply grief should be felt? Understanding, not criticism, was needed. But all her reasoning and sympathy could not banish the growing suspicion that something more was preying on him.

The sun was up now, angling through new leaves that fluttered in the stirring breeze and dappling the path with shadows. Blackbirds chirped and whistled, pigeons repeated their monotonous gargling coo, and iridescent mayflies danced over a puddle. Samson's ears twitched continuously at the rustlings in the grass and bushes edging the path and he tossed his head, dancing sideways, still full of energy.

Sharing his impatience, Melissa gathered up the reins again. She would ride on down to the yard. It was still early, but Tom would almost certainly be there. He could tell her if there was anything on which he needed a decision. Then, after speaking to her father at breakfast, she could relay any message when she rode out later.

'Go on, then,' she whispered, leaning forward, and laughed in delight as she felt the great muscles bunch and flex, and the horse stretched his long legs into a gallop. Ducking low to avoid overhanging branches, her hands light on the reins, she guided Samson along the path, exultant as he cleared two fallen trees without breaking his stride.

As they rounded a curve, still at full gallop, Melissa glimpsed something ahead blocking the path and shouted a warning as she hauled on the reins. Thoroughly startled by this sudden rough treatment as well as by the moving shape that was straightening into the tall figure of a man, Samson skidded, rearing up on his hind legs.

Instead of jumping back off the path and out of her way, the man dropped the bundle he was carrying and lunged forward. Melissa screamed in shock as he grabbed Samson's bridle and pulled the horse's head down, making it impossible for the frightened animal to lift his forelegs off the ground and unseat his rider.

Stroking the horse's arched, sweating neck with his other hand, he murmured softly. But the cracked, rasping sounds he made were barely human and did nothing to calm Melissa's unease or her anger, nor did his size. Tall, with heavily muscled shoulders stretching his coarse linen shirt, he was the biggest man she had ever seen, and made even more unnerving by a darkly bearded profile half-hidden by a wild mane of curly hair.

Still quivering and snorting, Samson had stopped trying to tear himself loose. The stark realisation that, on her own, she could not have achieved so swift a response punctured her fury. But this immediately flared again as it occurred to her that had this giant not been crouched in the middle of the path the entire incident would not have happened. Her tumbling emotions demanding release, she was about to unleash a torrent of wrath when the stranger glanced up.

In the shaft of sunlight she glimpsed oddly pale skin etched with deep lines of suffering above a curved nose and a hard mouth. But it was his eyes that stopped the words on her tongue and dried her throat. Not the colour: she had no idea what it was. Nor their shape for, facing the sun, they were narrowed. Yet even as they met hers they widened. She saw the brief flash, knew it was echoed in her own, and felt a jolt as severe as a physical blow. She did not know him, had never seen him before – and she would certainly have remembered a man of his size – so how could she sense recognition?

He looked down quickly, dipping his head as a servant to a superior, and released Samson's bridle. Then, raising one hand as if to tug his forelock – a gesture that seemed somehow off-key – he crouched to pick up the pieces of stiff and dirty sail canvas he must have salvaged from the beach, bending and folding them into a manageable bundle.

Swiftly shortening the reins, she kicked Samson into a canter, sensing the man watching her. In her mind's eye she still saw his hands – bearing old scars as well as fresh, jagged scratches – gentle and calming on Samson's muzzle and neck. And as she rounded the curve, out of his sight, she realised suddenly that they had not exchanged a single word.

Emerging from the path on to the road, Melissa turned toward the yard entrance, arriving to find one of the men fastening back the solid double gates.

'Morning, miss.' He raised one hand to his forehead: the salute an unwelcome reminder of the man in the woods. 'You're out some early.'

Still unnerved by the unexpected encounter, Melissa had to force a smile. 'Good morning, Walter. It's such a beautiful morning I thought I'd make the most of it. Has Mr Ferris arrived yet?'

'Yes. Down the slip, he is.' He pointed toward the hundred-foot hull supported by a framework of props. Towering above the quays, the packet dwarfed the single-storey sheds and buildings on either side. Fully planked, her decks laid, the gunports had been cut in her topsides and the superstructure was in place. Once the steering gear, capstans, and deck fittings had been installed, the two masts would be stepped and rigged.

Lifting her leg over the pommel, Melissa slid lightly to the ground. Flipping the reins over Samson's head, she looped them through the iron ring fastened to the wall of a small stone building. As she shook out the skirts of her riding dress, she saw the foreman approaching. Short and square, he wore a blue check shirt, a short waistcoat, breeches of the stout twilled cotton known as thickset, and leather gaiters.

'You're some early. Everything all right, is it?'

Tom Ferris had eyes as sharp as a kestrel's. It was one of the reasons he was such a good foreman.

'My mother's not well,' Melissa replied, relieved to have a legitimate, if not entirely truthful, excuse for her distraction.

'One of these here summer colds, is it? They do drag you down awful.'

'Dr Wherry says it's influenza.'

'The dear soul.' Tom clicked his tongue. 'You tell her I asked for her. I hope she do soon feel better.'

'Thank you, Tom. I know she'll appreciate your kind thoughts.'

His eyes were bright, his gaze sharp as he studied her. 'So, if your mother's sick, what you doing down here?'

'I'll probably be indoors all day, so I thought I'd take an early ride.'

He frowned. 'There was me hoping you'd brung me word from mister.'

Melissa shook her head. 'I'm sorry, Tom. I wondered if you had any messages you wanted taken back.'

'Come through the woods, did you?'

She nodded, her heart thumping hard as she swiftly banished startlingly vivid images of a tall, dark-haired man with a pain-scored face. 'I saw at least two big trees down. There are bound to be more.'

Men were starting to arrive, coming in through the gates in twos and threes. As they saw Melissa, all raised a finger to their foreheads and nodded in greeting, growling, 'Morning, miss.' She smiled, nodding in return.

Indicating the small stone building to which Samson was tethered, Tom lowered his voice. 'You'd best step inside a moment.'

Bending her head to avoid the thick oak lintel as she crossed the threshold into the room that served as the foreman's office, Melissa felt a tightening in her stomach that had nothing to do with hunger. She didn't wait for him to speak. 'Tom, you don't have to tell me: I know we should be using those trees.'

'Look, I'll speak blunt, miss. If mister don't do something soon, we're going to be in trouble. Not the packet,' he added quickly, 'we got enough wood to see she finished. But in all the years I been here, I never seen the store so low. This time of year he should be stacked high, ready for next summer. Even when we get all they trees boarded and planked, they still got to season, and that do take –'

'A year per inch of thickness. I know.' Melissa nodded. 'That was one of the reasons I came down through the woods, to see the storm damage for myself. There's some useful timber there, Tom. I'll see my father at breakfast. And I really will do my best to impress upon him the urgency of the situation.' But will he listen? Even more important, will he act?

'Much obliged, miss. But see, 'tisn't as if that's the only

problem.' Tom rubbed his grey-stubbled chin with gnarled fingers.

Apprehension slid like melting ice down Melissa's spine. 'No?'

Tom shook his head, his expression deeply troubled. 'What else?' She searched his blue-grey eyes.

He shifted uncomfortably. 'Look, you know 'tisn't that I don't trust you. But by rights I shouldn't say aught to anyone but mister.'

Melissa folded her hands, gripping one tightly with the other. 'I understand, and I respect your desire to do things the proper way. But truly, Tom, I have no idea when my father will be free to come down to the yard. He has been riding to Truro almost every other day. So unless you will come up to the house and speak to him yourself –'

'I can't do that, miss!' The foreman's weathered face registered shock. 'Have people thinking there's something wrong, or I can't do me job? No. Wouldn't be right nor proper, me coming up there. Not at all, it wouldn't.'

'Then you must tell me, and I'll tell him.'

Frowning, he shook his head. 'I can't say I like it.' He glanced up. 'No offence, miss. It's not that I think you'd say it wrong, or nothing like that. Truth is you're more like to put it better than I can. I haven't got no gift for words.'

'I'll be as diplomatic as possible,' Melissa promised. 'But I do think it's wiser that my father is fully informed. Whatever the problems are, the longer they are left the worse they'll get.' Despite the brave words, her disquiet was rapidly evolving into anxiety.

'Dear life –' he rolled his eyes '– don't you say such things. 'Tis bad enough already and that's no lie.' He sniffed. Then, walking round to the far side of the cluttered table that served as a desk, he moved things aimlessly from one place to another.

'Please tell me,' she urged quietly.

''Tis the suppliers,' he blurted, flicking a glance at her from beneath bushy grey brows.

Melissa didn't understand. 'What about them?'

Tom turned away to glare at the small, grimy window, clearly embarrassed. 'They don't want to let us have no more stuff, not till something's been paid off the account.'

As the implications began to sink in, Melissa felt heat climb her throat and burn her cheeks. She swallowed hard, fighting to keep her voice level. 'Is this just one or two suppliers, Tom? Or all of them?'

His relief was visible. She felt a pang of mingled hurt and amusement that he should have feared she would fall into hysterics. Did he really not know her better than that? Then her sense of fairness asserted itself. Never before had he been forced to give her such news.

'Well, 'tis mainly Keast's, over the cordage. But when young Billy come back from Eddyvean's he said they told'n they weren't letting no more sails out of the loft till they seen some money.'

Melissa's chin rose as indignation bubbled up inside her. 'Did they indeed? Well, they had no right to involve Billy in a matter which can be settled only between Mr Eddyvean and my father.'

'True, Miss, and so I told him. But –'

'I'll speak to my father as soon as I get home.' She smoothed her York tan gloves over her fingers, anger warring with burgeoning dismay. It was understandable that her father had spent less time on the business since Adrian's death. Yet with Tom running things it should have made little practical difference. But the fact that accounts clearly long overdue had not been settled was not only a deeply unpleasant shock, it was completely out of character. 'Don't worry, Tom. I promise I'll be tactful.'

He followed her out, rubbing his knuckles as she untied Samson and led him to the mounting block. 'I'm some sorry, miss. I don't like putting it on you. If there was another way ...'

Swinging herself into the saddle, Melissa quickly arranged her skirts, then gathered up the reins. 'I know, Tom. But there isn't.'

Back in the house, Melissa managed to reach her room

without seeing anyone. Two such different yet profoundly unsettling events in such a short space of time had left her badly shaken and she needed to regain her emotional balance before facing her father. But on opening the door she found Sarah waiting.

'Morning, miss,' she beamed. 'Nice ride, was it? I knew soon as I seen the sunshine that's where you'd gone. Bath's all ready and your clothes laid out.' She peered closer, her sharp little face puckering in concern. 'All right, are you?'

'Yes, I'm fine.' With a brief smile, Melissa turned away, unbuttoning her dress. Too independent to enjoy being fussed over, she had always resisted having a personal maid or dresser. It hadn't been easy to convince her mother that her needs fitted in perfectly with Sarah's duties as senior housemaid, but the obvious success of the arrangement had proved her point. 'Samson was a bit full of himself this morning, that's all.'

Sarah shuddered. 'Great thing he is. He do terrify me.'

'Oh Sarah. He's as gentle as a lamb.'

'He might be for you. I heard John say he do try and nip Mr Hocking.'

Melissa had a startling mental picture of shaggy black curls, and Samson's ears twitching then pointing forward in response to the strange sounds the man was making.

'I put out your blue.' Sarah scooped up the riding dress and bore it off, calling over her shoulder, 'Soon as you've bathed, I'll give your hair a good brush. Look like you been pulled through a hedge backwards, you do.'

'Thank you, Sarah,' said Melissa dryly as she twisted her hair into a large knot on top of her head and secured it with several pins. She stepped into the bath and lowered herself into the warm water.

But instead of relaxing against the high back and allowing herself the usual few minutes' relaxation and daydreaming, she reached immediately for the soap and cloth. With so much to do, the sooner she got started the better. Despite the importance of the conversation she must have with her father, she sensed that unless she kept her thoughts focused they would stray on to paths that were both dangerous and futile.

Fresh and cool in a full-skirted gown of pale blue muslin with a dark-blue sash below a deep double frill edging the low, round neck, her hair brushed to a gleaming ebony cascade, Melissa knocked lightly on her mother's door and went in. The room smelled slightly stale and the curtains were still half drawn.

She tiptoed to the bed where Emma lay against a bank of pillows, grape-coloured shadows beneath her closed eyes.

'Good morning, Mama,' she whispered.

Emma Tregonning's eyelids flickered open. She tried to smile but the effort was too great.

Addey waddled across, carrying a bundle of crumpled linen. 'Tossed and turned all night, she did. Got some nasty cough. The fever haven't broke yet. But I've just gived her a nice wash and she's more comfortable.'

'Do you think we might open the window for a few minutes?' Melissa suggested.

Addey frowned. 'Oooh, I don't know about that. If she was to get in a draught you don't know what –'

'Just to change the air. It's a beautiful morning. In fact,' Melissa added as inspiration struck, 'it's warmer outside than it is in here. So I really don't think she'll be in any danger.'

Addey hesitated for a moment, then sighed, her chin jutting. 'Only for a few minutes, mind.'

As Melissa pushed back the curtains, she saw the postman trotting up the drive. A letter from George would do more to restore her mother's health than any prescription of Dr Wherry's. But knowing better than to mention it she simply stood at the window, pretending difficulty with the catch. She wouldn't open it until the postman had gone.

'Melissa?' At the sound of her mother's voice, weak and slightly hoarse, Melissa turned and went to her side.

'Would you like some more lemon barley? Or maybe a cup of beef tea?'

Emma Tregonning's eyes were open and she was staring at the window. She clutched her daughter's hand. 'Is that the postman's horse?'

Reluctantly Melissa nodded. Since her brothers had first entered the navy, her father had paid a pound a year to ensure early delivery of the mail. 'I'll go and see if there's anything for you, shall I?'

Lobb was in the hall. He had placed the letters – one with a distinctive green seal – on a silver salver and was about to take them into the dining- room for her father to read over breakfast. He glanced up, saw her midway down the stairs and, knowing her errand, shook his head.

'I'm sorry, miss.'

'So am I, Lobb. It would have made all the difference. Is my father down yet?'

'He is, miss. Will you be joining him for breakfast?'

'Yes. Would you tell him I'll be with him in just a few minutes?' Turning, Melissa went back upstairs. Before re-entering her mother's room she paused to take a deep breath and steel herself against the disappointment her mother would make a valiant effort to hide.

As she slipped inside, Addey looked up; the naked hope on her plump face fading quickly as Melissa made a brief negative gesture.

'Pity,' Addey muttered for Melissa's ears alone. ''T would have bucked her up good and proper. Oh well, least said soonest mended. You go on down and have your breakfast. There isn't no more you can do for now. I daresay your father will be glad of a bit of company. I only hope he don't go down with it. Not like hisself at all he isn't, nor haven't been for weeks.'

'Well, it's not an easy time for either of them.' The matters she had to discuss with him would add even more pressure, Melissa acknowledged as she walked downstairs and crossed the hall to the dining room. But they could not be put off any longer.

Francis Tregonning was seated at the head of the table, gazing fixedly at the letter he held. It trembled slightly in his grasp, the broken edge of green wax visible at the top. The other lay read and discarded on the table. A napkin was tucked into his striped waistcoat, and a half-eaten plate of kedgeree lay congealing in front of him.

'Good morning, Papa.'

The butler set a dish of raspberries in front of her. 'Mrs Betts sent these up for you, miss.'

'How kind. Will you thank her, Lobb? I shall enjoy them.'

'Would you like the kedgeree, miss? Or perhaps some eggs?'

'One poached egg, a slice of toast, and a cup of hot chocolate, please.' The ride had been invigorating, but she wasn't as hungry as usual. Perhaps once she started eating her appetite would return.

'Just one egg?' The question betrayed Lobb's surprise.

'Just one, thank you.'

'Very good, miss. You're quite well?'

That was the trouble with long-serving trusted staff. They fussed.

'I'm perfectly well, thank you, Lobb. I had a most enjoyable ride this morning and I have a busy day ahead.' Melissa flashed him a meaningful smile.

'Quite so. Then you'll be needing a good breakfast, miss,' the butler responded blandly, turning away to the sideboard.

Melissa picked up her napkin. Her father seemed unaware she had entered the room. 'Papa?' She leant forward slightly. 'Is everything all right?'

Francis Tregonning raised his head. 'Melissa?'

Melissa wondered for an instant if he could see her, for he seemed tentative and confused, as if the room was dark instead of bright with morning sunshine.

Concerned, she reached out and touched his hand. 'What is it, Papa? Have you had bad news?'

He blinked, and made a brave effort to pull himself together. 'No. Everything is fine. It's nothing at all. Well, just a minor matter I have to sort out. But nothing to worry about.' Swiftly refolding the letter in his hand, he laid it on top of the one on the table, pressing both flat. 'Have you seen your mother this morning? How is she?' He reached for his cup, but his hand was shaking so badly the coffee slopped over the rim into the saucer. 'Damn it, Lobb!' he roared. 'Why must you fill the cup to the brim? Makes a dreadful mess.'

'I beg your pardon, sir. I'll bring you a fresh cup immediately.'

'Yes, do that. And don't fill it so full this time.'

Melissa caught the butler's eye, and read in Lobb's carefully blank expression understanding of the strain the anniversary of Adrian's death and his wife's illness had placed on his master. She turned to her father.

'Mama still has a fever. She was hoping so much that the postman might have brought a letter from George. I'm sure if one arrived her recovery would be twice as swift.'

'I wish he was here,' her father murmured with a desperation that wrenched Melissa's heart.

'Indeed, we all do, Papa.' If George were here he would be dealing with all the problems and she would not be facing the most difficult moments of her life. After a short pause to screw up her courage and choose her words, she began. 'I went for a ride this morning.' She grieved at the effort it cost him to appear interested.

'That's nice.' His smile was a travesty. And his fingers fretted at the edge of the folded letter.

'I gave Samson a gallop across the park and through the woods.'

'How's that strained tendon?'

'Fine, Papa. He's perfectly sound. But the gales have brought down two trees across the path. And I'm almost certain I saw more storm damage further in. The thing is, Papa, Tom is becoming really concerned.'

'He's got enough wood to finish the packet, hasn't he?' His unexpected belligerence was startling.

'Yes.' She knew his anger wasn't directed at her. But this uncharacteristic outburst forced her to recognise the truth of his claim that the yard and estate had become too heavy a burden for him to manage alone. 'There's also enough for the keel and frame of the next ship. But the store must be replenished soon.'

'I *know,* dammit!' Leaning forward and resting his elbows on the table, her father rubbed his forehead. 'I'm trying, but there are other ... Look, tell Tom ...' He winced, pressing his fingertips to his temple. 'Tell him … Tell him … Oh …' Je gasped as his right arm buckled, sliding off the mahogany. As he slumped forward his head hit the table with a thud that made the china jump and the cutlery rattle.

For a split second Melissa simply stared, too shocked to move. Then, thrusting her chair back, she ran to him with Lobb only a pace behind.

'Papa?'

As the butler gripped his shoulders and pulled him upright, Francis Tregonning's head flopped sideways. Melissa cupped her father's face. The right side seemed to have slipped, like wax that had melted. His eyes were closed, and a silver thread drooled from one corner of his mouth.

'Papa? What's wrong?'

'I fear your father has had a stroke, miss. I recognise the signs. Mrs Betts's brother, Henry, was taken the same way. If you'll ring for Gilbert we'll get him up to his room while you call the doctor.'

'What?' The floor seemed to tilt, and the butler's voice echoed strangely as fear rampaged through her. How serious was it? How was she to tell her mother? Who would take control now? What of the yard, the farm, the suppliers …

'Come along now, Miss Melissa.' Lobb's voice, quiet but firm, pulled her back from the edge of panic. 'Master wouldn't want anyone to see him like this. Best if we get him upstairs as quick as we can.'

'Yes. Of course.' Sucking in a deep breath, she pressed clammy hands to her cheeks as she crossed the room to tug the bell rope. As soon as Gilbert arrived, she went to the kitchen to tell Sarah and Mrs Betts that her father had been taken ill, then sent Agnes to fetch John. Back in the hall, on her way to write a note for Dr Wherry, she was halted by the appalling spectacle of her proud father, the front of his breeches wet, hanging limp and undignified between the two men struggling up the stairs.

# Chapter Four

Dawn had just broken when Gabriel woke. The rain had stopped and all around he could hear the drip of water from the leaves; too much of it dripping into the roofless part of the shack. The air smelled of wet earth and decaying vegetation. Dressing quickly, he had hurried to the beach for more remnants of sail canvas. He had found them, only to be severely jolted by an unexpected encounter with a startled horse and rider as he returned along the path.

Back at the shack, slamming a mental door on desires too dangerous even to contemplate, he had washed his face and hands. Then, using his dagger to fashion a crude comb from a piece of wood, had worked most of the tangles from his hair before tying it back once more.

He had never been a vain man, and had little patience with the extravagances of fashion. Some of his friends sported shirt points so high and stiff that turning the head was impossible without risking loss of an eye. Their jackets were cut so close that to put one on required the assistance of a valet and two servants. They admired buttons the size of saucers, and intricately arranged neckcloths that might take an hour and several attempts to achieve.

When they chided him for his lack of style he merely shrugged, replying that they had his blessing to do as they wished. For himself, he believed life was too short to be wasted in front of a mirror. While he trusted Berryman with his boots, his razor, and his life, he was perfectly capable of dressing himself, and in truth he preferred to do so.

Would he ever see any of them again? Even if he did, things could never be the same. For though he had been absent a little less than a year he was no longer the man they had known.

Aware that he had not yet fully recovered, and the day would tax his strength to its limit, Gabriel deliberately ate a hearty breakfast. It was, he decided as he finished all that remained of the food, an act of faith: faith in himself. He had stolen because he'd had no choice. And he had been lucky, for had he been caught, the outcome, once his identity was known, would be death. So if he wanted to eat again, that day or any other, obtaining work was imperative.

After hiding the bucket and cooking pot out of sight with his blanket and spare clothes, he set off for the yard. Once on the path, the sights, smells, and sounds of the summer morning were lost on him as his desperate barriers were demolished by a rushing torrent of vivid memory. Images flooded his mind: no helpless, frightened girl, but a strong, athletic young woman, her face aglow with pleasure and hair flying like a flag as her horse had hurtled round the bend. Though she had cried out a startled warning, she had not panicked, and her reactions had been lightning fast.

His own move to seize the bridle in case the alarmed animal threw her off had been instinctive, though unwise. A person of his supposed low class would have been more likely to stumble back out of the way. The suddenness of the encounter meant his impressions had necessarily been brief. But her trim waist belied her undoubted strength, for her mount was a huge brute that even he, in his former life, would not have scorned. Her open-skirted riding dress of garnet red revealed a white petticoat. And a rippling cascade of dark hair framed her face, pale above the fluted cambric covering her full bosom.

But when he had stilled the fractious horse and glanced up, seeing her properly had stopped his breath. As he looked into those magnificent emerald eyes his heart had turned over. He had watched her gaze widen and swift colour warm her cheeks as she caught her breath. Immediately looking away, his heart racing as it had not done since his capture, he had cursed himself for a fool. Was he not in enough danger? He sensed – knew – the attraction was mutual, profound. And hopeless. The best thing, the only thing, was to ignore it, forget it, and pretend it had never happened.

Keeping his gaze lowered, he had knuckled his forehead in time-honoured fashion, then bent to gather up the dropped canvas. But, as she kicked her mount on, he had not been able to resist lifting his head to watch her go.

Now, as he walked, he searched his memory for every tiny detail, recalling the light dusting of freckles across her nose and the golden tint beneath her rosy blush. Few women of his acquaintance would be so careless of their complexion. But then, few women he knew could have handled the big thoroughbred with such gentle expertise. The beast must have stood a good 18 hands. So how tall was she?

As for the rest of her features, he seemed to remember a neat, straight nose, a generous mouth too wide for classical beauty, and a firm, resolute chin. Slashing in frustration at a stand of nettles, he hurled the stick away. Why torment himself? As Lord Roland Stratton he could have asked friends to arrange an introduction, for she was obviously a gentleman's daughter, but as Gabriel Ennis, his inferior station in life put her far beyond his reach.

The boatyard was below him. Knowing he would provoke at best curiosity, at worst suspicion, were he to arrive from the beach, he remained on the path and followed it to the village, as he had done the other night.

Approaching the big wooden gates, now open and fastened back, he caught the sound of voices just inside. '… Only food? You sure?'

'That's what I heard. Don't make no sense, do it? Who'd break into an inn and not help hisself to a drink?'

'A bleddy fool, that's who. More hair than brains. Lest he's a Methodist, of course. Right, come on, pick 'n up.'

The realisation that the two men were discussing him broke Gabriel's stride, but only for an instant. He had, in every sense, come too far to turn back. Also, it was more than likely they had heard his footsteps. Though the arrival of a stranger in this small backwater was bound to arouse interest, there was nothing to connect him directly to the theft. It was to be hoped the villagers would find it impossible to conceive of a thief bold enough, or stupid enough, to return in broad daylight and ask for a job.

Subtly altering his appearance by lowering his head and hunching his shoulders, he walked through the gate. The two men he had heard talking were heading away, one each end of a long wooden ladder, toward the slip on which a framework of props and wooden scaffolding surrounded the hull of a newly built ship. Slowing his step, Gabriel peered about him, signalling his uncertainty.

'Looking for someone?' The suspicious shout was accompanied by a sudden loud hiss.

Glancing round, he saw clouds of steam billowing from the open doorway of a squat stone building with a slate roof and a wide doorway. Made of weathered vertical planks, the door was mounted on two wheels that ran along an iron rail parallel to the front wall. The steam evaporated to reveal a thickset man wearing a filthy leather apron that covered him from chin to ankles. In the background, Gabriel saw glowing coals on the forge hearth. An anvil and a large water butt stood on the beaten earth floor, and metal of varying lengths, shapes, and sizes was propped against the walls or lay in small, rusting piles. The sleeves of the blacksmith's shirt were rolled up, exposing brawny forearms, and in one huge fist he held a long-handled pair of tongs that gripped a still-steaming bar of metal.

Softly Gabriel cleared his damaged throat before calling out, 'Foreman?'

The blacksmith stared hard at him for a moment, then gestured with the bar to a similar building opposite.

With a nod, Gabriel crossed to it, and knocked on the open door.

'Yo!' The voice was gruff and preoccupied. Ducking his head, Gabriel paused in the doorway.

'Come in if you're coming. I can't see a bleddy thing with you blocking the light.'

Gabriel stepped inside. The small room contained a big table, a battered cupboard, and a scarred wooden armchair on whose seat was a crushed cushion of faded pattern and indeterminate colour. The table was strewn with half-models of ships, each mounted on a flat piece of wood a few inches larger; two broken blocks, an assortment of copper bolts, a sailmaker's metal palm, a fid for splicing rope, and some pieces of wood. Several leather-bound ledgers were stacked untidily on the cupboard's top.

A year ago he would have been surprised at the lack of paper, for there were no drawings or plans, but he was wiser now. The navy might use drawings, but small shipyards worked from three-dimensional half-hulls that showed the desired length, width, depth, and sheer. These were then scaled up; the lines of the model drawn out full size on the lofting floor, after which wooden templates were made of the principal timbers such as frames and stem and stern pieces.

Standing behind the table, scratching his scalp through the wiry grey frizz that surrounded his head like a halo, the foreman looked up, gave a slight start, and muttered, 'God a'mighty.' Planting his knuckles on the table, he stuck out a pugnacious chin. 'Well? What do you want?'

Aware that short men found his size both intimidating and a challenge, Gabriel did not approach the cluttered table, remaining instead at the back of the small room. 'A job.' Wincing inwardly at the hoarse growl that was all he could manage, he saw that beneath the bushy brows the foreman's pale-blue eyes were as sharp as a gutting knife as they swept over him from his coarse linen shirt, battered leather waistcoat, and stained breeches to his topboots. The foreman's gaze lingered a fraction too long; as it flicked up once more, Gabriel recognised suspicion and waited for the question. To his surprise, it didn't come, but the foreman's voice was terse.

'Wassamatter with your voice? Got a sore throat?'

Gabriel's lips twitched. He gave a brief, ironic nod as he leant forward and turned down the top of the bandage just enough to reveal the edge of the horrific wound.

'Bleddy 'ell.' The foreman grimaced. 'How did you get that?'

'Prisoner,' Gabriel rasped. 'In France. Stole the boots when I escaped.'

'Ah.' The foreman nodded, 'I was wond'ring about they.

Not from round here, are you? How haven't you gone home?'

Gabriel was ready for this. 'Can't. Press gang.' The cracked sounds emerging from his throat sounded more painful than they now felt. It occurred to him then that the limitations imposed on his speech were an asset rather than a liability. For, though he was Cornish-born, he had none of the working men's rolling burr.

The foreman's eyes rounded. 'They'd take you again?'

'They'd try.'

'Got a name?'

'Ennis. Gabriel Ennis.'

The foreman sniffed. 'What's your trade?'

Mentally crossing his fingers, Gabriel rasped, 'I'm a carpenter.' He dare not say shipwright. For though that was the work he had been doing in the French yards, in England he would have been exempted from the press by the need for new ships and trained men to build them. 'I worked on a big estate.'

The foreman scrabbled about in the clutter, picked up a broken block and two other pieces of wood, and tossed them, one after the other, at Gabriel, whose swift reflexes, honed by months surviving in an enemy country, enabled him to catch them easily.

It was a test. Glancing at each piece as he felt the grain and assessed the colour, Gabriel felt his tension ease. 'The block is ash. This is oak, a split treenail.' He pronounced it "trennal", as the foreman would have done. 'The broken spar is pine.'

The foreman sniffed again. 'When can you start?'

'Now.'

'You got somewhere to stay?'

Gabriel nodded.

'You heard what happened last night? The thieving?'

Gabriel nodded again.

'What you got to say about it?'

Recognising the foreman's suspicions, Gabriel held his gaze. 'I'd guess whoever did it was starving. A man in work has no need to steal.'

'I don't suppose you got a farthing to your name, you just back from France and all.' He frowned at Gabriel, who met the piercing eyes and waited, saying nothing. 'So you give me a good day's work, and I'll pay you tonight instead of the end of the week. We got good shops in the village. Willy Bowden'll see you right. He's the grocer. Mrs Mitchell run the bakehouse since her Cyrus passed away last year. Tell them Tom Ferris sent you.'

Gabriel knuckled his forehead. 'Much obliged.' Those two words didn't even begin to express his relief and gratitude. But to say more risked compromising his identity and therefore his safety.

Tom glared at him. 'I won't have no trouble.'

'You'll get none from me.'

After a long moment and another hard stare, Tom nodded abruptly. 'C'mon then, can't hang around here burning daylight.' With a sniff and a jerk of his head to indicate Gabriel should follow, the foreman set off across the yard to a long wooden shed with double doors at each end currently hooked back to admit maximum light.

Bent over trestles and wooden cradles, two shipwrights assisted by two young apprentices were shaping spars amid a thick carpet of golden sawdust and pale shavings. As he inhaled the sweet, resinous scent of pine, Gabriel recalled the Swiss forests, and fought a rush of memories both pleasant and painful.

Maintaining his slightly stooped, self-effacing posture, he quickly scanned the big shed. Each man's tool bag sat on the heavy bench that ran the length of one wall. Other tools – saws, adzes, and chisels – were slotted in a wooden rack above the bench. On the opposite side of the airy shed were stacked different types, shapes, and sizes of wood. The stacks were lower than Gabriel expected. Much would have gone into the hull shored up on the slipway. Presumably there was another store from which they drew seasoned wood.

'Here, you two, I got another carpenter. Name of –' He turned to Gabriel. 'Got a head like a sieve, I have. What did you say you was called again?'

Another test? 'Ennis. Gabriel Ennis.'

At the hoarse rasp the two men exchanged a glance before

51

eyeing him uncertainly.

Tom addressed them in a confiding tone. 'In prison in France, he was. They near enough cut his throat, poor bugger, that's how he can't speak proper.' He turned to Gabriel. 'Show 'em what they done to you.'

Reluctant, but aware it would aid his acceptance, which was no doubt what the shrewd foreman intended, Gabriel leant forward and pulled down the edge of the bandage, swiftly replacing it as both men grimaced and studied him with new respect.

Tom continued, 'He got back here, but he can't go home 'cos the press gang will have him again.' He turned to Gabriel. 'This here's Walter Keverne, he'll tell you what to do. This is Tansey, and his boy, Billy. And that there beanpole is Joseph. All right?'

'Hang on a minute,' Walter said. 'What about the wood, then? You seen mister?'

'No. But Miss Melissa come down this morning. I told she 'tis urgent.'

'So long as she remember to tell her father.'

'She will.'

Melissa. Gabriel cleared his throat. 'Any logs not cut?'

Walter nodded, sucking his teeth. 'A few. Stacked out the back they are. But since Charlie near hacked his leg off, there haven't been no one to go down the pit. Billy's willing, but he can't do it by his self. And with the packet to finish, none of we got time.'

Knowing it was an unpopular task, and hoping the welts on his back would stand the stretching, Gabriel shrugged. 'I'll do it.'

Tansey grinned, showing a mouthful of blackened teeth. 'Now I call that handsome. Come just the right time you have.'

'You want it quarter sawn?' Gabriel asked.

Exchanging a slow grin of relief, Tom and Walter both nodded.

'I'll need help,' Gabriel reminded.

'I'll go,' Billy volunteered. Stocky like his father, he had muscular arms and powerful shoulders. 'All right, father?'

Tansey shrugged. 'All right with you, Walter?'

'Get on, the both of you. What are you waiting for? God knows we do need it.'

Surprised, Gabriel indicated the reduced stacks of wood. 'That's all?'

Walter and Tansey nodded, Walter adding, 'Never seen 'un in this state, not in all the years I been here.'

'The wood, or mister?' Tansey muttered darkly.

'All right, all right,' Tom broke in. 'I don't want to hear no more of that. What if it had been your Billy?' He turned to Gabriel. 'Mister's eldest boy got hisself killed last year. A lieutenant in the navy, he was.'

'Mister?' Gabriel repeated.

'Mr Tregonning. Own the yard, he do. Got another boy out by Jamaica or some such place.'

'No word from he for months neither,' Walter added, shaking his head.

'I know what I think,' Tansey muttered darkly.

'Yes, well, you keep it to yourself,' Tom snapped. 'Family got enough trouble. They don't want you making it worse.'

''Tisn't only they who'll have trouble if we don't get more wood,' Tansey grumbled.

Wondering if Mr Tregonning was the owner of the woodland above the yard, Gabriel kept silent.

'You said your piece, now shut your yap,' Tom snapped. 'C'mon, move yourselves. Time's wasting.'

Gabriel followed Billy, hoping the youth wouldn't ply him with questions. In fact, he hardly spoke at all. But he worked. By late morning they had hauled a two foot thick and eight foot long log from the pile, stripped off the bark with small axes, marked the main divisions, and made the first cut.

When the others stopped for their dinner, Gabriel sent Billy to join them, saying he wasn't hungry and would wedge the log ready for the second cut. But within ten minutes Billy was back, a stone jar dangling from one large fist. His young face fiery, he thrust a thick wedge of meat and potato pie at Gabriel.

'Walter sent it. Said his missus always give him too much. Fat as a pup he'd be if he ate it all hisself.'

Wiping his hands on the sweat-soaked and sawdust-sprinkled shirt he preferred to retain rather than excite curiosity by exposing the welts that striped his back, Gabriel took the pie, touched by the boy's thoughtfulness and tact. 'Much obliged.'

Billy gazed into the distance while Gabriel ate, then thrust the jar toward him. 'Here, 'tis good ale. Falmouth brewed.'

Raising the jar to his lips, Gabriel drank deeply. The bitter beer, cool and delicious, quenched his thirst and gave him new strength. Wiping his mouth with the back of his hand, he returned the jar. 'Know anyone who might lend me a boat?' Watching Billy's face reflect tumbling thoughts, he added, 'For fishing, Billy. Nothing more.'

Blushing, Billy shrugged. 'I never thought you was one o' the *gentlemen*.'

'Too risky. I'll pay for the loan with half my catch.'

Billy thought. 'Jack got a boat. But he don't go out much now. Want me to ask him, do you?'

'Thanks.' Gabriel started back toward the saw pit.

It was mid-afternoon when, for the second time in two days, Melissa walked with the doctor to his horse. She waited until they were out of earshot of the house to ask the question, dreading his answer.

'How … How ill is my father?'

Dr Wherry stopped, raising his eyes to hers. His expression was sombre, his gaze compassionate. 'I think your brother should come home as soon as possible.'

Catching her lip, she nodded, not trusting herself to speak, understanding all his response implied. George was in the navy, and there was a war on. But George was also her father's heir and would be the new head of the family, responsible for her mother and herself. It was clear the doctor did not expect her father to recover. She forced the words past the lump in her throat.

'How long …?'

The doctor moved his shoulders. 'It's difficult to say. His strong constitution, active lifestyle, and moderate habits must count in his favour. But I'm afraid the toll of the last 12 months ...' He shook his head. 'I'm so sorry, my dear.'

Melissa returned to the house to find Sarah waiting for her.

'Please, miss. These was left on the dining room table.'

'Thank you.' Taking the folded letters, Melissa started toward her father's study.

'Beggin' your pardon, miss, but if you don't mind me asking, we was all wondering, how's master going on?'

Melissa swallowed the aching tightness in her throat. 'Not good, Sarah.'

The maid's eyes brimmed. 'I'm some sorry, miss.'

'Thank you. Could you bring me some tea? I'll be in the study.'

Sitting in her father's high-backed leather chair, she gazed out of the window. The sun shone from an azure sky dotted with puffs of cloud. Swifts dipped and swooped after insects. The garden was fragrant with roses and in the farm meadows the last of the clover would have been cut. Soon it would be the turn of the grass. Tall and lush, it would make good hay. The breeze made it ripple like water. Down in the yard, the new packet-ship was well on its way to completion. Once the masts had been stepped, the internal fitting could begin. Nothing had changed yet everything was different. And the suppliers had not been paid.

She had not yet told her mother of her father's collapse. The fever had reached its height at midday and in her delirium Emma had cried out for both her sons. Then, without warning, a drenching sweat had beaded her face and trickled down her temples and neck, soaking her hair, the pillow, her nightgown, and the sheets. Greatly relieved, Melissa and Addey had moved her to the couch. And while Addey bathed her mistress, crooning softly as if Emma Tregonning were still the child she had once nursed, Melissa aided Sarah in stripping and changing the bed. Her mother was sleeping peacefully now, aided by one of Dr Wherry's draughts. She would need all her strength to bear this latest blow. All the more reason for delaying as long as possible.

'Pour a cup for you shall I, miss?' Sarah enquired, setting

the tray down in the space Melissa had hastily cleared.

'No, it's all right, Sarah. I can manage.' Leaning forward to gather up the letters and papers strewn over the desktop, Melissa gave the maid a brief smile. 'I'll ring if I need anything.'

Still Sarah dithered, reluctant to leave. 'Want for me to send John over to Pencoombe, do you?'

Melissa's head flew up. 'What on earth for?'

'Well, 'tisn't right you having to do everything all by yourself.'

Melissa's eyebrows rose. 'Sarah, I'm perfectly capable of –'

''Course you are. No one could say otherwise. But we got eyes in our heads. We all know how much you bin doing to help master. So we was just thinking, what with your mother so ill an' all, and now your dear father took bad, maybe your Uncle Marcus or Uncle Brinley could –'

Melissa bit her tongue, knowing the suggestion sprang from concern for her well-being. The same age as herself, Sarah had come into service at the age of ten. Like the rest of the staff, her connection with the family was of long standing, as her parents and grandparents had also worked for Tregonnings. This long-established tradition had resulted in the servants adopting the family as their own. So while respectful and scrupulously attentive to every detail of their duties, when, in their opinion, the occasion warranted, they felt free to ignore normal boundaries and speak their minds.

'Sarah, if my uncles are sent for, my aunts will come as well. It would be impossible to keep them away. Even if they respected my father's privacy, just think what it would mean for my mother. She wouldn't have a moment's peace. Yet that's exactly what she needs right now. So, much as I appreciate your offer, and I do, truly, I would rather not involve my uncles for the time being.'

A fiery blush scalded the maid's face and she dipped her head. 'Beg pardon, miss. I shouldn't have spoke out of turn. It was just –'

'It's all right. I do understand. And I'm not angry. How could I be when I know you were only trying to help?'

'That's the truth, miss, as God's my judge. Sure you don't want nothing else?'

'Not for the moment.' She smiled and Sarah, still very pink, bobbed a curtsy and bustled out.

Pouring herself some tea, Melissa placed the cup and saucer within easy reach and, sitting down in her father's chair, drew a fresh sheet of paper and the inkstand toward her, and picked up a pen. After several moments' thought she began writing.

Once she had started, it was less difficult than she had feared. She kept the letter brief, setting out the facts just as the doctor had given them to her. Then she reassured her brother that she would manage everything until his return. To add to his burden by confessing her fears and anxieties would be both selfish and unfair. It would take several weeks for the letter to reach him, and several more for him to get home. And by that time it was probable ... No: she would think no further than tomorrow.

Signing her name, she took another sheet and wrote a second, identical letter. When she had finished she folded both and sealed them, and addressed one to Lieutenant George Tregonning, His Majesty's Ship *Defiant*, c/o Admiralty House, London, to be sent out on one of the navy sloops. After writing her brother's name and that of his ship on the other, she hesitated. Then, remembering him telling her that following a terrible storm in 1784 the Custom House and Public Offices had been moved from Port Royal, she addressed it instead to Kingston. This letter would go from Falmouth on the Jamaica packet, so even if one went astray, hopefully the other would reach him safely.

As Gilbert left with the letters, closing the door behind him, Melissa let her head fall back against the dark, shiny leather. Sarah's reminder of her uncles was like a thorn under her skin. While waiting for the doctor to arrive, she had wrestled with the question of when to tell them.

Naturally they would have to be informed. But surely it would do no harm to wait a little? It wasn't as if they could actually do anything. According to Dr Wherry the next 48 hours were critical, and a calm, quiet atmosphere must be maintained. If noise and fuss were to be avoided, then so were her uncles and their wives.

Straightening in the chair, Melissa swivelled it to face the desk, took a sip of her tea, and drew the pile of letters and papers toward her. She needed to keep busy. If she stopped, fear for her father would take over. For all their sakes she could not afford to let that happen. Instead, she would make herself useful. Her father had always dealt with the paperwork, though it now appeared even that had proved too much for him. It surely could not be so difficult? If it wasn't, then he had simply lost the will, or the ability, to concentrate.

Blinking away tears, she drew a deep breath. The more she could do to help, the less he would have to worry about. Maybe if she were able to reassure him … She bit her lip hard. She must not hope. Dr Wherry had been brutally frank.

'He may not die. But the damage is so great –'

'Are you saying it would be better if he did?'

'I am saying his physical and mental abilities would be severely impaired. You know your father: would he wish to live like that, do you think?'

Memories had whirled through her mind: going neck or nothing alongside him with the hunt; riding with him over the farm, listening to his plans to grow new crops such as swedes and mangel-wurzels, and maybe to invest in the new Tullian seed drill; accompanying him and Tom through the yard, listening as they discussed progress on a boat.

She could not imagine a more terrible life for her father than to be deprived of movement or understanding. Or worse: to retain awareness yet find himself unable to communicate. So she had shaken her head, her chest hurting as she choked down sobs, her hands clasped so tightly her knuckles ached.

Taking another sip of tea, she forced her attention back to the pile of letters and documents. Replacing her cup, she leafed through them, intending first to simply divide them into business and personal before deciding what action each required. But almost at once she came across three from Williams' Bank in Truro.

Several minutes later, tea forgotten, she raised her head and stared blindly at the book-lined wall opposite. Despite the summer sunshine flooding the room with warmth and light, she was cold to the marrow of her bones.

How had things reached such a pass? Why had he allowed it to go on so long, get so out of hand? Why had he not confided in her? Her breath caught on a shuddering sigh. That at least was easily answered. A proud man, he could not have borne to admit the extent to which he had lost control of his financial affairs, particularly to his own daughter who, at 12, had proclaimed him her hero.

Checking the dates, she saw that the letters had been written over a period of six weeks. Each began by regretting that Mr Tregonning had not responded either by letter or in person to previous communications. They continued, in increasingly stern tones, by requesting immediate repayment of at least a portion of the outstanding loan. The most recent letter made it clear that further delay was unacceptable, and should he not appear in person to discuss the matter, then regretfully the bank would have no alternative but to foreclose and take whatever steps necessary to recover their money, or goods to the value thereof.

Melissa shivered, then burned with mortification on his behalf as she imagined his shame, the terrible anxiety, and his fear of exposing the family, especially her mother, to the gossip and censure that would inevitably attend such a process. Why had he not replied to the letters? And if his recent visits to Truro had not been to the bank, then where had he gone?

Setting those letters aside, she picked up the rest of the papers and glanced through them. There were letters from shareholders in the new packet-ship, and from insurance companies. There were invoices and represented accounts marked with red ink from paint shop, rope store, sail maker and foundry, and others concerning the farm.

Dividing them into piles, not allowing herself to look at the totals – she would face that later – she scanned the desktop to make sure nothing had been missed, and glimpsed the distinctive green seal on a folded sheet partially hidden beneath the tray. As she opened and read it, her heart gave a convulsive lurch that left her dizzy and nauseous. This, surely, was what had pushed her father over the edge.

Expressing sincere remorse, aware that the timing was most unfortunate, Thomas Vincent deeply regretted that in view of his own suddenly straitened circumstances due to the unfortunate failure of a business investment, he had no choice but to request most urgently the immediate refund of his loan.

Her father was in debt to a moneylender as well as to the bank? Reading the sum due, Melissa gasped, and sat frozen as fear broke over her in a crushing, suffocating wave. The foundations of her world had shifted. Everything she believed firm and solid had suddenly turned to quicksand. She felt dazed and breathless. A knock on the door made her start violently. She looked up, trying to compose herself, as Addey peered in.

'There you are. Your mother's asking for you. Ever so much better she is. Still weak, but I reckon she's over the worst now. You going to be long in here?'

Melissa had to clear her throat before any sound would emerge from her constricted throat. 'No. I'll – I'll be up in just a moment.' As the nurse withdrew, Melissa placed her hands flat on the edge of the desktop and pushed herself to her feet.

What was she to do? She had to do something. If she didn't, her father's good name would be ruined, and her mother become an object of pity and scorn, gossiped about at assemblies on whose guest lists the Tregonning name would appear less and less. But do what?

She could, of course, call in her uncles, lay the situation before them, and ask for their help. But pride and a determination to protect her father – for clearly he had not confided in them himself – put that out of the question. So did the thought of her aunts' reactions.

If she could somehow manage to hold things together until George got home … Yet even if there were no delay in the letters reaching him, it would be at least three months before he returned to Cornwall. Neither the bank nor Thomas Vincent would wait that long. Which meant that somehow *she* must raise the money to repay the debts. But how was she to do that? And keep her uncles from finding out?

# Chapter Five

By late afternoon, Melissa was exhausted. She had spent the day either in her father's study struggling to bring order to the chaos and make a list of how much and to whom money was owed, or sitting with her mother while Addey bustled about seeing to her mistress's comfort. It wasn't so much the tasks themselves that Melissa found draining, but the effort of hiding her shock and anxiety at the size of the financial disaster.

'Looking proper hagged, you are,' the old nurse announced, returning with a fresh jug of lemonade. 'How don't you get a breath of air? Don't you go telling me you haven't got time. What with poor master like he is, and your dear mother weak as a kitten, there isn't that much for you to do.'

Oh Addey, if you only knew.

'Anyhow, I don't want you getting ill.'

'I'm never ill.' Melissa flexed her shoulders and rubbed the back of her neck to ease the tight band of tension that had formed there.

'Dear life! Don't go saying things like that!' the old nurse scolded, looking quickly round for the nearest wood and tapping the bedside table. 'Don't you argue neither. I'll stay with mistress. She's sleeping lovely now. Mind you, I reckon she'll have the aches for a few days yet. And she'll be limp as a rag for a fortnight. But now the fever has broke, the worst is over. Gilbert says master's sleeping so there isn't no call for you to feel you got to go and sit with he. You get off out, but mind you take a shawl. The sun might be out, but there's still an edge to that there wind.'

Tying the ribbons of a chip straw hat under her chin, Melissa swung the fringed silk over her shoulders and set off

61

down the drive. She would have preferred to ride, but that would have meant changing her dress. And as the household kept country hours and dined early, she wouldn't have time on her return to bathe and change again.

She did not relish the task ahead. But it was only fair that Tom be told of her father's illness. A far thornier question, and one she had not yet resolved, was whether she should confide to him the financial catastrophe facing the family. It would inevitably affect the yard.

Tom Ferris had worked for Tregonning's for 40 years. Totally honest, he had never pulled his punches with her father during their private discussions. She had grown quite accustomed to hear them bellowing at one another. But when the men were about, Tom invariably stood firm behind her father and backed his decisions. Though she had seen him literally chewing his tongue on occasions.

The sound of hooves broke into her thoughts. Glancing up, Melissa saw her Uncle Brinley's gig approaching, drawn by a showy, high-stepping chestnut. Suppressing the flutter of apprehension in her chest, she continued walking toward him, stretching her mouth into a smile of welcome as her thoughts darted in all directions like sparks from a spitting log.

He did not return her smile, his expression set. She curled her fingers into her palm, refusing to speculate on the cause. She would find out soon enough.

'Ah Melissa, I was just coming to – Whoa there! Stand still, damn you!' He hauled on the reins and the chestnut danced on the spot, tossing its head and mouthing the bit that sawed at the corners of a foam-flecked mouth that would soon be hard as leather.

Placing one hand on the soft muzzle, Melissa murmured soothingly to the sweating animal. Heavy-handed and impatient, her uncle quickly ruined every new horse he bought, and got rid of them at a huge loss, cursing their poor breeding and the morals of whoever had sold him such rubbish.

'Your Aunt Louisa was taken ill during the night. I've had the doctor to her, and he says it's this damned influenza. Thought I'd better warn your mother. Know she's not up to snuff at the moment.'

'That was kind of you, Uncle Brinley. Unfortunately –' she made a wry face '– your warning comes a little too late I'm afraid.'

'Already got it, has she? Not surprised. Nothing to her. Like a feather in a breeze. Bad, is she?'

'Not as bad as we might have expected. The fever has broken, and she's resting comfortably.'

'Glad to hear it. You off somewhere in particular? No, don't suppose you can be or you'd be aboard that great brute of yours. Hardly a suitable mount for a young lady. Still, I don't suppose it would be easy to find something to fit, you being like you are.'

Too used to his blunt manner to take offence, and ignoring the insinuation that her height was some kind of deformity, which was evidently how he perceived it, Melissa shook her head. 'I was just getting some fresh air. I've been indoors all day.'

'Father at home? May as well have a chat with him now I'm here. Haven't seen much of him lately. In fact, I'm beginning to wonder if he isn't avoiding us.'

Her insides giving a sudden and painful lurch, Melissa shook her head again. 'Oh Uncle Brinley, how can you think such a thing? It's just that he's been particularly busy at the yard. But I'm afraid you won't be able to see him today.'

Brinley Tregonning's fleshy features drew together in a frown. 'Oh? Don't tell me he's not here again.'

'No, he's at home. But he's not receiving visitors. I'm afraid he's ill.'

'He got the influenza as well?'

Still stroking the chestnut's nose, Melissa blinked away the sharp sting of tears. 'No, he's had a stroke.'

'*What?* Are you sure? I suppose you must be. Had the doctor? Yes, of course you have. Well, what a thing. Damned sorry to hear it.' His frown sharpened and he stretched his chin forward in the mannerism she knew all too well. 'Just a minute, when did this happen? Why wasn't I informed? My brother suffers a stroke, and you're wandering around out here, taking the air? If I hadn't come to call on your mother, how long would you have waited before bothering to let me know? What about Marcus? Has he been told?'

'No, of course not. What I mean is I would never have informed him and not you.' Watching a little of the tension leave him, she understood why, given the rivalry between the brothers, her father had not felt able to confide in either of them. 'Uncle Brinley, I can only apologise. It only happened this morning. Naturally I sent for Dr Wherry at once –'

'Don't like the fellow myself, got some odd notions. But Louisa seems happy with him, and from what she tells me he's been kind to your mother.'

'Indeed, without his understanding I really don't know if my mother would –' Cutting herself short, Melissa drew a deep breath. 'My father was taken ill at breakfast. Dr Wherry came within the hour. I cannot speak highly enough –' She stopped again, swallowing hard. 'He advised me to send for George.'

Her uncle's face slackened as he recognised the implication. 'Did he now?' He cleared his throat several times. 'Does he say –? Did he give any indication – how long?'

'He's coming back tomorrow morning.'

Brinley nodded. 'How's your mother taken it?'

Melissa moistened her lips. 'I haven't told her yet. The fever – she's still very weak. I didn't want – it seemed wiser to wait a day or two, let her recover her strength.'

He pursed his lips. 'Hmm. I daresay that's best. An event like this, on top of what happened a twelvemonth ago – well, you know what I mean.'

'I was going to write to Uncle Marcus this evening and ask young John to take it round. But I think perhaps Aunt Lucy in Plymouth should be told as well.'

'Yes, well, no need to trouble yourself over Marcus. I'll drive over now and tell him myself. I'll drop your Aunt Lucy a line as well if you like. Daresay you've got more than enough to do.'

'You're sure you don't mind, Uncle Brinley? It's really my responsibility.'

'Nothing of the kind. Don't give it another thought. You

have quite enough on your plate. Wherry's coming back tomorrow morning, you say? Then I'll do the same. Maybe have a word with him myself.' He gathered in the reins, and Melissa winced inwardly as the chestnut's head was jerked up, its eye rolling nervously and showing white. 'Can I give you a ride back to the house?'

Melissa would have liked to decline. But if she refused, her uncle would probably try to turn the gig in the drive and he lacked the skill to do so without terrifying the horse and resorting to the whip. Besides, the time their conversation had taken meant that it was too late now for her to walk to the yard. She would have to see Tom tomorrow instead. After all, it was unlikely there would be any change between now and then.

'Thank you, Uncle Brinley. That's very kind.' She climbed up quickly beside him. After circling the wide, paved sweep, he dropped her off at the front steps.

'Tell your mother I called, and that I'll look in tomorrow to see how she is.'

Thanking him once more, she watched him drive away at a spanking pace, and knew her uncle to be saddened by the news while still relishing the fact that being first to know allowed him particular authority as he conveyed the tidings to the rest of the family.

After rinsing the film of sweat and sawdust from his face, Gabriel slipped the braces from his shoulders, pulled his shirt free, and flapped it to shake off the shavings. This would be the first time he'd been seen in the village. There was no chance of his presence going unremarked. His height and the fact that he was a stranger were all too obvious.

Though with his stubble, long hair, and working clothes he might appear to be just another shipyard worker, to arrive filthy and unkempt would hardly allay the villagers' suspicion. Wiping his face on his shirt tail, he tucked it once more into his breeches and, shouldering his braces, slipped on his waistcoat. Then, loosing his hair, he raked it through with his home-made comb and tied it back again.

'Dear life!' Tansey hooted. 'What're you up to? Going

looking for a lightskirt, are you?'

'Father!' Billy blushed scarlet.

'It's all right, Billy,' Gabriel said. 'Just ask your father how I buy food if they won't let me in the shop?'

'Well, I tell you, pretty yourself up any more and they won't let you out again!' Tansey gave a great cackle of laughter.

'Gabe Ennis!' Tom shouted from the doorway of his office. 'Here a minute.'

'Want for us to wait, do you?' Walter grunted, as the two shipwrights and two apprentices started for the gate. Men from other parts of the yard and the packet were already on their way out.

'No,' Gabriel shook his head. 'You go on.'

'Right, well, see you tomorrow.' Clicking his tongue, Tansey winked. 'And if you're late, we'll know –'

'Shut up, father,' Billy growled, flushing.

'Git on, boy. Just because you don't know what it's for don't mean Gabe got to spend his nights alone.'

'He knows,' Gabriel replied, winning a look of desperate gratitude from the youth whose blush belied his powerful build. 'He's just choosy.' Cuffing Billy lightly on the shoulder, he murmured, 'Best way to be.' Then, leaving them, he crossed to the foreman's office.

Taking coins from a small box, Tom dropped them onto Gabriel's palm, then closed the lid and turned the key. 'You done all right.'

With a brief nod, Gabriel slipped the money into his pocket. 'You make that?' Made of oak bound with iron, the box was a perfectly crafted miniature of a seaman's chest.

Tom shrugged. ''Tisn't nothing special.'

Gabriel raised his eyes to meet the foreman's. 'It is. You made any more?'

'A couple. Me missus wanted one for her sewing. Why? What's it to you? '

'Nothing, except it's a beautiful piece of work.' He raised a hand. 'See you in the morning.'

There were still plenty of people about, more than he would

have wished. As he walked along the cobbled street, head down and shoulders slightly hunched, he sensed their curiosity. Who was he? Where had he come from? Why was he here? What did he want? A number of villagers would have the answers within an hour as men from the yard told their families about the newcomer. By this time tomorrow, human nature would have ensured that the news had spread to everyone else.

A gasp and muffled giggles made him glance up and he stopped abruptly, just in time to avoid a collision with two girls. Both wore calico skirts, one a rusty orange, the other light blue, with matching low-necked cotton bodices. And each had a white muslin kerchief about her shoulders, crossed over her bosom and tied at the back.

Their hair, a mass of short, frizzy curls over the top and sides, had been left long at the back and tortured into two thick ringlets that hung over each shoulder: a style that society women had begun to abandon at least five years ago. Yet these girls, so bold with their knowing eyes and teasing smiles, clearly thought themselves to be highly fashionable.

'Beg pardon,' he growled, knuckling his forehead, and stepped out into the road, careful not to meet their eyes. He heard whispers then more muffled giggles as they went on their way. It was only to be expected. The same thing had happened in France. A male stranger who was neither green youth nor old curmudgeon, and apparently without ties, was likely to have money to spend and was therefore an attractive proposition no matter what he looked like.

The street slanted inward to the middle where a narrow channel carried away rainwater and anything else flung into it from the cottages, ale houses, and shops that lined both sides. Stepping over it, Gabriel ducked his head and walked in through the open door of the bakery. Even at this late hour the scent of fresh bread still hung in the air, overlaid by the mouth-watering, hunger-sharpening aroma of hot savoury pasties.

A short, plump woman wearing a white apron over a grey dimity gown, sleeves pushed up to her elbows, was bent over a large sack of flour, struggling to move it from just inside the door to the area behind the counter where several others were already stacked against the wall.

Stepping forward, Gabriel muttered, 'By your leave,' lifted the sack from her hands and in two strides placed it against the others, then retreated to stand just inside the door. 'Mrs Mitchell?'

'My dear soul! Where'd you spring from then?' A light coating of flour clung to her round, rosy face now glowing crimson from her exertions. Straightening up, she puffed out her breath as she pressed her hands to the small of her back, then tucked up the wisps and tendrils that had worked free from the loose bun high on her head. '

'Haven't seen you round here before.' Her gaze was shrewd.

Gabriel gave her a brief, cool smile, sensing he would achieve more with reserve than by trying to ingratiate himself. 'Not been here before. I'm working at the yard.' He reached into his pocket.

Hearing the clink and jingle of coins, the woman's eyes brightened, but she was still suspicious. 'Some bad cold you got.'

Sighing inwardly, he shook his head and lifted his chin to reveal the bandage. 'Prisoner in France, escaped.'

'Dear life! They never tried to cut your throat?'

He shook his head. 'Irons, chained to a wall.' He held out his wrists.

One hand flew to her bosom. 'You poor soul. What you doing here? 'How haven't you gone back where you belong?'

'Can't. Press gang.'

Anger drew her brows together and she clicked her tongue. 'That's never right. Shouldn't be allowed. Dear life! '

Physically exhausted, stomach cramping with hunger, Gabriel knew the sympathy and indignation were kindly meant. But he couldn't take any more. He needed food, but craved the peace and solitude of the woods. 'Tom Ferris said –'

'Tom sent you? Well, why didn't you say? Now, just give me a moment.' Wiping her hands on her apron, she bustled around behind the counter.

Gabriel laid his money on the top and watched with

increasing concern as Mrs Mitchell packed a basket with a loaf, a saffron cake, and a steaming, golden pasty.

'Wait. Beg pardon, ma'am, but I can't –'

Placing the basket on the counter, she pushed the coins toward him. 'You put they back in your pocket. Better still, buy yourself a pitcher of ale to wash down the pasty.' She winked, sighing fondly. 'My Cyrus did used to love a glass of ale with his pasty.'

Scooping up the coins and picking up the basket, Gabriel saluted her. 'Very kind of you.'

Her flustered response – shooing him away with flapping hands – suggested she had little experience of compliments or gratitude. 'Get on. No such thing.' Then concern and curiosity reasserted themselves. 'Where you staying to?'

Moving easily toward the door, Gabriel smiled. 'I'm all right.'

'In the village, are you?'

'Not far.' He jerked a thumb vaguely.

'You be in again?'

'If you'll take my money.'

She threw up her hands, laughing. 'Some hard man you are.'

'But fair.'

Her chuckles remained with him as he hesitated outside a small stone cottage with a weathered board nailed above the doorway. The painted name had long since faded to illegibility. Tiny windows were thrown open to the evening, but whether to let fresh air in, or the smell of stale beer, wet sawdust, and tobacco smoke out, only the landlord knew. After a moment's hesitation, Gabriel ducked inside. It had been a long, hard day, and though brandy or a fine claret would have been his choice, he would gladly settle for a jar of ale.

In one corner, a wizened old man sucked on a clay pipe. Another two were hunched over a table talking quietly together. They all looked round to see who had come in, and remained silent, watching, until Gabriel left with the basket in one hand, a stone jar of ale in the other, and all too few coins left in his pocket.

*   *   *

Deeply asleep, Melissa wove the sounds into her dream. But the soft persistent knocking grew increasingly urgent. She turned over. The grey light percolating through the summer curtains told her it was too early. Even the sun wasn't up yet. Still tired, she rubbed her eyes. Then the knocking came again. She heard hurried footsteps and anxious whispers outside her door. Addey and Lobb.

Throwing back the covers, almost tripping over her long, white nightdress, Melissa hurled herself at the door and wrenched it open. Butler and nurse jumped violently. Both were fully dressed, but it was clear that while Addey had slept in her clothes, keeping vigil beside her mistress, Lobb's dishevelled air betrayed a recent hasty rousing from his bed.

Addey's hands covered her mouth as if to stop any sound escaping, but her eyes were wide and wet with tears.

''Tis the master, Miss Melissa,' Lobb said gently.

'What happened? Is he worse?' Melissa would have started along the passage. But, to her astonishment, Lobb stepped in front of her, grave and gentle.

'I'm ever so sorry, miss. I'm afraid he's gone.'

She rocked as if he had hit her. Her throat suddenly dried, so when she swallowed it felt sharp and painful. 'You're sure? I mean, it couldn't be just –?'

'Quite sure, miss. It was sudden but very peaceful. Gilbert will tell you himself.'

'He was there?' At least her father had not died alone.

'He was, miss. I'd only just gone to my bed. We – Gilbert and me – have been taking turns to sit with master. Anyway, it can't have been no more than half an hour after I'd left the room when Gilbert comes to tell me master's gone. It happened that quick, Gilbert didn't even have time to get out of the chair. So, with respect, miss, don't you start fretting about no one from the family being with him, for he couldn't have known nothing about it. All over in a breath, it was. That's the honest truth.'

Melissa searched his face, but his gaze, though shocked and sad, never wavered. She glanced from Lobb to Addey. 'Does my mother know?'

The old nurse's face crumpled as, hands still clamped over her mouth, she gave a muffled squeak before shaking her head.

'I must go to her.' The passage floor felt as though it was heaving beneath Melissa's feet as she hurried to her mother's room. This wasn't happening. It was just a nightmare. Only it wasn't her imagination run riot, a terrible dream from which waking would rescue her: it was real. And there was no escape.

Emma Tregonning lay on her side with only her head above the bedclothes. A frilled lawn nightcap tied with strings beneath her chin covered her hair, so that in the dim light her face looked small, almost childlike on the pillow. Her slow breathing indicated deep sleep.

Reaching out to touch her mother's shoulder, Melissa hesitated, then withdrew her hand, instead clasping her arms across her chest. What purpose would it serve? Would it not be wiser, kinder, to let her sleep as long as possible? Why wake her now and burden her with yet more grief? It could not change what had happened. Stepping back from the bed, Melissa turned to the old nurse who had followed her in.

'You stay here, Addey. I'll ask Sarah or Agnes to bring you up some tea.'

'Tea?' Addey whispered, shocked. 'This time of the morning?'

Melissa drew a deep shaking breath. 'Why not? I think we'll both feel better for something hot to drink.'

'Yes, well, perhaps you're right. I tell you, 'tis going to be some awful day.' Her face crumpled again, and she pressed both hands to her wet cheeks. 'What am I going to say to the poor dear soul when she do wake?'

'Nothing, Addey. You don't have to say anything.' Melissa put an arm around the shaking shoulders. 'The moment she opens her eyes, you come and fetch me. I'll tell her. But I hope, for her sake, she sleeps for another few hours. Now come and sit down here.' Pressing her gently into a high-backed chair upholstered in rose velvet, Melissa crouched to pick up the soft rug from the floor where it had dropped, and laid it over the old woman's knees.

'Where will you be?' The anxiety in Addey's face and her clutching hand startled Melissa for an instant. A skipped heartbeat and welling fear accompanied her realisation that, from this moment, everyone in the household would look to her for reassurance, decisions and orders. It was too much. How would she cope?

'I won't be far away. Lobb or Sarah will find me. Try to rest now. My mother will need you to be strong, Addey. And so shall I.'

Returning to her room, Melissa flung back the curtains and looked out on to a mist-shrouded world. Beyond the trees and curving hillside, the rising sun had washed the eastern sky pale primrose. It was going to be a beautiful day.

Closing her eyes tightly and swallowing the agonising stiffness in her throat, Melissa took another deep breath. Dr Wherry had warned her, and in her heart of hearts she knew it was for the best. It had been a swift passing, no pain or struggle, no gradual decline that would have robber her father of dignity. It was just – too soon.

Reaching into her closet, she took out a robe. She was slipping her arms into it when Sarah peered round the door, round-eyed with shock. Melissa didn't wait for her to speak.

'Sarah, before you run my bath, would you make a pot of tea and bring a cup for me and one for Miss Addey? She's sitting with my mother.'

Sarah nodded quickly. 'Shall I bring one for mistress as well?'

'No, she's asleep so please be as quiet as you can.'

Following Sarah out, still tying the belt of her robe, Melissa walked along the passage to her father's room. After a brief pause outside to gather her strength, she tapped very gently to warn Gilbert of her presence, then entered.

Seated on the chest at the foot of the large oak bed, his head in his hands, Gilbert looked up, his eyes red-rimmed, and shot to his feet.

'Oh miss –' His voice broke.

Melissa linked her fingers tightly. 'There's nothing you could have done, Gilbert. But you were here. That's what matters. He wasn't alone.'

'Twenty years.' The valet struggled for control. 'Started as a bootboy, then Mr Lobb trained me up for manservant. Said if master was willing I could learn to be a valet. These last five years –' He glanced over his shoulder and spread his hands, inarticulate in his grief. 'The best.'

'Why don't you go down to the kitchen? Mrs Betts is making some tea.' Seeing he was about to protest, she added gently, 'I'd like a few moments alone with my father.' As he bowed and stumbled out, his head down, she went to the bed.

Looking down at her father, she was struck by how peaceful he looked. The lines and grooves that stress had etched so deep, death had smoothed away. But though the signs of suffering had been erased, so too had the subtle features that had given his face its unique character.

Sitting on the bed, she took his hand in hers. It was cold and felt unnaturally heavy. 'I won't let it go, Papa,' she whispered. 'I'll hold on until George gets home.' Even as she spoke she wondered how on earth she could keep such a vow. Yet just saying the words, making the promise, stiffened her determination.

With a quiet tap on the door, Lobb entered. 'Time to come away now, miss. Master has to be washed and laid out proper.'

Releasing her father's hand, Melissa leant down and kissed his forehead. The skin felt cool and waxy. She knew then that though the figure looked like her father, this body was only a husk, a shell. The essence and spirit of the man she had loved and admired had gone.

A dagger-thrust of loss pierced her: loneliness so deep, so acute, it made her gasp. An instant later, anger erupted with volcanic force. How could he do this? She knew he had loved her. But he had bequeathed her a burden of responsibility she had neither the strength nor the knowledge to discharge.

'Miss Melissa?'

Roused by Lobb's quiet prompting, she stood up, drained by the violence of her feelings. Though physically she felt week and shaky, the emotional storm had cleared her mind. She would not, could not, give up.

# Chapter Six

Emma Tregonning did not stir until after nine. Addey came immediately to fetch Melissa who had put on her lilac muslin, deeming it wiser, in view of her mother's fragile state, not to don her black until after she had broken the news. But the nurse's tear-swollen eyes and hurried exit must have alerted her mistress to the fact that something dreadful had occurred.

Melissa entered the room to find her mother sitting on the edge of the bed, propping herself on her arms, too weak to stand, her gaunt face ashen, eyes huge with fear. 'What is it?' she croaked. 'What's happened? Has there been a letter?'

'No, Mama. No letters. Come now, you mustn't get cold. You're not well enough to get up yet.' Gently easing her mother back into bed, Melissa drew the covers over the frail, trembling figure. Then, to the accompaniment of Addey's stifled sobs, her own voice less than steady, she told her mother of her father's stroke and his death that morning.

She had prepared herself for an outburst of grief, even hysterics. But after a minute's stunned silence, during which Melissa watched her mother visibly shrivel like a flower in an unexpected frost, Emma Tregonning's only reaction was a cracked whisper. 'Too much.' Since then, she had lain blank-faced and completely unresponsive. The moment the doctor arrived he guessed what had happened, and Melissa told him what she knew of the circumstances as she led him upstairs to her mother.

'You have my deepest sympathy. But try not to mourn his passing, my dear. Be thankful instead that it was so easy. In truth, with virtually no hope of recovery, his death was a blessing.'

Bowing her head, Melissa had bitten the inside of her lower lip. How could she tell him it wasn't so much the fact of her father's death she found shattering? Though she would miss him terribly she could not have borne to watch him die by inches, trapped in a body he could not control. Without recognition or means of expression, what would he have been left with but bewilderment or, even worse, fear? What grieved her, filling her with trepidation that required all her strength and energy to keep hidden, was the devastation he had left behind.

After a brief examination to check that Emma's influenza was not developing into anything more serious, the doctor had drawn Melissa away from the bedside and, opening his case, taken out a small dark bottle.

'There is little I, or any doctor, can do for her at present. All I can offer is a stronger sedative. Sleep is the greatest healer. It will aid her physical recovery. But more important, it allows her an escape from the pain of losing her life's partner. After your elder brother was killed last year, your mother relied heavily on your father for support. Now he has gone as well ...' He shrugged.

What about me? The cry echoed inside Melissa's head. It's my loss, too. Who can I lean on? But she remained silent. The doctor could make her mother comfortable, and for that she must be thankful. As for the rest, in the absence of her brother she must shoulder responsibility.

A little while later, the doctor left. She watched him ride away, the sun warm on her face, the house at her back dark and heavy with sorrow. Then she turned and went inside.

It was midday. She wasn't hungry, but with Sarah and Lobb both urging her to eat, citing the need to keep up her own strength, she had not the heart or the will to refuse. And by the time she had finished the cold meat and fruit she did feel stronger. Rising from the table, she started toward the stairs. There had been so much to do she had not had time to change into the black muslin and crepe Sarah had retrieved from storage. But Lobb stopped her in the hall.

'Sarah has just informed me that Mr Brinley Tregonning

and Mr Marcus Tregonning are on their way up the drive. Are you at home, miss?'

Drawing herself up, knowing this was only the first of many tests she would have to face, Melissa tilted her chin. 'Yes, Lobb. Please show them into the drawing-room. And you had better bring some brandy. I believe my uncles would prefer it to Madeira.'

Seating herself in a chair half turned from the window so the sun would not be directly on her face, she picked up some white-work. But the tremor in her hands made tiny stitches impossible. Rather than risk betraying her agitation with a pricked finger and bloodstains on the embroidered handkerchief, she simply held it on her lap.

As well as being the oldest, her father had also been the tallest of the three brothers. It had embarrassed her and irritated them when she too surpassed them in height. The difference was slight, and though her Uncle Brinley took little notice except when Aunt Louisa reminded him of it, regarding it more as an inconvenience to her than a reflection on himself, with her Uncle Marcus it was different. He seemed to regard her regal build as both an affront and a challenge to his own lack of inches. Torn between amusement and annoyance – for it was neither her choice nor her fault – Melissa had learnt simply to ignore his prickliness. After all, she could not change the situation. Nor did she feel inclined now to spend all her time in his presence sitting down, a tactic she had employed when younger and far less sure of herself.

Her heart thumping uncomfortably as she waited for Lobb to show them in, she recognised the nervousness, the same self-conscious unease, that had attended those long-ago visits. Catching herself, she straightened her back, deliberately lowering her shoulders and lifting her chin. She was no longer a child, and this was no time for weakness. In order to convince her uncles that her primary concern at this tragic time was her mother's health, she not only had to lie, but do so fluently and without a tremor. And once started there could be no turning back. She had been brought up to value honesty above all things. It seemed bitterly ironic that from today, from this moment, honesty had to be sacrificed if she was to protect her father's reputation and the family's good name.

To prepare herself, mentally and physically, she drew several deep breaths. The door opened.

'Mr Brinley Tregonning and Mr Marcus Tregonning,' Lobb announced, withdrawing and closing the door quietly behind him as her uncles strode into the room. They wore the attire of country gentlemen. Both had chosen a double-breasted riding frock of fine cloth cut shorter than the normal tailcoat, Brinley's in dark blue, while Marcus favoured a light brown, over striped linen waistcoats, breeches, and topboots.

Though many gentlemen had begun to abandon their wigs, Melissa could not imagine seeing either of her uncles without their familiar toupees with the hair swept back full and wavy from forehead and temples with a loose roll curl covering the ears and a short pigtail queue. Both were conservative traditionalists who viewed change with suspicion and clung determinedly to the old ways.

'How are they?' Brinley demanded the moment greetings had been exchanged. As Melissa resumed her seat, he dropped heavily onto a brocaded sofa. Marcus lowered himself onto a Queen Anne chair upholstered in dark-green velvet, brushing dust from his breeches and regarding her with a look of frowning enquiry.

Tightly gripping the thumb of one hand concealed beneath the other, Melissa moistened her lips. 'My mother's condition is slightly improved, but –'

'Doctor been again, has he?' Brinley demanded.

'Yes. He left about an hour ago, but –'

'Told you we should come earlier,' he snapped at Marcus. 'Wanted a word. Too late now.' He turned back to Melissa. 'So what does he say about your father, then?'

Swallowing, Melissa glanced at them in turn. 'M-my father passed away just before dawn this morning.'

'*What?*' Brinley blurted.

Marcus stared at her in disbelief. 'But – he can't have.'

Melissa understood his reaction. She had had several hours to get used to the idea. Yet though her mind knew it to be so, her heart was still unwilling to accept.

'It was very sudden, but very peaceful. Gilbert, his manservant was sitting with him. He just – stopped.' She shrugged helplessly, the swelling in her throat making further speech impossible.

Her heart felt like a lump of lead, physically heavy in her chest, and her sense of loss was an intense ache that made her want to curl over and hug herself. Her attempted deep breath caught in a sob and she cleared her throat in an effort at disguise. Her uncles might make allowance if she wept, weeping was something women did. But it would make them uncomfortable and could cost her their respect. It was vital she maintained a façade of dignity, and filial concern for her mother.

'Good God,' Brinley shook his head. 'Francis dead. Hard to believe.' He pushed himself to his feet. Marcus followed suit. 'Like to see him. Pay my respects.'

Melissa rose quickly. 'Of course.'

She would have led the way, but Marcus stepped in front of her. 'No need for you … Lobb can … Difficult time, Emma ill. You stay here.'

They reached the door just as Lobb entered with the tray.

'My uncles wish to pay their respects. Would you take them up, Lobb?'

Swiftly setting the tray down on a side table, the butler bowed. 'Of course, miss. If you'll follow me, gentlemen?'

Melissa walked over to the window. Crossing her arms, pressing them against the ache, she gazed out over terrace and fields. In the sunshine the treetops were every shade of green imaginable. But the way the land sloped away meant that from here she could see little of the woods. Abruptly she turned away, using rejection of the view to shut off a brief but vivid memory of dark, knowing eyes.

A few moments later, her uncles re-entered the room. Both were subtly different: the changes more sensed than seen. Following them in, Lobb went unobtrusively to the table and poured brandy into two glasses.

'Sad business,' Brinley muttered, taking a glass from the

proffered tray and shaking his head. 'No age. Damn me if he don't look better than the last time I saw him.'

'For God's sake, Brinley,' his brother hissed, also taking a glass. 'Man's dead. Can't possibly look better.'

But Melissa knew what her uncle meant. Death had released her father from a burden that had become intolerable, and smoothed the torment from his features. Catching her eye and responding with an infinitesimal nod, Lobb bowed and withdrew.

'Anyway,' Marcus continued, warming the glass between his palms then swirling the spirit, 'the point is even if Emma were well I don't think she'd be up to dealing with things. As matters stand, I see no alternative but for us to take over.' He raised the glass to his lips.

'Tregidgo or Morley?' Brinley frowned. 'Favour Morley myself. Does a good funeral.'

Melissa glanced from one to the other. They were talking as if she wasn't even there.

Marcus shrugged. 'As you like. You speak to Morley, and make sure everyone is notified – use Lang's in Boscawen Street to print the cards. I'll see the lawyers and handle the legal business.'

Melissa stiffened as anger and anxiety fizzed along her limbs, making her heart skip a beat. 'If I may say something?' They both turned to her, clearly surprised at the interruption. She pushed her tongue between her teeth and upper lip to free it. 'It is most kind of you to offer your assistance with the funeral.'

Brinley waved aside her thanks. 'Least we can do.' He turned away to resume his conversation with his brother.

'On my mother's behalf I accept with gratitude,' she continued, forcing a smile as their expressions reflected mingled astonishment and irritation. 'For I fear the shock of her sudden loss, coupled with her ill-health, will make it impossible for her to take an active part in the preparations. I know we may rely on you to ensure my father receives a fitting send-off. Though, naturally, I will write personal letters to our relations informing them of the sad news, you are far better acquainted with his many friends and business associates.'

'Yes, of course we are. Now if you will –' Marcus began testily, but Melissa did not intend to be silenced.

'However, given the time and effort involved in arranging the funeral and letting everyone know, it would be most unfair if my mother and I were to impose further. You have your own lives and families to consider. So, while I truly appreciate your offer regarding business and legal matters, I feel I should deal with those myself.' She gave the smallest of self-deprecating shrugs. 'They will be minimal, I'm sure.' She watched their astonishment deepen to shock and dismay.

'Can't have that,' Brinley exploded. 'Good God. No, indeed. Not at all the thing.'

'My dear Melissa, such an action, were we to permit it, would exceed all bounds of propriety.' Marcus's brows furrowed in anxiety. 'Your presumption astonishes me.'

'Can't blame the girl,' Brinley grunted in response. 'Francis's fault. Odd ideas. Comes of educating females. Always said so.'

'Never mind that,' Marcus snapped. 'How do you suppose we'd look if it were to get out? It wouldn't be Francis and his progressive ideas they'd be discussing. Oh no. It's we who'd be the butt of the jokes and gossip. Allowing a woman – a young, unmarried woman – to handle legal matters? Out of the question. Women and business don't mix. Never have, never will.' He swung back to Melissa. 'My dear, I'm sure you think you could manage. But the fact is –'

'Oh dear.' Melissa pressed her palms together, resting the tips of her fingers against her mouth. 'I am so sorry. I have not explained myself clearly. Uncle Brinley, Uncle Marcus, what I meant to say, what I thought you would realise, is that in dealing with the lawyers I am not doing so on my own account, but on behalf of my brother George, who is now head of our family. Naturally, if my mother were well enough she, and not I, would be doing it.' She watched them digest this.

'Yes, but George is out in Jamaica or some such place, isn't he?' Marcus demanded.

'Indeed he *was*,' Melissa answered carefully, 'but we have

been expecting word from him this past fortnight.'

'Oh. Well, if he's on his way home ...'

That wasn't what she had said. But she considered it neither necessary nor wise to correct the assumption. After all, it wasn't impossible that George might be on his way home. They had heard nothing to the contrary. They had heard *nothing*.

'Solves a problem,' Brinley agreed.

'Yes, but what about the yard?' Marcus frowned. 'Can that foreman fellow be relied upon?'

Melissa smothered flaring anger. Until this moment neither of them had ever given a moment's thought to the yard or the men who worked there. She had no intention of allowing them to interfere now.

'Tom Ferris has worked for Tregonning's for 40 years, Uncle Marcus. He has always enjoyed my father's complete trust and confidence. I am quite certain he will have no difficulty keeping everything running smoothly until my brother's return.' She could see her uncles were reluctant, but their reasons for intervening had been demolished by her explanations. They really had no choice but to accept.

Swallowing the last of their drinks, they stood up, preparing to take their leave. With perfect timing, Lobb entered, ready to show them out.

Melissa rose with them. 'Will you forgive me if I don't come with you to the door? I have been too long away from my mother. I know how grateful and relieved she will be that the funeral arrangements will be in such excellent hands. Thank you both so much. Might I make one small request? I will be delighted to welcome to the funeral all those who might wish to attend. But given my brother's absence, and my mother's delicate state of health, my own feeling is that we should limit those returning here afterwards to immediate family. What is your opinion?'

Exchanging a glance, both brothers grunted their assent. Following them into the hall, Melissa made a brief formal curtsy of farewell then, as Lobb accompanied them to the door, she lifted the skirts of her gown with fingers stiff and aching from accumulated tension and hurried up the stairs.

'She haven't moved,' Addey whispered, as Melissa entered her mother's bedroom. 'Not one inch. If it wasn't for that cough, I swear you wouldn't know she was breathing.' Gazing at her mistress, she shook her head. 'I don't think he should have gived her that stuff.'

Knowing *he* referred to the doctor, whom Addey mistrusted yet depended upon for her mistress's physical health, Melissa simply ignored the last remark. 'Why don't you go and get some fresh air? I'll stay for a while.'

'I'm all right,' Addey replied staunchly.

'Addey, go,' Melissa pointed to the door. 'And while you're downstairs, make sure you have something to eat and drink.'

The old nurse's eyes filled again. 'I know what it is. You don't think I'm looking after her proper.'

'Addey! Don't be so foolish.' Hurrying to her, Melissa hugged the old woman. 'No one has ever been given more love and attention. You couldn't have prevented her getting influenza, or – or any of the other things that have happened.'

Clinging to Melissa's arm, Addey raised a tear-streaked face. 'I've cared for that dear soul since she was in her cradle. I seen her married, and I seen her three babbies born. There isn't nothing I wouldn't do for she, and that's God's own truth. But I can't reach her, and I dunno what else to do.'

Tightening her grip on the old woman's shaking shoulders, Melissa fought down her own worry. 'It's the shock, Addey. Dr Wherry says she needs time, and sleep. We just have to be patient. I know it's not easy. It's terrible seeing her like this. I feel just as helpless as you do. In fact, to be honest, I think I'm far less use to her than you. I don't understand illness and such things the way you do. That's why I want you to have a short rest. How on earth would I cope if you fell ill? I'd be in terrible trouble.'

Dabbing her eyes, Addey looked up, the fear in her tired, bloodshot eyes giving way to realisation and a glimmer of pride. 'You would too.' She nodded, sniffing loudly as she heaved a shuddering sigh. 'Well, perhaps a few minutes wouldn't do no harm. Truth is,' she admitted, 'I could do with a bite of something. I reckon my stomach do think my throat's been cut. A nice cup of tea would set me up a treat.' As Melissa released her she moved away, straightening her cap and her smoothing her apron. 'But I won't be gone long, so no need for you to worry.'

Loath to in any way offend or hurt the old woman, Melissa simply nodded. She sat beside the bed for almost an hour, talking quietly to her mother, describing her uncles' visit and their offer to arrange the funeral and notify all friends and distant relatives. When that failed to elicit any response, she talked about the garden, and about Samson's leg, now fully healed. Then she talked about the farm: the broken plough that had been mended by the blacksmith at the yard; the cabbage and broccoli planted in seedbeds at the beginning of May and now starting to show. And how, when they had reached a height of nine inches in August or early September, they would be pulled up in bunches of a hundred and planted out in the fields.

Though her mother's eyes were half open, they remained unfocused. Not a flicker of expression crossed her face, which was as pale as wood-ash. Had it not been for the faint sound of her breath, catching occasionally on a rattling cough, she might have been carved from marble.

Melissa felt anxiety stir but ruthlessly suppressed it. Between them, Addey and the doctor would do everything possible to make her mother comfortable. She had to concentrate on what she *could* do, rather than waste valuable energy fretting about things over which she had no control.

When Addey returned, visibly restored, she brought a request from Mrs Betts for a few moments of Miss Melissa's time. Anxiety spiked again as Melissa went downstairs. What now? Not the household bills? No, it couldn't be. Her mother had only been ill a few days. Had there been a problem, surely her mother would have known? But even if she had known, would she have confided in her daughter? Had the gentle pressure to marry been because of financial problems her parents had not wished her to know about?

'I know how busy you are, miss, so that's why I thought I'd

catch you now. Then it'd be one less thing for you to be worried about, see?'

Melissa tried to look encouraging. 'What is it, Mrs Betts?'

'Well, I was wond'ring like, if you'd thought how many will be coming back here after the funeral?'

'That's why you wanted to see me?' Relief left Melissa weak.

'Yes.' The puzzlement on the cook's homely face faded as she explained. 'We want to do it proper, see, and give master a good send-off. But what with mistress ill and all, I didn't know what you'd be doing.' She lifted her plump shoulders. 'Should I cook for two dozen? Forty?'

'My uncles are taking care of the details and arranging the service. I don't even know if my mother will be well enough to attend. In any case, with her so recently confined to bed, I think it wiser to restrict the funeral tea to a cold collation for immediate family only.'

Mrs Betts nodded. 'That's what I was thinking. Say 20, then, just to be sure.' She bobbed a curtsy. 'I won't keep you, miss. I expect you're busy.'

Watching her waddle away, Melissa felt her heart sink at the prospect of acting hostess over the gathering.

After dinner, desperate for some fresh air and to get away from the house, she changed her kid slippers for the half boots she wore when riding, threw a fine silk and wool shawl about her shoulders, and walked across to the stables. The horses had been fed and watered, and released into the back field. She watched Samson for a moment, debating whether to bring him in and saddle him up for a ride. But the evening's warmth and the aftermath of the day's events decided her against it.

Turning back toward the house, she walked round the side onto the terrace and looked down toward the woods and the creek. Someone would have to assess the full extent of the storm damage. And as Tom couldn't spare anyone from the yard, it would have to be her. At least it would be cooler under the trees.

She walked briskly down across the fields, her gaze drifting over tangled hedgerows of satin-budded brambles, pink ragged robin, and white wild roses to fields of grass bright with red sorrel. Above the soft rustling and sighing of the wind-stirred leaves she could hear the hum of bees and the saw-like chirping of crickets, and for a while forgot everything but the pleasure of being outside in surroundings she loved.

Entering the woods, she ignored the main track along which she usually rode, choosing instead a network of smaller, fainter paths. It wasn't long before she glimpsed further evidence of the gale's ferocity. As she carried on, studying the trees and undergrowth around the path, changing direction when it met another trail so as to cover as wide an area as possible, her anxiety seeped back.

Not only was it vital that the desperate financial situation should be resolved, news of it had to be kept from the men at the yard. If word got out, they would abandon Tregonning's to seek work elsewhere. And with families to feed and clothe, who could blame them? Yet unless the packet was completed it would be impossible to sell the family shareholding and recoup that money. But to keep the men working she had to be able to pay them. How was she to do that?

Deep in thought, she rejoined the main track and picked her way across the rutted, muddy stretch where water from a spring ran across the path and trickled into the undergrowth on the lower side. The sound of stone scraping against stone followed by a thud and a grunt of irritation made her start. Her head flew up and she stopped dead. Though he was facing away from her, she recognised him instantly. He was several yards ahead, a few feet off the path in the undergrowth. He seemed to be doing something to the tumbledown shack once used by the preventive officers. Only it wasn't a ruin any more. How long had he been here?

Watching him, too shaken to move, a strange shiver left her flushed with heat at the play of dappled sunlight and shadow on his naked, muscular back. But if he wore no shirt, what were those dark stripes?

Her soft gasp of realisation made him whirl round. For an instant neither one moved. Then he snatched up his discarded shirt and pulled it over his head.

'Beg pardon, ma'am.' Though cracked and hoarse, the words were clear enough. He dipped his head, avoiding her gaze as he touched the thick lock of black hair falling over his forehead.

Melissa was drawn forward. He was the first man she had ever met who was taller than she was. It felt strange to look upward rather than down. Quickly she turned to examine the shack, her curiosity increasing as she saw how, having rebuilt the walls, he had replaced the collapsed roof with branches covering old canvas held in place by heavy stones. 'Are you living here?'

His head was bent, his shoulders hunched as he fiddled with the loose cuffs of his shirt, drawing them down over filthy bandages that bound his wrists. 'Ma'am.'

'Why? Are you hiding?' When he remained silent, staring at his boots, she thought of the stripes on his back and asked gently, 'Are you a deserter?'

He glanced up at that. Though his eyes met hers for the briefest of moments, the blazing awareness, the powerful, wrenching tug of attraction, dried her mouth. She felt hot then cold. This was wrong.

'No, ma'am,' he rasped. 'Not a deserter. Prefer my own company, that's all.'

As he looked down again she saw another bandage around his throat. Perhaps that explained his voice.

'What happened to your back?'

Turning away, he folded his arms. 'I was a prisoner in France. They wanted information from me. But I escaped before ...' He broke off, frowning, as if angry with himself for saying too much. 'I've got work. I'll pay rent.' He was terse, strained. 'I just want to be left alone.'

The rebuff stung like a slap. Her cheeks flaming, Melissa stiffened. 'Rent won't be necessary. It's your efforts that have made it habitable. And as this is private land your solitude will not be disturbed. Good evening.' With a cool nod she turned back the way she had come, back straight, head high, torn between anger and tears and totally confused.

86

# Chapter Seven

After a night that had begun with restless tossing and ended with her waking suddenly from dream-filled sleep and sitting bolt upright, heart pounding, Melissa rested her elbows on humped knees, her head in her hands as she wondered what madness had possessed her. If her father with all his knowledge and experience had slithered into a financial quagmire, what made her think she could redeem the situation? It was ridiculous. Impossible.

The alternative? Acceptance. Oddly enough, society would blame her less for admitting defeat than for meddling in matters that were a male preserve. Her uncles had stated it clearly enough: women were totally unsuited to business or finance. They were simply voicing what every right-minded person – man and woman – knew to be true. Each sex had its own spheres of interest and influence, and the interests of all were best served by ensuring they remained separate.

She had always been separate. Set apart from her contemporaries by her unusual education, by a father who indulged her interest in the boat yard and, inevitably, by her height, it was too late now to start conforming. Nor, in her heart of hearts, despite being deeply apprehensive, did she wish to.

As for the man on the path, she could not afford to spend precious time and energy on pointless speculation. He was welcome to his solitude. But he was on her family's land. If convenience, or business matters, took her through the woods then it was up to him if he wished to avoid her.

Jumping out of bed to escape unsettling thoughts of him and an even more unsettling reaction to those thoughts, she went to the window and drew back the curtains. The sky was a peerless blue. But pink streaks of high cloud and the unusual clarity of distant sound on the crystal air warned of rain to come.

Hearing the door open, Melissa looked round as Sarah entered. Dressed in the black bombazine of mourning, she was carrying a cup of hot chocolate.

'Morning, miss.'

'Good morning, Sarah. I meant to ask you yesterday, did you get my black habit out of storage?'

'I did, miss. I thought it likely you'd be needing it. 'Tis brushed and aired and hanging in the closet. Want it today, do you?'

'Please.'

'Bath's all ready for you.'

Less than an hour later Melissa was on her way downstairs. A puff of white spotted muslin filled the gap between the large, pointed lapels of a close-fitting black jacket that curved back to short, rounded coat tails. Her petticoat, cut from the same fine black cloth, was long and plain.

She had caused her mother some concern by dispensing with the usual short train. But by pointing out that, as she wore the habit for walking as well as riding, the bottom of the skirt would fray, not to mention being constantly dirty, she had won reluctant acquiescence to this departure from accepted fashion.

In deference to her bereavement, instead of leaving her hair loose she had Sarah draw it back into a heavy coil. Despite escaping tendrils that curled on her temples and in front of her ears, the style, coupled with her pallor and the unrelieved black and white of her ensemble, made her look older. Her reflection suggested calm capability. But Melissa knew the façade to be eggshell thin. Behind it she was lonely and frightened.

Knowing her first task would be to go to the yard and tell Tom of her father's death, she had little appetite. But apparently deaf to her request for tea and toast, Lobb set in front of her a dish of fresh raspberries followed by some lightly scrambled eggs. Her astonished glance was met with a bland smile.

'With all you'll have to do today, miss, you need a good

breakfast.'

'I really don't –'

'I know it's a difficult time, miss. Things will be hard for you till Mr George gets home. So it's important to keep your strength up. Not just for your sake.'

Glancing up, she met his warning gaze, and, without another word, picked up her spoon. With exquisite tact he had reminded her that the entire household was relying on her leadership. She could not afford to indulge in self-pity or difficult behaviour.

As she crossed the stable yard, she saw her father's two hunters tied up outside; John grooming one, and Hocking the other.

'Morning, miss.' They returned her greeting. But both were subdued and there was none of the usual banter. She understood that this was out of respect and consideration. Though as she thought of what lay ahead at the yard she would have welcomed the usual cheeky remark from John or a gruff warning from Hocking about her biting off more than she could chew with Samson.

Yet they too must be anxious about the future. 'He's inside.' Hocking jerked a thumb toward the stalls. 'You stay there while I do saddle 'un up for you. Can't have you getting covered in hair.' He nodded at her black habit. 'Else Sarah will still be trying to brush 'un clean come Christmas.'

He helped her mount up, then with a brief salute returned to his task as she trotted Samson out of the yard.

Melissa told herself she was simply being mindful of her dress when she guided Samson onto the drive instead of taking him through the field gate. Well aware that their different stations in life ruled out anything but civility, she still smarted from the stranger's rebuff. Which was utterly ridiculous. He was a mere workman. Of what possible interest to her was his good opinion? Besides, she had received snubs and slights enough to be well accustomed to them by now. So why should this one matter? It didn't. Not in the least.

The road between Bosvane and the village was little used except by those coming to the Tregonning house, and this morning Melissa reached the yard without seeing even the postman. As she rode through the gates, Tom Ferris came out of the carpenter's shed. Seeing her, he raised a hand and hurried forward.

'I'm some glad you've come,' he said in greeting, as she dismounted and looped Samson's reins through the iron ring. 'Come on in here a minute. I got to talk to you.' He gestured for her to precede him. Ducking her head to avoid the low lintel, Melissa entered the cluttered room, turning as he followed.

'Have mister paid they suppliers yet?' he asked urgently before she could utter a word. 'Only we can't –'

'Tom, wait,' Melissa interrupted. 'My father is dead.'

Shock wiped all expression from the foreman's face. 'Dead?' His voice mirrored disbelief.

'Early yesterday morning. He had a stroke and ... It was very sudden. In fact it's all been so – I still can't –' She stopped, gave her head a quick shake, and cleared her throat. 'I tried to come down yesterday, but my uncles arrived. And with mother ill, there was just so much to do. But I wanted to tell you myself. It wouldn't have been right, you hearing the news from anyone else.'

'Good of you, miss. I appreciate that, I do. But bleddy hell.' He caught himself. 'Beg pardon, miss.'

'No need to apologise.' A tired smile briefly tilted the corners of her mouth. She envied him the freedom to express his feelings. She wasn't even sure what hers were. Only that she dare not examine them for fear of being overwhelmed.

'I'm some sorry. We shan't see the like of him again, dear of 'un.'

'I've written to George, but it could be weeks – maybe months – before he can get back. In the meantime, we have to keep the yard going.'

'But what about –? I mean – look, there isn't no way to pretty this up: did you get chance to ask mister about the suppliers?'

She shook her head. 'No, but I spent a large part of yesterday in his study going through all the books and accounts. Tom, we're in trouble.'

'How deep?'

She bit her lip, slowly shaking her head.

'Dear life!' As he rubbed his grizzled face, bushy brows drawn down, she heard the rasp of stubble against his calloused palm. His eyes searched hers. 'What are you going to do?'

'Fight.' She pressed her palms together. 'My great-grandfather set up this yard. Tregonnings have been building ships here for three generations. With a war on, the country needs ships. It needs yards like this. I've got to keep it going until George gets home.'

'That's the stuff, girl.' Tom Ferris rubbed his hands, a grin splitting his face. 'Never lacked for spirit, you haven't. You know I'm with you all the way. But how are you going to manage?'

'Not me, Tom: us.' She flashed him a weary grin. 'Well, you really, like you always have.'

He sniffed. 'Yes. Well, I'm all right with the practical stuff. But mister held the purse strings and kept the books and all. Not meaning to be disrespectful, miss. I thought the world of your pa, and that's God's truth, but these past weeks even when he did come down I couldn't get a word of sense out of 'un.'

Melissa nodded. She had found it difficult being the messenger. But how much more frustrating it must have been for Tom, waiting for replies that never came; watching precious stores dwindle by the day, the shock of learning that replacements were being withheld because of unpaid accounts, yet still unable to pin her father down.

'Well, as far as money is concerned, there isn't any. So we have to raise some as quickly as possible. But I can't sell land or property, not even that owned solely by my mother.'

'How can't you? Surely that would –?'

'Don't you see how it would look, Tom? My father barely cold in his grave and his widow is selling off parts of the estate? Within 24 hours it would be spread all over Truro that we were bankrupt, the gossips would see to that.'

'That bad, is it?' he asked quietly.

She met his gaze squarely. 'It's worse. Far worse.' She swallowed. 'It's not just a few unpaid bills. Tom, promise me you won't breathe a word of this.'

Anger darkened his face. 'You should know better than that.'

'I do. Of course I do. It's just – my father – there are debts. Tom, we could lose the yard.' She looked away as she fought for control. 'But on no account must my uncles, or anyone else, discover the true state of our financial affairs.'

'All right, my handsome. Don't you fret now. Us'll come about.'

Blinking, she forced a watery smile. Was he saying it to offer comfort? Did he really believe it? Either way, it was still she who would have to provide a solution. 'As far as I can see, the only saleable asset that no one will question is timber. We can use some of the fallen trees to replenish the store here. Once sawn and stacked they'll be seasoning ready for next year. But I was thinking, what about a programme of felling? I don't understand how my father couldn't see the possibilities. I did try to suggest it but –'

'He wasn't hisself, my bird. Nor haven't been for months. Now don't you go getting upset and thinking you could've changed anything, 'cos you couldn't. He was a fine man, but you know so well as I do that if he didn't like what you was saying, he wouldn't bleddy listen.'

With a muffled sound that was half-laugh, half-sob, Melissa pulled a handkerchief from her sleeve and wiped her nose. 'I did love him, Tom.'

'And he thought the world of you. Told me more'n once you was as good as a son any day.'

'He did?' A painful mix of pride and grief wrenched Melissa. Even her beloved father had judged her not on her own merits, but in comparison to her brothers, though neither had ever shown the slightest interest in the yard. Yet here she was, about to take on a man's job and shoulder a man's responsibilities. So perhaps it was a compliment after all.

'We could keep what wood we need for our own use and sell the rest. But what we really need is someone with experience –'

'Hang on a minute,' Tom waved her to silence. 'I reckon I know just the man. Don't you move.' Pointing a warning finger at her, he stepped outside and bellowed, 'Billy!'

'Yo!' The answering shout was faint.

'Tell Gabe Ennis I want 'un.'

'What, now? Only he's –'

'I don't care what he's doing,' Tom roared. 'I want 'un right this minute.' He stepped back inside, rubbing his hands. "He's the man. Carpenter, he was, on a large estate. Know timber, he do. And he's a hard worker. Just spent two days in the saw pit. Don't say much, but then he can't –'

The sunlight was suddenly blocked by a tall figure in the doorway, and Melissa choked down a gasp as she recognised him.

'This here's Gabriel Ennis, miss. Started here couple of days ago. Escaped from France.' Tom lowered his voice. 'Chained up by the neck 'e was, so he can't talk proper.' He turned to the newcomer, looking up. 'This here is Miss Tregonning. Her father own the yard. Well, he did: Mr Tregonning passed away sudden yesterday.'

There was a pause, and Melissa felt her muscles tighten. But though he must have recognised her, Gabriel Ennis gave no sign of doing so. Knuckling his forehead he rasped, 'Condolences, ma'am.' He turned to Tom, waiting to be told why he'd been sent for.

'Go on, miss,' Tom encouraged. 'Tell 'un what you got in mind.'

Melissa cleared her throat. If he had worked on a large estate, he must recognise how badly the woods had been neglected. Though relieved that he was acting as if this were their first meeting, she found it impossible to banish the vivid impressions of their previous encounters. These memories, plus the conflict between loyalty to her father and having to admit his many recent failings to a stranger, increased her confusion.

'I – I –' She stopped abruptly. Taking a breath, and a moment to marshal her thoughts, she began again. 'The woodland above the yard covers a large area and is, I believe, a valuable resource. Tom says you know about these things. What would be needed to set up a felling programme?'

As he shot her a brief glance from beneath dark brows she was grateful for the dimness. Was it intuition or fear that warned her he had immediately guessed why she was asking?

'To sell? Or to store for use in the yard?'

She swallowed. 'Both.'

'I'd need horses and chains, and at least eight men.'

'Can't do it,' Tom said flatly. 'Not eight.'

Melissa turned to him. 'How many can you spare?'

'Five, six at a pinch.' Tom sucked his teeth. 'Though only if we set aside all repair work. I'll have to shift around the men on the packet, mind.'

Melissa addressed Gabriel. 'You can have two shire horses from the farm. I'll drive one, so that will free another man for felling.'

'You can't do that!' Tom hissed.

'Tom, if I can handle Samson and his moods –'

'That isn't what I mean, and you know it. I daresay there isn't a horse foaled you couldn't handle. What I mean is, it isn't proper for you to be doing such things.'

She shot him a meaningful glance. 'No choice, Tom.'

'I don't like it.' He glared at her.

'But you can't spare any more men.'

'Some stubborn you are. All right.' He clicked his tongue. 'When do you want to start?'

'How long will it take to reorganise the work here?'

He shrugged. 'Tomorrow?'

Gabriel shook his head. 'Can't start felling until the trees have been chosen and marked.'

'How long will that take?' Melissa tried to keep the anxiety from her voice.

'Depends on the number. Those already down can be hauled to the nearest path. We'll need a track to the road. Opposite the yard gates is reasonably central. Easy for the haulier's wagons too.'

Ashamed that none of these points had occurred to her, she gave what she hoped was a decisive nod. 'That will be fine.

Please see to it.' She turned to the foreman. 'Tom, will you call the men together at noon tomorrow so I can talk to them?'

'Listen there's no need for that. I'll tell them what's happened. You been through enough already. And I daresay there'll be more to come.'

'I don't doubt it. But I have to speak to them myself. If the men aren't told what we're planning they'll think the worst and start looking elsewhere for work.'

Tom sighed, his expression morose as he scratched his head through the frizzy halo. 'Could be they'll do that anyway.'

Melissa smoothed the fingers of her gloves. 'I know it's a risk. But I have to convince them the yard will continue, with or without them. They've got to be persuaded that it's as important to me as it was to my father. If that means doing things I've never done before, then the sooner I get used to it the better.'

When he finished work late that afternoon Gabriel went into the village. His thoughts were full of Melissa Tregonning. Her father's sudden death had clearly rocked the foundations of her world. Mourning clothes and a severe hairstyle would make anyone appear older. But the change he divined in her went far deeper.

Her shyness and naiveté, still so appealing, had been overlaid by determination. It was obvious that she needed money. So Mr Tregonning's untimely death had clearly left his family with considerable financial problems. His daughter's determination to resolve these showed rare and undoubted courage. But she could have no idea of what she was taking on.

The yard had the necessary land for expansion, plus an experienced workforce. And with the war increasing the demand for ships, it would quickly rival any of the yards in Truro or Falmouth. For anyone with spare capital it was an ideal investment and would quickly show an excellent return. Once more he felt the bitter irony of his situation.

Acknowledging his name and status would allow him to increase his own fortune while improving those of everyone connected with the yard. But in solving her problem he would create too many for himself. He should leave this place. But how could he when he owed her the roof over his head? Besides, no one else possessed the knowledge she needed.

'Hallo, my handsome.' Mrs Mitchell's face lit up as he entered the bakery. 'I was just thinking of you. Here, do me a favour, would you?'

'If I can,' Gabriel croaked.

'No one better. Look, 'tis this sack of flour. I only opened 'un this morning. Now, what do you see?'

Bending, Gabriel peered into the sack. His voice cracked in surprise. 'It's moving.'

'Mites,' Mrs Mitchell announced angrily. 'Nothing wrong with my eyes. Well, I aren't having it. I paid for fresh-ground flour.'

Realising he was poised at the top of a slippery slope, Gabriel stifled a groan. He could not afford to become embroiled in village life. Yet what would have become of him had it not been for Tom Ferris's trust? Tom had guessed he was the thief, yet had still been willing to give him a job. On Tom's say-so, Mrs Mitchell had given him more food than he could pay for. The day he started at the yard Billy had noticed he had no dinner, and had brought him some. And Jack was willing to lend him a boat to go fishing. Not become involved? It was far too late.

'You want me to take the flour back?'

'All I want for you to do is carry the sack. You don't have to say nothing. Just stand there like. I aren't afeared of no man, but it don't do no harm to show I got friends. I aren't no fool, and so Joe Sweet will know when I've finished with 'un. Sell me stale flour, would he? Bleddy cheek! I'll put 'un straight, you see if I don't.'

Struggling to keep a straight face, wishing he could tell her it would be an honour as well as a genuine pleasure to accompany her, Gabriel said simply, 'Now?'

'Well, seeing you're here.' Quickly tying up the sack's neck, she pulled off her apron, took a shawl from a hook on the back of the door and swirled it around her shoulders. Then, holding the door while Gabriel picked up the sack, she locked it behind them.

Forty minutes later they were back in the shop with a fresh sack of flour. While Mrs Mitchell had given Joe Sweet her opinion of people who tried to take advantage of a decent widow-woman doing her best to run an honest business, the miller had darted frequent sidelong glances at Gabriel, who had simply gazed back. He had not said a word. There had been no need. Mrs Mitchell in full flow was not to be interrupted, nor did she require help.

Joe Sweet's abject apologies, his plea that it had been an honest mistake, a mix-up of sacks by his boy who would feel the back of his hand the moment he caught up with him, had followed them for several yards along the street.

'Well, that's done.' Mrs Mitchell beamed up at him as he straightened after setting the flour down. 'Now, my handsome, how about a nice pie for your tea? I don't want no money. You done me a kindness and Daisy Mitchell always pay her debts.' She quickly wrapped a saffron bun and a piece of hevva cake and pushed them into his hands. 'Bit o' something for later.'

Gabriel looked down at her. 'Thank you.'

'Dear life! ' Suddenly pink, she fiddled with the puffed muslin covering her bolster-like bosom. 'Charm the birds off the trees with that smile, you would. Go on, then. I got work to do. Be in tomorrow, will you?'

'Another job?'

'And if there is?'

'I'll be in.'

'Right, then.' At the door, Gabriel hesitated. 'Where can I buy a razor?' He rubbed his palm over a beard that was growing thicker by the day. In Brittany he had adopted the custom of all working men and shaved only once or twice a week. But in prison even that had become impossible. The captain of the fishing boat, knowing a full beard would betray his passenger as an escaped prisoner, had found him an old razor. Gabriel had scraped off as much as he could without touching his throat. But that had been well over a week ago. To leave it much longer would invite curiosity.

'You wait right there,' Daisy commanded. 'Don't you move

now.' She bustled out and he could hear her in the back room, muttering to herself. She returned a few moments later carrying a worn black leather case and a small white china bowl in which lay a stubby badger-hair shaving brush.

'These belonged to my Cyrus, bless his heart. 'Tis daft just to leave them sitting there. He wouldn't mind me giving them to you.' She thrust them at Gabriel, her eyes bright with unshed tears. 'If we'd had a son … Still, that's the way of it.'

He had expected directions, not another gift, especially one that had been an integral part of her married life. But refusal was out of the question. It would be throwing her generosity back in her face. And he really did need the razor. Deeply touched, he took the bowl and case, then leant down and dropped a swift kiss on the plump, floury cheek. 'You're a kind woman, Mrs Mitchell.'

'Oh!' Daisy pressed a hand to each side of her bright pink face. 'Dear life! Here, there's no way you're going to carry all that without dropping something. Now, I know I got an old …' Opening a cupboard she bent over and rummaged about. 'There!' She emerged, beaming and triumphant, and flourished a battered wicker basket. 'I wouldn't trust the handle. That's how I don't use 'un myself. But I expect you can fix 'un up good as new.' Setting the basket down, she quickly put in the bowl and razor case, followed by the bun and cake, and lastly the pie. 'There now. Off you go.'

'Yes, Mother.' Gabriel grinned. He knew older village women were often called this by people not their children. It was a term of familiarity, respect, and endearment. He used it for all those reasons, also because he recognised her unfulfilled longing and knew how much it would mean to her.

'That's enough of your cheek! Get on out of it!' Her waving arm shooing him away was belied by the delight in her smile.

'See you tomorrow.' Gabriel touched his forehead in salute, and closed the door behind him. He was still smiling as he started back along the street in the direction of the yard and the woods. Ahead of him, four women stood chatting. One saw him approach and murmured to the others, who turned their heads to look at him. Wary, he moved out to the centre of the narrow street, head down, eyes lowered, intending to pass by.

'Hello, Gabe,' one blurted, then giggled.

'Come on, Gabe. Where's your manners?' another demanded. 'Say hello.'

Unprepared, Gabriel didn't know how best to respond. To ignore them would give offence. But to stop and chat would signal encouragement, a situation fraught with danger. He knew an instant's longing for a time when no lady would have dreamt of speaking to Lord Stratton without first having been formally introduced. But these were not ladies, and such memories belonged to another life.

Glancing up, he gave a brief nod and made to pass by. Too late, he realised it would have been wiser to feign deafness. Immediately they pressed close, blocking his path.

'How do you like it here, then?' The one addressing him was clearly the ringleader of the group. She had dark hair, and bold brown eyes. Her dimity gown was cut low, and the grubby kerchief crossed over her bosom and tied behind revealed an opulent cleavage thrust forward to attract his attention.

Swiftly averting his eyes he shrugged, head down, shoulders defensive.

'Cat got your tongue?' one of the others piped up.

'Dicked in the knob, he is,' another scoffed.

'Here,' the third tried, 'need someone to do a bit of cooking and washing, do you?'

'Look like he got someone cooking for 'un already.' The bold one nodded toward the basket. 'No, what he need is company of a night.'

'Sal!' one of the other young women gasped.

Reaching out, bold Sal ran a finger down the front of Gabriel's shirt. Involuntarily, he stepped back.

'Aw, he's shy, the dear of him.' Someone giggled.

Sal took a pace forward, once more closing the distance between them and tilting her head provocatively. He could smell the sweet pungency of her sweat.

'Tis no fun alone in a cold bed. I should know, with my man away fishing all hours of the day and night.'

'Sal!'

'Aw, shut up, Lizzie. What Jed don't know can't hurt un. If he'd rather be out on his bleddy boat than home with me, well, while the cat's away ...' Grinning, she waggled the tip of her tongue at Gabriel.

The joke, if it was a joke, had gone far enough. With a brief shake of his head, Gabriel sidestepped the group and continued on his way. A chorus of mockery followed him. But he was not the target.

'Look like he don't fancy you, Sal.'

'What if Jed had heard you?'

'Losing your touch, you are, girl.'

## Chapter Eight

Swallowing the last mouthful of pie, Gabriel washed it down with spring water, then heaved himself to his feet, brushing the crumbs from his breeches.

After another day in the saw pit he would have given much for a hot bath to soothe his aching muscles, then hours and hours of dreamless sleep. But with wind and rain indicated by the mares' tails stretching across the paling sky, he needed to make his roof more secure. He also wanted to cut fir branches while they were still dry. Dense, springy, and virtually draught-proof, they would make a softer bed than earth and grass.

If this was to be his home for the foreseeable future then he might as well make it as comfortable as possible. Though small, it afforded him solitude and freedom. After the terror of his year in France culminating in the filthy, crowded prison cell, these were luxuries in themselves.

Once the fir branches were piled inside along the driest wall, a fire lit, wood stacked for burning, and the filled pot set to heat, he went back to a fallen elm he had noticed earlier and used the axe to peel off long lengths of bark. Sitting beside the fire, he cut the bark into thin, flexible strips. These he twisted and plaited into thick, strong cords, and tied them around the heavy stones left over from his rebuilding. Then, making holes with his dagger in the edges, he began to fasten the stones to the canvas, fixing each weight on opposite sides so the canvas was held down more firmly and not pulled off.

Coming round to the front again, he heard the crack of a twig and looked up to see Melissa Tregonning coming down the path. Dressed in the black habit she had worn that morning and carrying an oblong basket, she held herself rigidly erect.

As he remained still, watching her approach, he wondered what caused her such displeasure. But, as she came closer, he realised that her heightened colour and stern, almost defiant expression were not anger at all. He had seen her handle a horse many men would think twice about mounting, yet here, on foot, she was nervous. Why?

'Good evening, Gabriel.'

Intrigued by her refusal to look directly at him, he remembered just in time to tug his forelock. 'Miss Tregonning.'

She cleared her throat. 'I have no wish to intrude on your privacy; I know how you value it. However, it occurred to me that you might find these useful.' She thrust the basket at him. As he took it he saw that her hand was trembling. 'There are candles, another blanket, clean linen, and a pot of salve for your wounds.' She clasped her hands together, looking anywhere but at him, her cheeks a deep rose.

'Much obliged, ma'am.' Her opening words registered, and he realised she had totally misread his claim to prefer solitude. He had intended it as an explanation for choosing to live away from the village and other people. She had interpreted it as a personal rebuff. Yet why should she? Unless rejection was something experience had taught her to expect.

What isolated her from other people was their instinctive recognition of her as different. They might put it down to her height – though in his eyes she was simply magnificent – but what really set her apart was her strength and courage. And the modesty that made her oblivious to her appeal.

But if she was accustomed to being cold-shouldered, why should his perceived rejection matter? Unless – unless the lightning flash of awareness and attraction had affected her as profoundly as it had him. Gazing at her, he felt a stirring of deeper, hitherto untouched emotions.

She shrugged, awkwardly self-conscious. 'As I need your help it was the least I could do. I'll leave you now.' She turned away.

'No.' She mustn't go. Not until he had led her to realise that she had been mistaken. Hazardous it might be, foolhardy it most certainly was, and he would have to tread with infinite care. 'Beg pardon, ma'am,' he said quickly as she turned back. Deliberately averting his gaze, he feigned shyness so she would not feel threatened. 'But I was thinking … What about cutting other trees, not just the oaks?'

He watched her hesitate, considering his suggestion. Then she shook her head. 'There isn't enough time. We need oak for the yard. And the current shortage, we know oak will sell.'

'True, miss, but with respect, alder always fetches high prices. It's used for mill-cogs and waterwheels, where constant wetting and drying would rot most woods. It also makes excellent charcoal. Furniture makers are always looking for beech. Cornish elm is wanted for flooring and tool handles. Large sycamores are always in demand. The wood can be scrubbed without the grain lifting, so it's ideal for kitchen tables and chopping boards. And sycamore is also sought after for musical instruments because it polishes well.'

He had talked far more than usual that day and his voice kept cracking. 'Obviously the oak will sell as baulks or planks, but you can also sell the bark. The tannery in Truro would buy it, so would fishermen, for preserving their nets.' He glanced up to see Melissa gazing at him, her self-consciousness forgotten.

'Truly? I had no idea. About any of it.' Her delight gave way to uncertainty. 'But to cut so much … Wouldn't that destroy the wood?'

Gabriel shook his head. 'It badly needs thinning, to allow the young trees space and light to grow.'

She looked directly at him, and he felt the shock all over again. Not only had he never met a woman whose gaze was almost level with his own – a relief and pleasure in itself – he had never met a young woman of such contrasts: vibrant yet shy, courageous yet self-effacing. Her wariness momentarily forgotten, she studied him, puzzled and curious. 'Where did you learn all this?'

'Before I was taken prisoner –' He hesitated. He didn't want to lie to her. Though with his current life one enormous lie, what could another possibly matter? But it did. So he told her

103

the truth, though not quite all of it.

'I used to work on a large estate where forest and woodland were managed as a business to generate wealth. The owner was very astute, forward-looking.' Looking away, he studied the trees around them.

She cleared her throat. 'I know it's been neglected. My father – has been under great strain.'

He turned back to her. Her father's concerns could not be her fault or responsibility, yet she was behaving as though they were. Why had she shouldered this burden? He nodded. 'Tom – Mr Ferris – told me your eldest brother was lost in a naval battle last year. A tragedy for your family, ma'am. My condolences.'

Her gaze was clear and candid, and a tiny frown puckered her forehead. 'You sound different.'

He smiled briefly. 'Not used to talking so much.'

'No, I don't mean your voice; I mean your mode of speech.'

He bent his head, clenching his teeth as tension cramped his gut. In France, speaking only Breton, his disguise a matter of life and death, it had been easy to remain in character. But here, in his home county, and with her ... Looking up, he shrugged. 'You're right, miss. I used to work closely with the master. I wanted to better myself, so I picked up his way of talking. No offence intended.'

'No, no, I didn't mean – it was not a criticism, Gabriel, merely an observation. One I should not have made.' Embarrassment smothered both suspicion and uncertainty.

Torn between relief at having avoided potential danger and anger at his carelessness, he deliberately steered the conversation away from the past. 'May I wish you well for tomorrow?'

She drew a deep breath. 'I'll be glad when it's over.'

'No need to be nervous, miss. You know what you're doing.'

'I hope so.' It was heartfelt, anxious. After a moment she admitted, 'My uncles don't share your confidence.'

'You know why, don't you?' He saw anxiety cloud her face. 'You are attempting something men believe can only be done by another man.' One corner of his mouth lifted in irony. 'This is a severe threat to their dignity.'

She was silent for a moment, then tossed her head. 'If their dignity is so fragile it must rest on very shaky foundations.'

'It does,' he confided. 'And that is a secret all men would prefer to remain hidden.'

Her eyes widened. 'Really? No, you are not serious.'

'Indeed I am.'

Seeing his rueful smile, she gasped and blushed, covering her mouth with her fingertips. 'You really should not say such things.'

'Perhaps. But there will be occasions when you find that knowledge helpful.'

Watching her visible struggle as she recollected herself and withdrew from his unexpected and startling candour he realised that, despite being out in society, she had not acquired the usual veneer of arch sophistication he would have expected in a young woman of her background. He found himself fiercely glad.

She cleared her throat. 'About – about the wood ...'

It was a deliberate if reluctant retreat from an intimacy he should have resisted. Gabriel knew he must let her go. He turned away and set the basket on the ground. 'Why don't you take a day or two to think about it, miss?'

'But what you said – about the other trees being more valuable. Would they really raise a lot of money quickly?'

Watching her blush deepen and her lashes flutter as she realised how much her query revealed, Gabriel wondered just how desperate a financial crisis her father had left her to deal with. Picking up the last stone he began tying it on to the corner of the canvas, careful not to look at her.

'They would, miss. And with proper management these woods will still be generating income a hundred years from now.'

'Truly?' She sounded stunned. 'Thank you, Gabriel. Thank you very much.'

His hands grew still as he watched her move quickly away up the path, her long stride peculiarly graceful, her self-consciousness forgotten now she had so many more important matters to occupy her.

That evening, after washing himself and his filthy shirt, he shaved carefully. With no mirror he had to work by touch alone. It took a long time, and he did not dare go too close to the wound on his throat. But tentative fingertip examination when he removed the bandage told him the honey had done its work, and healing had begun. Smearing a fresh cloth with the sweet-smelling salve, he bound up his throat once more. Passing a hand over his almost-smooth jaw when he had finished, he smiled. No doubt Berryman would shudder at his efforts. But not only did he feel cleaner than he had for months, he also felt ridiculously proud and self-satisfied.

When the men assembled at midday, the overnight rain was just a memory. The sun shone from a sky the colour of cornflowers dotted with thistledown clouds. The yard was buzzing. The news that Francis Tregonning was dead and his wife ill had spread like flames in a gale. All were anxious about the yard and their jobs. But there was mixed reaction to the rumour that George Tregonning had been sent for.

What did he know about shipbuilding, or about the yard for that matter? He was a lieutenant in His Majesty's Navy. As Sam Laity's wife's brother delivered the post, everyone knew it was months since his last letter had arrived. Possible reasons for the delay of more recent letters were suggested and rejected. Missing in action? That was as good as saying he was dead. In prison in France? Same thing. If either of those were the case, it was time to start looking elsewhere for work.

The discussions and arguments subsided as Melissa rode into the yard on Samson. Wearing her black habit and a matching small beaver hat with a narrow rolled brim over her up-swept hair, she was very pale, but appeared calm as she dismounted. Standing to one side near the back, his arms folded, Gabriel watched her turn from the crowd to fasten the rein to the iron ring. Seeing how her hands trembled, his clenched in sympathy. Even as he willed her to be strong, he mocked himself. Remaining here was sheer madness. If he had begun to care in this short time … Was he not in enough peril?

Tom had organised a small platform for her to stand on, and helped her up. 'All right, you lot,' he bellowed. 'Let's have a bit of quiet. This here is Miss Tregonning –'

'We don't need telling who she is,' a voice yelled. 'We've knowed her since she was a cheeld.'

'Yes, well, she isn't a cheeld no more,' Tom barked. 'So shut your yap and show a bit of respect.' He turned to Melissa. 'Go on, now, my handsome,' he murmured with an encouraging smile.

Melissa's gaze swept over the assembled men. Her eyes met Gabriel's, flicked over his recently shaved jaw, and widened. She recovered instantly and, as her gaze moved on, he saw her inhale slowly. She lifted her chin and, by waiting, revealed both determination and a self-control that had him silently applauding in admiration. Only when the rumble of conversation had died away completely did she begin to speak.

'My great-grandfather set up this yard. In those days Tregonning's built small fishing boats, quay punts, and the occasional trading schooner. As the yard expanded over the years new sheds were added and the quay was enlarged. Then, when my father took over, the yard grew bigger still. Sons followed their fathers and grandfathers to learn their trade here. We started building bigger boats, fruit schooners and packet-ships.' She paused as heads nodded, allowing them time to remember.

'My father was a wise man. He believed in employing excellent craftsmen and allowing them to get on with the job. Though he's no longer with us –' Her voice faltered, and Gabriel caught his breath. But once again she managed to rein in her emotions. 'My brother will be home soon to take up where my father left off. This yard has a reputation for building first-class ships. That reputation is due to you. With the war increasing demand for new ships we will be busier than ever. Because we cannot wait any longer for imported timber to get through the blockades, during the next week Tom will be organising a gang to cut from our own woods to ensure we have a continuous supply.'

'I dunno how mister didn't think to do that months ago,'

someone grumbled.

'Never mind that. Who's going to be running the yard between now and when your brother get home?' someone else shouted. The mutters that followed showed the questioner was not alone in wanting reassurance.

Gabriel saw Melissa swallow, but her lifted brows conveyed mild surprise, as if the question was superfluous and the answer self-evident. 'Tom will handle all practical matters, just as he always has. Until my brother's arrival, I will deal with finance and administration.' She raised her voice slightly, drowning the rustle of whispers. 'You said yourselves you have seen me come here with my father since I was a small child. Over the years, I have learnt a great deal about the business. However, I understand your concern. Since my elder brother was killed last year, my father has not been –' She swallowed again. 'Grief, and anxiety about my mother's health, weighed heavily on him. Eventually this began to affect his own health.' She looked away for a moment. Then raised her head once more. 'I know how the yard works, and I know what is needed. I hope, I trust, that you will honour my father's memory by building on the past and on your fathers' achievements to give Tregonning's an even brighter future, for yourselves and for your children. Thank you.'

Taking Tom's hand, she stepped down. With a brief wave and a smile that acknowledged the warm applause, she released Samson, mounted from the block and, with her back straight and head high, walked the huge horse out of the yard.

She had given a superb performance. But as Gabriel listened to the murmurs, he hoped Lieutenant George Tregonning's arrival would not be long delayed.

Gabriel didn't leave with the others when work finished for the day. Instead, he went to the pile of old and broken tools dumped in one corner of the carpenter's shed. After ten minutes careful sorting he had found a mallet and an axe with broken handles, a plane with a chipped and rusty blade, and two chisels, one wide, one narrow. He looked up to see Tom watching him.

'All right if I take these?'

'They're broke.'

'I can mend them.'

'What do you want them for?'

'Repairs. Where I'm living.'

Tom sniffed. 'I suppose you'll need a saw.' He gestured toward the rack above the bench. 'Might as well take what you need from there. All the others got their own kit. Should be a sharpening stone there somewhere, and there's plane blades in that tin, though they might want a drop of oil.'

'Thanks.'

'When are you going to start looking at they trees?'

Gabriel recognised the deal, and the implied urgency. It was clear that Tom knew how things stood. But had she told him, or had he guessed?

'This evening. I'll need paint to mark them.'

'I'll fetch it,' Tom said. He hurried away, returning a few minutes later to add a tin and brush to Gabriel's already laden basket.

A few days later the men gathered once more, but this time in the churchyard. Most of the village had turned out to pay their last respects and watch Francis Tregonning laid to rest. It was a day of bright sunshine and blustery showers.

As they left the church, Melissa followed her mother, who clung to Addey's supporting arm. She wore a black velvet close-fitting jacket over a black silk petticoat and a hat without the veil that hid her mother's frozen countenance from both the sympathetic and the curious.

As Emma walked with painful dignity toward the waiting carriage, Melissa's gaze moved past friends of her parents from Truro, past Tom and the men from the yard and the farm. She told herself it was merely interest to see who had attended. But her conscience forced her to acknowledge the shameful truth. She was searching.

She found him, at the back as always, his dark head above the rest, his lean face still pale compared with the weathered complexions of the other men and, as their eyes met across the distance, she felt again the shock of recognition. Suddenly she was stronger, less isolated.

Acutely aware of her aunts' critical scrutiny, she hurried forward and slipped a comforting arm around her mother's thin shoulders, heat in her cheeks the only visible legacy of the brief exchange of glances. No one could see her pounding heart. No one could feel the fluttering in her stomach that felt like a dozen frantic butterflies, or the liquid weakness in her legs.

Since the age of 17 she had not met anyone taller than herself. For her, looking up into a man's face was strange. It made her feel vulnerable, threatened. But by what? Apart from that first occasion when he had seized Samson's reins to prevent him rearing, Gabriel Ennis had been polite to the point of diffidence. Considering his lowly background, his manners were remarkable, as was his speech, though he had explained that.

Most men considered her height a handicap, presumably because they were used to having that advantage. She had no idea why they should feel threatened, yet apparently they did, and it made them abrupt and aggressive. But he was so tall it was inevitable that he should look down on almost as many men as he did women.

Was this then the reason for their apparent affinity? How could it be anything else, given their different stations in life? Yet as she recalled the startling intimacy of their conversations she felt again the heated shiver and strange quickening. Surely such feelings must spring from something deeper than mere physical parity? Even if they did, what difference could it make? She closed her eyes against sudden inexplicable tears.

Back at the house, where tables groaned under the weight of Mrs Bett's cold collation, Addey led her mistress to a chair and made her comfortable while Melissa acted hostess in her mother's place. Lobb and Gilbert served sherry or Madeira to the gentlemen and ratafia to the ladies.

Very soon, with no outsiders to inhibit the family, conversations lost their hushed tone. Reminiscences gradually gave way to speculation about the future.

When quizzed, Melissa's expression conveyed mild surprise as she responded that naturally everything would carry on as normal while they waited for George's return. Then, with a self-effacing smile, she excused herself to fetch more food or refill someone's teacup.

Emma Tregonning sat in a high-backed armchair. Addey had placed a light rug over her knees. Despite the sunshine streaming in through the windows to warm the room, she looked pinched and cold. She had lost weight during her illness, and her skin had a waxy translucence.

Assailed by renewed anxiety, Melissa made her way across the room. 'Forgive me interrupting, Aunt Louisa, I must speak with Dr Wherry. I won't keep him long, I promise.' Slipping her arm through the doctor's, and ignoring her aunt's protests, she drew him away.

'Thank you, my dear,' he smiled. 'Was my hope of rescue so obvious?'

'Oh goodness, I'm so sorry. I hadn't realised. Was it that bad?'

'Don't distress yourself. With my long experience I should be perfectly capable of extricating myself from a difficult encounter without relying on external help. You have enough to concern you without worrying about me. However, I have to say that your Aunt Louisa is quite the most *adhesive* woman I have ever met.'

Suppressing a smile at his remarkably apt description, Melissa stopped beside one of the long windows and, checking to ensure they were out of earshot, turned to face him.

'Doctor Wherry, I know you have done everything possible for my mother. I would not have you think my anxiety is in any way a reflection on your treatment –'

'Say no more, my dear.' He patted her arm. 'I perfectly understand your concern. Physically, your mother's recovery is normal, if a little slow. Though that is only to be expected. The fact that she has responded so well is a tribute to the care you and Miss Addey have lavished upon her. But I must admit her complete withdrawal is causing me considerable disquiet.'

Melissa shrugged helplessly. 'I don't know what to do. I have sat with her and talked until I am hoarse. I've tried remaining silent, just holding her hand, or stroking it to let her know I am there. But nothing –' She broke off, shaking her head, angry at the hovering tears, at her own weakness and at her mother's passive rejection of the comfort she herself craved.

The doctor lowered his voice. 'In my opinion she should go away. I know how attached she is to Bosvane, but during this past 12 months the house has become associated in her mind with grief and loss. Right now, the best possible thing for her would be a complete change.'

Just for an instant, Melissa wished fervently that she too could simply hand over all the problems and worries to someone else. Only she couldn't, because there wasn't anyone. Instead, she focused on the doctor's suggestion.

The more she thought about it, the more it appealed. Now her mother no longer needed round the clock nursing Addey would be perfectly able to cope alone. And it would greatly ease her own burden. The effort of maintaining a façade in front of her mother was absorbing more strength than she could spare.

'Aunt Lucy is returning home tomorrow. I'm sure she would be delighted to take Mama back with her to Torquay. Naturally, Addey would accompany them. It's an excellent idea, doctor. Thank you.'

His sober expression befitted the occasion, but as he glanced up she glimpsed a twinkle in the depths of his tired eyes. 'Naturally, your mother's well-being was my first concern, but it occurs to me that you too might benefit from her absence for a few weeks.'

Melissa caught her breath and her heart gave an unpleasant lurch as perspiration prickled her skin. How much did he know? How had he found out?

He leant in. 'Fewer visits from overbearing relations.'

Mingled guilt and relief erupted in giggles she fought hard to hide, for who would understand? 'One can but hope,' she whispered back.

At 11 the next morning, John and Gilbert loaded the wagonette. On the journey down, Aunt Lucy had contrived space in her barouche for both her maid and her luggage. But with two more passengers for the return trip the boxes and trunks would have to be carried separately. Uncle Brinley, with whom Aunt Lucy had been staying, had been adamant that as soon as Emma and her old nurse arrived at Gyllan House, Hocking and John were to return with the carriage to Bosvane, and thus be available for any errands Melissa might require of them. One of his own grooms would drive the wagonette to Torquay.

There were fewer valises and trunks than Addey considered necessary for her mistress's comfort, but many more than Melissa believed would fit in the wagonette even with the seats folded out of the way.

'Addey, my mother is in mourning. She will not be out in company. Besides, she's only going for a few weeks. It cannot be necessary to take her entire wardrobe.'

'Nor am I, as you well know,' Addey retorted. 'But what if the weather turn bad, and her just out of her sickbed? I need to be sure she've got enough for warm weather or cold. She might not be out in company, but 'tis likely your aunt's close friends will call to pay their respects. She can't go up there looking like some poor relation. That would be an insult to your dear father's memory.'

Eventually, consensus of a sort had been reached. The packing completed, they had retired, exhausted, to bed.

Standing on the drive, clasping her mother's gloved hands, Melissa looked down into the pale, impassive face. There was no sign of recognition in Emma Tregonning's gaze. She had shut herself away, out of reach of further hurt, and thus beyond comfort.

'Hocking will drive you to Uncle Brinley's house, Mama, where you'll change from our carriage to Aunt Lucy's barouche for the rest of the journey. Though you'll have two overnight stops, Aunt Lucy says the inns are very comfortable, with soft beds and food of excellent quality.' After a moment, ashamed of her selfishness in hoping for a response, Melissa kissed the cool cheek, and handed her mother up into the carriage where Addey waited.

After tucking a soft rug around her mistress, and checking

the hot brick at her feet, the old nurse leant out of the door.

'Don't you fret now. I'll take good care of her.'

'I know you will, Addey.'

'Mind you look after yourself while we're gone. Worst is over now. You get some rest. Looking proper done up you are.'

'Thank you, Addey.' Melissa smiled wryly.

'You know what I mean.' The old nurse pursed her lips.

Melissa stepped back, allowing Hocking to close the door.

'You mind what I say, now,' Addey called as Hocking clicked his tongue and the horse started forward.

'Stop fussing. I'll be fine.' Melissa watched the carriage until it vanished from sight, then turned and went back into the house.

It felt different. Of course it did. She drew her shawl more closely about her, cold despite the brilliant sunshine, and walked swiftly toward the stairs. She had some sorting of her own to do, and yet more letters to write.

Gabriel and Billy were planking the quarter-sawn oak trunk. But this time Billy was in the pit, using his strength to pull the long two-handled saw, while Gabriel stood at the top, pushing and guiding the blade in long, rhythmic strokes.

'You asked Tom?' Billy called, breathing hard.

'Yes.'

'What did he say? Will he let me go with you?'

Gabriel raised his voice above the slow rasp of the saw. 'He wasn't keen. He was going to put you on the packet.'

'Aw, I don't want –'

'I told him you'd be more use in the woods.'

'What did he say to that?'

'He said I'd better have you.'

'Yo!' Billy shouted. 'Just oak, is it?'

'No, ash, larch, elm, sycamore, and beech.'

'We don't want all that in the yard.'

'It's not all for the yard. The ash will be sold for barrel hoops. The larch can be planked for decking, or sold for ladder uprights. The beech – ever heard of bodgers?'

'No,' Billy shook his head, scattering golden sawdust.

114

'What are they, then?'

'Bodgers make chair legs. In large beech woods, they work in camps until all the wood from one felling is used up. Then they move on to a new camp.'

'They don't go home of a night?'

'They make a home of sorts wherever they happen to be.' As he had done.

Billy was silent for a moment. 'No, I wouldn't like that. Father do drive me mad sometimes. But I'd miss 'un awful. And me ma. Don't you miss your family?'

Caught unawares by the question, Gabriel didn't answer at once. As he thought of his parents, his elder brother and his two younger sisters, it struck him with chilling force that though he respected his parents he had never experienced the feelings Billy described.

# Chapter Nine

After work, Gabriel walked to the village with Billy, Tansey, Walter and Joseph. He remained silent, enjoying their company and the banter. Reaching Daisy Mitchell's, he raised a hand in farewell, and immediately became the butt of their teasing as they alternated warnings about lonely widows with a wistful exchange of reminiscences concerning her renowned cooking: an important feature of village fêtes and feast days. He simply grinned, waved them away, and ducked in through the open door.

Daisy greeted him with a beaming smile. 'All right, my handsome? Well, look at you. Some smart you are. Far better without all that there beard.' She studied him. 'You missed a bit, there.' She pointed.

Gabriel ran a hand down his face, feeling the unevenness of his stubble, and gave a wry shrug. 'Did it by touch.'

'What do you mean? Haven't you got no mirror?'

'Broken,' Gabriel lied quickly.

'I got one you can have. 'Tis only small, mind. But –'

'Mrs Mitchell, I can't go on taking things from you.'

She stared at him. 'What are you on about? You aren't taking nothing. I'm *giving* it to you.'

'You know what I mean,' Gabriel said.

'You've come here to work, haven't you?'

'If you have a job for me.'

'Then 'tis fair exchange, isn't it? I got a pile of wood outside need chopping up. Axe is out there, and if he need sharpening, the stone's on the shelf in the back house.'

It took Gabriel less than half an hour to reduce the thick rings to a manageable size for the range. He wondered if they had come from Tregonning land. Perhaps the villagers had a long-term arrangement with Mr Tregonning allowing them to take fallen trees from a certain area for their own use.

His own father had agreed such an arrangement with the estate staff and local village. Or perhaps they simply helped themselves, assuming that as the woods were so neglected no one would notice or care. It was really none of his business.

When he went back inside, the basket she had given him stood on the kitchen table. He lifted a corner of the checked cloth. Apart from the usual pie and buns there was a dish of lettuce and fresh peas, one of strawberries, and a small mirror in a painted wooden frame.

Daisy appeared from the other room. 'Dear life! You was quick.' She pushed the basket into his hands, tapping the handle where he had mended it and reinforced it with elm-bark cord.

'Done a good job with that, you did. Go on then, off you go. I don't want no thanks,' she added quickly, seeing him about to speak. 'Like I said, 'tis fair exchange.'

'I'll drop the dishes in tomorrow.'

'All right, my handsome.'

He picked up the basket and turned to the door.

'Here, Gabriel –?'

As he turned, she shook her head and waved him away. 'No, don't matter. You go on.'

'What?' He moved toward her. 'Is something wrong?'

'No, well, not *wrong,* but – I was going to ask you – I aren't sure, see? Of course, there'll be talk, but that don't bother me.' She looked up, flustered. 'Hark at me gabbling on.'

He waited: taut, expressionless, his mind racing.

'Look, 'tis like this: Joe Sweet's wife died last year, not long after my Cyrus.'

As she spoke, and he realised he was not the cause of her concern, Gabriel felt himself relax.

'Well, Joe and me, we've knowed each other since we was children. Truth is there was a time … But I met my Cyrus, and Joe married Nell. Anyhow, the long and the short of it is, Joe was in here today. Only asked if he could come calling.

Brought me a bunch of forget-me-nots.' She shook her head in amazement. 'Carried them all the way through the street he did. 'Course he wouldn't never have got up the nerve if you hadn't come with me to take that flour back. So, what do you think?'

Gabriel struggled hard to conceal his amusement, enquiring gently, 'About the flowers? Well, it was –'

'No!' Daisy rolled her eyes. 'About him coming courting.'

'Why are you asking me?'

'Well –' She shrugged, fiddling with her apron. 'There isn't no one else. I got no family. And I don't want to go making a fool of myself. So I thought I'd ask you. I trust you, see?'

He winced inwardly as the unwitting blade drove deep. 'Would Joe treat you well?'

'Oh yes.' She dimpled. 'If he know what's good for 'un he will. A decent man, Joe is. He haven't been taking proper care of hisself since Nell died. That boy of his do try his best, but they both need looking after.'

Gabriel smiled. 'Mrs Mitchell, you're a treasure.'

'Aw, get on! You think I should tell 'un yes?'

He lifted one shoulder. 'Do what will make you happy. As for the talk: your friends will be pleased for you. The others don't matter.'

She stared hard at him, clasped hands pressed to her bosom. Then gave a decisive nod. 'There now, if that isn't the truth. Thank you, my handsome.'

He shook his head and indicated the basket. 'It's I who should thank you.'

She sighed, beaming happily. 'Got some lovely way with words, you have.' She leant toward him, suddenly confidential. 'Here, I'm just thinking, my bakery and Joe's flour mill? Putting they two together will make a nice little business. Yes, I think we'll do very well.'

Battling with laughter, Gabriel picked up his basket. About to head for the door, he noticed she had tilted her head awkwardly to present a pink-tinged cheek. He kissed it lightly. 'Goodnight, Mother.'

Cloud had rolled in from the west. As he reached the shack, the first drops pattered onto the leaves above his head. After eating, he bathed, then rebound his wounds with clean cloths spread with the soothing salve. The rain continued on and off for much of the night. Warm and dry between the two blankets on his fir bed, Gabriel lay awake, listening to the sighing wind and the drip of water onto earth, his thoughts drifting between past and present.

Two weeks ago he had not known this place or these people existed. What quirk of fate had decreed he should land here and nowhere else? Against his better judgement he had been inexorably drawn into village life. Educated by the best tutors, he would, not so long ago, have ridiculed the suggestion that he might learn anything of value from people of a class so far beneath his own. He was wiser now. Or was he? To play with fire risked being consumed should it flare out of control. But he could not bring himself to leave.

Just before daybreak next morning, after ten minutes spent digging up lugworms from the soft mud of a small inlet, Gabriel rowed Jack's boat out toward the mouth of the creek, baited three rusty hooks, and tossed the line over the side. Half an hour later he rowed back with a catch of six large, gleaming blue-grey and silver striped mackerel. By the time he had beached the boat and threaded four of the fish onto a strip of elm bark cord, the sun had risen.

Leaving two fish in the shack out of reach of scavengers, he followed the path eastward: the direction from which Melissa Tregonning had come. The only people yet awake in the house would be servants, and they would be too busy to notice him. He was curious to see where she lived, this gentleman's daughter so unlike any other of his acquaintance.

He had watched her gallop her enormous thoroughbred in the woods, and address a crowd of restless men. He had seen her shy, spirited, and withdrawn. He'd give a king's ransom to see her laugh. Meanwhile, he wanted to picture her in her home.

He arrived and departed unchallenged, the fish left hanging over the back door where they could not be missed: his thanks for her gifts.

* * *

'Mrs Betts is just frying up some mackerel for you, miss,' Lobb announced as Melissa took her place at the breakfast table.

'Mackerel?' Melissa repeated in surprise.

'Don't you worry. Mrs Betts checked they were fresh. She reckons they haven't been out of the water much above an hour.'

Melissa wasn't really listening. She had slept deeply; but it had not been peaceful. Her vivid dreams were filled with a nameless yearning and she had woken feeling bereft and jittery. Food was a necessity, but the thought of eating made her feel queasy. 'Lobb, I really don't think –'

'Now, Miss Melissa. You can't be living on fruit and fresh air. How do you think your dear mother would feel if she knew you were starving yourself?'

'Don't be ridiculous. I'm not starving myself.'

'Well, a dish of raspberries and one egg is no proper start to the day, not for someone rushing about the way you are.'

Melissa controlled herself with an effort, torn between amusement at his scolding and irritation at being treated like a child. 'That's enough, Lobb.'

'Beg pardon, miss, I'm sure. However, I should just like to say that it's been my privilege and pleasure to work for this family since before you were born. Now master's gone, and mistress's health has taken her away, I'd be failing in my duty if I didn't keep an eye to your well-being. If mistress was to come back and find you ill, she'd turn me off without a character. Though that would be no more than I deserve for not –'

'Enough.' Pressing her lips together, refusing to let him see her smile, Melissa threw up her hands, helpless against such outrageous blackmail. 'Serve the mackerel,' she allowed wearily. 'I'm sure they will be delicious. Who brought them?'

'That I can't say, miss. They were left by the back door. Hung up by a bit of elm-bark cord, Mrs Betts said.' A reminiscent smile hovered about his mouth. ''Tis years since I've seen elm-bark cord. I had an old uncle used to make it. Swore it was just as strong as hemp or sisal. I'll fetch your breakfast, miss.'

'Thank you,' Melissa managed. As the door closed behind him, she pressed her napkin to her mouth, burning with the sudden heat of realisation as she pictured, with stark clarity, the stone shack, its roof of ancient canvas and branches weighted by stones tied with elm-bark cord.

After breakfast, she rode to the yard, oblivious to the scenery as she rehearsed what she would say. As she turned in through the gateway she saw Tom coming up from the slip.

'Good morning, Tom. I'm going into Truro later and I need to know how many wagons –'

'You'll have to talk to Gabriel about that, miss. Only he isn't here. He've taken the gang up the woods to start clearing a track down to the road. Want me to send someone up for 'un, do you?'

'No. You're short-handed enough already. Don't worry, I'll find him.'

'You shouldn't have no trouble, not with the row they lot will be making.'

Following the path toward the source of the noise, she noticed various trees marked with different signs in yellow paint. If Gabriel had done this alone – and no one else would have known which trees to mark – he must have been walking the woods each evening until the light faded, having already worked a full day at the yard. She must ensure his wages reflected the extra time he had worked. Sudden fear clenched icy fingers around her heart. The wages. She had found no money in her father's desk. How was she to pay the wages?

The shouts of the men, the crash of saplings falling, the crackle of wood burning and sharp scent of drifting smoke were making Samson increasingly restless. By the time Melissa reached the men the huge horse was skittering sideways on the path, tossing his head as he fought the bit.

In the middle of the clearing a large bonfire surrounded by powdery grey ash had been newly capped with a fresh heap of undergrowth and wood débris. Hungry flames licked around the edges of the pile while clouds of thick blue smoke belched from the top. She was about to call out when Billy saw her.

'Dear life, miss! Made me jump you did.' He turned. 'Gabe! Miss Tregonning's here.'

Gabriel emerged from a dense thicket, a large axe dangling from one hand. He knuckled his forehead.

'Miss Tregonning.'

Her increased nervousness communicated itself to Samson, who plunged and snorted. She saw Gabriel tense. But before he could move she turned the horse in a tight circle, using the brief hiatus to collect her wits.

Then, lifting her leg over the pommel, she quickly slid to the ground, holding the bridle with one hand while she stroked the horse's sweat-darkened coat with the other. Horribly aware of her heightened colour, hoping he would attribute it to her battle with the fractious horse, she swallowed to moisten her throat.

'I'm sorry to interrupt. I know you have a great deal to do and I won't keep you. But as I'm going into Truro shortly it would be an ideal opportunity to order the wagons. But I'm not sure –'

'Of course, miss. If you'll give me a moment.' While he turned to Billy with brief instructions, Melissa took a folded sheet of paper from a pocket in her skirt. As Billy loped away toward the lower side of the clearing where most of the activity was taking place, Gabriel faced her again. 'If you are selling direct to a timber merchant, miss, then they will supply the wagons. But they may try using that fact to negotiate a lower price.'

She nodded slowly. 'How did your master deal with this? Did he use the merchant's wagons or hire an independent haulier?'

'Both, miss, it was a much larger enterprise. But you would be wise to compare prices.'

'I will, Gabriel. Thank you.' She hesitated, reluctant to reveal the extent of her ignorance. Yet without the necessary information, how was she to do business at all? She took a breath and hurried on, 'I – I've written out a list of the different types of wood to be sold, but I have no idea about current prices. What is the correct procedure in matters of negotiation?'

He bowed his head, but she had glimpsed his frown. As he scuffed the freshly bared earth with the toe of his boot, she could not see his eyes or read his expression. A dark tide of panic threatened to choke her. She had depended on him to tell her. Surely he must know? If he didn't she would be – not lost, but certainly at a grave disadvantage.

He glanced sideways, still frowning. 'You must deal with this yourself?'

She stiffened. 'I do not wish to bother my uncles. Naturally, as soon as my brother returns he will take over. In the meantime, I must act for him.

'No offence intended, ma'am. But it is not usual. You might find the wood merchant – surprised, possibly reluctant.'

Her chin lifted, determined and defiant. 'His prejudices are of no interest to me. If he wishes to buy our wood he will overcome them.'

'Indeed, ma'am.' His lips quivered. 'May I make some suggestions?'

'If you please.' She gave him a brief, tentative smile, a spilling over of relief and gratitude.

He looked away. 'First: say as little as possible. You tell him what you told me, that you are acting on behalf of your brother. You have wood to sell. Does he wish to buy? He will ask what you are selling and the prices you want. You tell him –'

'Oak, elm, beech, alder, ash, and larch,' Melissa read from the list.

Gabriel nodded. 'You ask him what price he is offering. When he tells you, you thank him for his time and prepare to leave.'

'*What?* But –' She bit her lip. 'Forgive me. Please go on.'

'Before you have reached the door, or the gate, he will stop you. He will be full of apologies. He may claim he was distracted by this unprecedented situation, or by your beauty.' As her cheeks flamed, Gabriel warned, 'While this may indeed be true, it will also be a ploy to distract you. So be prepared. Then he will ask if you have a price in mind.'

Melissa gazed at him, fascinated by this insight into aspects of commerce she had never imagined. 'Do I?'

Gabriel nodded. 'Twice what he offered.'

She gasped. 'He'll never accept that.'

'You don't expect him to.'

'I don't?'

'No. He will then suggest a price perhaps a quarter above his original offer. You regret that is unacceptable. He will suggest you wish to ruin him, and take the very bread from his children's mouths.'

As Melissa's hand went to her mouth he continued, 'Do not react. Above all, do not speak. Smile. You have a lovely smile.' His gaze flickered as her blush deepened once more. He cleared his throat. 'He might also ask why he should be expected to pay such a price for wood he has not seen. At this you allow yourself a small frown of impatience. You point out that –'

'He would take imported wood on trust, if it were available. I suggest that perhaps he would prefer to wait for ships bringing new supplies to find a way through the blockade? If so, I will not take up any more of his time. I have other merchants to see in – in Falmouth.'

Her triumph evaporated into uncertainty as she studied his face. 'Was that not right?'

His lips twitched, but his tone was grave. 'Indeed, miss, it was excellent. For *perfection* might I suggest a touch more detachment? A coolness of manner?'

She drew herself up, and, thinking of visits by her aunts, succeeded in blanking all expression from her face. 'Like this?'

His eyes narrowed fractionally. 'Just so. Now he will make his final offer: a sum halfway between his original price and your demand.'

She nodded. 'What do I do then?'

'Do you wish to accept it?'

'Oh yes. Indeed.' She hesitated. 'Don't I?'

'It will be a fair price. One he is unlikely to improve on. You request that his clerk set out the agreed terms as a contract with both of you signing and retaining a copy. As that document will take a little time to prepare you could offer to complete your other business in town first, then return for it before you come home.'

'Right. Thank you.' As she tried to remember all he had said, her misgiving blossomed into mouth-drying fear. 'Gabriel, considering your experience in these matters, would it not be more sensible –?'

'No.' His interruption and its forcefulness took her by surprise. 'No, miss,' he repeated more gently. 'That wouldn't do at all.' His features softened. 'You addressed the men: you can do this.'

Melissa moistened her lips. 'When will the first wagonload be ready?'

'Depends on the weather, but, all being well, in about two weeks.'

So long? She tried not to let her disappointment show. 'Thank you, Gabriel. I-I'm very grateful.' Preparing to mount, she gathered up the reins.

'I wish –' he began, and stopped abruptly.

Startled by the intensity even his hoarseness could not disguise, she glanced back, oddly breathless as her heart gave an extra beat. 'Yes?'

The brooding, troubled expression faded, leaving his face blank. It was like watching an ebbing wave wipe footprints from sand. 'Nothing. Good luck, miss.' He had retreated, his whole manner different. No less polite, but deliberately distanced.

He knuckled his forehead. 'Help you up?' Bending forward, he linked his hands. She placed her booted foot in them and he tossed her up into the saddle. Without waiting for thanks, and avoiding her eye, he gave a final salute and strode away across the clearing.


'Miss, you can't. It wouldn't be right nor proper.' The groom's glare was a mixture of anxiety and defiance.

'For goodness' sake, Hocking, I've driven myself into Truro countless times.'

His gesture encompassed her black habit, white brocaded

waistcoat, and black beaver hat. 'Not wearing full mourning and your dear father laid to rest only days ago you haven't. I know you don't care what others think, and most times I'd say you was right to ignore them –'

'But not this time.'

'No, miss. Not this time, especially not with your mother away. Don't you go thinking it don't make no difference. You know as well as I do there's some spiteful tongues in Truro. Appearances is more important than ever just now.' He met and held her gaze.

Melissa was the first to look away. Which appearances did he mean? Surely she hadn't betrayed herself? Her reaction to Gabriel Ennis was so deeply unsettling she had taken particular care to hide it.

Or was he referring to the truth about her father? About the family's situation? Did all the servants know? But how could they? And if they did, how had they found out? She couldn't ask, for to do so would only alert him to the very facts she wished to remain hidden. Discretion left her no choice but retreat.

'You're right, Hocking. I wasn't thinking.'

'No wonder, miss. Some time you've 'ad of it these past weeks.' He cleared his throat. 'I think it best if I drive you myself, miss. No reflection on young John, he's a good lad. But seeing this is your first visit to Truro since … Well, I just think it's best.'

Touched by his concern, Melissa nodded. 'Indeed, I think so too. People will see that not only I am observing all the proprieties, but that I have proper protection.'

He shot her a dry glance. 'You aren't that much taller than me when we're both sitting down. I'll bring the gig to the front door, miss.'

'You won't be long, will you? Only I have –'

'Two shakes of a lamb's tail.'

Returning to the house, she went to her father's study and closed the door. Opening the glass-fronted bookcase, she pulled out the fourth volume from the end of the second shelf and retrieved from behind it a velvet-wrapped package. As she was in mourning, her action should remain undiscovered for several weeks at least. Meanwhile the contents of the package would, she hoped, buy her what she most needed: time.

# Chapter Ten

Melissa sat straight-backed in the gig alongside Hocking, too absorbed in what lay ahead to take note of the countryside through which they drove.

'Where to first, miss?' the groom enquired as they reached the bottom of Lemon Street.

'The timber merchant on the Quay.'

'Which one, miss?'

Melissa's heart sank. She should have asked Tom which merchant her father purchased wood from. Perhaps he had bought from more than one. When checking the bills she had been concentrating on the amounts owed rather than the names of the suppliers. What if the timber yards were owed money? If they were, she would find out soon enough. Despite the sunshine, she shivered.

Why had she not thought to ask Gabriel if he knew the best one to approach? What was she doing here? She had believed herself so well prepared. But the truth was – the truth was she had no choice. She was here because a timber merchant offered the only hope of protecting her father's good name and saving the boatyard from closure.

'Which is the largest?' Surely that would be the one most in need of fresh supplies?

The groom thought for a moment. 'Nankivell's, miss.'

'You wouldn't happen to know if my father bought from them, I suppose?'

The groom whistled through his teeth. 'That I can't say, miss. Not my line of work, see?'

'Never mind. Take me there, please.' Though she glimpsed Hocking's glance out of the corner of her eye, she continued to gaze straight ahead. Whatever questions were trembling on the tip of his tongue, he took the hint, remaining silent as they turned into Boscawen Street, then along Princes Street until they crossed the broad junction and drove onto the open area of the quay. The tide was out and the foul stench of sewage-tainted mud was thick in her nostrils.

'Come in with you, shall I, miss?' Hocking enquired, clearly expecting his offer to be accepted.

'No, thank you,' Melissa replied, stepping down onto the cobbles. 'I shouldn't be above quarter of an hour. But if I am, then please walk the horse. It will do him no good to be standing –'

'Never mind the horse,' Hocking blurted, as concern got the better of him. 'You shouldn't be going in such places alone. What would mistress say?'

'I would very much prefer,' Melissa said deliberately, 'that for her peace of mind she doesn't ever hear of it.'

'What are you doing down here anyhow?' he growled, his leathery face creased with anxiety.

'I'm hoping – no, I *intend* to sell Mr Nankivell timber from our woods. As I haven't conducted business with him before –' they both knew she hadn't conducted business with anyone before '– I am a little nervous. So please don't make it any more difficult for me.'

'I don't want to cause you no trouble, miss. 'Tis just –' He broke off as she raised a coolly enquiring eyebrow. 'Beg pardon, miss, I'm sure. No doubt you know what you're doing.' His tone implied the opposite.

'Of course,' Melissa responded with a calm completely at odds with the apprehension that had loosened her knees and gripped her stomach with sharp claws. She walked briskly across the quay to the Queen Anne building. On one side of it an alley led to the timber yard.

It occurred to her that for Mr Nankivell to operate from such imposing premises his business must be thriving. For it to continue doing so in these troubled times he needed wood to sell. Clinging to that thought and clutching the list, she stepped inside.

She emerged half an hour later, her face flushed, her heart thudding against her ribs. She stood for a moment in the wide doorway, smoothing her gloves as she tried to control an elation that fizzed and bubbled like champagne and left her feeling as light-headed.

When she introduced herself he said he recognised the name. Having heard of her father's demise he offered his condolences. Then, to her immense relief – for it meant Tregonning's did not owe him money – he asked how he might be of service. Thereafter the interview had proceeded exactly as Gabriel said it would.

When the merchant, unable to entirely conceal his annoyance, had suggested that the price she was asking seemed to indicate a lack of understanding of the current situation, Melissa had derived intense pleasure from telling him, with exquisite politeness and a dazzling smile, that, on the contrary, she understood perfectly. If he preferred to wait for ships presently delayed by the blockade to arrive, she would take her leave and offer her timber elsewhere.

Accepting his final offer, on condition that it included transport, she had watched his initial frozen shock melt into reluctant admiration.

'You drive a hard bargain, Miss Tregonning.'

Not sure whether it was proper to thank him, or if his remark was intended as a compliment, Melissa decided to play safe, and simply inclined her head. Then, recalling the last of Gabriel's instructions, she asked the merchant to be kind enough to have a paper drawn up specifying the agreed terms. To spare him any inconvenience she would complete the rest of her business before calling back for it in, say, two hours?

His expression as he took her proffered hand had been one of bemusement. But she had not lingered to enjoy her triumph, all too aware that without Gabriel's coaching her chances of success would have equalled those of a lamb trying to persuade a wolf that grass was tastier.

'Everything go all right, miss?' Hocking enquired, as she settled herself on the gig's padded seat. His anxiety evaporated in the glow of her delighted smile.

'Yes, thank you, Hocking. It went perfectly. Mr Nankivell is going to buy all the wood we can supply.'

'Glad to hear it, miss. Where do you want to go now?'

'To see Mr Rogers, my father's lawyer.'

Turning the gig, the groom pointed it back toward Princes Street.

'Hocking, you're acquainted with the gentlemen my father used to hunt with. Do you think you could find out, tactfully of course, if any of them might be looking for new mounts for the coming season?'

He darted a look at her. 'Selling the hunters, are you, miss? You won't have no problem there. Master was known to keep only the best blood and bone. A word in the right ear and you'll have buyers queuing up. Be long with Mr Rogers, will you, miss?'

'At least an hour.'

'All right if I go and see Mr Sibley's groom, then? He's an old friend, and got a good eye.'

'Please do, Hocking. But –'

'Don't you fret, miss. He won't even know he've been told they're for sale.'

At the lawyer's office, Melissa announced herself to an elderly clerk, one of several moving with quiet purpose between a number of panelled doors leading off a spacious reception area. Tall and slightly stooped, he wore an old fashioned suit of black cloth shiny with wear, and a tie wig.

'If you will be seated, Miss –?'

'Tregonning.'

'Miss Tregonning,' he repeated with slow gravity, 'I shall ascertain whether Mr Rogers is currently engaged.' He bowed and withdrew. Glancing around the elegantly furnished room, Melissa perched bolt upright on a Queen Anne armchair upholstered in green and gold brocade. Renewed tension quickened her breathing and her pulse. He returned a few moments later.

'If you will accompany me, Miss Tregonning, Mr Rogers will receive you.'

The clerk wore his collarless coat unbuttoned over his long

waistcoat and knee breeches. As she followed the austere figure, Melissa noticed that his white stockings were a little too loose for his thin legs and his black shoes with their square steel buckles, though well polished, bore unmistakable signs of age. A frugal man, she decided, as neat and sparing in his habits as he was in his dress. Had he ever loved?

As she recognised the source from which the thought had sprung, shock and shame broke over her in a hot, drenching wave. Her cheeks burned and her clothes clung uncomfortably to suddenly damp skin. Concealed behind the clerk, she withdrew a small handkerchief of cambric and lace from her sleeve and surreptitiously wiped her forehead and upper lip.

'My dear Miss Tregonning.' Glendon Woodford Rogers greeted her with an outstretched hand. Though his clerks adhered to a mode of dress popular 20 years ago, Mr Rogers clearly preferred a more modern look. Of portly build, he had wisely remained in breeches instead of adopting the thigh-hugging pantaloons that among younger men were considered the epitome of style. His close-fitting frock coat of blue cloth sported large mother-of-pearl buttons and was cut away at the hip and thigh so that the skirts were little more than square-cut tails that reached to the back of his knees. His double-breasted waistcoat of cream and blue striped silk strained across a barrel-shaped paunch. Pale yellow silk stockings and low-heeled, long-toed shoes tied with narrow ribbons completed his ensemble. The magnificence of his raiment conveyed, as was no doubt intended, his success and consequent wealth.

Drawing a deep breath, Melissa extended her hand. 'Good afternoon, Mr Rogers. I'm very grateful to you for seeing me at such short notice.'

Taking her hand, he bowed. The brief but ominous creaking that accompanied this movement indicated his reliance on a corset to hold his corpulence in check. Biting hard on the inside of her lip, Melissa seated herself carefully on a chair of carved walnut upholstered in crimson velvet that was slightly too low for comfort, and smoothed the skirts of her habit.

Flicking his coat tails up, the lawyer resumed his own chair – padded leather and mahogany – beside a large ornate bureau. The lid was rolled back to reveal rows of drawers and tiny cubbyholes, and the writing surface was covered with documents penned in elaborate script and bearing important seals.

'Now,' he smiled, leaning slightly forward. 'How may I help you? Though before you begin, I should perhaps make it clear that if you have come to see me in connection with your father's will –'

'Actually, I haven't. Though I am aware of the terms. We discussed it after – when he had the new document drawn up.'

Mr Rogers sat back in his chair. Resting his elbows on the arms, he made a steeple of his spread fingers. 'Then what is the problem?' Melissa told him, watching his expression alter from avuncular encouragement through thoughtfulness to frowning concern. 'My advice, Miss Tregonning,' he said when she had finished, 'is to confide in your uncles. They are the people best placed to –'

'No,' she said firmly, shaking her head. 'Forgive me, Mr Rogers, but that is quite simply out of the question. Even my mother does not know the full extent of my father's – commitments. As he is now no longer – no longer your client, the interests you represent are those of my mother, my brother, and myself.'

The dark crimson of his anger was alarming against the snowy points of his shirt collar. 'Are you presuming to lecture me on confidentiality? I have never heard such gross impertinence. I need no such reminder. Especially from you, young lady.'

Once more, embarrassment surged through Melissa. Her skin oozed with mortification. Why especially from her? 'I'm so sorry. I didn't mean – Mr Rogers, I cannot apologise enough. Truly, I meant no offence. It's just that – if my uncles are informed, my aunts will learn of it. If it became public – which it would – my mother – can you imagine –?' Helpless, she shook her head, blinking away tears. 'I really am most terribly sorry. It – it has all been such a shock.'

He unbent slightly. 'Yes. Yes, I can see that it must have been. But I do not see how, without your uncles' help, you can hope to come about. You have no immediately convertible assets.'

Melissa's head flew up. 'But I do.' Plunging a hand into the pocket of her skirt, she passed him the velvet-wrapped package, watching anxiously as he opened it.

'My grandmother left me the rubies. The pearls, garnets, and other smaller pieces were gifts.'

He glanced sideways. 'The sapphires?'

'My 21st birthday.' She swallowed. 'I want to sell it. All of it. So I was wondering … Actually, I hoped … Of course, you will need some kind of proof of their ownership and origin, so …' Fumbling in her other pocket she extracted a slim wad of tightly folded papers. 'I have written it all down. I thought – I hoped, maybe you could take them to Plymouth? Surely they will fetch a far better price there than they would here? And even if you are known there, no one would know who you were selling them for.'

His gaze was sympathetic. 'Miss Tregonning, you came to me for advice. Well, my advice is this: take your jewellery home.'

She felt as if he had slammed a door in her face. 'Is it not – will it not sell?'

'Oh yes, it would sell. I have no doubt of that. You have some very nice pieces. My point is –'

Melissa shook her head, urgency overriding good manners. 'Forgive me, Mr Rogers, but I must sell. I have no choice. I need the money. Besides, what use are necklaces, bracelets, and rings to me when everything my father, grandfather, and great-grandfather worked to build is in danger of being lost? I do not receive many invitations, Mr Rogers. So opportunities to wear elaborate jewellery are rare. If it became public knowledge that my father died on the verge of bankruptcy, even those invitations would quickly cease. Besides, how could I ever again appear in such gems knowing their value would have kept the yard going and men in work?'

'Unfortunately, it wouldn't,' he countered gravely. 'I applaud your sentiments, and your courage. But although what you have here might partially clear the debts, it will do no more. So if you were counting on that alone –'

'I wasn't. I have just come from Mr Nankivell, the timber merchant on the quay. He has agreed to buy all the wood we can supply. Even now, a team is at work felling trees under the direction of an experienced woodsman.'

He was staring at her, openly astonished. 'Is your brother aware of your activities, Miss Tregonning?'

'I have written to him,' Melissa replied truthfully. 'But as he is at sea and, it is to be hoped, on his way home, he will not be aware of all that has been achieved until he sees it for himself. When he does,' she added with a defiance born of nervous tension, 'I have no doubt at all that he will be delighted. Mr Rogers, if I do nothing, my brother's arrival will be greeted with foreclosure by the bank and a writ from a moneylender.'

The lawyer inhaled deeply. 'As you have chosen to ignore my advice, I see no point in trying to persuade you otherwise.' Melissa clenched her hands in her lap. 'I consider the course of action upon which you have embarked to be fraught with risk.' He frowned at her. With a sudden understanding of how a fox must feel when cornered, she tried to work some saliva into a mouth so dry it was too painful to swallow. 'However, in the face of such initiative, foolhardy though it may be, I feel bound to offer my assistance. As it happens, I am already travelling to Plymouth over the weekend.'

For a moment she could only stare at him. 'You are?'

'I am.'

'Thank you, Mr Rogers.' The release of tension left Melissa feeling shaky. 'I can't tell you how grateful I am. There is just one more favour I have to ask.'

His brows climbed, and there was a touch of asperity in his tone. 'My goodness, Miss Tregonning, you are very free with your requests.'

She dipped her head, accepting the criticism, but plunged on. 'It's not for me, sir. Not directly, at any rate. But until the jewellery is sold, or I receive the first payment for the wood, I have no money to pay the men's wages. I can probably stave off the demands of the bank and Mr Vincent for a little while longer, once I tell them of the business arrangement with Mr Nankivell regarding his purchase of our trees. I intend to write to them as soon as I get home so they will know that money will soon be available. But the men cannot wait. They need their wages. They have families to feed and clothe.'

His brows had almost disappeared beneath the pointed peak of his pig-tailed wig. 'You want me to give you money?'

'No, sir,' she corrected with dignity. 'I ask for no gift, merely a loan, to be repaid upon your return from Plymouth with money from the sale of my jewellery.'

He sighed, shaking his head as if astonished at his own behaviour. 'What sum do you require, Miss Tregonning?'

Climbing into the gig, she told Hocking to drive her to the various shipyard suppliers. Paying each one something on account, she promised full settlement by the end of the month. 'I have to wait until then for money to be released,' she explained as truthfully as she dared.

All three nodded, telling her they understood, offered their condolences once more, and sympathised with the time it took to complete legal matters.

She inclined her head, grateful for their assumptions. 'I do not anticipate any further delay. But if one should occur, I will pay interest on what is owed, on condition you begin supplying the yard again immediately.'

Each time there was an instant's hesitation. But, given such a promise, what could they lose? With smiles, bows, and much hand-washing, she was assured that the items requested would be dispatched that very afternoon.

As Hocking drove the gig back to Bosvane, Melissa closed her eyes. She had achieved everything she set out to do. But the strain had been intense and reaction was setting in. Though she had been more successful than she dared hope, she felt totally drained.

In one hand she clutched a soft leather bag, the remaining coins hard, reassuring, against her palm. In the other, two papers: one a copy of the agreement signed by Mr Nankivell and herself, the other a receipt for her jewellery from Mr

Rogers.

Hocking dropped her off at the front door. As she walked into the house, Lobb took one look, pursed his lips, and announced he would have a tray brought to her. Where would she be?

Realising she must look as weary as she felt, and that part of her exhaustion was due to simple hunger, she didn't argue. 'In the study, Lobb. Thank you.'

In her room she removed her hat and habit, rinsed her face and hands, then put on a simple gown of lavender muslin. Cooler and much refreshed, she tidied her hair and went back downstairs. Entering the study, she saw on the side table a silver tray containing a jug of lemonade, thin slices of ham and beef, rolls and butter, cheese, and a dish of fruit compote. The sight of the food made her mouth water and she ate where she stood, looking out of the window at the view and trying not to think at all.

She had just finished and was dabbing her mouth with a napkin when Lobb entered. After a flickering glance at the empty dishes, he picked up the tray, totally expressionless. 'Will there be anything, else, miss?'

Sensing his satisfaction, she matched his composure. 'Not for the moment, Lobb.' She waited until he reached the door. 'Thank you.'

'I'll tell Mrs Betts, miss. She will be most gratified.' He sailed out.

Seated at her father's desk, she took up a fresh sheet of paper, dipped a pen in the inkstand, and began her letter to Mr Edmund Turner of the Commercial Bank. But after writing the address she stopped, turning the pen in her fingers as she mentally tested, then discarded, various phrases.

Informed of her father's death by her uncles, Mr Turner had sent one of his clerks to the house to leave a card of condolence. He had not come in person. Nor had he attended the funeral. Doubtless he was a very busy man. But her father's association with the bank had begun before she was born, and until last year the two men had often hunted and dined together in Truro on excellent terms.

She dipped the pen once more and resumed writing. She would not apologise for her father. No doubt the bank had been within its rights to demand immediate repayment of the money owed. But Mr Turner had known about Adrian's death, and must also have been aware of its aftermath of devastation. To pile even more pressure on a man trying to deal with his grief while caring for a wife incapacitated by her loss seemed unduly callous.

No, she would not apologise. But nor would she betray her anger. With careful dignity, she wrote that she regretted any inconvenience caused by her father's lack of response to the bank's letters. She stated that, unknown to anyone, he had been suffering from illness kept hidden to spare the family further worry. She would come in person later the following week to make, on her brother's behalf as the new head of the family, a substantial reduction to the outstanding loan.

Signing the letter, she set it to one side, and began another to Thomas Vincent, undertaking to repay his loan in full by the end of the month. As she sealed them both she prayed the sale of her jewellery and the first load of wood would realise enough.

The following morning, she rode Samson up to the farm. Glistening spider-webs festooned the hedgerows, spangled with raindrops from an early shower. The clouds had rolled away, leaving the air clear and the sky a freshly washed blue. In a field adjoining those in which small, hardy black cattle were grazing, pigs rooted among thick stalks; all that remained of the winter kale.

In other fields, the earth's acid sourness had been enriched with sand, seaweed, and Devon limestone burned in kilns all along the Cornish coast. Here ripening oats that would feed the horses rippled in the breeze, as did wheat, providing grain for the miller and straw for thatching or bedding for the cattle.

Grass, now long and juicy, would be cut with scythe and sickle over the next two to three weeks. Lifted and turned to dry in the sun, it would then be raked up, loaded onto the high-sided cart, and carried to the stack, a fodder smelling sweetly of warm summer days for both horses and cattle through the winter. Sheaves of cut wheat would be set up in shocks, carried to the rick-yard, then threshed with flails to release the grain.

Brown and white hens clucked quietly, ignoring the large cockerel strutting amongst them as they scratched and pecked grain from the earth in a large pen at one side of the thatched farmhouse. A chicken-shed divided inside into three tiers of snug, open-fronted boxes stood in the shade of two apple trees. The door, now standing wide open, would be closed at sunset, the chickens inside, safe from prowling foxes.

Dismounting outside the small gate, Melissa tied Samson to a tree and knocked on the open door before calling out. Up and working since dawn, Edgar would now be having his dinner.

'I'm so sorry to interrupt your meal, but I wanted to catch Edgar at home.' She pulled off her gloves as Becky jumped up from her seat at the scrubbed table, shooing a cat off the spare chair and dusting it with her apron before inviting Melissa to sit down.

'Nothing wrong is there, miss?' Edgar's knife and fork looked toy-like in his huge, sun-darkened hands.

'No, I've come because I need to borrow the horses to drag out trees we're having felled in the woods. Can you manage with the oxen and let me have Captain and Duchess?'

The farmer and his wife exchanged a glance. 'I suppose so, miss,' Edgar said slowly. 'We haven't started cutting the hay yet.'

'They're both fit?'

Edgar nodded. 'You'd best work Captain in blinkers though. He do jump at his own shadow when the mood's on 'un.'

'I won't forget.' Smiling, she stood up. 'Thanks, Edgar. I'll bring John with me to collect them on Sunday afternoon.'

'On the Sabbath?' Becky gasped, visibly shocked.

Melissa grimaced. 'I know. But they have to be in the woods to start work early Monday morning.'

'Well, I don't know, miss.' Becky was more anxious than disapproving. ''Tis to be hoped nobody see you, that's all I can say.'

'They won't,' Melissa promised. The only people to see her

with the great draught horses would be the people whose jobs she was trying to protect. They would understand. Bidding them goodbye, she remounted Samson and rode to the yard to pay the wages.

Tom had cleared a space on the cluttered table to make room for the ledger in which he marked men present or absent each day. It lay open, the pen and inkwell alongside, ready for each man to make his mark, or sign his name if he could write.

'Here, you sit down,' he insisted, indicating the only chair. 'Looking fagged to death you are.'

She sat, and Tom stood at her shoulder, just as he used to when her father … She shut off the thought. 'When I was in Truro yesterday I saw the suppliers and –'

'I should think you did. I dunno what you said to them, but stuff have been coming in all morning.'

Trying to hide her rush of relief, Melissa simply nodded as if she had expected no less. She gazed at the ledger, the figures a blur. 'Gabriel must have put in a lot of additional work marking the trees. I think he should be paid for that time.'

'I was going to suggest it, miss. I tell you straight, I dunno how we'd have managed if he hadn't come when he did. Fate, it was.'

All the tasks and responsibilities she had assumed since her father's stroke flashed through Melissa's mind. Yet none of it would have been possible without Gabriel's knowledge and physical strength.

'You're right.' Taking the heavy leather purse from her pocket, she placed it on the table and loosened the drawstrings. 'How much will you need altogether? '

He indicated the total at the bottom of the page with a blunt and ragged fingernail. 'And say half a day extra for Gabe.'

Counting out the coins, she checked them again. Then, as Tom scooped them into his box ready to pay the men at the end of the day, Melissa returned the remainder to the purse, noting how little was left, and stood up to leave.

'When Gabriel comes in, will you tell him John and I will bring the shires down first thing Monday morning?' Seeing Tom's frown, she didn't give him the chance to speak. 'I've struck a new agreement with the suppliers. So there will be no problems about anything you need for the packet.'

A grin split Tom's face as he shook his head in admiration. 'Dear life! You got spirit, girl. Be some proud of you, your pa would.'

As Melissa rode back to the house she wondered. Would her father be proud? Or would he be turning in his grave at the desperate risks she was taking?

## Chapter Eleven

Arriving home, and greeted by Lobb with the news that her aunts had called, Melissa sagged. 'Oh dear.'

'Quite so, miss. Both ladies made no secret of their surprise not to find you here. They could not imagine where you might have gone. I, of course, was unable to enlighten them.'

Her brief smile reflected her gratitude. 'No doubt they were less than pleased.'

'As you say, miss. I was instructed to tell you they would call again.'

Managing not to grimace, Melissa thanked him. In her father's study she put the remaining money in one of the desk drawers. Then, taking up a pen and a fresh sheet of paper, she wrote a swift letter to her Aunt Louisa saying how sorry she was to have missed both her and Aunt Sophie. She hoped they would understand that at present most of her time and all her energies were devoted to making sure everything would be ready for her brother's arrival home.

She reread the lines, tapping the end of the pen against her teeth. Would they recognise the hint and stay away? Neither of them was known for their tact or subtlety. But she dare not be more direct. For, ever vigilant in matters of etiquette, they would perceive rudeness and she would have handed them another stick with which to beat her.

Adding her best wishes for their continued good health, she signed and sealed the letter. Then, giving it to Lobb for John to deliver, she went upstairs to change.

Sarah had laid out a black silk dinner gown. Looking at it, Melissa shook her head. 'Not tonight, Sarah. There is no one to see me. I'll wear the lavender instead.' Since coming out of black after Adrian's death she had worn little else but the muted shades of half-mourning.

Her father's passing demanded she resume black once more. So she would, in public. Abandoning it while at home alone did not signify that she missed or mourned him any less. But black silk and bombazine were so constant and forceful a reminder, they rendered her helpless: trapped in memory, despair, and hopeless longing for a time now gone forever. That left her unable to concentrate, or to plan.

Success – *survival* – depended on her doing both to a degree beyond anything she had previously imagined or attempted.

As Sarah brushed out her hair, Melissa reviewed all the tasks she had completed. Then as she thought of those that lay ahead, she remembered.

'Sarah, where's my blue sporting petticoat?'

The maid paused. 'In one of the trunks in the attic, I believe, miss. Whatever do you want that old thing for?'

'*Because* it's old. So it won't matter if it gets torn or dirty. As it's shorter than a riding habit I'm not going to trip, or catch my feet in it.'

'Dear life, miss! What are you going to be doing to get torn and dirty?'

Melissa drew a breath and looked at Sarah in the mirror. 'Leading Captain while he drags trees out of the woods. The ground is certain to get churned up and muddy.'

'You're never –' Sarah began, but, seeing Melissa's eyebrows climbing, she folded her lips. 'Whatever you say, miss. What have you got in mind to wear with 'un?'

'Do I still have that blue muslin pierrot jacket?'

'Yes, miss.'

'And my old riding boots?'

'Yes, miss.'

'Do you think you could have them all aired and ready for Monday morning?'

'Yes, miss.'

'Thank you, Sarah.'

'I don't know as you should be thanking me, miss. 'Tisn't right nor proper, what you're doing,' she muttered, sweeping the brush through Melissa's thick tresses with brisk, angry strokes. 'I dread to think what Missus would say if she knew.'

'That's enough, Sarah,' Melissa said lightly. 'Or I won't have any hair left.'

Monday morning came. By the time Melissa left the house, the team in the woods had been hard at work for over two hours.

They had started on those trees brought down by the storms. Zeb Rickard, Ned Philpot, Joe Pengelly, and Will Sparrow – known to all as Chirp – had set to under Gabriel's direction, using small axes or saws to lop off branches, separating those thick enough to be useful from débris to be burned.

The waste was hauled off to the bonfire where ash and embers had already spread to cover a large area of the clearing. Here, oak branches were stripped and their bark put into canvas sacks.

It was hard, hot, thirsty work, and one of the beer kegs had already been emptied.

Gabriel and Billy, being bigger, stronger, and younger than the others, were felling the marked trees, wielding axes with heads almost a foot wide and shafts nearly four feet long.

After showing Billy how to decide on the best place for a tree to fall, Gabriel chipped a long, shallow nick to weaken the trunk and ensure it fell in that direction. Then he moved round to the opposite side to hack out the deep wedge that would sever the tree from its roots. Working together on the first, Gabriel stood by as Billy tackled the second, then left him to get on by himself and started on the bigger or more awkwardly placed trees.

The wood echoed to the thuds of axes, the rustle of foliage, voices raised in terse, dry banter, then the warning shout, the slow creak and crash of a tree's fall, and the deep, vibrating thud as it hit the ground.

Gabriel swung his axe, using its weight to add force to his own strength; his gaze fixed on the deepening cut. The impact of each blow drove the air from his lungs in a soft grunt. Sliding the axe through his hands ready for the next swing, he sucked in a deep breath. The air was vivid with smells: the sweet, resinous fragrance of the timber; the acrid bite of bonfire smoke; the thick, dark reek of leaf mould and raw earth; the juicy sharpness of trampled undergrowth, and the musk of his own sweat.

Though the hard physical work demanded of him since joining the yard had been exhausting at first, it had proved a blessing in more ways than one. Not only was he sleeping like the dead and growing stronger each day, the gaol-induced weakness was now little more than a memory. If he focused on the swing of the axe, the strike and bite, the flying chips of heartwood and the next cut, he didn't have to think. He couldn't afford to think. The thoughts that crowded the edges of his mind, waiting for a chance to demand attention, were far too dangerous.

He swung one last time, heard the creak, bellowed a warning, and stood back watching as, with a series of loud, splintering cracks, the tree slowly toppled. Gathering momentum, it crashed through some sycamore saplings and undergrowth to land with a shuddering thump that travelled up through the soles of his boots.

Sliding his calloused palm down the smooth haft of the axe so it was balanced in his hand, he started toward the next tree. Then he realised all sounds of work had stopped.

Having become used to noise its absence was eerie, as though the wood and everything in it was holding a collective breath. Hearing the thud of hooves and the jingle of harness he understood the reason for the unexpected quiet. He turned toward the clearing, trying to ignore the sudden leap in his chest.

As he reached it from one side, Melissa and John arrived from the other. She was in front, leading one of two huge, black, heavily built draught horses with large heads and soft, intelligent eyes: though Captain's were shielded at the side by leather squares attached to the face strap of his bridle. Sturdy legs ended in hooves the size of dinner plates, thickly fringed with long white hair. The bar and chains with which they would drag the logs had been looped up and roped to their leather harness for the walk down. Also tied to each harness was a nosebag full of oats, and an empty canvas bucket for water.

The five men had left their jobs and now hovered uncertainly.

Gabriel waved them forward. 'Get the chains down.'

As he started toward Melissa, she turned to the boy. 'I'll hold Duchess. You get on with unfastening the nosebags and buckets.'

'Where shall I put them, miss?'

'Over there.' Gabriel pointed to where the beer kegs stood alongside the bag or basket that contained each man's dinner. He remembered to raise his index finger to his forehead.

'Good morning, miss.'

'Good morning, Gabriel.' Her cheeks were pink, and her eyes met his only for a moment before sliding away to gaze around the clearing. 'Where would you like us to start?'

'With the trees the storm brought down. The trunks are clean.'

'Clean?'

'The branches have been lopped and the tops and root plates sawn off,' he explained. 'The oaks should be brought here so their bark can be stripped. The rest can be dragged straight down to the collection area.' He lowered his voice. 'Are you sure the boy can manage? He looks – small.'

She glanced up at him, smiling. 'Appearances can be deceptive.'

'As you say, miss,' he murmured.

'John,' she continued, her colour deepening, 'could ride before he could walk. Duchess will do exactly as he tells her.'

A novelty indeed among the titled ladies of his acquaintance. 'Miss.' Giving a polite nod, he turned to the waiting men. 'Billy, you carry on felling. Zeb, you and Chirp work that side with young John.' He turned. 'Joe, you and I will work this side with Miss Tregonning. Ned, you stay here to release the logs. If you need a hand –'

'I'll shout,' Ned grunted, and, with a rough salute to Melissa, he trudged away.

For the next two hours, Gabriel worked fiercely. After

felling a marked tree he left Joe to lop the branches and saw off the top while he moved on to the next. Each time Melissa came for the log he paused so as not to unsettle the big horse whose ears flattened at every unexpected noise.

Her boots were gradually caking with mud and leaf-mould, her skirt acquiring an increasing number of smears and snags. He watched her turn Captain and manoeuvre him backward. While Joe fastened the chains, she ran her gloved hand over Captain's thick neck, talking softly while she studied the area and worked out the best route, allowing for the length of the trunk, to the nearest path then back to the clearing.

When the chain was secure and Joe gave the word, she clicked her tongue, Captain took the strain, and the huge log began its slow journey over the woodland floor. She had just arrived to collect the fourth tree when the faint sound of a horn brought Captain's head up, his ears twitching. Coming from the yard, it signalled the dinner hour. She glanced round as Gabriel came toward her, Joe following behind.

'I'll just take this one –'

'No, miss.' Speaking quietly Gabriel cut her short. 'If you keep working the men will feel obliged to do the same, and they've been here since seven this morning.' A flood of colour to her cheeks revealed her embarrassment, and he wished he could have spared her.

'Oh. Of course. I-I didn't – I'm sorry, I should have realised.'

'Don't concern yourself. No harm done.' At her tentative smile he grew brisk, very aware of Joe Pengelly listening to every word. 'You go on home, now, miss,' he urged. 'I'll take the horse back and make sure he's fed and watered.' He saw her expression flicker.

'Thank you, Gabriel. That's most kind. I'll be back –'

'No hurry, miss. In fact, if you've had enough today –'

'No.' She stiffened. 'I appreciate your concern, but I'm neither exhausted nor incompetent, and so –'

'Beg pardon, miss. No offence meant.' He took hold of the bridle. Melissa immediately let go and Captain tossed his great head. Placing one hand on the dark muzzle, Gabriel blew gently into the flaring nostrils, glancing toward her as the horse calmed.

'I see Captain is in good hands. I will be back. Though I may be a little longer than an hour as I have further to walk. I'll make more suitable arrangements tomorrow.'

With a brief nod, she turned and walked swiftly away.

Beside him, Joe Pengelly released his breath in a low whistle. 'I dunno.' He shook his head. 'She's some brave maid, but this isn't no place for the likes of she. Blessed if I know what she think she's doing of, coming down here like this.'

With a noncommittal grunt, Gabriel clicked his tongue and, with the great horse lumbering along beside him, followed in Melissa's wake.

The next day, when she arrived with John and the horses, he was not surprised to see her carrying a basket containing food and a bottle of lemonade. When the horn sounded and everyone stopped for dinner, she collected her basket and tactfully sat some distance away.

Subdued by her presence, the men were unable to relax. Though Gabriel longed to go and sit with her, doing so would not only cause comment, it risked creating suspicion and bad feeling. So he remained near the group. Yet he was not part of it. Everyone seemed relieved when it was time to resume work.

During the next four days, more than two dozen trees were felled, stripped, moved to the collection area, then sorted and marked according to type. The sacks of oak bark were stacked up ready for the tannery wagons.

Gabriel watched as Melissa valiantly kept pace with the men, clearly thinking they had grown used to her presence and were able to accept it. But it was plain to him they found her constant proximity inhibiting, and were becoming increasingly uncomfortable. He was himself, though for very different reasons.

She had just left, leading Captain back to the collection area with another sycamore bole, when Joe's distraction burst out like beer from a newly broached barrel. 'I don't care what nobody say, this isn't right. She got no business down here. 'Tisn't proper for a lady to be doing such things. I know she's different from the rest, but that's no excuse.'

Resting on his axe, Gabriel chose his words carefully. 'She's working as hard as any man. Why do you think she's doing it?'

'Blessed if I know, and that's the truth. There must be something going on we don't know about.'

'Money troubles?' Gabriel suggested. 'Yet we're still getting our wages.'

'Yes, but for how long? Mister have got two brothers. I dunno how she haven't asked they in to take over.'

'Are they in the same business?'

'No,' Joe allowed grudgingly.

'Would they do any better, then? Anyway, why should they care about us? But she does. Remember her speech? She promised to build a strong future for the yard.'

'Yes, so she did,' Joe was testy. 'But I don't suppose none of us thought to see her getting her own hands dirty. I still say that can't be right.'

Gabriel said no more. If the others shared Joe's opinion, which was all too likely, it could lead to trouble. Melissa had to be warned. As she approached with Captain, ready to hitch up the next log, she passed Joe who was returning to the clearing to borrow a sharpening stone, his having unaccountably gone missing into Gabriel's pocket. For a couple of minutes at least they would not be overheard.

Letting the head of his axe rest on the ground, he watched as she drew nearer. She still carried herself straight, even after four days of leading the draught horse increasing distances across gouged and rutted earth. But the effort it was costing her showed. Her face was pale and drawn and there were shadows like purple bruises beneath her eyes.

'Beg pardon, miss.' Though there was no one around, he kept his voice low.

'Yes, Gabriel?' Her voice sounded flat, its usual vibrant timbre dulled by weariness. She continued moving as if she dared not stop and started to turn the horse. Letting the axe fall onto the thick churned-up leaf-mould, he took a couple of strides forward and placed a restraining hand on the bridle.

Startled, she looked up. He heard her breath catch, saw twin spots of colour appear on her cheekbones. 'What? Is something wrong?'

He hesitated, not wanting to alarm her. 'I need to speak to you. Privately.' Shock widened her eyes, blanking her features for an instant. 'It concerns –' he made a small tight gesture '– all this. But not now, not here.'

She moistened her lips, turning her head away to avoid looking at him, her pallor replaced by a painful blush.

'Very well.' Even her earlobes had turned deep rose. 'This evening?'

'Thank you.' There was an awkward pause. Gabriel agonised over his next question, acutely conscious both of its significance, and the risks if she accepted.

She cleared her throat. 'Where –?'

'Will you –? After you, ma'am.'

'No, please, you were saying?' It was little more than a whisper.

Tension roughened his voice. 'For your sake we should not be seen together. Will you do me the honour of coming to … Where I live.'

Her head still averted, she gave a brief nod. He released the bridle, allowing her to continue turning the horse. As Joe stumped back, frowning and preoccupied, whistling tunelessly through the gaps in his teeth, Gabriel held out the sharpening stone. 'This yours?'

Joe clicked his tongue. 'I knew he couldn't have gone far.'

That evening, after a strip wash, Gabriel laundered his sweat-soaked clothes and hung them up to dry. The lowering sun was still warm, and a light breeze whispered among the leaves. He redressed his wounds, raked the crude comb through his tangled hair before tying it back neatly, and put on his clean shirt. With no idea what time she would come, he had delayed eating until he had cleaned himself up.

But now, though he was ready, his stomach had contracted into a tight, hard knot, and despite the day's exertions his appetite had vanished. Crouching to add more wood to the embers, he mocked his nervousness. He was a grown man, not some callow, moon-struck youth.

Socially adept with women – his father had entrusted this aspect of his education to a kindly, tactful widow of good breeding whose late husband had gambled away her inheritance – he had met many, flirted with some, and been intimate with a few: advisedly choosing married ladies who understood the rules of such encounters. But he had never loved. And could not, must not, now.

He heard a twig snap and looked up to see her walking down the path toward him. She too had bathed; her grubby working clothes replaced by lavender silk over satin with a fluting of fine white lawn filling the low neckline. The silk shawl clasped about her was, he guessed, more an indication of nervous tension than a need for warmth. She wore no hat and her hair rippled, dark and glossy, down her back.

Though her skin had a delicate rose lustre, her features were taut. As she came closer he detected the faint, flowery scent of her soap. He wanted to press his face into the curve of her neck and shoulder and fill his lungs with her fragrance. The urge to touch her was so strong his fingers curled into his palms. He saw her throat work as she swallowed.

'Good evening, Gabriel.' Her gaze fell away, lighting on the crude chair he had spent several evenings making. A blanket was folded to cover its back and seat and it stood against the wall of the shack where it caught the dying sunlight.

'Good evening, miss.'

She gestured. 'May I?'

'If you please.'

She sat, aware of him watching as she adjusted her skirts and her shawl, putting off the moment when good manners demanded she look at him.

'Ma'am.'

She glanced up. 'Please, Gabriel. Will you not sit?' She attempted a smile. 'To look up so far is something of a strain. I am not used to it, you see.'

'Forgive me.' He sat in the doorway a yard from her, leaning against the frame, his fingers linked loosely about his knees.

'You said –' she cleared her throat '– you said you needed to speak to me privately?'

'Yes. It concerns your daily presence in the woods. Miss Tregonning …' He hesitated, and she watched him search for words. 'May I suggest, with the greatest respect, that it might be time to let someone else take your place?'

As she looked at him, snatches of the past week tumbled across her mind. Every morning before leaving the house she had looked for the postman. There had been no letter from Mr Rogers, though it was now a week since she had seen him. She dare not take time off to drive into Truro, but as each day passed without word, her anxiety grew.

Lobb and Sarah, disapproving of her activities, were treating her with the punctilious formality they usually reserved for visitors. Though she had thought herself fit, the sheer physical effort of spending hours each day leading Captain back and forward over the soft, uneven ground was proving far more tiring than she had expected.

She drew herself up, seething with anger, frustration, and injustice. Presumably he had a reason, but she would not make it easy for him.

'Why?'

'Ma'am, there is no easy way to say this, but your presence is unsettling for the men.'

'Do they imagine this is my idea of fun? That spending every day filthy and tired is some kind of game to me? Perhaps they think I am simply trying to prove a point.'

As she leapt up from the chair, her fury demanding the release of action, he uncoiled, rising swiftly to his feet. But he remained at a respectful distance.

'Were none of them listening? They heard Tom say he could not spare another man. Who, out of all of them, could handle Captain like I do?' She had to force the words past the swelling lump in her throat. 'I thought they understood. This isn't only for me, or for the family, it's for *them*. Surely – don't they *want* –? I am asking nothing more of them than I am willing to do myself. Is it not enough?'

She shook her head as a sob caught in her chest and, biting

hard on her lower lip to stop its treacherous quiver, turned away, her arms clasped tightly across her body as she struggled for control.

'It is too much,' he said quietly. 'That is the point. Try to see it through their eyes.'

'I *can't*.' Tears of hurt and exhaustion were blurring her vision. She fought desperately but they spilled over, leaving cool tracks down her burning face. 'Don't you see?' She whirled round, not realising he had moved, and they almost collided.

Gasping, she stumbled back and would have fallen onto the embers of the fire had he not caught her. She had never been this close to any man save her father. His grasp was firm, his face inches from hers.

'See what?' His voice was low, little more than a hoarse murmur.

'I've no strength left,' she whispered, lost, helpless.

His grip tightened on her upper arms. 'That's not true,' he said harshly. 'Of course you're tired. No one could have done all you have done since your father died – and before that, for all I know – and not be tired. But that is only on the surface. Underneath you are still strong, and growing stronger every day. Look at me. *Look at me.*'

She shook her head, her chest heaving. 'I have always so despised women who weep in public.'

His voice was gentle. 'There is no one here.'

She raised her eyes, helpless to stop the tears still spilling over her lashes. 'You are.'

'You need rest, and proper sleep.'

'I need money.' The words were out before she could stop them. Shame and embarrassment bathed her whole body, and her clothes clung, hot and damp.

'Close your eyes.' He spoke quietly but in such a tone it didn't occur to her to disobey. 'Picture all the logs waiting to be collected. That's money. There will be the same number next week, and the following week, and the one after that. You know this,' he chided softly. 'You arranged it. You made it happen.'

Steadied, reassured, she opened her eyes. The naked longing on his face stopped her breath for it mirrored feelings in herself she had refused to acknowledge. But in an instant it had vanished and his whole manner changed so completely she was disoriented. She must have imagined ... But the thought that she had reflected her own fevered dreams and wishes on to him; that he might have seen, might guess ...

Hands flying to her burning cheeks, she turned her head away. Concerned and diffident, he released her at once. But the imprint and warmth of his grasp lingered, and she ached.

'All right now, miss?'

She nodded, another lie, and swiftly, neatly, wiped her cheeks. He had called her strong. So she was, and would continue to be. Drawing a deep breath she faced him.

'Thank you for telling me of the men's concern.' She swallowed, drawing her shawl over her shoulders. 'I think perhaps I did not make it clear to the men that in my mother's absence and until my brother returns I am, in effect, their employer. I am also doing my best to ensure the continuing viability of the yard. Current circumstances require particular measures: measures they may find unusual, maybe even a little discomfiting. However, these are of a temporary nature, as I hope soon to be in a position to employ permanent workers for the woods. But if any man feels unable to accept the situation then, naturally, he is free to seek employment elsewhere, and I will gladly supply him with a reference.' She cleared her throat. 'As this meeting has not taken place, obviously it won't be possible for you to explain my reasons for continuing to work. Indeed it is not your responsibility to do so.'

He tugged his forelock. 'Just so, miss,' he said gravely, meeting her gaze for an instant, before dipping his head.

Glimpsing admiration and warmed by it, she turned away. It wasn't until she was crossing the park that she realised, startled and intrigued. What she had also seen was amusement.

Instead of entering the house through the front door, she walked round to the terrace to enjoy the last rays of the sun and the fragrance of the honeysuckle, always stronger in the evening. The French windows stood open and she could hear voices. She paused. Not visitors surely? Bad news? Her heart in her mouth, she hurried into the drawing room. The door to the hall stood open and she could hear Sarah, her voice sharp with anxiety.

'No good telling me, Mr Lobb. She won't listen to nothing I say. Why don't you try?'

Melissa heard the deep rumble of Lobb's reply, and though she could not make out the words, his tone held the same worried disapproval as Sarah's.

Stiffening her spine, Melissa pulled the door wider. The two in the hall spun round, startled.

Lobb took a step toward her. 'Not wishing to be impertinent, miss, but what is going on? The way you've been this last week, a blind man could see something's wrong.'

Melissa nodded. 'Are all the servants in?'

'I believe so, miss.'

'Then will you ask all of them, and that includes Hocking and young John, to come to the morning-room?'

'When, miss?'

'As soon as possible. Ten minutes?'

'Certainly, miss.' He turned to Sarah. 'If you will inform Mrs Betts and young Agnes, I'll send Gilbert across to the stables.'

Twenty minutes later, having told them the unvarnished truth about the desperate financial situation, she stood dry-mouthed, her folded arms pressed against her aching stomach, scanning faces she had known all her life. They looked stunned, disbelieving. Some frowned. Mrs Betts had tears in her eyes. How would they react? She soon found out. They were angry.

'How come you never told us?'

'Why did you keep it to yourself for so long?'

'Didn't you trust us?

'What did you think we'd do? Walk out? When our families have worked for this family for generations?'

'Poor opinion you got of us and no mistake if you could think we'd do that.'

'I still can't like to think of you working in they woods,'

Sarah sighed. 'But at least now we know why.'

Lobb raised a hand for silence. 'Not a word of this is to go beyond the four walls of this room.'

This provoked angry mutters. 'As if we would!'

'We don't need telling that.'

'If anyone asks after Miss Melissa,' Lobb added, waiting until they fell silent again, 'friends or relatives in the village, or visitors to this house, you refer them to me.' He turned. 'All right, miss?'

Melissa nodded. 'Thank you, Lobb. Thank you all. I'm really – I don't know how –'

'That's all right, miss,' Sarah interrupted briskly. 'Been a long day for you, it have. I expect you're ready for a nice hot drink. If you'd like to go on up, I'll bring 'un to you.'

Unable to speak, Melissa flashed them all a grateful if tremulous smile, and started up the stairs. That night, for the first time in weeks, she slept long and deep.

# Chapter Twelve

Next morning, in spite of her determination and the changed attitude of the household staff who had relaxed once more into the occasionally irritating – but so much missed – familiarity tempered with respect, Melissa felt apprehensive as she set out for the wood. On impulse, thinking of the day's work ahead, she pulled Captain over to the mounting block in the yard and swung herself on to his broad back.

Seeing John watching, wide-eyed, she shrugged. 'You can walk if you would prefer it.'

'Not likely.' Not bothering with the block, he scrambled up on to Duchess, who swung her great head but stood still, as solid and dependable as a rock.

Comfortable on Captain's broad back, Melissa led the way across the park and down through the woods. Pulling him up a short distance from the entrance opposite the yard, she jumped down, not wishing to shock the men further by being seen astride the draught horse. Foolish perhaps, when she was already breaking so many far more important rules. But they didn't know about those. And it was easier for everyone if she adhered as far as possible to the behaviour expected of a well-bred young woman.

John slid off at the same time and they led the horses up into the clearing. Almost immediately she sensed a different atmosphere. She was greeted with tugged forelocks and an audible "Morning, miss" instead of the grunts, frowns, and avoiding eyes of the last few days. Resentment had given way to a well-intentioned if clumsy friendliness, evident in the occasional dry comment thrown her way as they passed. Somehow, without compromising her, Gabriel had told the men what their choices were. It looked as though they had chosen to stay.

There was no sign of him when she arrived. As Joe emerged to take her to the first of that day's logs to be pulled out, she heard the crack, groan, and crash of a falling tree. Gabriel appeared a few minutes later, a formidable figure in stained breeches and mud-smeared boots, shirtsleeves rolled up muscular arms now golden-brown against the narrow bandages, and a lock of black hair falling over his sweat-beaded forehead.

'Good morning, miss.' He made his usual salute. 'Everything all right?'

'Good morning, Gabriel. Everything is fine, thank you.' She met his gaze full on, wanting to convey the gratitude she could not voice. 'I was just wondering –'

'Yes, miss?' She sensed sudden alertness beneath his bland expression.

'Why is the bonfire not lit? There's a huge pile of brush and clippings.'

'Indeed, miss. But with your permission they will be kept for tonight.'

'Tonight?'

'St Peter's Tide, miss?' he prompted gently.

She had forgotten. 'Oh. Of course. Perhaps if it was divided up, and the separate piles bound with rope, the horses could haul them as far as the new entrance. Then the men would only have to drag them across the road and down to the beach.'

'That's very kind, miss.'

'Not at all. Most of the men in this village are connected with the sea, as fishermen or sailors, or building boats. Midsummer might be the high point of the year for West Cornwall, but for us St Peter's Tide is far more important.'

Normally the bonfire and celebrations were the only topic of conversation among the household during the week leading up to the festival. But how could they have talked of celebrations with her father so recently dead? 'Have the men in the yard made up tar barrels?'

'I believe so, miss. Will we see you there?'

The yearning was so strong she could almost taste it. But she could not go. She would be the spectre at the feast, her presence awkward for everyone else. It wouldn't be fair. Nor would it be fitting while she was in full mourning. Choking down her disappointment, she shook her head.

'No. But I hope you all have a marvellous time. As tomorrow is feast day work will stop early. Something for everyone to look forward to.'

Not her, though. An early finish meant less work completed. Less work meant less money. She still hadn't heard from Mr Rogers.

Late that afternoon, after finishing in the woods and dragging the roped bundles of lopped branches to the entrance, Melissa led the way back through the woods toward Bosvane, tired and dejected. Behind her, John tried valiantly to suppress his brimming excitement.

Hocking was already waiting when they reached the yard. He too would be going down to the beach, and wanted to get the shires brushed, fed, and turned out as soon as possible.

The same air of expectation pervaded the house. Sarah hummed to herself as she prepared Melissa's bath. Afterwards, having brushed out her mistress's hair and helped her dress, she finished tidying the room. She stopped suddenly, turning to Melissa, her arms full.

'I wish you was coming down, miss. No disrespect to your dear father, God rest him, but it would do you good to have a bit of fun. You know what they do say about all work and no play.'

'Yes, it makes you extremely tired.' Melissa smiled. 'It's a kind thought, Sarah, and I thank you for it. But it wouldn't do, you know. I really am very weary. I must be walking miles every day. You go along, now. You won't want to be late.'

'But I haven't –'

'Whatever it is, I'm sure it will keep until the morning. And Sarah?'

'Yes, miss?'

'Enjoy yourself.'

Eyes bright with excitement, Sarah grinned. 'I will, miss.'

Alone in the dining room, waited on by Lobb, aware of his unspoken sympathy and his determination to see she kept up her strength, she ate a reasonable meal. Enough to satisfy him anyway, for when she said she had had enough, he did not press her.

She rose from the table. 'Thank you, Lobb. Please tell Mrs Betts how much I enjoyed it. I must admit that after all the fresh air and exercise of recent days I'm really looking forward to a quiet evening.'

He smiled gently. 'There's always next year, miss.'

Two hours later, her embroidery discarded on a chair, the book she had tried to read abandoned on a side table, unable to face the work awaiting her in the study, she fetched a shawl from her room and walked out on to the terrace.

The sun had set in a glory of gold and crimson. The vivid splendour had paled to shades of rose, then turquoise, and now dusk was falling. The breeze had dropped and the air was sweetly perfumed. In the stillness she could hear distant shouts and laughter. She turned, grasping the handles of the French windows, and stood with her head bent. After a long moment, she took a deep breath and closed them quietly.

Then, crossing the terrace, she walked down through the park and took the lower path that led to the beach near the mouth of the creek.

The tide was beginning to ebb, and where the beach was widest near the yard, an enormous bonfire sent showers of sparks and orange tongues of flame leaping into the air. Beyond it, lighted tar barrels mounted on poles illuminated the laughing faces of the gathered men, women, and children.

Melissa sensed the rising excitement as the fire, which had clearly been burning for some time, began to subside. Standing in the shadows out of sight, she watched men and boys begin to dance around the fire.

Then one young man, boosting his courage with a yell, leapt through the flames. The watching crowd gasped, then roared encouragement. A man jumped the fire, followed by another youth.

Movement a few yards away at the water's edge caught

Melissa's attention. Someone climbed out of a boat and started dragging it up the beach, unrecognisable in the shadows cast by the bright flames and dancing figures. But once he reached high water mark and straightened up, her heart gave a painful lurch.

Leaning into the boat, Gabriel Ennis lifted out several fish strung on a length of cord.

She heard a shout, and saw Billy break from the circle of dancers. He ran toward Gabriel, beckoning him to join in. He shook his head, but Billy pleaded, gesticulating as he urged Gabriel toward the fire. Fending him off, Gabriel turned away and froze, looking directly at her.

Catching her breath, she stepped back. He surely could not recognise her. She was too far away, and in shadow.

Billy caught his arm. A new circle had formed. Now women had joined the men, holding hands as they wove like a snake jumping through the dying flames. A buxom young woman in a low-cut dress raced down, grabbed Gabriel's hand, and tugged him back to the circle.

Unable to watch, Melissa turned her back on the merriment. She stumbled over the rough stones and tangled seaweed toward the welcome darkness of the wood. There no one would see her stupid tears, or mock her foolish, aching envy to be part of the circle, to dance with her hand in Gabriel's, to leap the flames and trust the ancient gods to protect her for the coming year.

Reaching the low cliff, she seized exposed roots to pull herself up into the trees. Straightening her dress and wiping her eyes, she started up the path. But a few moments later she heard the crack of a twig and stopped. The footsteps came on, a man's footsteps, not running but moving fast.

Had he heard her? Should she call out or remain silent? She had every right to be here. But she was alone, it was very dark beneath the trees, and no well brought-up young woman with a care for her reputation went wandering in woods at night. She pressed a hand to her stomach, her heart beating so hard and fast she felt sick.

'Miss Tregonning?' The breath she had been holding

exploded in a soft gasp and she reached blindly for a tree as her legs threatened to give way. Relief was followed by anger.

'Gabriel! You frightened me!' She drew a shaky breath as he loomed out of the blackness.

'Indeed.' He bit the word off. His anger, matching her own, was disconcerting. What right had he to be angry? 'You will permit me to see you safely home.'

'You forget yourself,' she shot back. 'I am perfectly able to walk home without assistance. Nor am I used to being addressed with such ...' Authority. It was the only word to describe his tone, not that she would tell him so. What authority could a man like Gabriel claim?

'I most humbly beg your pardon.' The strange, hard note had gone. 'It was wrong of me –'

'Yes, it was.'

'The thing is, I don't doubt your *courage,* miss; but the *wisdom* of walking alone in the woods on a night when spirits are high and beer flowing freely, *that* I might question. With respect. However,' he added, as she caught her breath, fighting the knowledge that his criticism was justified even as she struggled to frame a suitably crushing retort, 'you are not alone now.'

'True.' But the confusion she experienced in his presence was anything but a comfort. 'Why did you not stay on the beach?'

'Hunger.' He held up the fish. ' My d – evening meal.'

'How many did you catch?'

'Six. Too many even for me. Would you – it would give me great pleasure if you would accept half.'

'You are very kind, but I cannot. Mackerel are best eaten fresh. With all the staff, including Mrs Betts, at the celebrations –' She shrugged.

'There is no one at home to cook them?'

'Exactly.' Her eyes had grown used to the darkness now and she could see him more clearly: a tall, solid presence that unnerved as much as it reassured.

'Then allow me.'

'What?' Wary, not sure what he meant, she gazed up at the

pale blur of his face.

'Billy told me how important St Peter's Tide is to the village. You wouldn't have wanted to miss it even if you couldn't take part.'

'Even so, perhaps I shouldn't – But I thought if I was careful –'

He shook her head. 'You were not seen.' He sounded so sure.

'Except by you.'

He was silent for a moment. 'Miss Tregonning, would you do me the honour of dining with me?'

Now she was silent, biting her tongue hard. She wanted to. She mustn't. Yet was she not beholden to him? Without his practical help and advice she would be in straits far more desperate than those she currently faced, and with no hope of retrieving the situation, or keeping it secret.

'It must be several hours since you last ate. You have just told me there is no one at home to prepare your supper.'

'You make me sound helpless,' she objected, starting to tremble and uncertain why. 'Anyway, Mrs Betts will have left me something cold on a tray.'

'Ahh,' Gabriel murmured dryly. 'That does indeed sound more appetising than freshly caught fish.'

'No it doesn't, and so you know.' She swallowed nervously. 'I really –' Ought, should, must. She drew a deep, shaky breath and, as loneliness defied the clamour of good sense, blurted, 'Thank you.'

'You will?'

'Perhaps you have changed your mind.'

'No. It was just – I hardly dared hope. This way, miss. I know a short cut.'

When they reached the shack he asked her politely to wait while he went inside. She heard him strike flint against stone, saw the glow of lamplight, and a moment later he re-emerged carrying the lantern. Hanging it from a stick wedged high up on one side of the door, he went back into the shack, fetched the chair, set it down against the wall and, after covering it with a blanket, he indicated with a gesture and a smile that she should sit.

Meanwhile, bombarded by doubts, but aware that to leave now would be the height of rudeness, Melissa was determined to behave exactly as she would have had he been the cream of Truro society. A guest had certain obligations, and having accepted his invitation she would honour them.

Swiftly, she reviewed possible topics of conversation. But though he did not seem ill at ease, nor was he inclined to talk as he moved about. So, taking her cue from him, she lapsed into silence, watching as he quickly kindled a fire within a low semi-circle of blackened stones. With no demands being made of her, no expectations to meet, she began slowly to relax.

Neatly gutting the fish, he wiped them dry with a clean piece of muslin and threaded each one through the gills on to a peeled oak twig.

'How did it get hot so fast?' Melissa asked, gazing into the heart of the fire where the burning wood was a brilliant golden-orange with almost clear flames. 'There's hardly any smoke at all.'

'Dry wood doesn't make smoke. Hard woods such as oak or maple – that's oak – burn much hotter than soft wood like pine or poplar.' Gabriel laid the twig across the fire, supporting it on two notched sticks driven into the earth. 'Won't be long now.' He glanced up with a quick smile of such sweetness that she jumped, her heart turning over. Instinctively attempting to disguise her reaction, she adjusted her shawl. It was hunger, nothing more. 'I'll turn them in five minutes. They'll be ready in ten.'

'Where did you learn all this?'

Turning away, he shrugged. 'It's woodcraft. For example, if you are lost a tree can tell you where north is.'

'Really?' He hadn't answered her question but it would be impolite to press. 'How?'

'You look for moss. It usually grows thicker on the north side of a tree. But you must choose a tree that is out in the open, not one in a damp, shady spot. Or you can chop into the trunk. The side that has the thickest bark will be north, though you should check several trees to be sure.' He turned the fish over, the firelight casting his strong profile in bronze. 'Folklore has it that if you want to make your dearest wish come true, you write it on a piece of beech wood and bury it.'

Melissa sighed. 'If only it were so easy.'

'Indeed,' he murmured.

Straightening, he went into the shack and came back with two plates, chipped but clean; and a single fork that he used to push the fish off the stick and onto the plates.

'No, please,' Melissa cried as he was about to add a third. 'No more. Two is plenty.'

Handing her one plate and the fork, he paused to turn off the lantern before lowering himself to the ground beside her chair, resting his back against the wall.

She glanced at the lantern then back at him, her uncertainty returning. 'Why –?'

He raised a finger to his lips, saying quietly, 'You'll see. Eat. Please,' he added, but she sensed it was an afterthought added to soften the faint hint of command.

Flaking easily from the bone, the mackerel tasted delicious. The first mouthful made Melissa realise how hungry she was. She had almost finished the second fish when a shuffling in the undergrowth brought her head up. Immediately wary, she glanced at Gabriel.

With a reassuring smile he raised a finger to his lips again then pointed to the path. Melissa looked where he pointed, and for a moment saw nothing. Then a large badger trundled out of the shadows. He stopped, sniffed the air, then ambled forward, nose to the ground, to where Gabriel had left the fish guts. Fork poised, meal forgotten, Melissa watched, entranced, as his mate joined him. Two half-grown cubs rolled into view, tumbling over each other with soft grunts, then abandoned their game and pushed in beside their parents to share the feast.

A few moments later, after a quick snuffle round to make sure no scrap had been missed, the cubs resumed chasing one another, playing hide and seek, while their parents ambled off along the path and out of sight.

Turning to Gabriel, Melissa found him watching her. He smiled. She smiled back.

165

'That was amazing. I've never seen … How often do they come?'

'Most nights. But I don't always feed them. It would not be wise.'

'The wrong kind of food, you mean?'

He shook his head. 'No. If I fed them regularly they might become dependent. They might come to me for food instead of hunting for their own. Then if, for some reason, I could not feed them …' He moved his shoulders, allowing her to work out for herself the possible result.

What reason would prevent him feeding them? If he were no longer here … Melissa felt suddenly chilled. Setting down the plate, she stood up. She didn't want to go. All the more reason to leave at once.

'That really was delicious. I'm not simply being polite, as you can see.' She indicated the plate now containing nothing but bones and skin.

He grinned, uncoiling and rising to his feet. 'You were hungry.'

She nodded shyly. 'Thank you. I've so enjoyed –'

'Last year, did you jump through the flames?'

'Yes.' She smiled at the memory. 'There is no ceremony in the circle. Everyone is equal when they honour the old traditions and seek protection from witchcraft and evil for the coming year.'

'You need such protection?'

She raised her brows. 'You need to ask? Perhaps I am foolish, but in my current situation any help would be welcome.'

'Then we must honour tradition.'

'No,' she said quickly. 'I don't think –'

'You will risk evil?' he enquired softly. 'What of me?' he added. 'I too would welcome protection.'

As he pulled the notched sticks from the ground and tossed them aside, Melissa's glance fell on his bandages and she felt hot with shame. Absorbed in her difficulties it was all too easy to forget the suffering he – and others – had endured.

Kicking the embers into flickering life, he held out both

hands to her. The flames danced in his eyes and cast a glow across his lean, dark face. 'Your servant, ma'am?'

Her heart quickening, she tossed her shawl onto the chair, stepped forward, and placed her hands in his. With the fire between them, their hands clasped above it, they began to circle the flames, pulling against each other, gradually building up speed. Exhilaration vanquished shyness, and, as Gabriel smiled broadly, Melissa tossed her hair back and began to laugh. Faster and faster they whirled.

'Now!' he cried, and swung her over the flames so she landed lightly by his side. Releasing one hand he leapt across the fire. Their hands rejoined, and after another circle, he swung her though again. Rockets fizzed skyward from the beach below, and Melissa heard the pop of firecrackers exploding.

'Don't let go!' he warned, his eyes gleaming. 'You know what they say: "bad luck to weak hands".'

'I'll hold fast,' she vowed.

In turn they leapt to and fro, trampling out the fire. When the last flames had died, both were out of breath and the darkness shrouded them like a blanket.

'Now you are safe for another year,' he murmured softly.

'You too,' she replied. Her heart thudded so loudly she feared he would hear it. Her hand was still clasped in his. She knew she should withdraw it, for the ritual was over now, but it was warm and strong, and she felt *safe,* which was ridiculous. She was permitting a liberty beyond all that was proper. She cleared her throat.

'I should – I really – Thank you. I don't mean just for this: the fish and the badgers and – I mean for all your help. If you hadn't –' Her breath caught in a tiny gasp as he laid a calloused finger gently against her lips.

'It was my privilege.' His finger moved lightly across her cheek and freed a damp, clinging curl.

Glad of the darkness that hid her fiery blush, she knew she should move away, berate him for his impertinence. But, trembling in the grip of something outside her experience and beyond her control, she did neither.

She heard him swallow, could feel the heat emanating from his body so close, so very close, to hers. He drew her like iron is drawn to a lodestone: an attraction as elemental as that holding the moon to earth, and as impossible to break.

He made a sound, too brief to be a groan, and stepped back, releasing her hand. She pressed it to her midriff, trying to retain the fading sensation of his touch, of his infusing strength.

'I'll see you home, miss.' His voice was as harsh and strained as it had been the day they had first met here on this same path.

Her eyes pricked and her throat was stiff with loss, and bewilderment at her reactions. 'There's no need.'

'Just to the park, miss. For your safety.'

Not trusting herself to speak, she simply nodded.

Night wrapped them in velvet darkness, and though stars could be glimpsed through the tree canopy, the moon had not yet risen. She was not afraid of the dark, but nor could she easily see the ruts and dips in the path, and tripped twice. But instantly his hand was at her elbow to steady and reassure.

They reached the edge of the woods and he stopped. She knew he could not see her face, but she forced a smile anyway. A smile would alter her voice and mask feelings she could not explain and feared would shame her. She did not want him thinking … What didn't she want him to think? Why should it matter what he thought? Who was he anyway? All this raced through her mind as she turned toward him, clutching her shawl as she drew a deep, careful breath.

'Thank you, Gabriel.'

'No, miss.' His voice was a gravelly rasp. 'Thank *you* for the honour of your company.'

On impulse, she offered her hand. It was what she would have done on taking leave of someone of her own class. But he wasn't, and she shouldn't have. Before she could withdraw, he took it. Instead of a brief, polite shake, her hand was raised and her heart stopped at the warm pressure of his lips on her knuckles. Then he was gone.

Reaching the terrace she paused and looked back. In the distance she could hear shouting and laughter, drums and

168

singing, punctuated by more firecrackers. A rocket, trailing brilliant sparks, shot high into the sky.

The next day was feast day. While the men worked, women would be down on the quay setting up stalls to sell sweets, ribbons, trinkets, fruit, and pastries. When the men finished work and joined them, there would be games and singing, and fiddlers would play for those who enjoyed dancing.

From late afternoon until dusk, sailing boats, rowing boats, and gigs would take groups of villagers aboard for short trips out of the creek and into the Carrick Roads. In the evening, there would be a ram roast, and drinking, and more fireworks.

Picturing it all, drawing on memories of other years, still vivid, she stayed at home.

# Chapter Thirteen

When Melissa arrived at the clearing on Monday morning the atmosphere was noticeably subdued. After offering a brief salute or mumbled greeting, the men went about their work in silence, the after-effects of two days of celebrations painfully obvious.

Seeing Joe wince and shudder at the crash of a falling tree, and glimpsing Billy bent over behind a bush, Melissa maintained a tactful distance, appearing not to notice pallid faces and hands that shook. It wasn't difficult with so much on her mind, not least the prospect of seeing Gabriel again.

Following the direction of Ned's trembling finger, she led Captain toward the newly felled trees beset by vivid memories: the meal she and Gabriel had shared, and their own private honouring of St Peter's Tide.

In the short time she had known him, an unspoken agreement had evolved between them. When they were alone the guarded formality so carefully maintained in the presence of others might be lowered. How this had happened she wasn't sure. But the ease with which she found herself confiding in him took her aback.

Rarely conscious of it at the time, it was only at the day's end, when she lay in bed replaying their conversations, that it would occur to her how freely she had spoken. Then she was shocked at how much she had told him.

When she saw him with the other men he was as self-effacing as it was possible for a man of his size to be, remaining silent unless directly addressed. Yet when they were alone, though he volunteered little about his past, and virtually nothing of a personal nature, his posture, his speech, and his manner seemed to her to undergo a subtle change.

There was still constraint – given the difference in their circumstances how could it be otherwise? – but that too altered in a mysterious way, though a barrier remained beyond which she could not see.

He did not press her to talk. If some of his rare questions might, on other lips, have sounded impertinent, somehow from him they did not. His understanding, when she found herself blurting out her anxieties, was far beyond what she would have expected.

With his acceptance of responsibility and skilful organizing of men renowned both for their independence and their suspicion of strangers, he must surely have been a great asset to his previous employer. Why then had he left? Why had he gone to France? How had he ended up in prison? What secrets had he known and kept that warranted such dreadful torture?

Holding Captain while Ned unfastened the chains around the second log of the morning, she was almost knocked backwards when the big shire jerked his head up, ears pricked as he whinnied softly. Trying to ignore the sudden quickening of her heart, she released her breath, kept her face carefully expressionless, and waited, soothing the shire whose tense muscles quivered beneath her unsteady hand.

A moment later, she heard the thunder of galloping hooves and, glancing round, saw Hocking hurtle into the clearing on Samson. Seeing her, he hauled frantically on the reins, bringing the huge thoroughbred to a skidding halt.

'Miss, you got to get up to the house right away!' he gasped.

'What is it? Is there a letter?' Her brother? Her mother?

Panting for breath, the groom shook his head. ''Tis your aunts, miss. Mr Lobb done his best, but they say they aren't leaving till they seen you.'

She shut her eyes. Oh no. It was too much.

'Give me a moment.' Her thoughts raced.

'Why has everyone stopped?' Gabriel demanded, striding from dense undergrowth and wiping his sweating face with his neckerchief.

'Miss is needed at home urgent,' Hocking explained, throwing himself off Samson's back and grabbing the bridle as the thoroughbred danced sideways, nostrils flaring, sides heaving like bellows as he mouthed the foam-flecked bit.

'Not bad news, I hope?'

Melissa grimaced. 'Unwelcome visitors.' She turned to the groom. 'Will you ride behind me?'

'No, miss. That beast don't like me no more than I like him. Tried to pitch me off twice he did. I'd sooner walk. Bleddy animal,' he muttered, glaring at the object of his loathing. 'Go on, don't you wait for me. Just leave 'un in the stable.'

Melissa switched her gaze from Samson to the big shire whose bridle she held. 'But – what about Captain? He's too strong for John.'

Handing his axe to Ned, Gabriel strode forward and took the rein from her suddenly nerveless fingers. 'I'll drive him. Go home,' he urged.

'Best not linger, miss,' Hocking warned. 'Time's wasting, and you can't go in to them looking like that.'

'Yes. No. You're right.' Biting her lip, Melissa hurried to Samson, gathered up the reins, and put her mud-caked boot into Hocking's cupped hands. As she threw her leg over his back the highly-strung thoroughbred sprang forward, scattering the watching men. Giving him his head, she crouched in the saddle and raced back through the wood. If Lobb had sent a message to Hocking to fetch her, surely he would also have had the foresight to guide her aunts into the small parlour, whose windows faced the garden and not the park.

Shutting Samson – still saddled and bridled – in his stall, she raced across the yard and into the house through a rear door. Wrenching off her filthy boots, she left them on the flagged floor of the passage and sprinted up the back stairs. Sarah was waiting for her with hot water, clean stockings, kid slippers, and a demure black gown.

Ten minutes later, washed and changed, her hair brushed and pinned into a neat chignon with soft curls fringing her forehead and in front of her ears, Melissa stood in front of the mirror and pressed her hands to shiny glowing cheeks.

'I look like a beetroot!'

'Shall I fetch some of master's wig powder, miss? That would take off the shine a bit.'

Melissa shook her head. 'Aunt Louisa would be bound to notice. She does not approve of cosmetics. In her opinion, one should be neither too proud nor too humble to present to the world whatever complexion one has been blessed with by nature.'

Sarah snorted. 'One rule for she, and another for everyone else, is it?'

'Sarah!' Melissa admonished.

'Well, I aren't so stupid to believe nature made her hair that colour. I swear each time she come calling 'tis a different shade.'

Melissa scrutinised her reflection. 'I must go. I dare not keep them waiting any longer. Do I look all right?'

Clutching Melissa's discarded skirt and jacket, Sarah gazed critically at her young mistress. 'You do look handsome. If you got a bit of colour 'tis no surprise, seeing how you just walked up quick from the park.'

'Yes. Of course!' Flashing a grateful smile, Melissa hurried out to the landing, and peered over the balustrade. Waiting in the hall below, Lobb glanced up and nodded.

Running swiftly down the stairs, her slippers silent on the wide, carpeted treads, Melissa paused outside the door of the morning room to square her shoulders and lift her chin. Then, taking a deep breath, she opened the door.

'Aunt Louisa! Aunt Sophie! What a lovely surprise! How kind of you to call again so soon. I'm so sorry I wasn't here to welcome you. It's such a lovely morning I thought I should get some fresh air. I had planned to go no further than the garden, but when Medlyn told me about the damage, I thought I should take a look.'

'What damage?' demanded Aunt Louisa, elder and more forceful of the two sisters-in-law, resplendent in black satin with quantities of lace.

'The horse chestnut in the park,' Melissa replied, her gaze straying involuntarily to that part of her aunt's elaborate

173

coiffure not hidden by the plumes decorating her hat. Sarah was right. Normally brown, the carefully dressed curls had acquired a definite hint of red. 'The recent heavy rain has caused a large branch to break off. I understand,' she plunged on, trusting in her aunt's total lack of interest in any subject not of her own choosing, 'that the gales we had in early June have brought down a number of trees in the wood.'

'Indeed?' her aunt interrupted. 'Well, I'm sure your brother will take care of it when he returns.'

The door opened and Lobb appeared with a silver tray bearing ratafia and a dish of macaroons. 'I trust you'll forgive the liberty, miss, but I thought the ladies might welcome some refreshment after their journey.'

'Thank you, Lobb.' Melissa's smile was heartfelt. 'I was just about to ring.'

'Will there be anything else, miss?'

'Not at the moment.' With a stately bow, the butler made his exit.

'Takes a lot upon himself.' Aunt Louisa frowned as the door closed.

'I'm sure his intention is good,' her sister-in-law placated. Smaller, plumper, and ever conciliatory, Sophie hated what she termed "upsets". But as she was her sister-in-law's confidante and companion, accompanying her on the morning-calls required by civility, and less formal visits to various members of the family, she spent much of her time smoothing the ruffled feathers Louisa invariably left in her wake.

'He is invaluable, Aunt Sophie,' Melissa said with unfeigned warmth. 'I don't know how I should have managed without him these past weeks.'

'Yes, well, never mind that.' Louisa was dismissive. 'Let me look at you.'

Melissa regarded her aunt, her brows slightly raised as she waited for the inevitable criticism.

'You're looking tired,' her aunt observed. 'And you have a high colour. I hope you are not starting a fever. These summer colds can be most unpleasant. Fortunately I am rarely troubled by the minor afflictions to which so many of our acquaintance succumb.'

Melissa wondered if the illnesses claimed by her aunt's friends were on occasion more diplomatic than real: the only way to limit the frequency and duration of her aunt's social calls.

'I am perfectly well, thank you. I confess I went into the garden without my bonnet. I had not intended to stay out above a few minutes. But then ...' She made a small helpless gesture. 'I fear I may have caught the sun a little.'

'A *little?*' sniffed Louisa, shaking her head. Sophie echoed the movement, though more in anxious concern than irritation. 'Melissa, such behaviour cannot be condoned. As one already disadvantaged you really cannot afford to be so careless. How can you hope to attract a husband when you are so unmindful of the things that matter?'

'Indeed, Aunt Louisa, you are perfectly right,' Melissa agreed humbly. 'I cannot see myself ever becoming the wife of a man who would choose his life partner on the basis of her complexion.'

Catching her Aunt Sophie's shocked and widening gaze for a fleeting instant, Melissa quickly lowered her eyes, waiting for Aunt Louisa's wrath to break over her deserving head. But, having made her point, the redoubtable lady's attention had already passed to more pressing matters.

'When is your mother coming home?'

'I don't know.'

'Has she not written to you?'

Melissa shook her head. 'Not yet. I am sure she will as soon as she is feeling better. Dr Wherry thinks it far wiser for her to remain with Aunt Lucy until she is properly recovered. I must agree with him, though I do miss her.'

It was the truth. She loved her mother very much. Perhaps not quite to the same extent that she had loved her father, for she had had more in common with him. Nor was it easy to love without reservation someone whose love for her daughter was less than her love for her sons, despite her efforts to pretend otherwise. It was the fact that she had to try so hard that hurt.

'I have found Dr Wherry to be a most able man,' Louisa

announced. 'Perhaps his manner on occasion tends toward the brusque. But that is not to be wondered at when so many people call upon him over trifling matters. However, though his advice concerning your mother may indeed be sound, I cannot feel it at all the thing for you to be alone in this house.'

Melissa masked her stirring alarm with a display of mild bewilderment. 'I do not understand you, Aunt. I am not alone. I have Lobb, and Mrs Betts, and Sarah, and Hocking in the stables, Medlyn in the garden, all taking excellent care of me.'

'So I should hope,' Louisa sniffed. 'That is their purpose. But that is not what I meant, and well you know it.'

'Indeed, Aunt, I hope you are not concerned on my account. Truly, I do not wish for company other than family just now. Besides, while I am in mourning, it would not be fitting.'

'I am glad to hear you say so. I must allow, Melissa, that your attitude does you credit. I would not have expected you to show such sensibility. Though it pains me to say so, and one hesitates to speak ill of the dead, in the matter of appropriate behaviour your father did not deal with you as he should. As a result you have too often shown a disturbing lack of decorum. However, if that is now all in the past, I yield to no one in my delight that you have recognised the error into which you had fallen.'

Trying desperately to ignore the swift succession of images of her appallingly indecorous behaviour, each one painfully vivid, Melissa dipped her head as guilt burned from her toes to the roots of her hair. 'You are too kind.'

'One should always give credit where it is due.' Louisa settled herself more comfortably and permitted herself a satisfied smile. 'Well, this is most pleasant.' She turned to her sister-in-law. 'Is this not delightful, Sophie?'

'Indeed, it is, Louisa. Such a pleasure.' She beamed at her niece. 'We see you so rarely, Melissa. Of course, I know how much you used to enjoy being with your dear father.'

Melissa winced inwardly. Her Aunt Sophie was totally without malice. But she could have said nothing more likely to provoke another tirade.

Louisa drew herself up. 'Yes, well, it is certainly not my

place to question the wisdom of my brother-in-law's actions. But I would be less than truthful if I did not admit to grave concern at the way he permitted – no, I would go so far as to say, *encouraged* – Melissa's interest in matters of no concern to members of our sex.'

Melissa had hoped their visit would be a short one, but neither of her aunts was showing any inclination to leave. Resigning herself to the inevitable, she forced a smile. 'I was just thinking, if you are not expected elsewhere, could I persuade you to stay a little longer and join me in a light luncheon?'

Thrown off her stride by the abrupt change of subject, Louisa blinked. But Sophie, acutely aware of her own *faux pas*, and visibly anxious to retrieve the situation, responded with instant and genuine pleasure.

'What a delightful idea, is it not, Louisa? That is most considerate of you, my dear. I'm sure we should enjoy it excessively.'

Louisa frowned. 'I am not generally in favour of eating at midday. However,' she added graciously, 'I am aware that the desire for frequent nourishment is more pronounced in young people, and those –' she glanced at her sister-in-law '– of less stringent habits than my own. But in a spirit of charity I daresay I could manage a morsel or two. For I am persuaded that having been without company these past weeks you will be glad to have us remain a while longer.'

'You are too good,' Melissa murmured and rose to tug the bell. The conversation turned to the sister-in-laws' own offspring, their families and social lives. By interspersing murmurs of interest with the occasional question, Melissa was able to maintain an appearance of interest and keep the conversation going while taking very little part in it, allowing her thoughts to drift. They strayed ever more frequently to the woods.

With Gabriel driving Captain, at least the stripped trunks could still be dragged out at the same rate. But if he was driving Captain he could not be felling. Billy by himself would not be able to fell quickly enough to keep both horses working …

She was jolted back to awareness by Lobb's arrival with the announcement that a cold collation had been set out in the dining room.

Mrs Betts had excelled herself, preparing an array of platters and dishes that occupied a large area of the table. As they took their seats, Louisa fixed her niece with a very speaking look, flicked her gaze toward the butler, and gave her head an infinitesimal jerk.

'You may go, Lobb,' Melissa said, wondering with some trepidation what her aunt wished to say that could not be mentioned in front of a servant. 'We will serve ourselves.'

He caught her eye as he bowed. 'Perhaps a tray of tea in the parlour in an hour, miss?'

'Yes, that will do very well.' Surely then they would leave? But would she have enough time to return to the wood? 'Thank you, Lobb.'

Knowing she needed fuel to maintain her strength, and hungry despite her anxiety, Melissa took a portion of pie and some thin slices of meat. She murmured agreement as Aunt Sophie complimented the succulence of the cold roast beef and the delightful piquancy of Mrs Betts's tomato pickle.

Aunt Louisa, determinedly overcoming her reluctance for midday eating, had helped herself from every bowl and dish on the table, and did not speak at all until she had devoured half the contents of her heaped plate. Then, knife and fork poised, she leant forward, her voice heavy with significance.

'I had not intended – indeed I would not mention it now, except that your mother gave me to understand – of course that was before the scandal – besides, it is better that you hear from us rather than from servants' gossip what is being said.'

Melissa tried to swallow, but the food had become a solid, choking lump. Setting down her fork, she reached for her glass. The lemonade lubricated her throat, allowing the lump to go down. She had to ask, though she dreaded the answer.

'What is being said, Aunt Louisa?'

'That Lord Stratton has returned to England.'

Is that all? She stopped the words just before they spilled

out. Her aunt clearly thought the news of great importance. At least it was nothing to do with her father, or his debts. Dizzy with relief, Melissa raised her glass again. The tremor in her hand rattled it against her teeth as she took another sip. 'Who is saying it?'

'The person who told me is connected to one of the families intimately involved in the unfortunate affair. More than that I cannot divulge, for it would betray a confidence.'

As it was highly unlikely Aunt Louisa was intimate with any of the Marquis of Lansdowne's family – for she would not have been able to resist boasting of the connection, however tenuous – her confidante must rank among the Poldyces.

Melissa shook her head. 'I must say I think it most unlikely, Aunt. Why would he return?'

'Conscience, perhaps. Who can tell with such a man?'

'He would need to have taken leave of his senses to risk coming back knowing the hangman's rope awaits him.'

Sophie sighed. 'There is something very romantic about a man who will not allow even the threat of death to keep him from the land of his birth. Or perhaps he has made this daring dash in order to wish his brother happy in his impending marriage.'

'The Earl of Roscarrock is getting married?' Melissa was startled. 'I understood him to be in poor health.'

'That's as may be,' Louisa sniffed. 'But with his younger son in disgrace, the marquis, quite properly in my view, intends to secure the succession. Grace Vyvyan is a strong, healthy girl. You've met her, Melissa. She came out the same year as Phoebe. When was that? Now let me see, Charlotte came out in –'

'Phoebe came out a year after me, Aunt Louisa,' Melissa cut in calmly. Her aunt's memory concerning her daughters' debuts into society was encyclopaedic. These apparent lapses, which occurred on every visit, were Aunt Louisa's opportunity to contrast Melissa's failure to secure a husband with her own daughters' success.

'So she did. Do you know I can hardly believe it? Both my girls married after their first season, and now mothers themselves.'

'I have always found Grace a pleasant young woman,' Sophie intervened, adroitly steering the conversation back to the original subject. 'But I cannot help feeling she lacks *sensibility*. For someone like poor Baron Roscarrock ...'

'She's got a level head on her shoulders, if that's what you mean,' Louisa retorted. 'So won't be expecting any of this romantic nonsense.'

'But what's wrong with a little *romance*?' Sophie pleaded.

Her sister-in-law gave a snort of disgust. 'For heaven's sake, Sophie. There's no place for such frippery when land, titles, and the continuation of the family name are at stake. The marquis needs a good breeder. Grace is one of five, all living, and her mother was one of seven. If Grace is the sensible girl I believe her to be, the marquis will be admiring his first grandchild within a twelvemonth.'

'Poor Roscarrock,' Melissa murmured. 'So great a weight of expectation. I hope it may not prove too much for his frail constitution.'

'It is such a pity Lord Stratton is not his father's heir,' Sophie sighed. 'For he always enjoyed excellent health. It's said he has great charm and –'

'Really, Sophie,' Louisa interrupted. 'Of what possible use would it be for him to be heir with the shadow of the gallows upon him and unable to show his face? In my opinion, even if he has come back to England, he would be foolish indeed to return to Cornwall.'

'Has anyone actually seen him?' Melissa enquired.

'No,' Louisa allowed. 'But he's not likely to advertise his presence.'

'It seems more probable this rumour is just that, a rumour,' Melissa asserted.

'Indeed you could be right,' Sophie agreed. 'All it needs is for someone to remark how sad it is that Lord Stratton will not be here to see his brother married. Then someone wonders if he *will* come. And before the cat can lick her ear everyone is whispering that indeed he *has* returned.'

'Yes, well,' Louisa was testy. 'The point I was wishing to

make – if I may be permitted to finish without further interruption – is this. Had Melissa been a little less headstrong, and a little more willing to listen to those with her best interests at heart, she might have stood at the altar in Grace Vyvyan's place.'

Staring at her aunt, Melissa was torn between wild laughter and welling anger. She and Roscarrock? Even her hopeful mother had accepted the impossibility of such a match. But the betrothal she yearned for in her most secret heart was equally impossible. Sudden scalding tears pricked against her eyelids. 'I think not, Aunt. Present circumstances –'

'Indeed, I need no reminder. Does it not occur to you, Melissa, that had your father not been so worried about securing the future of his only daughter, his health might not have collapsed under the strain?'

'Louisa!' Sophie gasped.

Raising a majestic hand that forbade interruption, Louisa continued. 'It is time certain things were said. Melissa, I would not have you think you alone are responsible. I just ask you to consider the possibility that your behaviour – the behaviour your father indulged, even I regret to say *encouraged* in you – has had consequences beyond those readily perceived.'

Gripping the napkin on her lap tightly, Melissa battled against the sharp stabbing of renewed grief. Her heart pounded sickeningly against her ribs and blackness hovered at the edge of her vision. She clenched her teeth. She must not say *anything,* for she would say too much. Once uttered, words could not be recalled. Like rocks tumbling into a pool, they would cause waves. Who knew how far the ripples would spread?

Then, with a blinding flash of intuition, she saw that her aunt was right, though not in the way she imagined. Melissa was almost certain that her father's collapse had resulted from the intolerable strain of his financial pressures. Yet had he not encouraged the interests her aunt so deprecated, she would not now be in a position to try and save his business and protect his reputation.

She looked up. 'Yes, I accept that possibility.'

Her quiet dignity left her Aunt Louisa bereft of words.

When they finally left it was too late and she was too drained and weary to return to the woods.

Next morning while she was at breakfast Lobb entered, bringing the long-awaited letter from Mr Rogers. Ever discreet, the lawyer simply requested that she visit his office at her earliest convenience.

'Will you send a message to Hocking? I shall want him to drive me into Truro within the hour. John is to inform Gabriel that I won't be down today as business takes me to town. But both horses will be back at work tomorrow as usual.'

As Lobb bowed and left to instruct Gilbert, Melissa gulped down the last of her hot chocolate and hurried back upstairs to change.

A short while later, decorous in black bombazine, her hair covered by a small white chip hat trimmed with black satin flowers and held in place by a black satin ribbon, Melissa sat beside Hocking as the gig bowled along toward Truro.

'Got a bit of news, miss. I saw Mr Sibley's groom down in the village the night of the bonfire. He always comes over to visit his sister for St Peter's Tide. He tells me Mr Sibley is not wishful to cause any distress at this sad time, but he was wondering if master's hunters might be coming up for sale.' Hocking kept his eyes on the road ahead. 'Didn't I say he wouldn't even know he'd been told?'

Melissa suppressed a smile. 'Indeed you did. Perhaps if you were to see him while I am engaged with Mr Rogers, you could confirm that they are.'

'Got a price in mind, have you, miss?' When she mentioned the figure, Hocking pursed his lips, frowning slightly. 'With respect, miss, if that's the sum you want – and 'tis a fair one – then I'd suggest you ask more. Mr Sibley is a great one for a bargain, so I hear. He never pay the asking price, 'tis a matter of pride with him. So he'll try to beat the price down.'

She should have remembered. Had Gabriel not given her exactly the same advice when she went to sell the wood? They discussed the amount of the increase and finally agreed a new figure. It sounded a large amount to Melissa. She was relieved that being in mourning, as well as her gender, required that she distance herself from the transaction.

'Tell your friend that if Mr Sibley is interested in proceeding, he should contact Mr Rogers, who will be handling the sale on behalf of my brother. After that I'd be obliged if you would call at the tannery and tell the foreman that Tregonning's Yard has two cartloads of oak bark for sale, and more will be available shortly. Should they wish to purchase, they may do so through Mr Rogers.'

This time she was not asked to wait, but was immediately escorted into the lawyer's office. She searched his face as he came forward, immaculate in a flatteringly cut frock coat of forest green worn over biscuit-coloured breeches and a crimson and silver waistcoat. He bowed briefly over her proffered hand. His smile held genuine warmth. But as a shadow of concern entered his sharp gaze she lowered her eyes.

'I must apologise for the brevity of my letter, Miss Tregonning, but I thought it wiser to commit to paper as little as possible.'

Melissa waved his apology aside. 'I understand completely, Mr Rogers. Indeed, I thank you for your discretion.' She sat down. As he resumed his own seat he leant forward.

'I hope I find you in good health?'

She allowed herself a wry smile. 'You mean, I think, that I do not look to be in high bloom, but as a gentleman you could not possibly say so. I admit, Mr Rogers, I am rather tired. Since I saw you last there has been a great deal to do. Plus the unexpected arrival of rather taxing visitors ...' She made a vague gesture, leaving the sentence unfinished.

'How are your aunts? Do they keep well?' he enquired with bland innocence, reminding her once again that behind a façade that could vary from aloofness to geniality according to circumstances he was exceptionally astute. Having acted for her father for most of her life, he was well acquainted with all the family.

'They seem so, thank you.'

'What of your mother? Have you received news of her progress?'

'Not yet, but –'

'I'm sure you will very soon.'

'I hope so. Mr Rogers.'

'Of course. Now you want to know how I fared with my mission. You will be pleased to hear that the news is most encouraging. I was able to negotiate an extremely good price for your jewellery. Better, in fact, than I had anticipated.' Reaching to the rear of the bureau he drew forward a leather pouch. It looked impressively large and clinked heavily as he set it down and loosened the thong.

As she glimpsed the gleam of gold, tension slid from Melissa's shoulders like a sloughed-off skin. 'That's wonderful! I'm so grateful. Naturally, the first deduction must be repayment of your loan.'

'Before we go into that, why don't you give me a progress report on all your schemes? Have you made any progress during my absence?'

'Indeed, I think you will be surprised, Mr Rogers.'

He was clearly impressed by the number of trees that had been felled and moved to the collection area. 'Is a figure brought to you at the end of each day?'

'No, not exactly.' She hesitated, then decided it would be easier to tell him the truth. 'The fact is, Mr Rogers, if the packet is to be finished quickly, few men can be spared from the yard. The five working in the woods must concentrate on felling and stripping. I borrowed two draught horses from the farm to move the logs, and the stable boy is driving one of them. The other is a more difficult beast, and requires a firmer hand, so …' She faltered, regretting her impulsive honesty, and glanced away from his gathering frown.

'Miss Tregonning, you cannot be telling me that –?

'I am doing what is necessary, Mr Rogers, that is all. My groom is at this moment informing Mr Nankivell that his wagons may begin collecting first load of logs at his earliest convenience. Tom Ferris, foreman at the yard, has sold several sacks of oak bark to the village fishermen. The rest is being offered to the tannery. Also I have learnt from my groom that a local gentleman is interested in purchasing my father's hunters.

I have instructed him that any interested parties should contact you. Oh, and by the way, I have set the price high to allow for negotiation.'

His brows had climbed higher and higher up his forehead during her recital. Now he shook his head, and gave a bark of laughter. 'Miss Tregonning, I am astonished. Astonished, and I have to admit, awed.'

Surprise, delight, and a hint of pride swelled in Melissa's chest.

'To say you have been busy is something of an understatement.' The lawyer drummed his fingers lightly on the paper-strewn surface of the open bureau. 'If I surmise correctly, you wish me to act on your behalf – in the temporary absence of your brother – regarding the sale of the wood bark, your father's horses, and so on?'

Melissa nodded. 'If you would be so kind.'

'It will be my pleasure, Miss Tregonning. In the circumstances I shall defer your repayment of my loan until Mr Nankivell and the tannery have made *their* first payments. My fees for the additional work will not be unreasonable and I'm sure repayment at that time will cause you less difficulty then than it would now. Naturally I will ensure a detailed record is kept of all transactions made on your behalf, and a copy will be sent to you at the end of each month, if that is acceptable?'

'Indeed, Mr Rogers. I am most grateful. I will use the money from my jewellery to repay Mr Vincent, and reduce the outstanding debts owed to the yard's suppliers.'

'That would indeed be wise. However, will you permit me to make one or two suggestions?

She regarded him warily. But when he raised his brows, clearly awaiting her reply, it dawned on her that his question had been entirely serious. 'Of c-course. Please.'

'Firstly, I think it might be wise if I were to review the figures relating to Mr Vincent's loan, just so we may be quite certain the interest has not been overestimated. I do not doubt that gentleman's honesty. But in matters of finance one cannot be too careful. A maxim I recommend you to adopt, Miss Tregonning. Once I have checked all is as it should be, I will make the repayment on your behalf and send you a signed receipt of settlement, if that is acceptable?'

'Perfectly.'

He gave a brief nod. 'Secondly, rather than deposit the jewellery money in the bank where Mr Williams might consider it a redemption of your father's debt, I believe it would be more sensible to allow it to remain here in my safe, where you will have access to it.'

'Can I do that?' Melissa felt her eyes widen.

'Miss Tregonning, it is yours. You may do with it whatever you wish.'

'In that case, Mr Rogers, I accept your offer with gratitude. Naturally, I intend to repay the bank as quickly as possible, but –'

'The amount and frequency of repayments must be at a time of *your* choosing,' he finished smoothly. 'I understand perfectly. In the meantime –' he picked up a sheet of thick paper and handed it to her '– you will see each item of jewellery is listed, plus the amount it fetched.'

Melissa caught her breath and her heart leapt as she scanned the paper. 'I can hardly believe –' She raised her eyes. 'Mr Rogers, I don't know what to say. I never dreamt … Of course, I was hopeful, but I never could have expected … Thank you so much. You don't know what this means.'

'Oh, I believe I do, Miss Tregonning. Had our discussions during your last visit to this office failed to impress, then what you have achieved since then has left me in no doubt of your determination. Now.' His manner grew brisk. 'Doubtless you have incidental expenses to meet.' Reaching into a small drawer in the bureau, he withdrew a small kid purse. 'I trust this will be sufficient until your next visit. Should you require more, you have only to ask.'

'Thank you.' Blessing his foresight and his tact, she reached for the purse and would simply have put it into her bag, a black velvet pouch drawn in with a black satin ribbon.

He stopped her with a gesture. 'Please count it, Miss Tregonning.'

'Oh but –'

'You will be signing a receipt,' he reminded. 'You must always check.'

After counting and signing, Melissa put the purse and both folded papers into her bag and rose to her feet, extending her hand. 'Thank you, Mr Rogers. With all my heart.'

Taking her hand, he bowed over it, creaking faintly. 'Your servant, ma'am. I trust you will not be offended if I confess I have never had dealings with a lady of such enterprise.'

Her lips twitched. 'I hope you do not find it too uncomfortable?'

He smiled. 'Miss Tregonning, it is an education as rewarding as it was unexpected.'

Hocking was waiting with the gig. As soon as she was settled, he clicked his tongue and the horse broke into a smart trot.

'How did you get on with Mr Sibley's groom?' Melissa enquired.

'Just as I expected, miss. 'He said the price was too high. But I just shrugged and told him never mind as the word had got around and other gentlemen was showing interest. 'Course, then he starts begging me to hold them off till he'd had a chance to speak to his master.' Hocking's eyes narrowed in a grin of satisfaction. 'Deal's as good as done, miss.'

As they headed home Melissa reviewed the progress she was making. Bees droned lazily over tall foxgloves, and hedgerows laced with white convolvulus. At the edge of the road, young fronds of bright green bracken uncurled. Blue harebells, yellow agrimony, pinkish-white yarrow, and purple scabious brightened grassy banks and ditches, and the air was fragrant with meadowsweet.

As the sun's warmth seeped into her bones, for the first time in weeks Melissa allowed herself to relax. It really did look as though everything was going to be all right.

# Chapter Fourteen

The following morning brought even better news: a letter from Aunt Lucy to say that her mother was showing slight signs of improvement. That this took the form of Addey twice coming upon her mistress "weeping fit to break her heart" filled Melissa with dismay. How could Aunt Lucy possibly imagine that to be improvement?

But, after several minutes' anxious reflection, she was able to accept the truth of her aunt's assertion that emotions frozen by shock and grief had at last begun to thaw. Picturing her mother's abject misery, her own eyes filled in sympathy. Blinking hard, for she could not spare the time to be weak and self-indulgent, she set the letter aside and glanced at the others.

One was addressed in Aunt Louisa's bold scrawl. She left it. The third gave her a start as she recognised Robert's writing. Swiftly breaking the seal, she unfolded the sheet. The date showed it to have been written on the 9th March: almost four months ago. Why had it taken so long to get here? Of course, it was unlikely to have been sent the same day it was written. Robert might have had to wait weeks for the ship's mail to be taken ashore, or collected by a passing packet-brig.

She skimmed through the close lines of small, neat script, noted Sir Edward Pellew's name, read that he had been in action against the French, but little of it registered. All she could think of was that if Robert's letter had got through at last, then she might soon hear from George.

Finding it impossible to concentrate, she refolded the letter to read later. It occurred to her that not so long ago a letter from Robert would have been the highlight of her week. She would have read and re-read it with her atlas close at hand, the easier to trace the movements of his ship.

Her life now was so different, and bore no resemblance to her life then. Her new responsibilities made such demands that she could summon little interest for what might be happening in the Channel.

Taking a deep breath, recognising as she did so that contact of any kind with Aunt Louisa required her to mentally brace herself, she picked up the remaining letter once more. It was an invitation to a picnic the following afternoon. Though the prospect did not fill her with enthusiasm, her first inclination, for the sake of peace, was to accept. Then she read on.

'... *You have shut yourself away for long enough. An observance of what is proper is one thing, but complete withdrawal from even close family shows an excess of sensibility and I cannot think it healthy. Naturally you miss your father, as indeed we all do, but life must go on. It is of the utmost importance that your behaviour at this sad time does not give rise to rumour and speculation. To be labelled reclusive must damage even further your prospects of marriage. You know that I have only your good at heart when I point out that you have difficulties enough already.'*

Melissa's hand clenched, crushing the sheet. She stood up so abruptly that her chair almost fell over.

'Is everything all right, miss?' Lobb enquired sharply.

'My esteemed aunt –' she began furiously, then caught herself.

'Ah,' said Lobb, and tactfully turned away to the sideboard.

Gathering up the other letters, she started toward the door, pausing as she drew level with him. 'I know you will be glad to hear that my mother is beginning to show signs of recovery.'

'Oh miss, that is indeed good news. Do you know when she might be coming home?'

Melissa shook her head. 'I don't think it will be for a while yet, but Aunt Lucy is convinced a corner has been turned.'

'I'm delighted to hear it, miss. With your permission I shall impart the good news to the rest of the household.'

'Thank you, Lobb. I'd be most grateful.'

He opened the door for her. 'At least that's one weight off

your mind.'

Passing him, Melissa made a wry face. 'I wish the others might be so easily lifted.'

In her father's study, she sat at his desk. Her initial intention was to dash off a swift note thanking her aunt for the invitation but regretting that she must decline. She would claim that, as her aunt surmised, her high colour had indicated the development of a summer cold and it would be unfair of her to risk spreading the infection.

But even as she dipped the pen she knew she could not do it. She would have to go. Putting down the pen, she smoothed the crumpled sheet. It was plain as she read on that Aunt Louisa's concern was less for her than for public opinion.

'... *By rejecting the support of those who wish only to comfort and advise you at this tragic time, you invite society to accuse us, your family, of neglect. I have already heard whispers of astonishment that your mother is not facing her loss with the fortitude expected from one of her breeding. You are not alone in your mourning, Melissa, and family gatherings cannot be considered going into society. I shall put my trust in your loyalty and good sense, and look forward to seeing you.'*

Eyes closed, teeth clenched, Melissa battled anger and intense frustration. Then, taking up the pen, she wrote her acceptance. After folding and sealing the sheet, she left it on the tray in the hall and went upstairs to change out of her morning gown into her working clothes.

Collecting the basket containing her lunch from Mrs Betts, she went to the stable yard. The shires were tacked up and ready, and John was tying Duchess's nosebag to the harness.

'Good morning,' she greeted them.

Man and boy glanced round, chorusing, 'Morning, miss.'

Captain shifted restlessly as Hocking checked the straps and chains, and the groom growled at him to stand still.

'What's the matter with him this morning?'

'Dunno, miss. Daft side out, he is.' Hocking grumbled.

Setting her basket down, Melissa approached the huge horse, talking to him in soothing murmurs while she looked first at his eyes and nose. He stood docile while she ran expert hands over him. 'He looks all right. Did you find any sores? Any heat in his legs?'

Hocking shook his head. 'Nothing. You sure you want to take him, miss? He isn't hisself. Got one on 'un today, he have.'

'He'll be fine once he starts work, won't you, fellow?' She rubbed the white blaze that stretched from forelock to muzzle, and the horse tossed his huge head, jingling the harness. 'Speaking of work, we had better get going. Will you give me a leg up, please?'

They reached the clearing in time to see the final log of the first load lifted onto Mr Nankivell's heavy four-wheeled wagon. As it pulled away, the team of horses straining under the weight, Gabriel turned. Catching sight of her, he came forward, saluting.

'Morning, miss.'

Her rebellious heart quickened as it did whenever she saw him. No other man of her acquaintance had affected her in this manner despite their indisputably greater eligibility. Though his manner and greeting were respectful, she glimpsed a brief flare of warmth in his eyes and knew it was echoed in her own. 'Good morning, Gabriel.'

'The driver will be back for a second load this afternoon.'

She gave a brief nod of acknowledgement, her grip tightening on Captain's bridle as he jerked his head and swung his quarters sideways. 'Be still,' she chided softly.

Gabriel's glance flicked to the horse. But, aware of his responsibilities, Melissa didn't want to delay him.

'Where would you like me to start?'

'One moment, miss, and I'll show you.' He moved past her to the boy, pointing as he issued directions. Nodding, John led Duchess off to where Chirp was waiting. Returning, Gabriel fell into step beside her.

'Two stripped boles are ready to be pulled out. Ned is clearing the débris and will chain them for you. Billy is helping me with a large sycamore. Once that's down we'll have finished in this area.'

'What happens then?'

'We move further in. That will mean extending the track.'

Melissa nodded. 'How big is the sycamore?'

'About ninety feet high and perhaps two and a half in diameter.'

'It must be very old.' She bit her lip. He must know what he was doing.

'It is. And showing signs of disease,' he explained quietly. She felt her colour rise. Could he read her mind? 'Better it's dropped now while most of the wood can be salvaged. If it's left and brought down by the winter gales, there will be a lot more destruction.'

She darted him a swift, apologetic smile. 'You're right, of course. Good luck.'

It was only as she led Captain away that she realised how deeply she dreaded the possibility that he might one day leave.

During the next two hours, against the slow, rhythmic *thunk* of the two axes biting alternately into the huge trunk, she twice passed John and Duchess. It was the first time the entire team had worked in the same area. Captain's restlessness kept her on her guard. But once a log was chained to his harness he appeared to settle down.

She drove him from behind, walking slightly to one side and using the long traces to guide him. But going in toward the logs with the chains looped up he was jittery and hard to handle. So she held either his bridle, or the reins close beneath his chin, though his frequent head tossing made her arm and shoulder ache.

She was leading him past some shrubbery when a pair of wood pigeons suddenly exploded out of the bushes in a violent flutter of wings. Snorting in panic, Captain reared back on his haunches, almost pulling her arm from its socket, his forelegs flailing. Fortunately Melissa had a firm grip and jerked down hard, stepping smartly back from the plunging hooves.

'Steady, now. Steady. It's all right,' she crooned, trying to sound calm and reassuring despite the eye-watering pain in her wrenched shoulder. Nostrils distended, his eyes showing white behind the blinkers, Captain snorted, champing on the bit as foam flew from the corners of his mouth.

'What's the matter with you, you silly old thing?' She stroked his nose, tightening her grip on the bridle as the sound of the axes ceased, and Gabriel's warning shout echoed through the wood.

After a loud groan, the splintering cracks echoed like gunshots. Then came the crashing thud as the sycamore fell. The earth vibrated and Captain flinched. But though tremors ran through him he remained still as she continued to stroke, talking softly. When the sounds of axes and saws resumed she coaxed Captain forward.

The fallen sycamore was a giant: some of its branches as big as whole trees. There was no possibility of hauling it out in one piece. Even cut into sections, the weight of each would be as much as one horse could manage.

Though Gabriel had lined up its fall with care, the size and spread were so great that it had inevitably damaged other trees on its way down. Sunlight streamed through the wide gap in the canopy and Melissa glimpsed blue sky and puffs of fluffy white cloud. A short distance away, Billy was cutting down a partly uprooted alder presently leaning across the path. Ned and Chirp were already hard at work on the sycamore's branches.

Standing at Captain's head, she coaxed the huge horse backward, toward a roped bundle of branches from the trees felled earlier that morning. Hearing her, Zeb glanced up then straightened, ready to help. But Gabriel was closer. Telling the others to carry on, he dropped his axe and strode forward to release the looped-up chains.

Captain twitched, swinging his hindquarters sideways. Slapping his rump, Gabriel pushed him back. As he bent and picked up one of the chains, Billy cried out. But the warning was lost as the alder fell and another tree, uprooted by the falling sycamore, gave a rending creak and toppled across the crown.

The violent rustling and shaking of foliage were too much for Captain. With a shrill whinny he reared up, throwing Melissa backwards and tearing free of her grip. She tripped, lost her balance, and fell with a breath-stopping thump.

Zeb tried to reach the other rein but couldn't get past the foliage of the fallen tree. Desperately scrambling to her feet, Melissa saw Gabriel hurl himself forward to grab the loose rein, wrapping it round his hand for greater purchase as he dug his heels into the soft ground. She wanted to shout at him to let go, but was terrified of scaring the huge horse even more.

Thoroughly frightened, Captain reared, pawing the air as he fought the rein. One of the chains flicked like a whiplash, catching Gabriel a glancing blow as the horse lunged forward. The rein tightened. Unable to free himself, Gabriel was pulled off his feet. Melissa could only watch as, face down and dangerously close to the horse's massive hooves, he was dragged over the débris-strewn earth.

'Billy!' Melissa screamed, deafened by the thunder of her heartbeat, her mouth dust-dry with fear. 'Go that way! Try to head him off!' Hoisting up her skirts, she raced after the runaway horse. Though it could not have been more than a few seconds, it felt like an eternity. Then, as Billy charged in from the side, John and Duchess came up from the clearing.

His path blocked, Captain's headlong dash slowed just enough for Melissa to hurl herself forward and grab his bridle. Using strength she didn't know she possessed, she forced him to a halt.

Both were trembling uncontrollably. Captain's nostrils were distended, his eyes wild. Melissa gasped breath into her tortured lungs. The others arrived at a run. Billy stopped beside Melissa and they stared at the figure sprawled face down and unmoving on the trampled earth.

Grabbing Billy's hand, Melissa clamped it onto the bridle. 'Hold him.' Her heart hammering painfully, she dropped to her knees beside Gabriel. Carefully unwinding the leather rein from his fist, she bit back a wince at the livid bruise down the inside of his forearm.

She looked up at the uncertain, anxious men. Gabriel had organised and directed them, and now they were rudderless. Everyone had looked to him. Now they were looking at her: as if she would know what to do. Hysteria bubbled, heady and dangerous. She fought it. She had to be strong for his sake.

194

'Help me –' Tremulous and cracking with strain, her voice was almost inaudible. She coughed. 'Help me turn him over.'

His eyes were closed, his face smeared with blood and dirt, bits of leaf and twig entangled in his hair. His boots and breeches were ingrained with earth, and through the rips in his filthy shirt she could see blood-stippled welts and grazes streaking his skin.

'Best if we get him home, miss. Know where he live, do you?'

Her thoughts raced. Rather than live in the village he had sought out a ruined tumbledown shack so he might have privacy and solitude. He had trusted her. She could not – would not – betray him.

'N-no,' she lied. 'Besides, as we don't know how badly he's hurt he must be taken up to the house, in case – in case he needs a doctor.'

'Yes, but how are us going to get 'un up there?' Chirp asked. 'He won't be walking nowhere, that's for sure. I suppose we could carry 'un.'

'Not if he've broke something,' Billy warned.

'A stretcher. We need some kind of stretcher.' Quickly, Melissa looked around.

'Don't you fret, miss. Us can do that,' Zeb announced, surprising everyone. 'Have 'un ready in no time, we will. Chirp, you fetch over that there rope. Joe, cut a couple of they young birches: 12 to 15 foot long. John, do you run back to the clearing and fetch that there bit of canvas we was using to keep the rain off.'

'What about me?' Billy said urgently. 'What can I do?'

'You stay right where you're to and keep hold of that there horse,' Zeb said. 'We'll need he in a minute.'

While the men worked, Melissa remained on her knees beside Gabriel. Stripping off her gloves, she pressed her folded handkerchief against the long cut above his right eye. Had Captain's hoof done that? It might have broken his neck.

The thin fabric was soon saturated, and each time she lifted it, blood welled from the wound and trickled down his temple into his hair. She choked down terror. Beneath the dirt and blood and rapidly colouring bruises, he was alarmingly pale.

Turning her back on the busy men, she pulled the fine muslin kerchief from about her neck and bosom. Laying it across her thighs, she folded it into a long, narrow strip. Binding it tightly around his head, she tied the two ends, blinking away tears of shock and fear. Let him be all right. Please let him be all right.

Within a short time, two long poles had been braced apart by cross members and the canvas fastened between them. The men lifted Gabriel's inert body onto the makeshift stretcher. Melissa turned Captain, now docile, his head low. With two men on each side, the top ends of the poles were lifted and fastened to the harness. Though the lower ends would drag along the ground, Gabriel was clear of the earth and a safe distance from Captain's heavy hooves.

Dropping the bloody handkerchief beside him, Melissa pulled on her gloves and picked up the reins. Her chest felt tight and she had to fight for breath. But she had to be strong and keep going. She glanced at the men, who avoided looking at her as they waited to be told what to do next.

Hysteria threatened once more. Only days ago they had disapproved of her being here. Now, though embarrassed by her *décolletage*, they still expected her to give them directions. So she must, for who else was there? She sucked in a breath, strove for calm.

'Thank you all very much. It must be nearly dinner time, so I suggest you take your break now. I understand Mr Nankivell's wagon will be back for the second load of logs this afternoon. The sycamore must be stripped and sawn into sections and hauled out to the collection area. Once that has been done, the track must be widened and pushed through to the new felling area.' That was as much as Gabriel had had time to tell her. She turned to Billy. 'Did Gabriel – do you know where that will be?'

Billy nodded, and knuckled his forehead. 'Yes, miss. Gabe said it would be best if we –'

'That's fine,' she interrupted quickly. 'You carry on then. Do exactly as he told you.'

Walking behind Captain as he hauled his precious burden through the wood and across the park, she fought the urge to hurry him along. What if Gabriel's injuries were worse than they appeared? Why was he still unconscious? What if ... A sob caught in her throat and tears spilled down her cheeks. *Stop it.* Wiping her eyes on her sleeve, she swallowed hard.

As she reached the drive, Lobb, who must have seen her through one of the windows, hurried out of the front door.

'Dear life, miss! Whatever's happened?'

'There's been an accident. Captain bolted and Gabriel was dragged. I think he must have been kicked. He's been unconscious for ages.' Hearing a gasp, she glanced round. 'Sarah, go and fetch Hocking. Captain's badly scratched. Tell him I'll be along later.'

'Miss,' hissed Sarah, eyeing Melissa's half-exposed bosom. 'Where's your –?'

'I needed a bandage.' She turned back to the butler. 'Please fetch Gilbert, then take Gabriel up to Mr Adrian's room. I'm going to –'

'Mr Adrian's room?' Lobb repeated, visibly startled.

'Just do it!' Biting her lip as she fought for calm, she met his concerned gaze. 'Please?' Then she crouched beside the stretcher, anxiously searching for signs of returning awareness.

'Very well, miss.' As soon as the butler returned with Gilbert in tow, Melissa left them and ran into the house as Agnes hurried down the hall.

'P-please, miss,' she stuttered, 'Mrs Betts says to tell you she's sent hot water and clean towels up to Mr Adrian's room, and she's making some beef tea.'

For a moment Melissa couldn't speak for the suffocating lump in her throat. Beef tea had been her father's sovereign remedy for falls on the hunting field. 'Thank her for me, Agnes,' she said unsteadily. 'As soon as Sarah comes back tell her to bring salve and bandages.'

Bobbing a curtsy, Agnes ran back to the kitchen. Watching Lobb and Gilbert struggle up the stairs with the tall figure of Gabriel sagging between them Melissa pressed her fingers against her trembling mouth, her chest heaving painfully.

Scalding tears splintered her vision. She had watched this same scene only a few short weeks ago. Then it had been her father. He had died. Shaking her head violently, she banished the memory. Then followed them up the stairs.

As he lay on his back on her brother's bed, Gabriel's eyes were still closed. The crimson streaks of dried blood were vivid against her white kerchief and his dark stubble. Purple bruises were forming around the grazes.

Barely glancing at her father's valet, Melissa crossed to the bedside. 'Thank you, Gilbert. That will be all.'

Startled and uncertain, the manservant hesitated. 'But, miss –'

Melissa glanced at Lobb, a brief look full of pleading.

'All right, Gilbert,' Lobb said. 'Off you go now.'

'Thank you,' Melissa whispered as the door closed.

'Is this wise, miss?' Lobb began.

'Why is he still unconscious? It must be half an hour at least. Surely he should be waking up by now?' She searched the butler's face, seeking reassurance. 'Lobb, it's my fault.'

After a long moment the butler switched his gaze to the man on the counterpane. Melissa sensed his dismay. In the same instant she realised its cause lay not in the man's possible injuries but in her passionate concern. But, to her intense relief, he chose, for the moment at least, not to comment.

'I don't see how it could be your fault, miss. But never mind that now. I daresay him still being out of it is the best thing. It won't have been a comfortable journey even on that stretcher. Anyway, it'll give me a chance to get him cleaned up. Now, if you'd just like to wait outside –'

'No.' Melissa's blurted refusal startled them both. But she was adamant. 'I'm not leaving until he shows some sign of regaining his senses. So either you help *me,* or I do it by myself.' She clasped her hands to her chest, her knuckles bone-white. 'Lobb, I owe this man more than I can ever repay. Had it not been for him …' Her voice broke and she couldn't continue.

Lobb moved briskly to the foot of the bed. 'In that case, miss, I suggest you attend to those cuts and grazes about his head, while I deal with the rest.'

Leaving her makeshift bandage in place for the moment, Melissa squeezed out a cloth in the hot water and began gently to clean the dirt and dried blood from Gabriel's face. There was a brief knock and the door opened to admit Sarah, eyes bright with curiosity, carrying linen strips and a pot of salve.

'Dear life, miss!' she gasped. 'Whatever are you doing? You shouldn't be –'

'Thank you, Sarah,' Lobb intervened before Melissa could utter a word. 'On the side table, if you please.'

'Want me to stay and help, do you?' she offered.

Melissa glanced up. 'No. Thank you.' She softened the refusal with a brief smile. 'But I'd be obliged if you would fetch one of my father's nightshirts, the largest you can find.' Gabriel's shoulders were far too wide to fit anything belonging to either of her brothers.

'Tell Gilbert to do what he can with these.' Lobb handed the mud-caked boots to Sarah, who held them at arm's length. 'And ask Mrs Betts to whip up an egg with some hot milk, sugar, and a dash of brandy.'

'Yes, Mr Lobb.' Sarah's cheeks were flushed, her tone pert, as she marched out and shut the door.

'What's the point? He won't be able –'

'It's not for him; it's for you. No, miss, don't turn round.' She heard the soft, dry sound of clothing being removed. 'You've had a nasty shock, what with Captain bolting, and everything. A warm, nourishing drink will settle your nerves. Help you to see things more clearly.'

She recognised his anxiety and its cause but, focused on unwinding the makeshift bandage without re-opening the cut, she didn't bother to reply. Dropping the blood-soaked kerchief onto a soiled towel she carefully washed around the deep gash. He would carry the scar for life. Then, smearing salve onto a thick pad of folded muslin, she fastened it firmly in place with a strip of clean linen. Behind her she heard a blanket shaken out, and felt the swish of air as the butler spread it over Gabriel.

'Lobb, will you help me with his shirt?'

'Not much of it left,' Lobb murmured as he moved round the bed. They eased the ripped garment up and freed Gabriel's arms. Lobb drew the unconscious man onto his side so Melissa could lift it carefully over his head. As Lobb pulled the shirt free he saw Gabriel's back. 'God a'mighty! What –?'

'He's not a deserter,' Melissa said quickly. Gently releasing Gabriel so he lay flat, Lobb frowned at her. 'How would you know that, miss?'

'Because I saw –' she gestured '– accidentally – at the yard,' she added, heat climbing her throat and face at the lie, 'and he told me.'

'So how *did* he get those stripes?'

'He was a prisoner in France,' Melissa said quietly. She unwound the filthy bandages from his wrists and added them to the pile on the towel. Then, with great care, began to release the dressing around his throat.

'They chained him to a wall and tortured him.'

'Dear life!' Horrified, Lobb glanced up from the scarred wrists. 'Why, for pity's sake? What had he done? I've never seen the like of that.'

'They wanted information.'

'What information? What could he know? A man like him. It don't make sense.'

'He didn't say. But it must have been important. Why else would they …? Oh God.' As she lifted the last covering, the livid wound across his throat was revealed, and Lobb inhaled sharply. Biting her lip hard against a surge of anger and compassion she dimly recognised as a mask hiding something far deeper, she dropped the stained and crusted linen onto the towel.

'Did he tell them?' Lobb's voice was barely audible.

As she sponged the worst of the mud and blood from Gabriel's chest and arms, Melissa shuddered. 'He says not. I believe him. He managed to escape.'

'Poor bugger should have got out sooner. Begging your pardon, miss.'

But Melissa wasn't listening. 'There's earth and grit embedded in these grazes.'

Another knock made them both jump. As Lobb started toward the door, Melissa laid a fresh towel gently across Gabriel's upper body, and Sarah entered, carrying a folded nightshirt and a cup and saucer. She handed them to Lobb, her gaze flickering to the figure on the bed.

'Anything else, miss?'

'Yes. More hot water, bread poultices, and burn these.' Bending, she made a loose parcel of the towel and its contents and handed it to the maid.

'Miss.' Sarah bustled out. Sitting on the edge of the bed, Melissa wrung out the cloth again, but before she could resume her sponging and drying, Lobb removed it, and handed her the cup and saucer.

'First things first.'

'I don't want –'

'Yes you do, miss. Believe me, you'll feel all the stronger for it. Come along now, while it's nice and hot.' He stood over her, encouraging but implacable.

Thick, sweet, and pungent with brandy, the creamy liquid slid down her throat and curled warmly in her stomach. But stopping allowed reaction to take hold.

Her eyes filled and her mouth began to tremble. Bending her head over the cup, she made herself keep on sipping and swallowing, forcing the choking lump down. The painful stiffness in her throat receded and she felt new strength spreading through her body.

'Now, isn't that better?' Lobb demanded as she handed him the empty cup.

She smiled back unsteadily, clinging by her fingertips to a veneer of control. Before she could speak, Sarah returned with a pitcher of hot water and the poultices.

By the time the remaining cuts and grazes had been thoroughly cleaned, poultices applied, and fresh dressings fastened around his throat and wrists, Gabriel was beginning to stir, his head turning on the pillow, restless and uneasy. Helping Lobb get her father's nightshirt over Gabriel's head, she rolled him toward her, holding him in her arms, inhaling his warmth, the scent of his skin mixed with the soap and salve, while the butler pulled the nightshirt down. Then they covered him once more with a sheet, blanket, and fresh counterpane.

About to sink onto the edge of the bed, Melissa found herself steered away: Lobb's hand cupped beneath her elbow as he deftly moved a chair forward.

'You'll find this more comfortable, miss.'

She sat, bone weary but unable to relax, watching Gabriel's black brows draw together in a frown as he began to mutter. He seemed worried, anxious. She yearned to stroke his hand, soothing him as she would a fractious horse, with gentle touch and soft words.

But a lifetime's conditioning, Lobb's presence, and her own innate shyness forbade it. So, instead of clasping his hand, she gripped her own. Her eyes drank him in, from the tousled curls, so dark against the white bandages, over the planes and hollows of his face to the stubborn line of his chin.

Everything she had achieved she owed to him. Without his advice, expertise, and hard physical work she, her mother, and brother would be facing financial disaster and her father's name and reputation would lie in ruins.

But despite his knowledge and practical experience, the difference in their class and background placed them on opposite sides of an unbridgeable chasm. Were he to share her feelings – feelings his accident had brought into agonising focus – and were they to act upon them, the resulting scandal would bring disgrace upon the whole family, thus destroying everything she had worked so hard to achieve. All her efforts, the appalling risks she had taken, the lies she had told and the brave face that had cost her so much to maintain, would have been for nothing. She would never be forgiven.

Right now she was not sure she cared, for had she not always been an outsider? But he would be forced to leave, the family would see to that. Had he not suffered enough? To admit what she felt would condemn them both. Nor did she know for certain what was in his heart. She sensed attraction, and friendship, and respect. Though she would always be grateful for those, she must never forget the price of seeking more. His face shimmered as her gaze blurred, and she looked away, clinging precariously to her self-control.

On the far side of the room, Lobb folded the towels and old counterpane ready to be taken downstairs for soaking in salt water to remove the bloodstains. It was a maid's work, but doing it gave him an excuse to stay. As long as he didn't suggest that she leave, Melissa found his presence oddly comforting.

Gabriel's frown deepened. His eyelids fluttered. Then, without warning, he sat bolt upright, taut as a coiled spring, eyes wide and unseeing. Startled, Melissa gasped. His head snapped round.

'You!' he croaked. 'Where – what –?' He stifled a groan, his face contorting.

'It's all right. You're safe.' She leant forward, trying to reassure him. 'Please, lie down. You're still very –'

'Can't – can't stay here. Must go.' Head bowed, his shoulders hunched against the pain, he struggled to get out of bed.

'Gabriel, you can't.' She tried to press him back. 'You're hurt.'

Still he resisted, ashen-lipped, his voice a rasp of desperation. 'You don't understand.'

'Miss is right,' Lobb announced, coming to her side. 'You couldn't even stand, let alone walk. So you just lie still now. What with one thing and another, you been through enough,' he finished gruffly.

Melissa knew she had to speak to Gabriel alone. She glanced round.

'Lobb, would you be kind enough to fetch the beef tea Mrs Betts promised? And send Agnes up for the washing? If it's left outside the door there'll be no need for her to come in. Gabriel will need his clothes to go home in.'

As she had hoped, her final words, hinting at their unexpected guest's early departure, were sufficient to overcome his reluctance to leave her without a chaperon. As soon as the door closed behind him she knelt beside the bed and looked up into the ravaged face.

'You *can't* go back to the shack alone. You're terribly

bruised, and that cut on your head – I think Captain kicked you. You've been unconscious for –' relief that he had finally come round vied with frantic anxiety and a tangle of other emotions to make her voice shake '– too long.'

His head swung slowly toward her, his eyes full of anguish. 'Melissa, I must go. I'll be all right.'

'All right?' The nervous strain was too much. 'Look at yourself! You're too weak even to stand.'

'I can't stay here. Your reputation –'

She swallowed a sob. He had called her by name and wasn't even aware of it. 'With Lobb to protect me? Anyway, my aunts would tell you it's too late to worry about that.' She fought to hold her voice steady. 'If I let you go back and anything were to happen – I can't, Gabriel. It's my fault you were hurt.'

'No.'

'And my responsibility – as your employer – to ensure you come to no further harm.' Biting her lip, she stood up. 'If you're well enough you may go home in the morning. But you must stay here tonight.'

'You don't understand,' he repeated, in a tone of such torment that her skin tightened in a shiver. Collapsing back onto the pillows, he covered his eyes with a bruised and bandaged forearm as Lobb returned with the beef tea.

'Now, miss, I expect you'd like to go and change. Sarah has prepared your bath. It will soon be time for dinner.'

Melissa glanced up, startled. Where had the afternoon gone?

'Don't you worry about – anything. Gilbert and I will take turns to sit. You go along now.'

Noting how adroitly the butler had avoided mentioning Gabriel, Melissa realised that further private speech would be impossible even if he were up to it. She nodded wearily.

'Thank you.' Closing the door behind her, she glanced down, and, for the first time, realised the extent of her own dishevelment, the mud and blood staining her skirt, and the gnawing ache in her strained shoulder.

After soaking in the hot, scented water while Sarah bustled about with pursed lips, radiating unsatisfied curiosity, Melissa sat at her dressing table, eyes closed, as the brush swept through her hair until it crackled. Then, dressed in one of her lavender gowns, a gauze shawl about her shoulders, she walked across to the stables.

Hocking looked up as she entered. Concern deepened the creases in his leathery skin. 'All right, are you, miss?'

She nodded. 'What about Captain?'

He gestured toward the stall. 'Butter wouldn't melt.' He rolled his eyes. 'Calm as a bleddy pond he is now.'

Melissa glanced over to where the big horse munched steadily on an evening feed of oats, his coat glossy from a thorough grooming. 'Was he badly cut?'

'Not as much as he deserved. A few scratches, that's all. They'll heal soon enough. He's limping on his near fore. I thought a turpentine poultice, and keep him in for tonight?'

When Melissa merely nodded, the groom peered at her. 'You sure you're all right?'

Before she had time to respond, the clatter of hooves announced the return of John with Duchess, and Melissa went out into the yard.

'Yes, miss, we got on fine.' John slid to the ground. 'Billy said to tell you the second load went, and the sycamore's cut but we haven't shifted it all yet. Ned and Chirp have started widening the track. How's Gabe, miss? Going to be all right, is he? Only it isn't the same without him.'

'He's – much better, John. I'll tell him you asked.'

When Melissa returned to the house she met Lobb at the bottom of the stairs.

'You go on into the dining room, miss. I'll just tell Mrs Betts you're back.'

'What about –?'

'He's sleeping now, miss. Had his beef tea and went out like a candle. Best thing. Rest is what he needs. Gilbert is with him. So all you need think about is your dinner.'

If only it were that simple. Something told her the butler knew it wasn't, but neither of them was going to acknowledge the fact.

'Thank you, Lobb.' She made a good meal of spinach soup,

roast lamb and green peas, and a strawberry tart. Then, after collecting some sewing from the morning room, she went back upstairs. Gilbert rose from his chair as she entered.

'Go and have your dinner, Gilbert. I'll stay and keep watch for a while.'

He hesitated. 'You sure, miss? Only –'

'Quite sure,' she said firmly. 'Now I'm here there's no reason for you to stay and miss your meal.'

'If you say so, miss.' He left, visibly reluctant, and she knew it would not be many minutes before Lobb arrived to see if she needed anything.

Taking the chair next to the bed, she turned it slightly, so she could more easily see Gabriel's face. She sat with her sewing untouched on her lap, watching him sleep. But though his eyes were closed, he was certainly not peaceful.

Perspiration filmed his face and the exposed skin of his neck and chest. It soaked the roots of his hair as his head moved restless and uneasy on the pillow. He muttered constantly, his fingers gripping and twisting the sheet, but the sounds were unintelligible.

Suddenly he moaned and shook his head, slamming it from side to side, clearly stressed as he repeated the same phrases over and over again: denying, explaining, only not in English. Fluent in French, Melissa recognised some of the words, but not the dialect. Was he saying "smuggler"?

Behind her, the door opened, and Lobb came in.

Before he could speak, she raised a hand for silence, and turned back to Gabriel as his face changed, fear-filled exhaustion replaced by hauteur, as startling as it was brief. 'You must allow me this, sir. Honour demands ...' he gasped. 'I must ...'

As his head rolled again, Melissa's hand flew to her mouth. He sounded so different. His features tightened and his lips drew back, his breath an indrawn hiss through bared teeth.

She glanced at Lobb, whose eyebrows registered his shock.

Gabriel flung up an arm to shield his face. Exhaustion had muted his groans, but the torment in them pierced her very soul. Despite her familiarity with his wild, unshaven appearance, despite their moments of closeness and mutual trust, he was suddenly a stranger. Unnerved, Melissa shivered. Who *was* he?

# Chapter Fifteen

Melissa slept little that night. Her busy brain allowed her weary body no peace. She could not lie still. Twice she got up and pulled back the curtains, gazing out across the park and woods to the moon-silvered waters of the Carrick Roads and the sea beyond. But the tranquil view offered no escape from the images that streamed through her mind: captivating, contradictory, confusing images of the man lying injured and restless in her brother's bed.

The night hours slowly passed, and eventually sheer exhaustion forced her to stop puzzling over a mystery that defied all attempts at unravelling. But she was still unable to relax. So, instead, she turned her thoughts to what might be achieved.

She owed him so much, and wanted to repay him. It would have to be done in a way that gave no hint of her true feelings. Nor must she intrude on his privacy. As she reviewed possible ideas, one stood out. She examined it carefully, searching for flaws, and found none. It seemed she had found the perfect solution. At last she slept.

It seemed only minutes later that Sarah arrived with her hot chocolate.

'Morning, miss. 'Tis a lovely one too.' She swept the curtains back, flooding the room with sunlight.

Melissa pushed herself up on her elbows as she forced open heavy-lidded eyes. 'Good morning, Sarah.' Her voice was thick with sleep. 'Has Lobb been in to see Gabriel yet?'

'In there most of the night he was, miss, so Gilbert says. Mr Lobb told Gilbert to go to bed and he'd call him to take over in a few hours. Only he never did. I suppose he fell asleep in the chair.'

Melissa sipped her chocolate, remaining silent while her mind raced. Had Lobb simply succumbed to tiredness and the demands of age? Or was his real reason for staying with Gabriel a determination to limit contact, and therefore speculation, even within the household? Only she and the butler had heard Gabriel's feverish ravings, and seen the startling, if short-lived, switch of personality. Clearly Lobb intended to keep it that way.

Bathed and dressed, her hair in long, loose curls down her back, she left her room and, after hesitating for a moment in the passage, resolutely turned away and went downstairs to the dining-room. Seeing Gilbert waiting to serve her, she realised that Lobb must still be upstairs with Gabriel.

'Good morning, Gilbert,' she smiled and took her seat. 'Scrambled eggs, toast, marmalade, and coffee, please. Then you may go.'

She forced herself to eat slowly. But as soon as she had finished, she went back upstairs. Pausing outside her brother's room, she smoothed the front of her gown, nervously fingered the pleated gauze at her bosom, took a deep breath, and tapped her knuckles against the panelled wood. To spare each one of them possible embarrassment, she waited for Lobb to open the door.

Though he looked tired he was freshly shaved, his coat and breeches immaculate, his linen pristine. Melissa was both moved and admiring of his determination to maintain standards no matter how demanding or unusual the circumstances.

'Good morning, miss.'

'Good morning, Lobb.' She kept her voice low. 'How is he?'

'As well as might be expected, miss. He was a bit restless during the early hours. Got quite upset, wandering in his mind. A few drops of laudanum took care of it and we were both able to enjoy a few hours' sleep. I decided that as Gilbert was under instructions to wake me should there be a turn for the worse, it was more sensible for me to remain and avoid a lot of disturbance.'

She nodded. 'Thank you. That was most thoughtful.'

'Not at all, miss. Last thing we want is gossip and wild talk. Family's been through enough without that.' Having delivered what she recognised as an anxiety-inspired warning, he stood back, allowing her to see the bed and its occupant.

Propped up on pillows, Gabriel turned his head. Above the black beard stubble, the upper half of his face was blotched with plum and purple bruises. His blue-grey eyes were shadowed and wary.

'Good morning,' Melissa smiled. 'I hope you are feeling a little better?'

'Much better, thank you, miss.' But his voice belied the claim. Lacking resonance, it was little more than a hoarse whisper. Melissa guessed he was in considerable pain. She turned to the butler.

'I think a hot drink and something to eat, Lobb, then perhaps another dose –'

'No,' Gabriel interrupted. 'It's very kind of you, miss. But I've imposed long enough. If I could have my clothes –'

Melissa ignored him. 'A tray, Lobb, if you please? And perhaps you would find out if Gabriel's clothes are dry?' She turned back to the bed. 'No one will keep you here against your will. But as it appears that at the moment you can hardly move I think you would be wiser to stay, certainly until you have eaten.' She heard the door close quietly behind her.

'Also, I wish – that is –' Swallowing the sudden dryness in her throat, she walked over to the window and stood beside the curtain, her back to the light so he should not see the blush she could feel creeping, hot and prickly, across her face. 'I have a proposition to put to you.'

He did not look at her, and remained silent.

'It occurs to me that, given your knowledge of woodland management, your talents are really not being used to best advantage at the boatyard. I have given this matter careful thought and –' Overcome by shyness, she half-turned toward the window, entwining her fingers. 'I was wondering – that is – I should like to offer you the position of estate manager.'

She found herself unable to look at him. When he still said

nothing, she hurried on, 'There would, of course, be an increase in pay, and you would be entitled to one of the estate cottages.'

He cleared his throat, but his voice still sounded as harsh and strained as the day they met. 'It's a kind offer, miss, and I don't want you to think I'm not grateful, but I can't.'

It had not occurred to her that he might refuse, and his words had the impact of a blow. She turned from the window, every muscle tight. 'May I ask why?'

He glanced at the door and the words burst from him in a fierce whisper. 'I'm a stranger here. Can you not imagine the comments? What of your family? That you should take such action without consulting them must inevitably provoke shock and censure. Do you not see? The repercussions for you would be –'

She stared at him, startled. Then raised a hand. 'Please, that is my concern, not yours. But if it will put your mind at rest, I can point out to them that while we wait for George's return, it is important to keep the estate functioning properly. Your knowledge and expertise will help achieve this. Surely they must recognise the necessity and good sense.' Would Aunt Louisa ever approve of anything she did? 'In any case, I am of age and do not require their consent.'

The tightness in her throat cut her short. She rubbed her hands, her palms slippery, her pulse beating loud and quick in her ears. As the silence lengthened she realised how desperately she wanted him to agree.

She accepted that their relationship could never develop beyond what it was now. But he was the first real friend she had ever had and she wanted to show him how much it meant to her. The tension in the room increased. She darted a glance at him and felt her heart clench like a fist at the bleakness in his face.

He would not meet her eyes. When he spoke, he was the public Gabriel: polite, self-effacing and *distant*.

'Thank you most kindly, miss. I'll help in any way I can until you find a proper woodsman. But I must go back to the yard. Tom Ferris has been very good to me. So, with your permission, I'll stay in the shack.'

She opened her mouth to argue, to persuade, to plead, when it suddenly dawned on her that she might have made a terrible mistake. The bond between them and the friendship she valued so highly might in fact exist only in her imagination. As embarrassment surged through her in a suffocating wave, she tried to mask it with cool civility.

'As you wish.' Refusing to acknowledge the fire in her cheeks or the clammy dampness that caused her clothes to cling uncomfortably, she moved toward the door. 'Be sure to eat well. It will assist your recovery. If the pain troubles you, tell Lobb, and he will bring you laudanum.' Her voice broke and turning quickly she left the room.

As the door closed Gabriel shut his eyes: teeth and fists clenched against an overwhelming desire to call out her name, beg her to come back. No drug could ease the pain of hurting her. She saw his refusal as rejection. And he was powerless to explain the real reason: that acceptance would focus too much attention on him and thus increase the risk of his being recognised.

The memory of her beloved face flooding scarlet with humiliation would haunt him for ever. But as an outlaw under sentence of death, he could not – dared not – admit his feelings for her. His suffering equalled, exceeded even, hers. For she was everything he admired, everything he had dreamt and despaired of finding. Yet better he should suffer that than she should be tainted by the scandal attached to his name.

Knowing how much extra work had fallen on the head groom because of John's absence in the wood, and her own trips to Truro, Melissa declined his offer to drive her over to her uncle's house in the gig.

'No, thank you, Hocking. I'd much prefer to ride, and Samson needs the exercise.'

'If you're sure, miss.' Visibly relieved, he didn't argue and stumped off to fetch Samson's tack.

She had changed into her black habit and her hair was drawn back into a low chignon. Her eyes were slightly red from her spell of secret weeping in the garden. Of course, Sarah had noticed and asked what was wrong.

'I'm just tired. There has been so much to do. Then Aunt Louisa … And I suppose too waiting to hear from George.'

'You'll hear soon. Bound to,' Sarah comforted. 'Bring you some witch hazel for your eyes shall I?'

'Oh Sarah, I should so much enjoy lying quiet for half an hour with pads on my eyes, but there just isn't time to spare.' She smiled wistfully. 'Fresh air will have to do instead.'

'All right then,' Sarah said. 'How about I pin a veil to your beaver hat? Shield your face lovely from prying eyes he will.'

'What an excellent idea! Aunt Louisa will compliment me on my good sense in taking such care of my complexion. She will also point out that I should have done so years ago, and what a shame it is that I have left it far too late.' The sigh was so deep it felt as if it came from her toes.

''Tis only for a couple of hours, miss,' Sarah comforted. 'Then you can come home again.' She set the hat on Melissa's head with the veil hanging down over her face, then drew the two long ends up, tied them over the brim at the back and let them hang down to her mistress's shoulders.

The ride to Gyllan House took almost half an hour. But controlling Samson, who was bursting with energy, allowed Melissa little time to brood on the events of the morning. Though desperately disappointed by Gabriel's refusal, she clung to the fact that though he had rejected her offer he still wanted to stay on at the yard.

As she trotted up the carriage drive to the front door, a stable boy ran out to take Samson, and Cardew, her Uncle Brinley's butler, welcomed her.

'Good afternoon, Miss Tregonning. May I say, on behalf of all the staff, how sorry we were to learn of your bereavement. Allow me to offer our sincere condolences. Your father was a fine man. He will be sadly missed.'

The unexpected tribute provoked a sharp pang of grief. Melissa forced a smile. 'How very kind. Thank you.'

'Everyone is down by the lake, miss. Shall I – ?'

'No, that's all right, Cardew. I'll find them.' She removed

her hat – the veil had served its purpose, her eyes no longer felt hot and gritty, and she was away from public gaze now – and handed it to him with her gloves and riding crop. Then she went back out into the sunshine. But the small puffs of cloud were moving faster and beginning to join together.

At the wide steps that led from the upper lawn she looked down toward the wide grassy area edging a reed-fringed lake and her heart sank. Aunt Louisa's invitations to the rest of the family had clearly been couched in terms similar to a royal decree, for there were at least a dozen people sitting in chairs or on rugs.

All in full mourning, they looked to Melissa like a flock of scavenging crows amid the white cloths spread with dishes of pastries, plates of cakes, and bowls of raspberries and strawberries. There were even fresh peaches from the succession house, a source of great pride to her aunt who delighted in being able to serve at her table a selection of fruits that must, she was convinced, be the envy of her neighbours. Several children were playing under the watchful eyes of nursemaids who maintained a respectful distance from the main group.

'Ah, there she is!'

Her aunt's voice rang out like an accusation, and, fighting an immediate and urgent desire to turn and run, Melissa raised a hand, and walked down to join the party.

As she moved around the group, pausing to exchange polite greetings, respond to enquiries after her mother's health and remarks concerning the delightful weather and wonderful view, she was aware of being watched. It was not one of the sidelong glances, accompanied by a sympathetic smile, of her aunts, uncles and cousins; she was being studied. Then she realised with anger and dismay there was a stranger present.

'Melissa, my dear, how delightful.' Remaining in her chair, Aunt Louisa grasped her niece's hands and pulled her down to kiss the air by her cheek. 'I knew you would not disappoint us. You can have no idea what a pleasure it is for me to see you here among the family.'

'Family, Aunt?' Melissa said quietly, furious that she had

been duped.

'Of course.' Louisa's brief frown conveyed surprise and irritation. 'Did I not say so? Ah. You refer to James. But indeed he is family, Melissa.' She beckoned to a plump, pleasant-faced man loitering just out of earshot and clearly awaiting this signal.

He was wearing the coat, breeches and boots of a country gentleman. Though Melissa hazarded his age to be approaching 40, his shirt points were starched, his cravat modishly tied, and he had discarded his wig in favour of a fashionable forward-brushed style that curled in front of his ears.

'You must,' Aunt Louisa insisted, 'remember my cousin, James Chenoweth? His mother is my father's youngest sister.'

Melissa would have denied the acquaintance, but he did not give her the chance.

'Miss Tregonning,' he bowed. 'I fear my aunt expects too much. We met but once, and that was many years ago. I have not been in Cornwall for some time. But I hope you will not be offended if I say that I share your sadness, and deeply regret the loss of your father. A most enterprising man as I remember.'

Melissa curtsied. 'Thank you, sir.'

'Charlotte.' Aunt Louisa leant over slightly, addressing her elder daughter. 'If you were to move that way a little ... Excellent. There, now there is plenty of room on the rug. Come now, Melissa. Do sit down. We do not wish to keep poor James standing on ceremony.'

Melissa had no choice but to sit in the space her aunt had arranged for her as James lowered himself down beside her with a soft grunt. Turning from him, she smiled at her cousin.

'You look very well, Charlotte.' As sleek and smug as a well-fed cat, Charlotte leant forward, her eyes bright as a blade. 'I am increasing again. Henry is delighted, of course. We hope it will be a girl this time.'

'That is wonderful news. My felicitations to you both.'

A small frown wrinkled Charlotte's smooth forehead as she tilted her head, observing Melissa with a critical gaze. 'I believed my mother to be worrying without cause, but I see

215

now her concern was justified. You are grown so thin! I have to say it does not become you. You being so tall. I can only suppose you have been terribly anxious about Aunt Emma.'

Drawing her legs up beside her, Melissa brushed her fingers lightly over the skirt of her habit. 'Indeed, I was, for a while. She and my father were very close, and his death came as a great shock. However, Aunt Lucy assures me in her latest letter that my mother is in much better spirits.'

Charlotte seemed unimpressed by this good news, preferring to dwell on matters of concern and anxiety. 'What of my cousin, George? Have you heard from him yet? Your situation must be really very difficult.'

Melissa had had enough. 'It is true, Charlotte,' she confided, 'I am quite at a loss.'

'You poor thing!' Charlotte's voice dripped sympathy, but the expression on her face did not reach her china-blue eyes. They were avid, hungry for misery. 'Tell me the worst. You may rely on my total discretion. I shall not breathe a word to a soul.'

'Oh, I will not swear you to secrecy,' Melissa said kindly. 'You see, what has startled – no, I may go so far as to say *overwhelmed* me – is the affectionate regard in which my father was held. Even more touching have been the many small acts of kindness I have received from people who knew him only by reputation. I do not know how I may thank them adequately. Then, with my mother taken ill and my brother not yet returned – though we expect word any time – I was quite fearful as to how I should manage. But by great good fortune our lawyer has been able to deal with everything with a minimum of fuss. So I'm sure you can imagine that with all my terrors coming to naught I feel very foolish.'

Charlotte's thin lips tightened as she sat back. 'Well, I am relieved to hear it has all gone so well for you, particularly as I understand there have been some very disquieting rumours.'

Disguising her flinch by moving slightly as if to be more comfortable, Melissa was too wise now to enquire about the content of the rumours and simply shrugged. 'It is a sad fact that success and popularity such as that enjoyed by my father often breeds jealousy.'

With a sniff strongly reminiscent of her mother's, Charlotte stretched her mouth into a smile that would have curdled milk. 'Indeed.' She turned away and called sharply to a harassed young nursemaid struggling to placate a fat two-year-old lying on his face, roaring loudly as he hammered the grass with feet and fists.

'Some tea, Miss Tregonning?'

She looked round. James Chenoweth was proffering a cup and saucer. 'I daresay you would welcome some refreshment.' His expression was all bland innocence. But though Melissa thought she detected a note of complicit sympathy she was not ready to relax her guard.

'Thank you, Mr Chenoweth.' She took the saucer carefully.

'James, please. Let us not stand on ceremony. We are family, after all.' He smiled, raising one eyebrow. 'I understand from my cousin Brinley that you are having the woods bordering the creek chopped down?'

Her start made the cup rattle. Then she saw the glint of humour in his eyes.

'Not quite all of them. Actually, it is work my father had planned before he – before he was taken ill.'

'It must surely confirm his reputation as an astute businessman, given the current difficulty of obtaining wood from abroad.' He smiled again. 'Such a project must require considerable organisation.'

Though she acknowledged the possibility he might simply be making conversation, the seed of doubt in Melissa's mind put out a tiny shoot.

'I imagine it must,' she agreed. 'I am sure Tom – that's Tom Ferris, our foreman – was vastly relieved that with the practical arrangements already in place, all that was required of him was to supply a team of men.'

Though she longed to give Gabriel the credit that was due to him, to mention a stranger's name was bound to invite questions. Given her aunt's nature, curiosity would inevitably turn into suspicion. 'When George gets home I have no doubt he will be both astonished and delighted that the yard and estate have continued to operate with such efficiency.'

'I do hope, Miss Tregonning ...' He hesitated, and she guessed he expected her to follow his lead and permit him use of her first name, as they were family. But when she did not speak, he continued smoothly, 'I beg you will not take it amiss if I express my most sincere admiration for the fortitude you are displaying in the wake of the tragic events that have befallen your family.'

His words had the effect of a needle pressed with slow deliberation into tender flesh. Fortitude? She was living on the edge of terror; staggering from one crisis to the next. Her eyes pricked, the view dissolved into a bright blur, and she lifted the cup to quivering lips, sipping and swallowing as she fought for control.

'But I wonder – and I beg you to believe I make this observation with only your best interests at heart – if you might be allowing hope to blind you to the very real possibility that your brother may not be on his way home. That he might, in fact, not come back at all.'

Icy rage stiffened her spine and tingled to her fingertips. Lowering the cup, she looked directly at him, tone and manner so cold they almost crackled. 'May I enquire your meaning, sir?'

'Forgive me,' he said quickly, his voice low. 'It was not my intention to cause you anxiety. Though the West Indies is, I am told, a most unhealthy place, I understand your brother to be blessed with a strong physique. No, the point I wished to make is that, as a naval officer in wartime, duty might prevent him leaving his ship.'

Melissa was silent for a moment. It was a fair point. But the way he had made it, deliberately invoking her worst fears, told her that whatever he claimed for his intentions, she would be wise to remain very much on her guard. 'I allow that this possibility has crossed my mind.'

'I could not help but overhear what you said to your cousin,' he confided. 'I am relieved and delighted to hear of the kindness that has been shown you at this sad time. But a great burden of responsibility has fallen on your shoulders. One you should not be carrying alone.'

Melissa gazed into the distance. 'Perhaps. But with my mother so much affected by grief and currently in poor health I have little choice at the moment. However –' she accompanied her brief glance with a polite smile '– I am fortunate in being blessed with the loving support of close friends, and family, of course.'

'That is all well and good, and just as it should be. But surely –' he edged slightly closer '– in such circumstances as yours, the ideal solution would be found in a husband who would remove the weight of responsibility from them and from you.'

Furious with him for his crass impertinence and with her aunt for deliberately contriving this meeting, Melissa struggled hard against a burning desire to slap the smug, knowing, and spuriously sympathetic face. But though he deserved no less, it was she who would be blamed, censured, accused of ill manners and ingratitude.

'My circumstances, sir, are that I am in mourning for a dearly loved father. Speaking purely for myself, I consider the idea of marrying simply to offload one's responsibilities on to someone else both selfish and reprehensible.' She nodded coolly. 'I will not detain you. As your visits are so rare no doubt you will wish to converse with the rest of the family.' She deliberately turned away and, after a few moments, heard him clamber to his feet and move off.

'Melissa! Come and sit by me.'

Glancing round, Melissa saw that the chair next to her aunt was indeed empty, the previous occupant having no doubt been sent on some errand expressly for the purpose of vacating it.

'So,' her aunt whispered, leaning toward her, 'how do you like James? I find him most charming. Such style and address.'

'I am glad he pleases you, Aunt. I found him tactless and totally lacking in consideration.'

Her aunt's features sharpened. 'Indeed, miss? It is clear something has upset you, though I cannot believe James to be the cause. He was most anxious to renew your acquaintance.'

'He is a stranger, Aunt. I do not remember ever meeting

him before.'

Louisa brushed this aside impatiently. 'Take heed, Melissa,' she hissed. 'Opportunities such as this do not present themselves often. With your father gone and your mother away for God knows how long, someone had to do something. I have put myself to some considerable trouble organising this afternoon.'

'I wish you had not.'

'Don't you take that tone with me. You should be on your knees giving thanks that someone in this family cares enough for your future welfare. James would make you an excellent husband.'

'Aunt Louisa, until George comes home, I cannot –'

'But will he come home? That he might not is a possibility you must consider. The newspapers are full of reports of fierce battles between the French and British over Guadaloupe and Martinique.'

Distracted for a moment, Melissa frowned. 'But they are in British hands. Our navy took them last year.'

'Well, the French want them back and are willing to fight. George's ship is out there. If anything happens to him, you are your parents' sole heir. You will be the target of every fortune hunter in the district.'

'Will I?' Melissa's short laugh was edged with bitterness. 'You mean my numerous disadvantages will matter less than the size of my inheritance?'

'Don't be missish,' her aunt snapped. 'That's the way these things work, as you know perfectly well. But none of this need trouble you if you accept James. I'm sure if your dear father were alive, it's what he would want: to keep it in the family.'

'That is what I intend doing, Aunt Louisa. Though as my father is dead, you cannot possibly know what his wishes would be. But my brother is alive, and until I receive an official letter to tell me differently, I shall continue making preparations to welcome him home. This is not a suitable time to be thinking of marriage, and I am astonished that you should think it so.'

'My dear Melissa, you quite mistake my intentions –'

'I am sure they are good, Aunt. No doubt you wish to see me as happily settled as your own daughters are.'

'Precisely so. Now –'

'I must beg you to excuse me, Aunt Louisa.' She stood up. 'I suddenly have a headache and must go home.' Making a brief curtsy, Melissa walked quickly away without a backward glance.

Gabriel winced, every muscle protesting as he pulled up his breeches and slowly tucked in his shirt. Washed clean of blood and dirt, the rips mended, it smelled fresh and felt soft – until the material rubbed against his raw flesh.

He caught his lip, biting hard. After Melissa's visit he had spent the rest of the morning painfully stretching and flexing; trying to loosen bruised and strained sinews. Gilbert had brought a tray of food and helped Lobb prop him up with pillows.

Dismissing Gilbert, Lobb had moved about the room, tidying. Constant stabs of pain made eating a slow, difficult business. But, aware of the butler's surreptitious glances, Gabriel took care to be even more awkward, as if unused to silver tableware, crisp napery, and fine china. The butler spoke little but his reserve was all too obvious.

While he ate, Gabriel's mind raced. What had he said while out of his senses? Not enough to betray his identity. But certainly sufficient to arouse suspicion and cause concern. His continued presence could only make matters worse.

'Mr Lobb?' he said as soon as he had finished. 'I don't want you to think I'm not grateful, but I shouldn't be here. So if I could have my clothes I'll get out of your way.'

'Miss doesn't think you're fit. Looking at you, I'd say she's right.'

'It looks worse than it feels,' Gabriel lied. 'I'll be fine once I'm moving. Miss Tregonning is a remarkable lady with a very kind heart. But you and I both know that her family wouldn't like it one bit if they knew she'd brought me back here. She's got problems enough without me adding more. You've been very good, Mr Lobb. I don't remember much of yesterday and last night, but if it was you who cleaned me up and dressed my wounds then I'm much obliged to you. Though I'm sure a man in your position has far more important things he should be doing.'

The butler regarded him steadily for several moments. 'Gilbert will bring your clothes. Miss is going over to her aunt's house this afternoon. Once she's gone I shall be busy downstairs.'

Getting out of bed had been accomplished in stages, with long pauses between while Gabriel waited for the nausea to subside and his head to stop swimming. The sweat of pain and weakness stuck the borrowed nightshirt to his scarred back. Beneath its bandage, the wound on his forehead throbbed, as loud and insistent as a drum. Eventually, fearful that she would be back before he managed to get away, he gritted his teeth, closed his eyes against the swirling blackness, and finished dressing.

Pulling on his boots, he crossed to the window to check that there was no one about, and caught sight of his reflection in the dressing-table mirror. He stared in shocked revulsion at the bruised, unshaven stranger whose eyes were full of shadows. Then, hearing a sound in the passage, he turned to the door as Lobb opened it.

'Ready?'

Gabriel nodded.

'The front door's open. Everyone's out the back.'

Seizing the butler's hand, Gabriel shook it hard. 'Thank you, Mr Lobb.'

'No need for that. What I did was for miss. You go on now.'

Walking down the stairs and out of the house was an agony that had nothing to do with physical pain. But it was, he told himself, for the best.

By the time he had crossed the park and entered the woods the stabs had moderated to twinges as exercise loosened him up. Even the pounding in his head had eased to a dull ache. Though by no means fully recovered, he felt well enough to call at the shack for some money then walk on to join the team in the wood. As well as reassuring them and getting everyone back to work, his presence would put a stop to the inevitable rumours and speculation.

## Chapter Sixteen

'Hey, look who's 'ere!' Chirp shouted across the clearing to Zeb, before turning back to Gabriel. 'Some glad to see you, we are. Young Billy been running round like a blue-arsed fly.'

'I haven't! No such thing! It just look like it because you're so bleddy slow!'

Gabriel grinned. 'And I was only gone a day.'

Ned stomped out of a thicket, wiping his sweating forehead. 'Long enough. How are you feeling?'

'How do I look?' Gabriel replied.

Ned shook his head. 'Bleddy awful. Want a drink, do you? There's still some ale in that there keg.'

'He won't want ale,' Zeb elbowed him, 'not now he been eating with the gentry up the big house.'

'What was it like?' Billy's young eyes were alight with curiosity. 'Did they give you rich food and wine and stuff?'

Sensing envy, Gabriel shook his head. 'No. They gave me beef tea.'

Ned grimaced. 'I tasted that once. Like's cat piss it was.'

'So how would you know what cat's piss taste like?' Zeb asked with interest. 'Got some strange habits you have, boy.'

'Did Miss Tregonning look after you herself?' Joe gazed, round-eyed, at Gabriel.

'Some worried she was,' Ned nodded.

Gabriel gave a brief laugh. 'Not about me!' For Melissa's sake they must never know the truth.

Zeb's forehead creased. 'What do you mean?'

'As soon as she got me back to the house she turned me over to the servants and went to check on the horse!'

The men loved it, slapping their thighs as they roared with

224

laughter.

'So who looked after you, then?' Zeb wanted to know.

'The butler and a manservant – so I was told later, I was still unconscious.'

'There was we thinking miss would be doing most of it herself.' Joe sighed.

'The gentry only do that for their own,' Gabriel pointed out with more truth than Joe, or Melissa, would ever realise. 'When I came around, my head ached fit to burst and I thought my arms had been pulled off.'

'All right now, are they?' Billy's expression mirrored concern as he hefted the huge axe in his left hand. 'Only they big trees is more than one man can –'

'Dear life, Billy!' Chirp elbowed him. 'Give him a chance. 'Tis a bleddy miracle he's upright.'

'I don't think I can swing an axe today, Billy,' Gabriel admitted. 'But I'd like to hear how far you've –'

'Tell you later.' Billy looked past him at the sound of multiple hooves and the creak of a wagon. 'I'll supervise the loading, shall I? I expect there's other things you want to get on with?'

Glimpsing the hope in Billy's eyes Gabriel nodded, glad to see the boy eager for responsibility. It was also a timely reminder that, once they could recognise which trees to fell, they would be able to manage without him. 'Go ahead. I'll fetch the paint and mark a few more.'

Arriving back at Bosvane, Melissa left Samson with Hocking, and hurried to the house, removing her hat and pulling off her gloves as she crossed the gravel. Lobb greeted her at the door.

'Good afternoon, miss. I hope you had a pleasant afternoon?'

Reawakened anger at James Chenoweth's insensitive behaviour and her aunt's meddling interference burned beneath her breastbone. 'No, Lobb. I did not.'

'Sorry to hear that, miss.'

'It's of no consequence. But I'm glad to be home.' They were in the hall now. Trying hard to sound casual, she enquired, 'How is Gabriel? Is he still in much discomfort?'

'I understand he is very much better, miss. Before he left he charged me most particularly to thank you for your great kindness.'

Melissa stopped in mid-stride, her hand on the banister, absolutely still as she repeated carefully, 'Before he left?'

'That's right, miss. He said he had given enough trouble, and that his presence in the house, if your family learnt of it, was bound to cause you more problems which he didn't want to happen especially after you'd been so good to him.'

'Oh.' Her throat closed. She swallowed painfully. 'I see. Thank you, Lobb.'

The butler took a step forward and, lowering his voice, said gently, 'It's all for the best, miss. That young man has secrets it's better we don't know about. He showed sense and consideration leaving like he did. With respect, miss, it's time you were thinking of other things. Indeed, though I've done my best during your absence these past days, the household needs your attention. Mrs Betts is most anxious to speak to you in connection with the pass books?'

The tradesmen's accounts. Melissa made a valiant effort. 'Of course. Thank you, Lobb. Would you bring some tea to the study? And kindly tell Mrs Betts she may come as soon as she wishes.'

He bowed. 'Yes, miss. Thank you, miss.'

Melissa spent the next hour with the cook-housekeeper discussing the repair and replacement of various domestic items. She checked the pass books for the butcher, baker, grocer, and hardware shop, and counted out the money into separate piles for Mrs Betts to take to the village the following morning to settle the monthly accounts.

Then it was time to change for dinner. Leaving Sarah tidying up, Melissa walked along the passage and opened the door to her brother's room. The bed had been stripped and re-made. The counterpane lay flat. The bedside table was bare. Apart from the faint herbal scent of the salves she had applied to his wounds, there was no sign that Gabriel had ever been there. The longer they spent in each other's company the less she knew him.

Last night she had held him, nursed him, listened to his feverish ramblings. Yet he was more of a stranger than ever. She knew she shouldn't. She knew it was wrong. But she missed him, and ached with the sense of loss. Closing the door quietly, she went downstairs.

Gabriel remained in the wood until the faint sound of the horn in the yard signalled the end of the working day. He walked wearily toward the clearing. His head throbbed and his shoulders were stiff and sore. But he had selected and marked 20 more trees. Bidding the others goodnight, he headed for Daisy Mitchell's to buy a pie for his evening meal.

The surprised pleasure on her rosy face as he ducked into the shop was swept aside by concern when she saw the rainbow-hued bruises and dark, lumpy scab above his eyebrow.

'Dear life, my handsome! You should never be out.'

'It's not as bad as it looks.'

She folded her arms. 'Think I'm stupid, do you?'

'Can I have a meat and potato pie?' Gabriel asked meekly.

'I'll get 'un. Now you sit down before you fall down,' Daisy ordered, nodding toward the wooden chair near the door used by older villagers whose legs needed a brief respite before setting off home again. 'White as a sheet you are. Well, parts of you. As for the rest …' She shook her head.

Gabriel folded his tall frame onto the chair, and rested his elbows on his knees. Though he had paced himself, the afternoon had taken more out of him than he'd expected. He sat, his head hanging, while Daisy bustled about. He heard the scrape of metal, the clink of china, the sound of liquid being poured, and brisk footsteps.

'Here.' Daisy was standing beside him. 'You get this down your throat. Look dreadful, you do.'

Gabriel glanced at the cup and saucer then up at her plump face. It was puckered with anxiety.

In his past life he had drunk tea without a moment's thought. Born into a wealthy family where luxury and quality were taken for granted, it would never have occurred to him to

227

ask the cost of the food or the wines that graced the table at every mealtime.

But this past year had taught him different values. As he looked at the strong, steaming tea, a treat hoarded for special occasions, he was touched and humbled by Daisy's generosity.

'Don't worry, Mother,' he tried to grin. 'It will take a lot more than a frightened horse to see me off.' He took the cup, surprised to see his hand shaking.

'Oh yes?' She tossed her head. 'Men! Haven't got the sense they was born with. Not going to go off in a swoon, are you?'

'Swoon? Me?' He was genuinely astonished. 'Of course not.'

'You can't see what I can see,' Daisy sniffed. 'You sure now? 'Cos I couldn't lift you up. And a great lump like you on the floor wouldn't do my business no good at all.'

'I'll be all right, Mother,' he promised.

She patted his shoulder, her brief grip saying far more than words, and waddled back behind the counter.

As he sipped the strong brew and felt his strength returning, he realised for the first time how close he had been to collapse.

'Was it right what I heard? About Miss Tregonning?'

'What did you hear?'

'That she led the horse what took you up to the big house? What was she doing down there in the first place, I'd like to know? Nothing against her, she's some lovely maid. If she wasn't so tall she'd be married long since. 'Tis a shame, dear of her.'

Besieged by unfamiliar and powerful emotions, Gabriel stared into the teacup, wondering who had talked. But it was too late to worry about that now. He shrugged, wincing at the knife-like twinge, and responded only to the first part of her question.

'You tell me. I was dead to the world. Don't remember a thing.' He stood up, and set the empty cup and saucer on the counter. 'Thank you, I needed that.' Taking money from his pocket, he laid it on the counter and picked up the pie and buns she pushed toward him.

'You should still be in your bed, not out scaring decent

folks to death.'

'I've got to eat.'

'What you need is a good woman to take care of you.'

'True.' Gabriel nodded, then winked at her. 'But I'm too late, you're already spoken for.'

'Get on with you.' She blushed, and came round the counter, pausing just long enough for him to drop a kiss on her cheek before she shooed him out.

Next morning, Melissa came downstairs to the news that if she so wished she could have mackerel for breakfast as six had been found outside the back door. As he imparted the information, Lobb's expression was carefully blank.

Matching it, Melissa tucked away her pleasure at the gift, whose significance she would ponder over when she had more time.

'Thank you, I should like that. A thoughtful token of thanks, don't you agree? Far more practical than – say – flowers.'

'Indeed, miss,' Lobb agreed blandly as he poured her coffee. 'It's nice to see that our efforts were appreciated. Though I can't help but wonder what we were being thanked for on the last occasion six fresh mackerel appeared on the doorstep.' Without giving her a chance to respond, he sailed out.

The postman brought a letter from Mr Rogers. When she came to Truro to collect the money for the men's pay, might she spare him a few minutes, as there were some minor matters he wished to discuss with her.

She decided to go that morning. Captain would be better for an extra day's rest. So would she. Reaction to the accident and its aftermath had left her more shaken than she cared to admit and feeling ridiculously vulnerable. With John and Duchess still working there would be enough trees cut, stripped, and stacked to keep the haulier's wagons busy for a couple more days at least.

Late that afternoon, Gabriel and the team left the woods, returned to the yard and joined the line to collect their pay.

Aware of the men watching as he reached the table, Gabriel wondered how Melissa would react to the curious and speculative glances. Hating his inability to make it easier for her, he kept his eyes lowered, the additional tension painful in his shoulders.

'Ah, Gabriel,' she said calmly, apparently oblivious to their avid audience, 'I am glad to see you recovered.'

'Thank you, miss.' Their eyes met for an instant before he looked quickly away, anxious not to unsettle her.

'Mr Rogers has heard from Mr Nankivell that next month he would like to increase the loads to three a day. Will your team be able to manage that?'

'We'll do our best, miss.' He knuckled his forehead and bent to sign the ledger. As he picked up his money and moved on, passing Tom with a nod, he could hear Melissa thanking a blushing, tongue-tied Billy. She was magnificent. He could only guess what the effort was costing her. Ahead of him, Tansey turned.

'Coming for a drink, are you? You look like you need it. Come on,' he urged as Gabriel hesitated. 'All the lads is going down.'

'I don't know, Tansey ...'

'Got something better to do have you?'

'Sleep.'

'Get on with you, plenty of time for that. What you want is a nice glass of Cousin Jacky. Ben have had a new delivery.' He tapped the side of his nose and winked. 'Take the pain away lovely that will. If it don't, well, least you won't care no more.'

Up early that morning to go fishing, now weary and aching, Gabriel longed for his bed. But refusing the invitation would seem churlish. Nor did he want to provoke even the mildest speculation. The thought of a glass of cognac was very tempting.

The tavern was crowded with men talking, laughing, and arguing. The atmosphere, a compound of ale, wet sawdust, and sweaty bodies, was thick enough to slice. Smoke curled from clay pipes toward the low-beamed, yellow-brown ceiling. The grimy windows were firmly closed, so the only fresh air came in with the customers down a short narrow passage from the open door.

In deference to Gabriel's injuries as well as his height, which meant he either had to stand with his head between the beams or hunched between his shoulders, he had been urged into one of the pew-like benches in a corner. The rest of the group had filled the remainder of that bench and the one at right angles to it, then closed the circle by drawing up stools.

After several minutes of serious drinking during which thirsts were quenched by tankards of ale, the order was given for Cousin Jacky. Gabriel struggled with disbelief and laughter as he listened to Walter, Zeb, Ned and Tansey arguing over the brandy's quality in the same thoughtful tones – if different vocabulary – used by connoisseur friends of his father. His father. Gabriel tried to picture the marquis's face were he to walk in here now and see his younger son. He failed. Then jumped as an elbow dug into his ribs.

'That's how you got back, wasn't it?' Tansey said expectantly.

'What was?' Gabriel said.

'Smuggler's boat. Revenue cutter from Falmouth have caught one off the Lizard.'

'They have?' One of the first things he had learnt working in the yard was, whenever possible, to answer one question with another, preferably a repetition of what had just been said. Doing this convinced the men of his interest while giving nothing away. It also allowed him a few precious moments to think.

Tansey nodded. 'Walter? Where did you hear about that boat?'

'From my cousin Moses. His wife's sister's husband is a crewman on the cutter.' He went back to his story. 'Seems when the Customs men searched the boat, as well as the Cousin Jacky they found a package of secret papers. The captain said they was for Lord Grenville.'

Gabriel froze, then lifted his glass and took a large mouthful of cognac, shuddering as it went down. It burned fiercely but sharpened his senses and helped steady his nerves.

'Who's he when he's at home?' Tansey demanded.

'How the hell should I know?' Walter shrugged. 'But he must be someone important.'

'I should think he is,' Zeb put in. 'He's only the bleddy Foreign Secretary, that's all. Live up Boconnoc near Liskeard, he do. When he's not up London.'

'Know 'un, do you?' Ned enquired drily.

'No, not personal. But I got a nephew in service with the family.'

'Well, what do he want with papers from France?' Tansey demanded. 'Sounds like a bleddy spy to me.'

'For once in your life you could be right.' Walter pointed his pipe at Tansey. 'But the spies is on our side. See, Moses said the captain told the Customs officer that without people like him willing to risk their lives bringing back information from agents in France, our government wouldn't know what was going on over the Channel. It could make the difference between winning the war or losing 'un. So instead of treating him like a criminal, they should be giving him a reward, 'cos he was a public benefactor.'

His heart thumping, Gabriel forced himself to join in the laughter.

'That Customs man have got some job,' Zeb grinned. 'Smuggling's against the law and the punishments is hard. But if they papers is real, then the captain is as like to be given a purse of gold sovereigns as a fine. And if the Customs officer don't deliver them, then it could be he that gets locked up.'

'Yes, but that isn't the end of it,' Walter announced, and all heads turned toward him. 'The captain and crew is all being kept in the gaol. They aren't allowed no visitors neither.'

'What? Why not?' Chirp frowned. 'That's never right.'

'All I know is that there's two men come down from London to ask them questions.'

'Here, Walter.' Isaac Bowden, another of the yard workers, broke in. 'Where did you say that boat was from?'

'Mullion.'

'Know the captain's name, do you? Only my wife got cousins down Mullion way what do a bit of free-trading.'

'I believe 'tis Janner Stevens.'

Isaac shook his head. 'No. Don't mean nothing to me.'

Gabriel stared at the remaining brandy in his glass. It shivered as his hands shook uncontrollably. Janner Stevens was captain of the boat that had brought him back to Cornwall. His head spun. The sweat of physical weakness and fear trickled down his temples and from under his arms. Though desperate to get out into the fresh air, where there was space and freedom, he dared not move. He tried to think.

There might be any number of reasons for government officials to question the smugglers. He was certainly not the only escapee helped by the free traders. His name while in France had been Pierre Durtelle. No one could connect that man with Gabriel Ennis.

But the harder he tried to dismiss his anxiety, the more it increased. It wasn't about the package of papers or the contraband government officials were questioning Janner Stevens: it was his live cargo they were interested in.

It was obvious from the way Walter and the others were talking that such a visit had never occurred before. So it had to him they were after. But whom were they trying to find, Pierre Durtelle or Lord Roland Stratton? How many people knew both were the same man? Was his escape known to whoever had betrayed him? Gabriel's sweat turned to ice as he realised that because he didn't know who had turned him in to the French, he had no idea who was hunting him, or why.

'Here,' Tansey nudged him. 'You all right? Look sick as a shag you do.'

Gabriel touched the thick scab above his eye. 'Don't feel so good,' he muttered. 'I think I need some air.'

'Be all right on your own, will you?'

'I'll be fine. My head's giving me hell, that's all.' Gabriel pushed himself up.

''Tis more than enough by the look of you,' said Tansey. 'You mind how you go.'

As Gabriel eased his way out through the crush of bodies he heard Tansey explaining his sudden departure.

'... Kicked in the head by a bleddy cart horse.'

Then he passed from the thick fug of the tavern into cool, fresh air. He stood for a few moments breathing deeply, waiting for his thundering heart to slow, and for his head to clear.

Daylight was fading to dusk, earlier tonight due to a thick blanket of cloud. The breeze blowing up from the south felt damp. Gabriel set off along the street. Already shivery from this new shock on top of the weakness resulting from his accident, he wanted to reach the protection of the shack before the rain began.

He'd gone only a few yards when behind him someone shouted, a man's voice, spoiling for a fight. Assuming a quarrel had spilled into the street from one of the many inns Gabriel ignored it. Another shout was followed by the sound of pounding boots coming closer, then his waistcoat was seized, jerking him round.

In the split second before a flailing fist caught him a glancing blow on the jaw, he recognised his assailant as one of two men roughly his own age who'd been drinking just inside the doorway of the tavern. He'd been aware of their glances, but their checked shirts, neckerchiefs, and trousers had identified them as fishermen and he'd thought no more about them, too concerned with Walter's news.

Instinctively he raised his hands to defend himself. 'What – ?' he began, but got no further as the second man punched him.

'Think I wouldn't find out?' the first man growled, his sun and wind-burned features vicious, narrowed eyes glittering with anger. 'You marked her, you bastard.'

Gabriel had been taught to box, but there was no science to this mauling. It was dirty and brutal, a deliberate attempt to inflict as much damage as possible.

'I don't know what you're talking about,' he shouted, trying desperately to parry the blows as they circled him, attacking with feet and fists. 'Listen to me –'

'Bleddy liar! She told me it was you!'

'Go on, Jed,' the second man urged. 'Kick the bugger where it hurt. If you don't, I will.'

'Stop this!' Gabriel roared so loudly his voice cracked,

lashing out and feeling pain shoot up his arm as his knuckles connected with the side of a skull.

As the man addressed as Jed reeled back, the other one charged in, head low, fists lower. 'Mess with my sister, would you?'

'I don't know your sister,' Gabriel gasped.

'That's not what she said,' his assailant hissed. 'Attacked her in her own home.'

'Oi! What's going on?' Walter bellowed. 'Jed Treen, what in God's name do you think you're doing of?'

As Billy, Zeb, Joseph, Chirp, and Ned grabbed the two panting men and hauled them off, still kicking and flailing, Gabriel staggered back and leant against a wall, his arms clasped across his stomach and ribs.

He sucked in rasping breaths as he fought waves of sickening dizziness. Blackness lapped at the edges of his mind, threatening to engulf him. He hung on grimly, forcing it back by sheer effort of will.

'That bastard attacked my Sal!' Jed spat.

'Is that so?' Walter said. 'She told you that, did she?'

'Too right she did, 'specially when I landed her one after I seen the bruises.'

*Sal.* Gabriel remembered: the bold, teasing girl in the group who had accosted him in the street, then tried to pull him into the circle dancing around the bonfire.

'What bruises was they then?' Tansey asked, pushing through the gathering crowd.

'All over her – never you bleddy mind where they was!'

'When was this attack supposed to have happened?' Walter demanded.

'What do you mean, *supposed*?' Sal's brother snarled. 'In some terrible state she was. Crying and all.'

'When, Jed?' Walter pressed.

'Night afore last.'

A murmur ran through the crowd. 'Where was you while all this was going on?' Walter enquired.

'Where do you think? Out fishing of course.'

'It wasn't Gabriel,' Walter said.

Jed glared around wildly. 'What do you mean it wasn't him? Sal said –'

'I don't give a bugger what Sal said,' Walter broke in.

'Here, you watch your mouth, that's my sister –'

'Shut up, Eddy,' Walter snapped. 'You're bleddy idiots, the pair of you. You got the wrong man.'

'Oh yeah?' Jed sneered. 'How would you know that?'

'Because,' Billy strode forward and glowered down at the fisherman, his fists clenched, 'two days ago Gabriel was took up to the big house on a stretcher. Kept there all night he was, unconscious. He only come away yesterday afternoon.'

Jed glared at the nodding men. 'You're having me on. I don't believe a word of it.'

Gabriel pushed himself away from the wall, pressing his bandaged wrist against his forehead to staunch the blood trickling down his face from the torn scab.

'Miss Tregonning's butler looked after me. He knows what time I left. Ask him.' There was more murmuring and heads nodded.

Tansey tapped Jed on the shoulder. 'If you was to spend a bit more time home, your missus wouldn't be running round the village like a bitch on heat.'

Ignoring the sniggers, Jed squared up to Tansey, as belligerent as a terrier. 'How's a man supposed to put food on the table if he don't work?'

'Get on, Jed,' Zeb jeered. 'You get off that boat and straight go in the Anchor. I reckon you do drink more than you eat.'

'So what's wrong with a man having a pint of ale when he come back after a hard day's fishing?' Jed snarled, but with less certainty. 'Tisn't none of your bleddy business anyhow.'

'It is when you beat up an innocent man,' Walter snapped.

'Come on, Jed,' Eddy muttered, putting his arm around his brother- in-law.

'Yeah, you get on home,' Tansey called amiably. 'And don't forget to ask your missus who really gived her they bruises.'

As Gabriel turned away, Billy touched his shoulder. 'You all right?'

Gabriel nodded. 'I will be when I've had some sleep.'

'See you home, shall I?'

'No. No, I'd rather be on my own.'

'I don't mind, honest.'

'No, Billy. Thanks all the same. You go on back with the others.'

'Night, then.'

'Good night.' Turning away, Gabriel pressed a hand to his bruised side, praying no ribs were broken, and concentrated on reaching the shack before he collapsed.

# Chapter Seventeen

The first large, slow drops burst on the leaves like overripe berries then slid off to hit the path beneath with a soft thud. Intermittent at first, they began falling faster, driven by a gusty wind that made the leaves whisper and sigh and the branches creak. By the time Gabriel reached the shack, staggering like a drunk and shivering as his temperature began to climb, his shirt was soaked, his hair hung in ropes, and rain dribbled in cold rivulets down his burning face.

Racked with pain from the beating, every movement agony as his bruised muscles stiffened, he shut the door and slid the wooden bar across. No fire would burn outside. It was too wet. If he tried to light one in here he would suffocate. In any case he hadn't the strength. Desperate to lie down, feeling too ill even to remove his wet clothes, he crawled beneath the blankets. Shaken by violent tremors, he slipped helplessly into a state between sleep and delirium.

His body had given up. But, deranged by rising fever, his mind whirled with vivid images, razor sharp and terrifying. Suddenly he was reliving his capture in the shipyard: the soldiers grabbing his arms, shouting at him while his erstwhile workmates drew back and turned away, dissociating themselves from him and whatever he was guilty of. He could feel his heart racing, his mouth sour with a metallic taste of fear as he protested in angry bewilderment, trying frantically to work out what had gone wrong, and how he had been found out. The images dissolved and reformed, taking him further back. Back to the incident that had driven him into exile and deadly danger.

In Plymouth, on business for his father, he had joined a

party of friends at a gentlemen's club near the dockyard. Stepping out into the street after a pleasant evening, they almost bumped into two young naval officers who were passing. One suddenly stopped.

'Good God, it's Stratton.' The young man's speech was slurred, his tone deriding. 'Lord Roland Stratton. Well met indeed.'

Gabriel turned. Not recognising either man, he addressed the one who had spoken. 'And you are?'

'Lieutenant Frederick Poldyce of His Majesty's ship *Audacious*.' He made an exaggerated bow. 'I believe you're acquainted with my elder brother, Richard. He mentioned meeting you at one of Lady St Cleer's routs. He's a second lieutenant aboard the *Queen Charlotte*. Was,' he corrected himself, face twisting with grief. 'Not any more. Dead, you see. Killed in battle. The Glorious First of June.' Biting cynicism edged the man's tone.

Gabriel dipped his head. 'You have my deepest sympathy.' Aware that no words of his could ease such loss, he turned away.

'Keep it!' Frederick Poldyce snarled. 'I don't want your damned sympathy!'

Startled, Gabriel and his friends glanced back. Poldyce's companion tried to take his arm, but was roughly shaken off. 'Why would I want sympathy from a man who stays safe at home and leaves others to fight for Britain's safety? Aye, and die for it.'

Gabriel stiffened, his sharply drawn breath hissing between his teeth at this stinging slight.

'Ignore him, Stratton,' one of his friends urged. 'The young fool's foxed. Brother's death so recent, bound to have hit him hard.'

'Especially as *Audacious* got separated from the rest of the fleet and didn't even take part in the battle,' another added. 'Come, let's go.'

Gabriel struggled to control his temper, for the abuse was unjust. He had been desperate to join the navy, but his father, citing a more urgent duty, had insisted he remain at home. It was vital that he remain alive and unharmed, for should his brother succumb to the weakness that had plagued him since childhood, the responsibility of the title, the estates, and the future of the family would fall to him.

Not trusting himself to speak, Gabriel turned with them to walk away, but Poldyce cried out again. 'You're a coward, Stratton, A craven coward. Even now you hide behind your friends.'

As his companions gasped at this blatant insult, Gabriel spun round, his voice taut with anger and disgust. 'Go home, Poldyce. You're drunk.'

Breaking free of his friend's restraining grasp, Frederick Poldyce hurled himself forward. 'Perhaps I am. But in the morning I'll be sober, whereas you will still be a coward.'

As Gabriel's fists clenched, his friends grabbed his arms. 'No, Stratton,' they pleaded. 'Don't give him the satis –'

Poldyce struck Gabriel an open-handed slap across the face. 'What price your honour, my Lord?' he taunted, his pallid sweating face distorted by a sneer. 'What does it take to –?'

'Enough,' Gabriel said with deadly calm. 'My friends will wait upon yours.'

When the seconds failed to reach agreement – Gabriel's friends acknowledged the insult to be beyond bearing, and Poldyce's refusal to apologise made a duel inescapable – a day and time were fixed. Gabriel found himself in a quiet park in the cool of a summer dawn, Trusting that, having had time to come to his senses, the young naval officer would wish the matter resolved in a manner that satisfied honour while causing no injury, Gabriel planned to fire into the air.

But Poldyce's second, offering him the pistol box and inviting him to choose his weapon, muttered a warning. Poldyce would shoot to kill. 'It's the shame, my Lord,' he whispered. 'He can't bear the shame.'

What shame? That his brother had died when his own ship, running off to avoid capture, had put into Plymouth and missed the battle? But what, Gabriel wondered, had that to do with him? The shock of realisation hit him like a fist. It had nothing whatever to do with him. In the wrong place at the wrong time, he was simply the means to an end. Frederick Poldyce had deliberately provoked the quarrel, issuing a challenge impossible to refuse, either to test his own courage, or because, for reasons Gabriel could not even guess at, he wanted to end his life but could not dishonour his family by committing suicide.

*So I am to do it for him?* Gabriel gazed at the pistol, coldly furious at being used, and for not having realised. Yet how could he have known? It was too late now. There was no going back.

They took their places, walked the requisite number of paces, turned, and fired. The loud reports, almost simultaneous, sent startled birds fluttering skyward. His own aim steady and true, Gabriel felt the searing heat of Poldyce's shot graze his arm, saw his opponent jerk and a crimson flower bloom high on the shoulder of his white shirt. Knees buckling, his face the colour of ashes, the young lieutenant crumpled to the grass and was quickly carried to the waiting carriage by two friends with the doctor in attendance.

'You aimed wide,' Gabriel's second accused.

Gabriel glanced up, surprised. 'Of course.'

'After what his man said? Poldyce meant to kill you.'

Gabriel's smile was bitter. 'No, he didn't. What he wanted was for me to kill him.'

He had not intended to tell his father anything about the incident. But the letter that arrived a few days later, shaking him to the core with its news of Frederick Poldyce's death, left him no choice.

The marquis aged 20 years in as many seconds. Alternately anguished and raging, he first entreated then commanded his son to flee the country. Although there had been no intent to kill, Stratton had fired the shot as a result of which the young man had died. The distinction was too fine to be risked, for murder meant the gallows. To protect the inheritance, he had to live. Therefore he must go. Accepting that he had no choice, Gabriel agreed, but insisted on calling upon Frederick's father first.

An intimate of Lord Grenville, Sir John Poldyce held an

influential position in the Foreign Office, and though he and the rnarquess had met on several occasions, acquaintance had not deepened into friendship. A cold man was how the marquis had described him, not easy to know and hard to like, though he enjoyed the trust of both Lord Grenville and the Prime Minister, William Pitt.

Waiting in the library while the butler went to announce his presence to the grieving father, Gabriel felt more nervous than he had when facing Frederick's pistol. At last, Sir John had appeared. A gaunt man dressed all in black with thinning, grizzled hair and eyes set deep beneath untidy brows, he carried himself ramrod straight. Though his face was grey and ravaged by grief, his voice as he greeted Gabriel betrayed no trace of emotion.

'Lord Stratton.' He inclined his head briefly.

'Thank you for seeing me, Sir John. Under the circumstances ...'

'Quite so. Why have you come?'

'I am to go abroad. But I could not leave without – Sir, I beg you will accept my sincere condolences. I am most dreadfully sorry.'

Sir John gave a brief nod, and the lines of suffering deepened. 'As I understand it, the quarrel was not of your making.'

'Even so –'

'Even so my son is dead. Both my sons ...' He shuddered, then turned and walked behind a large table that served as a desk.

'Sir, I would have eloped. But I was informed –' He could not say it. He could not tell this grieving man that his younger son had planned both murder and suicide. 'I was informed that such action would not be honourable. Believe me, I intended only a flesh wound.'

'Indeed.' In that one word Gabriel heard surprise, disbelief, and censure. He knew guilt was unwarranted – he had not sought the confrontation – yet it still weighed heavy. In the silence that followed, he felt growing helplessness and discomfort. He did not regret coming. Honour had demanded he face the consequences of his actions, even if they were entirely unforeseen. But perhaps it had not been wise.

'I think you must desire my absence, Sir John, so –'

'No. Not yet.' He indicated a chair. 'Please sit down.' Seating himself, Sir John lightly tapped his chin with steepled fingers, his brow deeply furrowed, seeming lost in thought.

Gabriel waited, not sure what was expected of him. The silence dragged on.

At last Sir John looked up. 'Tell me, was it you who brought back an important package from Switzerland after one of our agents was shot during a skirmish with French soldiers?'

Startled, for he had understood the matter to be one Lord Grenville had kept secret from his colleagues in the Foreign Office, Gabriel hesitated. But it had been some time ago and doubtless what was necessarily top secret then had since become common knowledge within the department. He nodded.

'It was.'

'How have you occupied yourself since your return?'

'On my father's estates. My purpose for being in Switzerland was to learn forest management. Since I came back I have been managing the woodland and coppices. You may be aware that my brother is not in good health –'

'Indeed.' Sir John cut him short. 'Is your role purely supervisory?'

'On the contrary, with so many men being pressed into the navy or joining the militia regiments forming to defend England against invasion, I've had little choice but to do much of the physical work myself. Though I'm fortunate in having an excellent aide in my father's estate manager. I've also learnt a great deal from the carpenters and shipwrights who buy wood from Trerose.'

Sir John's thin smile signalled satisfaction. 'You are fluent in French, presumably, but do you understand the Breton dialect?'

'Yes. I believe most Cornishmen do.'

'How very fortuitous. Such skills will provide the perfect disguise.'

'I beg your pardon?' Why would he need a disguise?

'For you to obtain work as a shipwright, first at Lorient, France's major merchant and naval shipbuilding centre, then at Brest, the chief naval base and dockyard for the French fleet operating in the Atlantic. As you're probably aware, Brest is currently under open blockade by the British Channel fleet. We, that is the government, need information on French coastal defences, and the number and current state of ships under construction or repair.'

Gabriel was startled. 'You want *me* – ?'

'You have to go abroad anyway. You could, at the same time, perform a valuable service.' The piercing gaze was intent. 'Can you do it? Will you do it?'

Gabriel stood up. 'Yes, Sir John, I will. And I thank you for the opportunity.'

A spasm crossed the older man's face. 'My own sons' service was so short.' He drew a deep breath. 'Do you have any questions?'

Gabriel thought quickly. 'Presumably you will want information on as regular a basis as possible. How am I to send it back to England?'

'You will find the Breton smugglers helpful. They liaise with their Cornish counterparts in mid-Channel. Any letters given to them will reach me.' He held out a fine-boned hand and Gabriel gripped it. 'God speed, Lord Stratton,' he said formally. 'And good luck.'

News of the fight between Jed Treen and Gabriel reached Bosvane early the next morning. Taking one of the carriage horses down the village early to have a loose shoe replaced, John overheard the blacksmith describing the incident to Edgar Rawling, who had arrived to pick up a mended ploughshare. Back in the stables, John related it to Hocking, who told Mrs Betts when he went across to the kitchen for his breakfast.

'He was in the middle of telling her when I went down for another pitcher of hot water to top up your bath, miss,' Sarah said, picking up the silver-backed brush. 'So I made him start again. I thought you'd want to know, seeing as how 'tis only a day or two since that great horse nearly done for Gabriel in the woods.'

Steeling herself not to show any reaction, and compressing her lips to hold back the flood of questions that would betray her and compromise him, Melissa sat down in front of the dressing-table mirror. Her silence was all the encouragement Sarah needed.

'That Sal Treen,' she snorted in disgust. 'Mother always said she'd come to a bad end. Even when we was small I wasn't allowed to play with her.' Taking the pins from her mistress's hair, she loosened the black tresses and began to sweep the brush through them.

Melissa gathered her silk and lace robe closer, as if she were cold. 'Mrs Treen said Gabriel attacked her? In her own home?' She should not be having this conversation. It was totally wrong to gossip with the servants. But this was different, she told herself. It involved someone employed on the estate. That alone justified her concern. But the fact that the incident involved Gabriel made it impossible not to ask. She had to know.

'That's what Jed said. But I don't believe a word of it.' Sarah was scornful. 'Sal can take care of herself. When she was 18 Jimmy Doidge took a shine to her but she wouldn't have him. So, one night when he seen her walking along the street, he hid in one of the op-ways. He wasn't going to do no harm; Jimmy wouldn't hurt a fly. He just wanted to give her a fright, pay her back, like. Jimmy isn't very tall, but he's broad and built like a brick privvy. But Sal punched him in the face and down he went. Out cold, he was.'

Despite her anxiety Melissa had to fight laughter at the picture conjured by Sarah's graphic description.

'That's how I don't believe it. There isn't a man in the village would dare put a finger on Sal 'less she said he could. I tell you what I think,' Sarah confided, lifting the thick, glossy hair off Melissa's neck with long, upward strokes, ''tis my guess Sal have got a new fancy man. Jed come home unexpected and nearly caught 'em. I think the chap made a run for it. That's the first bit of sense he showed if you ask me. But there's Sal looking like she've been tipped over the hedge. Well, she can't tell Jed what she've really been up to, so she tells him someone set on her.'

'But,' Melissa said blankly, 'if someone had assaulted her she would have bruises –'

'Exactly, miss,' Sarah said, her face wrinkling with distaste. 'That's why she said she'd been set on.'

Melissa was shocked. Though she'd never experienced it herself, among her acquaintances she had observed courtship to be a matter of formality and etiquette, depth of feeling indicated by lingering glances, small gifts, chaperoned rides and frequent calls. The concept of physical contact so close and so violent that it resembled a beating was beyond her imagination. She'd had no idea such things happened.

But why had this woman accused Gabriel? It couldn't have been him. How could she be so sure? After all, how well did she really know him? The truth was she didn't. All she had was intuition. But how reliable was that? Reaching into her heart and mind, he had awakened emotions and desires she never suspected were there, so how could she be objective? The idea of him with other women … She jerked her head to block the thought before it could translate into unbearable images, wincing as the brush tugged sharply. But at least she had an excuse for the springing tears that made her eyes glisten.

'Oh, I'm some sorry, miss. All right are you?'

'Yes. I'm fine.' She swallowed. 'Was – anyone hurt in the fight?'

'Well, they was both able to walk. But from what I hear Gabriel got the worst of it. Two against one, see? Billy wanted to take him home, but Gabriel wouldn't let him. Said he could manage by hisself. But I can't see him working today. Good job 'tis Sunday tomorrow: give him a chance to rest and get over it before he go back on Monday. There, all done.' She put down the brush and turned to pick up the lilac round gown.

Melissa remained silent during the rest of her toilette. But as she was leaving the room to go down to breakfast, she paused in the doorway. 'Lay out my riding habit and boots, will you, Sarah? I'll be going to the yard later.'

There were two letters beside her plate. Recognising Aunt Lucy's hand, she quickly broke the seal and unfolded the single sheet. The small writing and crossed lines made it difficult to read, but gradually she relaxed into a smile at the news of her mother's ongoing recovery.

*'It is a slow business,'* Aunt Lucy wrote, *'but I have persuaded her to drink a teaspoonful of my Aromatic tincture in a wineglass of water twice a day, and it has worked wonders.'* Recalling that Aunt Lucy's Aromatic tincture consisted of an ounce each of Peruvian bark and dried pressed orange peel infused for ten days in a pint of brandy, she was not surprised that her mother's spirits had begun to lift. She read on.

*'... Her cough lingered so long I was beginning to fear it might settle on her lungs. Though I daresay that was not to be wondered at considering her weakened state. But I made up a tea from linseed, liquorice root, and coltsfoot leaves sweetened with a little honey and it troubles her very little now and should be quite gone by next week. So you are not to concern yourself, for she is quite comfortable here and has at last begun to accept what has happened. I rely on you to let us know at once if you should receive any news of George. Meanwhile, take good care of yourself, my dear. Your mother sends her love. Ever your affectionate aunt, Lucy.*

Setting the letter aside with a slow exhalation that released part of the deep anxiety underlying her every action since her mother's departure, she picked up the second. She didn't recognise the writing and instantly the fear of more bad news, ever-present at the back of her mind, coiled like a snake about her heart and squeezed.

'Tea or coffee, miss?' Lobb's enquiry broke through her dread. Whatever the letter contained would have to be dealt with. Delay would not make it easier. The sooner she opened it, the sooner she would know. Steadying her fluttering nerves with a deep breath, she broke the seal with hands that trembled.

'Tea, please,' she said absently, as she scanned the sheet. Relief that it didn't concern her brother meant the true import of the words didn't immediately register. When she realised what the letter was saying, her gaze flew back to the beginning and she read it again, one hand flying to her mouth as she gasped.

'Not bad news I hope, miss?'

She glanced up as Lobb finished pouring. 'It's from Lieutenant Bracey's mother. He's been captured.'

'Dear life, miss! I'm sorry to hear that. I remember we had the pleasure of entertaining Lieutenant Bracey here last year. A very pleasant young gentleman, as I recall. May I enquire what happened?'

Melissa returned her gaze to the letter. 'His ship was involved in a battle with the French off Lorient. Good heavens.' She looked up at the butler. 'It was four months ago.' How swiftly the time had passed. And how much had happened. 'The squadron managed to take two French ships, but the *Defence* was sunk. Robert was captured, along with other officers and a large part of the crew, and is being held prisoner.'

'Now don't you go worrying, miss. I understand that captured officers are treated well. You know, with decent food and all. From what I hear, they don't all stay in prison either. I'm told that if they've got money and give their word of honour not to try and escape, they go and live in grand houses and castles and such-like.'

Melissa recalled the terrible wounds on Gabriel's throat and wrists, and the scars criss-crossing his back. He had told her little, and had even cut that short. But his damaged body was eloquent enough. He too had been a prisoner in France. Why had his treatment been so different? She shuddered and glanced up at the butler. 'But that's not like being in prison at all.'

'Except they can't leave, miss,' Lobb pointed out gently. 'They can't come home.'

An hour later, having picked up a pot of salve and more clean bandages, Melissa checked that Sarah was still upstairs and went to the kitchen. Mrs Betts had gone to the village and Agnes was out in the yard, beating rugs. Wrapping cold meat, bread rolls, cheese, and two raspberry tarts in a clean napkin, she packed them in a basket with the salve and linen. Then, carrying the basket into the study, she decanted some brandy into her father's silver hip flask. Leaving her hoard out of sight behind a chair, she went upstairs to change into her habit.

When she came down she picked up the basket. But instead of calling at the stables for Samson, she quickly crossed the terrace, walked down the garden, and climbed over the railings into the park.

The sun was warm, the sky a glorious forget-me-not blue, and the grass sparkled with droplets of moisture that glittered in the sunlight like a million scattered diamonds. In the wood the night's heavy rain lingered in water-filled ruts. Beneath the trees the air was cool and heavy with the loamy smell of vegetation, leaf mould, and damp earth. A fitful breeze had sprung up, shaking the leaves so that every so often a cascade of droplets pattered onto the ground.

The shack looked deserted. The door was closed. The hearthstones were cold and wet, as were the blackened remnants of previous blazes. She rapped gently on the rough wood. There was no reply. But she had no doubt he was there. She could sense his presence. She knocked again and, putting her face close to the door, called softly.

'Gabriel, it's me.' She thought she heard something. But it was so brief and faint it might have been the wind in the trees, or a bird. 'I heard what happened last night. I've brought you some food, and clean bandages.' She waited. After a long pause she heard the rustle of movement, then his voice, hoarse and low-pitched.

'Please, miss, go home. I-I'm not fit – You shouldn't have come.'

'Well, I'm here, and I'm not leaving until I've seen how you are.'

'I'm all right.'

'No, you're not. You're hurt. I can hear it in your voice.' More movement was followed by a groan, quickly smothered. 'Please, Gabriel, let me help.'

The wooden bar slid slowly back and the door opened a few inches. She waited, expecting to see his face appear in the gap. But it didn't. A heavy dragging sound, overlaid by harsh breathing, was followed by the soft thump of something falling. She pushed the door, and it opened to reveal Gabriel's prostrate form. He had collapsed onto his makeshift bed, a hand shielding his face, his head turned away. Filtered by the leaves, the dappled sunlight was still strong enough to reveal the purple bruises, the dark streaks and smears of dried blood on his arm, and the stain covering the front of his shirt. Melissa's stomach turned over and she swallowed.

'Faint,' he muttered. 'Sorry. You shouldn't –'

'Sshh. And don't try to move.' Compassion, vying with fury at those responsible for his injuries, enabled her to ignore her own queasiness. Kneeling beside him, she reached into the basket for the silver flask and unscrewed the top.

'Can you lift your head? I have brandy.' Her voice died as he lowered his arm and turned toward her. Runnels of dried blood caked one side of his face. The cut above his eyebrow had once more scabbed over. But beneath the crusting of blood his eye was swollen and plum-coloured, as was that side of his jaw. She bit her tongue hard to stop herself crying out. It was *he* who was hurt. Her shock and horror must be put aside.

'I don't –' he croaked. 'I can't –'

'It's all right. I'll help you,' she said with quiet calm that belied a thundering heart full of powerful, unnerving feelings. Slipping her hand behind his head, swallowing hard as her fingers encountered tangled hair stiff with dried blood, she gently raised him and put the flask to his lips. He took two deep swallows and shuddered. She laid him down again.

'Is there any water, or must I fetch it from the spring?'

'Bucket,' he rasped, and pointed.

Hauling the bucket over, she dipped a cup. 'Would you like a drink before I clean your face?'

'You can't –'

'Well, there's no one else. Do you want me to help you up again?'

'No.' Painfully he levered himself up on one elbow. With one eye crusted shut he couldn't focus and she had to place the cup in his trembling hand. After draining it he handed it back, and sank down again.

'Thank you.' This time he didn't turn away. 'How did you find out?'

'From Sarah, my maid. She heard it from the groom, who heard it from the blacksmith. So I imagine it's all over the village.' His question opened the floodgates, and all the yearning, anger, sadness, distrust, shame, and craving for reassurance that had been seething inside her since early that morning spilled over. 'I don't understand. Why did this woman accuse *you*? You would never –' She broke off, looking down quickly.

'How do you know?' he rasped, his voice too soft for her to detect any inflection.

'I – I just do,' she whispered. 'Am I wrong?'

His undamaged eye met hers. 'No. I did not touch her.'

'Then why?' But now the question was driven by puzzlement not awful doubt. 'Why say it was you?'

He started to shrug, and winced as his battered body protested. 'I don't know. Revenge, perhaps? May I have another drink?' She quickly passed him the refilled cup, watched him swallow, and saw his strength beginning to return. 'I've only spoken to her twice. The first time she was in the street with a group of her friends and would not let me pass. The second was the night of St Peter's Tide.'

'What's she like?'

'Pretty, lively, and very bold. She wanted to me to dance with her. But I declined.'

'Why?' It was out before Melissa could stop it. She felt a blush creep up her throat. She turned away to set the cup down, acutely aware of her hot colour and the impropriety of her question. Where was her dignity? 'I expect because she's married.'

'That is certainly reason enough. But even if she were not, my reaction would have been the same. I do not find her at all attractive.'

Ashamed of her relief, Melissa could no longer contain her anxiety and it burst out disguised as anger. 'Sarah said Billy offered to help but you wouldn't let him. What if you hadn't got back here? What if you had collapsed? You would have lain out in the rain all night.'

'But I didn't.'

'You took a terrible risk.'

'You know why I refused. I don't want anyone to know I live here. I don't want visitors dropping by.'

Melissa stared down at her hands, guilt-stricken as she realised what she had done. Showing as much tact and consideration as Aunt. Louisa, she had put her own need to see him, her own need for reassurance, above his already stated desire to be left alone. 'Oh. I'm so sorry,' she whispered, and started to scramble to her feet.

His hand shot out and grasped hers. 'No.'

She froze: gazing blindly at the floor, aware only of his touch, the strength of his grip. Hot shivers rippled over her skin. She couldn't catch her breath and felt a strange quaking deep inside. Twenty-one years of conditioning shrieked that this was wrong. But that wasn't how it felt.

'Don't you understand?' His voice was low and urgent. 'If they knew where I live, you could no longer –' He cut himself off, then started again. 'While no one knows that I am here, you are protected from rumour and gossip.'

Her gasp of ironic laughter was shaded with despair. 'If only that were true, but it isn't. Surely you have heard the men talking at the yard? Though I believe that, in general, they are kindly disposed toward me. But with my relatives it is different. My behaviour and my unmarried state are an embarrassment. The disappointing result – I am frequently reminded – of parental indulgence and my own wilfulness. I have only to exchange a few words with a member of the male sex, be it about the weather or the war, for gossip to fly. Then I am besieged by visits from my aunts, all agog with hope and speculation.'

She ought to withdraw her hand. But though her conscience was sending commands, her muscles would not respond. Nor did he move to release it. She could not, dare not, look at him for fear of what he might see. She was adrift, out of her depth. His touch had pushed her there. Yet while he held her she felt safe.

'Right now,' he said quietly, 'no one knows where either of us is. But have you thought about the risk you are taking?'

Sharply conscious of her attraction to him, of their clasped hands, her nerves leapt. She cleared her throat. 'You have never given me reason to consider myself in any danger.'

'Melissa,' he murmured. 'How little you understand your effect on a man. But I meant the risk to your reputation should it ever become known you are making your visits without a chaperon. Even though –' his voice grew harsh and strained '– you are here from motives of kindness and charity.'

Charity. Was that how he saw it? Was it not the wisest explanation for her presence? As she shook her bent head, her laugh held more pain than amusement. 'It's strange. Just weeks ago my aunt warned my mother that no man who valued his good name would wish to be associated with me.'

'Why? What terrible thing had you done? Ah. Of course. Your interest in the yard.'

She nodded. 'Since my father's death my unsuitable interests seem suddenly less of a problem. Perhaps the fact that, should my brother not return alive from the West Indies, I will inherit a considerable fortune makes it easier now for gentlemen to overlook my disadvantages.' Tension tightened her voice. 'James certainly finds it so.'

'James?'

'A distant cousin, or so my aunt describes him. Though I do not recall ever meeting him before. Even if I did like him, which I don't, for there is something deceitful in his manner, how could I think well of a man who would talk of marriage at our first meeting, and while I am in mourning?'

'How indeed?' His voice was oddly hollow.

'At least I may come and visit you without fear of receiving a marriage proposal.' She bent her head as hot tears stung her eyes. She had made herself to say it aloud, forced herself to face cruel reality. 'You can have no idea,' she babbled on, her throat aching, 'what it feels like to be courted and flattered for what you hold title to, and not for the person you are.'

'Can I not?' he muttered.

'I beg your pardon?'

'You are of age –' he was brusque '– so you are free to make your own choices. No one can force you into marriage against your will. To swim against the tide of convention demands great strength of character, but you have that in plenty. Take heed, though. For the more freedom you claim, the higher the price.'

'What is the price?'

His face changed, emotions passing like cloud shadows across his bruised and blood-streaked features as he regarded her. 'Loneliness.'

'Oh that,' she murmured, shrugging lightly, 'I've been paying for a long time.'

His fingers tightened for an instant, then releasing her hand he lay back, closing his good eye, his features drawn, whether in pain or exhaustion she couldn't tell. Pulling the bucket closer, she took the cloths and salve from the basket.

It took some time to clean all the blood from his face. As she sponged and wiped, taking great care not to reopen cuts or press too hard on bruised and swollen flesh, she rinsed the cloth over and over again and watched the water in the bucket turn pink, then red. While half of her concentrated on what she was doing, the other half shimmered with awareness of the man himself. On one hand it was a simple act of kindness. But on the other, because of her attraction to him, it was an act of great intimacy. Far greater than when she had nursed him at the house. Then he had been unconscious. Now he was not. Despite the coolness of the water she grew hot, and her hands began to tremble.

He lay unnaturally still, emanating tension, deep lines etched between his brows and either side of his mouth. Eventually she could stand it no longer. 'I'm so sorry,' she blurted. 'I really am trying to be gentle, but –'

'You're shaking.' His eyes snapped open. 'It is too much for you. I should never have let you –'

'No! No, you are mistaken. It's just – I –' She could not tell him, for their situation was impossible. She had no right to voice a truth that might embarrass him, and must surely shame her. 'You must forgive me, it's just that – I received a letter this morning with some disturbing news about a friend. He's in the navy, serving in one of the ships of the Channel squadron. Well, he was. His ship was sunk during an action and he's been taken prisoner. Please, lie back. I'm almost finished.'

He lay down again, and closed his eyes. 'Have you known him long?'

'About three years. He and my brothers were at Naval College together. But I met him at an assembly in Truro.'

'A local family?' His eyes were still closed, and she could detect nothing but polite interest in his tone. Perhaps he was asking simply to take her mind off the unpleasantness of her task. He couldn't know that though she wished he had not been hurt she was intensely glad to be able to do this for him. It was so little compared to all he had done for her.

'They live at Malpas. Robert is so much at sea that it is more a friendship of letters. Through him I learnt much about life aboard ship, about the battles, and the inevitable casualties.' His frown deepened. 'In truth,' she said quickly, 'I preferred that to his protestations of affection. Besides, though I do not think he intended it so, his letters in some measure prepared me for the day that we heard my elder brother had been killed in battle.' After a short silence, she took a deep breath. 'I'm nearly finished.' She opened the pot of salve and, with shaking fingers, smeared it carefully along the fresh scab. 'This will help the healing, but I fear you will always bear a scar.' She edged away, wiping the residue from her fingers.

He sat up, looking away from her. 'You must go.'

He was right. She had done all she could. She had no reason to stay longer. Lifting the napkin parcel from the basket, she laid it on the rumpled blanket.

'I thought – it will save you going to the village.'

He touched the napkin, and shook his head without speaking.

'Consider it thanks for the fish.' She forced herself to her feet, brushing the folds of her habit.

He stood up, moving with a care that clearly signalled pain.

They stood facing one another, barely a foot apart in the cramped space.

'I – thank you,' he said.

'I owe you so much.'

'You owe me nothing.' His fierceness made her jump. Tentatively she offered her hand.

He stared at it then pulled the door wider. 'For the love of God, Melissa.' His voice was hoarse. 'Go.'

# Chapter Eighteen

Leaving the shack, she walked to the yard, trying to ignore the throbbing in her temples, assuming it to be the result of shock at Gabriel's appearance and her own anxiety. But as she stood with Tom, discussing progress on the packet, a sudden dizziness assailed her. Though unpleasant, it was short-lived. Relieved that Tom hadn't noticed anything amiss, and not wanting to make a fuss though she didn't feel at all well, she left very soon after.

Brushing aside Sarah's observation that she looked pale, Melissa changed into a light muslin gown, soothed a scratchy throat and unusual thirst with two glasses of lemonade, and went to the study. She found it hard to concentrate, and by evening the throbbing had grown worse and felt like hammers pounding the inside of her skull. One minute she was dewed with perspiration, the next she felt chilled. Her eyes were hot and her nose had started to run. Unable to face her dinner, she sent apologies to Mrs Betts, and crawled into bed, forced to acknowledge Sarah was right. After priding herself on never being ill, she had caught the summer cold affecting the village.

Barely able to raise her head from the pillow, she spent most of the next three days sleeping. It was only now, forced to stop, that she realised how desperately tired she was and how much the past weeks had taken out of her. She woke only to drink glasses of lemon barley, and eat a few mouthfuls of the light, nourishing dishes Mrs Betts sent up on a tray.

By the fourth day she was feeling much better. While she was in her bath, Sarah changed the bed linen. Then, much refreshed though still weak, she slid between the fresh sheets. As she lay back against a pile of soft pillows encased in crisp, freshly ironed cotton, she thought of Gabriel's bed: a pile of branches stuffed with grass and bracken to raise him a few inches off the earth floor, and two rough blankets. She pictured him lying on it, bruised and bloodstained. Once more she was swept by compassion and anger, but it ebbed before the force of a yearning so strong and powerful she was frightened and sought escape.

'Have I missed anything while I've been ill? Is there any news from the village? '

Sarah glanced up. 'Only that Sal Treen is walking around with a black eye and telling anyone that asks it was Jed what give it to her.'

'She's *proud* of it?' Melissa was astonished.

Sarah rolled her eyes. 'You'd think it was a bunch of flowers. She say 'tis proof Jed love her. I think 'tis a warning to her, and to the men she been fooling with, of what Jed will do if he's pushed too far. Mind, she do look happier than she have for a long time. And why not? She got what she wanted: Jed haven't been out drinking since the night he set on Gabriel.'

'How is Gabriel?' It was perfectly reasonable that she ask. Impossible not to. But no one must know how much it mattered, especially Sarah, who was as sharp as a tack when it came to recognising things people preferred to keep secret. Melissa tugged a loose thread from one of the lace ruffles on her nightgown. 'Has anyone seen him?'

'They all have. John says he was back at work Monday morning just like normal. Got a face all colours of the rainbow, poor soul. But it haven't slowed him down. John says he's working like the devil was after him. He've been with Billy felling big trees on the north side. John have had some job –' She stopped, shook her head, and picked up a crumpled pillowcase which she folded.

'What? What has John had trouble with?'

'No, miss. I never said trouble. But with only one horse, 'tis taking him longer and he been fretting about not getting the logs to where they're to be picked up by the wagons.'

'It's my fault. I should –' Melissa started, but Sarah

wouldn't let her finish

'No such thing, miss. Begging your pardon. You couldn't help being ill.'

'Do the men know why I haven't been down?' Lying back, Melissa closed her eyes.

'I expect John have told them. He asked after you Monday when he came over to pick up his dinner. Mrs Betts told him you wouldn't be going nowhere 'cos you was bad with a cold and couldn't get out the bed. Anyway, Gabriel told John he wasn't to worry 'cos there was enough piled up for a few days yet. Once they had finished the big trees, Billy could carry on by hisself, and he would drive Captain.'

Had Gabriel guessed that whatever he said to John would find its way back to her? Was he reassuring her that everything was continuing as usual?

Sarah gathered up the rest of the bed linen to take downstairs. 'Dear life! I'd forget my head if it wasn't screwed on. Mrs Betts said to ask if you fancy a bit of fish for your dinner.'

Melissa opened her eyes. 'What kind of fish?'

'Plaice. Do you good it would, steamed with a bit of butter and a drop of lemon.' She opened the door, then turned back. 'She'd dearly love to know where it come from. Always fresh caught, it is.'

Melissa stretched, raising her arms above her head. 'Well, it's very kind of someone to go to so much trouble. Tell Mrs Betts I'd love some.'

'I thought you might,' Sarah said drily, closing the door behind her.

The following day Melissa insisted on getting up. But after bathing, dressing and eating her breakfast, a definite wobble in her legs forced her to accept that it would be another couple of days before she was fully recovered. In the meantime she would do as Lobb and Sarah suggested, and sit out on the terrace in the warm sunshine.

'I have no idea why I feel so weak,' she complained to Sarah from beneath the broad-brimmed hat that shaded her face and shielded her eyes from the sun's dazzle.

'We been telling you for weeks you're doing too much,' Sarah scolded. 'But would you listen? That's how you took ill. I reck'n you got off light. Could have been far worse. At least you haven't had the cough. Not like poor Mrs Betts. She got it awful. Making her throat some sore it is.'

'I didn't know. Why didn't you tell me?'

'You had enough to worry about. Anyhow, she's coming on. Just got this nasty old cough.'

'Is she taking anything for it?'

Sarah threw up her hands. 'What isn't she taking? She've tried all sorts. Her sister told her to slice an onion into a basin then put a layer of that there brown sugar between each slice. She was to leave it stand 24 hours then pour off the syrup and take a teaspoonful every whit and while.' Sarah sniffed. 'Well, she been swallowing the stuff since yesterday morning. It haven't stopped her cough, but her breath would strip paint.'

'Oh, the poor woman,' Melissa sympathised. 'I know a better remedy than that. It's one Aunt Lucy sent for my mother when she had a sore throat during that cold, wet spell we had back in the spring. Look, I'll come and –'

'No, miss, you won't, begging your pardon. You're only just getting over the cold. You never had the cough, and the last thing we want is for you to go catching it now, which you would, being as how you're still not properly right. What with Mr Lobb not looking at all hisself, the last place you should go is anywhere near the kitchen. So you tell me, and I'll tell her.'

'All right,' Melissa said reluctantly. 'It's very simple, and it really works. It's just equal quantities of treacle and vinegar in a small covered jar, set near a fire until they are fully dissolved. Then she must give the jar a good shake to make sure it's mixed, and take one teaspoonful three or four times a day.'

'I'll tell her.'

'Will you suggest to Mr Lobb that he takes it as well?'

'I'll tell him, miss, but whether he will or not …' She shrugged. 'You know what men are like. Master was just as bad, God rest him. Sooner suffer than admit there was anything wrong.' She caught herself. 'Still, like I say, you're on the mend now. You just take things easy for another week.'

'Sarah, I can't possibly lie around doing nothing for another week. I dread to think how much has piled up in just these last few days. Listen.' She held up her hand, effectively stopping her maid, whose lips had tightened ominously, from launching into another scolding. 'That must be the postman. It's too early for callers. Will you go and see? I'll stay here a bit longer. It's too nice to go inside just yet.'

Muttering under her breath, Sarah bustled away, returning a few moments later with a fat package from Mr Rogers, and a letter addressed in Aunt Louisa's bold hand. There was still nothing from George. Though Melissa had schooled herself not to waste time on useless speculation, her disappointment was still sharp.

'Thank you, Sarah.' As the maid returned to the house, Melissa opened Mr Rogers' package first. It enclosed a copy of Mr Sibley's agreement to buy the two hunters at the agreed price. A covering letter announced that, if convenient, his grooms would collect them the following day. Checking the date, Melissa realised that meant today. She set it aside as a reminder to go and warn Hocking so he would have time to make the necessary preparations.

Returning to the letter, she smiled, delighted to read that Mr Nankivell had paid for the first ten wagonloads of wood. Part of this money, Mr Rogers informed her, had been used to settle in full the outstanding amounts owed to the tradesmen supplying equipment for the packet, the rest to pay a further instalment off the debt to the bank. He would draw a proportion of his own fee – a detailed account enclosed herewith – from the sum paid by Mr Sibley for the horses. The remainder would be held in his safe for the men's next wages. A receipt signed by Thomas Vincent was also enclosed, showing his loan plus the interest to have been settled in full.

'Continuing frugality will be necessary in the months ahead,' the lawyer warned. 'But I have great pleasure in confirming that, due to your remarkable efforts, all the more astonishing in view of your youth and inexperience in matters of business, all fears of foreclosure may be laid to rest.'

Her fingers tightening on the letter, Melissa tilted her head back, closing her eyes as she lifted her face to the sun's warmth. Her heart swelled with relief and gratitude. She recalled Gabriel's instructions on how she should bargain with Mr Nankivell. Without his advice and his work in the woods – she shivered violently. It didn't bear thinking about. No matter what he said, she owed him more than she could ever repay. Why, then, had he said she owed him nothing?

Heaving a deep sigh, she refolded the letter and put it on the table at her elbow, and broke the seal on her aunt's.

*'My dear Melissa, my woman tells me you have been confined to bed with a cold. This really is most inconvenient as James will only be with us another week before important business necessitates his departure for London.'*

Melissa battled with frustration as she gazed across the terrace. Anyone would think she had contracted a cold specifically to cause maximum disruption to her aunt's plans. With a sigh, she acknowledged that she might have done, had such a thing been possible. Why wouldn't they just leave her alone? She read on.

*'As there is still no news from your brother, and we have no idea how long it may be before a letter is received (if at all) your Uncle Brinley is most concerned for your wellbeing. It was against his better judgement that he allowed you to persuade him you needed no assistance with legal and financial matters after your father died. Nothing will satisfy him but to have you reassure him in person everything is as it should be. I should tell you your Uncle Marcus and Aunt Sophie share our concern. Having discussed the matter, and in the light of your indisposition – from which I understand you are now making a good recovery ...'*

How does she obtain her information? Melissa wondered, more intrigued than angry. Anger cost effort and she had none to spare. After all, Aunt Louisa's bossiness and meddling were something she had lived with all her life. For the most part she had simply ignored them and gone her own way, encouraged by her father and secure in his love. Did they think, because he was no longer here, that she would be more easily manipulated? She picked up the letter once more.

'... we decided that, rather than jeopardise your recovery by asking you to drive over to dine with us, it would be far more sensible if we were to come to you. You will have been sadly short of company, so a happy family dinner must surely lift your spirits. And a quick look at your father's books will set your uncles' minds at rest. Having seen so little of you since your father's death, they have grown increasingly worried that there might be something amiss.'

Crushing the sheet, Melissa drew a deep breath, anger at her aunt's presumption shaded with anxiety. On no account could she allow them to examine her father's books.

'Everything all right?' Sarah asked, setting down a glass of lemon barley on the table at her elbow.

'My aunts and uncles have invited themselves to dinner.' Melissa smoothed out the sheet and frowned at it. 'Next Friday.'

'Ah,' Sarah replied, the brief sound loaded with meaning.

Melissa stood up. 'I'm just going to walk across to the stables and let Hocking know that Mr Sibley's men will be coming for father's two hunters this afternoon.'

'Don't you go overdoing it, mind,' Sarah warned.

'I won't,' Melissa grimaced, and waved Aunt Louisa's letter. 'I'm going to need all my strength.'

A quick look at her father's books. Over her dead body. They had not invested in the yard, only in the packet. They were free to see the ship, and discuss its progress with Tom, any time they wanted. But they hadn't bothered. If they wanted reassurance, she would give it. She could claim with total honesty that all accounts were paid up to date. But examining her father's ledgers and correspondence was out of the question. She would tell them it was all with Mr Rogers, for she suspected it was curiosity, linked with the arrival of James Chenoweth, that had precipitated this sudden rush of familial concern. Though Aunt Louisa had only mentioned his name as an aside, Melissa knew she had not given up. He would be one of the party. This sudden interest in the Tregonning finances was no doubt prompted by a desire to discover the potential size of her dowry.

Despite the heat of the late July sun, Melissa felt a brief chill as she contemplated the gathering. Then she straightened her back. "As you are of age you are free to make your own choices. No one can force you into marriage against your mill." Gabriel's words, his voice, echoed in her mind. Infused with new strength, she inhaled deeply, drawing into her lungs the sweet scents of the summer morning.

She had planned, as soon as she was fully recovered, to return to her work, driving Captain in the woods. Gabriel should be felling trees, not leading the horse that pulled them out. But when, after informing Hocking about the hunters, she told him of her plan, he shook his head.

'Won't be no need, miss. Not now.'

She stared at him. 'What do you mean?'

'Well, with the hunters gone, I'll have more time. So Mr Lobb and me – well, we both thought –'

She stiffened. 'You thought?'

'Well, miss,' he shuffled uncomfortably, 'it isn't right you being down there. I know you didn't 'ave no choice before. But now I aren't so pushed … Look, miss, just think what would happen if Mr Brinley or Mr Marcus got wind of it.'

Or Aunt Louisa. 'You have a point,' she conceded reluctantly. 'Thank you, Hocking.'

'That's all right, miss. We don't want to see you in no trouble.'

With a brief smile, she turned and went back to the house. They meant well, all of them: Lobb, Hocking, Sarah, and Mrs Betts. They truly wanted what was best for her. When would she see him again?

Over the next few days of hot sunshine, hazy horizons, and soft southerly breezes, Melissa regained her appetite, helped make jams and preserves for the winter, and built up her strength by riding Samson around the park. She filled every minute from when she got up until it was time to go to bed, keeping busy, trying not to think, not to yearn.

On the evening of the tenth day after she had fallen ill the clouds formed a mackerel pattern that the setting sun edged with flame. The sky was crystal clear; later that night, a golden ring surrounded the pale quarter moon. The next morning she woke with a start, and closed her eyes again as she remembered today was Friday, the day her relatives were coming to dinner. She forced herself to get out of bed and drew back the curtains. The sky was streaked with mare's tails.

This slowly thickened until, by the time she walked downstairs for breakfast, the entire sky was obscured with a milk-white veil. Through the landing window she glimpsed rooks, blown by the rising wind, wheeling low over the cut fields, before they landed to feed. In the garden, clouds of gnats hovered and spiralled beneath the trees. Scarlet pimpernel and daisies would be closing their petals. All sensed that the hot, dry weather was about to change.

As she took her seat at the dining-room table, Lobb came in. 'A letter for you, miss.' His voice sounded hoarse and nasal, and his nose looked red and sore.

'Thank you, Lobb.' Taking it, she studied him. 'You look as though you should be in bed.'

'I'm all right, miss, thank you.'

'Well, you certainly don't sound all right.' She frowned. 'I didn't hear the postman.'

'He hasn't been yet, miss. This was found outside the back door, weighed down by a stone.'

Melissa looked more closely at the letter. It was grubby and water-stained. Though the ink had run until the address was only just legible, the writing seemed vaguely familiar.

'About the wines for this evening, miss. What would you like –'

She glanced up. 'Lobb, I appreciate your courtesy in asking, but as we are both aware, you know far better than I do what is in the cellar, and what would be most suitable to offer my uncles.'

'May I inquire, miss, the impression you wish to make?'

She thought. 'I want them reassured. In fact, if it were possible to give an impression that everything is not just satisfactory but positively thriving, I should be very grateful.'

'You leave it with me, miss.' He paused, turning his head away, and covering his mouth as he gave a hacking cough.

'Beg pardon, miss. I'm sure I'll be able to find a couple of bottles that will please the most demanding palate.'

'That would be splendid. And Lobb?'

'Miss?'

'When you return to the kitchen, ask Mrs Betts to give you a dose of cough mixture. You are to repeat the dose every two hours. That is not a request.' She smiled, but her tone was firm. 'It's an order. You are far too valuable a member of this household for me to permit you to neglect yourself.'

'Whatever you say, miss,' he replied, wooden-faced. 'What would you like for your breakfast?'

'A dish of fruit, two poached eggs, toast, and coffee, please.'

As the butler left, struggling hard to suppress another bout of coughing, Melissa realised with a slight sense of shock that she was far more at ease giving orders now than she had been even a week ago. She pressed her lips together on an impish smile. She had never imagined herself a tyrant. Sighing, she turned her attention to the letter and, opening it, recognised the writing as Robert's.

As her gaze skimmed the lines, one hand crept upward to mask her open-mouthed shock as she read. He was on parole and, because of over-crowding and illness in the prison, had been moved to a big house on the outskirts of Le Conquet, a small town in the Chanel de Fort between the mainland and the island of Ushant. But, before leaving the prison, he had overheard something that hinted at the presence of a traitor in the British Government. He was willing to break his parole and forfeit the bond money to ensure this information reached the right hands, but he dared not commit it to paper.

*'Melissa, you must ask one of the local fishermen who have contact with free-traders to come to my aid. You may promise them, on my behalf, a large reward in return for picking me up and returning me to Cornwall. But, I beg you, be careful whom you trust. I am permitted to go fishing in a small inlet north of the town. I shall be there between seven and nine o'clock on the last night of July.'*

Realisation struck Melissa like a lightning bolt. That was

tomorrow night.

*'Do not fail me, Melissa. I may be moved again at any time, and will certainly be confined if it becomes known that I have tried to escape. But more important than that, more men will die who might have been saved.'*

Hearing the door open as Lobb returned with a tray, she quickly refolded the letter. Under the butler's watchful eye she ate her breakfast, barely aware of what she was doing and tasting nothing as she wrestled with the thorny task Robert had set her. The men at the yard would know who among the local fishermen were involved in free-trading. But she could hardly just walk up to them and ask.

When she had finished, she nodded to Lobb as he held open the door for her and, as always, asked him to convey her thanks to Mrs Betts.

'With pleasure, miss. She asked me to ask if she might have a quick word, when you have a moment? I believe it concerns the menu for tonight.'

'Of course. I'm just going up to change. Ask her to come to the study in 20 minutes.'

'So I thought, if you was in agreement, miss –' Mrs Betts's plump face was flushed and rosy beneath her frilled cap and her forehead puckered with concentration as she counted on red-knuckled fingers '– julienne soup and salmon with lobster sauce. Then, for an entrée, boiled fowls with bechamel sauce, and braised ham with broad beans, with side dishes of glazed carrots and spinach in a cream sauce. Then for the third course, roast duck with peas, a lobster salad, cherry tart, and cheesecakes, for they is something Mrs Marcus is very partial to. Mrs Louisa do dearly love strawberry cream, so I'll do a couple of they as well.'

'Mrs Betts, you're a marvel.' Melissa smiled. 'It sounds wonderful.'

'Well, I dunno 'bout being no marvel, though 'tis kind of you to say so, miss. Mistress might be away, but that don't mean things isn't as they should be. We don't none of us want no one thinking that just 'cos you're here on your own standards is slipping.'

'Indeed we don't. No one could possibly think that.' Familiar with Mrs Betts's strangled syntax, Melissa was deeply touched by this display of loyalty. All the servants seemed determined to protect her from criticism, even from within the family.

Mrs Betts winced, sucking in her breath through pursed lips.

'Is something wrong?'

'No, miss. 'Tis just my corns. Giving me gyp, they are. Always do when the weather's on the change. Be raining by tomorrow night, you mark my words.'

Melissa walked across to the stables wishing the change might have come sooner, then the dinner party could have been postponed and James would have returned to London without her having to meet him again.

As she rode down through the woods, past the yard, and on to the collection area, she tried to contain her excitement at the prospect of seeing Gabriel again. But it wasn't easy. Her heartbeat had quickened and her nervousness communicated itself to Samson, who jinked sideways, tossing his head. She could trust Gabriel to keep the secret. If he didn't know which fisherman to ask, he would be able to find out with far less risk than if she were to try.

Samson's ears pricked and, lifting his head, he whinnied. The answering squeal from Duchess was closer than she expected, and, a moment later, John appeared at the far side of the clearing. The sturdy mare was dragging part of a huge beech trunk.

'Good morning, John.'

'Morning, miss. Feeling better, are you? Been gone some long time you have.'

'I know.' Her smile was rueful. 'But I'm well again, thank you. I came to see how you've been getting on.'

'Been going on fine, we have.' His face clouded. 'Well, I say that, but see, with me being on me own –'

'It's all right. I understand. You couldn't possibly expect to haul the same number out as we did when there were two of us. Still, as soon as the hunters have gone, Hocking will bring

Captain down for a couple of hours each day.'

'Honest, miss? Mr Hocking's coming down here?'

'Yes. Why?'

An impish grin crossed the boy's face. 'Told me I was making something out of nothing when I said it was hard work, he did. Now he'll see for hisself how easy 'tis. I bet he won't need no rocking come bedtime.'

Melissa hid her smile and held her tongue. She had heard the groom chaffing John, telling the boy he didn't know what hard work was. It sounded easy enough, leading a horse into and out of various parts of the wood. The reality was very different, as Hocking would soon discover.

'How far have Billy and Gabriel got with the felling?'

'Couldn't tell you, miss.' He shrugged. 'I'm still pulling out trees they cut down last week. If you follow the track uplong you'll find Zeb and Chirp. They'll show you which way to go.'

Thanking the boy, Melissa guided Samson along the newly widened path whose surface had been churned to thick, stodgy mud by Duchess's hooves and the dragged logs. Clouds of gnats spiralled beneath the trees. There were no sunbeams slanting through the trees, no dappled shadows. Obscured by the milky-white veil of cloud the sun was a pearly ball. The sound of axes, the creak and rustle of branches being lopped, the eerie groan and shuddering crash of a tree falling all sounded uncannily near in the still air.

She exchanged greetings with Zeb and Chirp, thanked them for their kind enquiries and assured them she was very well, and followed their pointing fingers further into the wood. When she reached Ned and Joe their genuine pleasure as they greeted her, their mumbled confessions to missing her, and frowning concern as to whether she should be out yet, helped extinguish the spark of impatience. Ashamed, she reminded herself how lucky she was to have the respect and goodwill of these men.

'I suppose you'll want to see how they're getting on uplong.' Ned jerked his head toward the deeper part of the woods. 'Best go on foot, miss. 'Tis pretty thick through there, and you're like to get knocked off by low branches, or your 'skirt tore.' He indicated Samson. 'You tie 'un up over there. We'll keep an eye to 'un.'

Dismounting, she did as Ned suggested, and set off toward the rhythmic thuds that echoed on the damp, muggy air. Now she was so close to seeing Gabriel again, her mouth dried, making swallowing difficult, and her heartbeat was so loud it almost drowned the sound of the axes. Her habit kept getting snagged on thorns and twigs. Then, suddenly, there he was, only a few yards away. Stripped to the waist, muscles bunching and stretching as he swung the huge axe; his broad back was dewed with sweat, the stripes a darker pink against pale skin that still bore large patches of green-yellow bruising.

She swallowed, about to call out and let them know she was there, when Gabriel abruptly turned toward her. The thud of the axes and their grunting breaths would have masked any sound she had made. Had he sensed her presence? Her heart leapt as she saw his pleasure, swiftly concealed as he let his axe fall. Murmuring a warning to Billy, who leapt like a startled faun as he spun round, Gabriel scooped up his shirt and pulled it on over his head while he waited, as etiquette demanded, for Melissa to speak first.

'Good morning, Gabriel, Billy. I'm sorry to interrupt.'

'No trouble, miss.' Billy grinned. 'Glad to stop for a minute, and that's the truth. Feeling better, are you?'

'Yes, thank you. I'm quite recovered.'

'Some nasty cold that is.' He clicked his tongue. 'Mother had it. Some bad she was.'

'I'm sorry to hear that.' Melissa addressed Billy, but every cell in her body was aware of Gabriel's gaze. 'I hope she's recovering?'

'Coming on now.' Billy nodded, clutching the axe against his bare chest. 'Tis just the old cough. She isn't getting no sleep. Nor's father, and that's making 'un some itchy.'

'I've got something that will help. I'll send a bottle down. I didn't have the cough myself, but Mrs Betts did. The mixture got rid of it within a couple of days.'

'Be handsome, that would. Thank you kindly, miss. Much obliged, I'm sure.' Billy bobbed a bow. As he turned away and reached for the beer keg, Melissa's eyes met Gabriel's and she bit her lip.

'Good morning, miss.' Only a trace of huskiness remained in his deep voice. As he came toward her, she saw that the bruising on his face had almost disappeared, the swelling around his eye had gone, and the cut above his eyebrow had healed though the scar was still livid. She was suddenly aware of how many days had passed, and how much she had missed him. He still wore a bandage about his throat, but had discarded those from his wrists. Her gaze lingered on the puckered flesh and new skin and she felt a deep, wrenching tug of compassion. *Why* had he been tortured?

'Beg pardon, miss, but I think your skirt is caught ...' Gabriel leant forward and unhooked the material from a spike of blackthorn.

Her breath caught as she felt the heat radiating from his body and smelled the sweet, musky scent of his sweat. 'I must speak with you privately,' she whispered. 'It's urgent.'

Straightening, he took a respectful step backward, giving no sign he had heard her. 'I didn't want to bother you while you were ill, miss, but I think you should see how far we've gone with the felling.'

'Th-thank you.'

'Carry on, shall I, Gabe?' Billy asked, glancing toward the wide, shallow indentation of creamy-white, close-grained heartwood exposed by the axes. 'Tough old bugger, 'e is, begging your pardon, miss. Be another hour at least till he's ready to fall.'

Gabriel nodded. 'I won't be long.'

Following Gabriel, Melissa waited until she heard the thud of Billy's axe, then took Robert's letter from her pocket. As they reached an enormous sycamore, a fallen giant still shrouded in soft green summer foliage, and he turned, she held it out to him.

'This was left outside the back door, weighted down by a stone. It wasn't you who brought it?' When he shook his head, wiping his hands on his breeches before he took it, she gave a tentative smile. 'I didn't think so.' She hesitated. 'I didn't

271

know who else to ask.'

He unfolded it and swiftly scanned the lines, realising immediately that if it was genuine, and she clearly believed it was, then the fewer people who knew about it the better. He looked up, saw the tension in her stance, and anxiety in the way she was rubbing and squeezing her hands. A friend was how she had described Lieutenant Robert Bracey, but her manner suggested a deeper connection. They had known one another for three years. Their families were acquainted.

'I thought perhaps that working with the men you might have heard …' She gestured helplessly. 'It's an open secret that the villagers are involved with the free trade. But it's not something people talk about. If I were to walk into the yard and ask …' She shook her head. 'I was hoping you might know who I could approach?'

Gabriel didn't answer immediately. He read the letter again, his thoughts racing as he considered and discarded options and possibilities. If the information Bracey had obtained was genuine, and he clearly believed it was, then absolute secrecy was vital. That precluded telling any of the villagers. Smuggling spirits and avoiding the Customs boats went on all the time around the Cornish coast. It was risky, but the rewards made it worthwhile. Smuggling sensitive information was deadly dangerous, as he knew to his cost. He had escaped once. He would be insane to go back. What if he was caught? He folded the letter.

'Burn this as soon as you can. Do not speak of it to another living soul. I will bring Lieutenant Bracey back.'

# Chapter Nineteen

Melissa's face paled and Gabriel saw apprehension in her widening eyes. 'You cannot go alone.'

'I'll take Billy. He's –'

'You can't.' She shook her head violently. 'Tansey would never allow it, not unless you told him why. And once Tansey knew, so would the entire village within an hour. Besides, it's a working day tomorrow. Tom will expect to see you at the yard before you go to the woods. I can probably think of a reason for your absence that will satisfy him, but it would be difficult to find something that would require both you and Billy, especially at such short notice. In any case, he's too valuable where he is.' Her gloved fingers fretted with the leather loop on the handle of her riding crop.

Gabriel wiped a forearm across his sweat-beaded forehead and blew a frustrated sigh. 'You're right, unfortunately. I'd prefer to go alone, but I accept it isn't possible. Even with a favourable wind the crossing will take at least 20 hours. I'll need an extra hand to help with the boat. And in the event of any – problems.'

Her quick glance told him she realised how grave such problems might be.

He saw her chin lift and her features set in the expression of determination that had kindled first his admiration and then his love, for it did not entirely hide the fear underneath. As she opened her mouth tension gripped him, for he knew what she was going to say.

'I'll go with you.'

'No.' It was flat, definite.

Her expression did not alter. She met his gaze calmly, and

he wanted to shake her, to hold her close and protect her from the folly of her own courage. He looked away, balling his hands into fists as he fought the impulse.

'You don't have a choice.' She spoke quietly, but with a determination that matched his.

He turned on her, fear for her safety masquerading as anger. 'Do you know how to sail?'

She swallowed, steadfastly holding his gaze even as her face flushed a deep rose. 'No, but I have often been on the water. And you know better than anyone how quickly I learn. Look,' she pleaded, 'the weather is changing. If we are to reach the rendezvous with time to spare, we must go tonight. You said yourself you can't go alone. I'm truly grateful that you will go at all, and I understand about the risks.'

*'Risks?'* He pushed a hand through his hair. 'Melissa, this undertaking will be fraught with danger, which is why –'

'Why I, and no one else, must go with you,' she interrupted, flushing as she defied him. 'You've read the letter: secrecy is vital. But I cannot – I will not – ask someone else to brave dangers I am not prepared to face myself. Now, what will we need? I can bring food but what are we to do about water?'

He gazed at her, fear for her safety battling with wonderment at her courage and sheer practicality. He knew he could trust her, knew also that she trusted him. But what was driving her to do this? How deep were her feelings for Robert Bracey?

If he answered her it was tacit acceptance that she would accompany him. Imagining the hazards they might encounter chilled his blood, and, despite the heat and closeness of the air, his skin tightened as he shivered. But he saw no alternative.

'There's sure to be an empty cask in the yard,' he said abruptly. 'I'll fill it at the spring. Will you bring some brandy? For medicinal purposes?'

She nodded, and the true state of her nerves was revealed in an anxious giggle. 'What shall we do for a boat? You weren't planning to use the one you go fishing in, were you?'

'We may as well put to sea in a bath. No, there's a 28-foot gaff cutter moored in the inlet just round the headland.'

'I know the one you mean. It belongs to Henry Glasson. As he's confined to bed with inflammation of the lungs, he won't need it for a few days.'

'Let's hope no one tells him it's missing.' He studied her, anxiety tightening the muscles at the back of his neck. What was he thinking of, letting her risk her life like this?

'I know what you're thinking,' she said quietly.

'I doubt it.' His brief, hard laugh contained little humour.

'Answer me honestly,' she challenged. 'Is there anyone in the village you trust more than me?'

Her question took him aback. As he hesitated, he saw her relax slightly for she had her answer. She smiled.

'I'm perfectly well, and have recovered my strength. You need have no fears for me, Gabriel. I won't let you down.'

He bent his head, biting his lips to stop himself saying things he had no right to say, words of love that once voiced could not be recalled. The urge to speak, to touch, to tell her everything, was unbearable, and his heartbeat pounded like thunder in his ears.

'Gabriel?'

Pulling himself together, he met her gaze. 'Yes?' It emerged as a harsh rasp.

'I –' She glanced away, her cheeks scarlet. 'What time do you want to leave? My aunts and uncles are coming to dinner tonight, but they do not keep late hours and should be gone by half-past ten.'

'What about Lobb, and your maid? How will you –'

'I'll manage. Don't concern yourself. Is there anything else we'll need?'

'No.' It wasn't true. They would need a compass. With the weather about to change, thick cloud was likely which would make it impossible to steer by the stars. But she had enough to worry about. One way or another he would find anything else they might require. 'I'd like to set off before midnight.'

'Shall I meet you at the boat? I'm familiar with the path down to the inlet.'

'Are you sure you can manage with what you have to carry?'

'Yes.' She sounded strained, and he guessed that, having made her decision and obtained his agreement, she was beginning to recognise the enormity of undertaking. She nodded and turned away. 'We should go. Billy will be starting to wonder why we are taking so long.'

'Melissa?' She looked round, visibly startled at his use of her name.

'Please be careful.' It wasn't what he wanted to say, but as her eyes searched his he feared he had already said too much, that she would see, and know. But she gave a brief nod and, picking up her skirts, set off back toward Billy.

He followed, watching her move with swift, easy strides along the rough path. He had not seen her for ten days. Each morning, not daring to ask, he had eavesdropped shamelessly, desperate for any word about her. He knew better than anyone the weight of the burden she was carrying. Every day he had worked himself to exhaustion, and every night sleep had eluded him as he agonised over what he should do. She was without doubt the most remarkable young woman he had ever met. And he, who had dallied and flirted and amused himself with willing female companions, was deeply in love with a girl he had never even kissed. And never would.

As soon as he had brought Robert Bracey safely back to Cornwall, he must leave. He had stayed too long already, and would not be able to contain his feelings if he remained. Whether in his guise as Gabriel Ennis, or unmasked as Lord Roland Stratton, the consequences for her should their liaison be discovered could only be disastrous. He could not risk it. He loved her too much. Perhaps she would find happiness with Bracey. The very thought was like a thousand blades piercing his soul. But it would be better for her. All he could offer was disgrace.

After leaving Gabriel and Billy, Melissa returned briefly to the house, then rode into Truro where she spent an hour with Mr Rogers signing various receipts and collecting the men's wages. He was deeply perturbed that she had made the journey alone.

'Miss Tregonning, I beg you, for the sake of your safety and my peace of mind, to ensure you bring a footman or groom with you whenever you intend to carry large sums of money.' He waved a silk handkerchief in front of his face and seemed genuinely dismayed. 'I shall send young Webber to accompany you as far as the crossroads.'

'There's really no need.'

'Indeed there is!' He was shocked. 'I have a certain reputation in the town, Miss Tregonning. One it has taken some years to acquire. I do not wish it lost overnight, which it certainly would be should it become known that I had permitted you to leave these premises unaccompanied while carrying a purse of that size. The very idea!'

Melissa had apologised, and drunk the cup of tea Mr Rogers procured for her while the tallest and burliest of his junior clerks was sent to the nearest posting inn to hire a hack for an hour.

Now, as she rode into the yard, she guessed it must be almost four o'clock. Dismounting, she tethered Samson to the iron ring and lifted the leather purse from the bag strapped to her saddle.

'All right, my handsome?' Tom beamed, rubbing his hands as he emerged from the office. 'Better now, are you? Some worried we was. ''Tisn't like you to get ill. Been doing too much, you have.'

'Don't fuss, Tom.' She smiled. 'It was just a cold, nothing serious. I'm fine again now.' In fact, she was already slightly weary. But with the most demanding of the day's activities still some hours ahead, and dinner with her aunts to be got through first, she could not afford even to think of feeling tired.

He studied her. Beneath straggling, bushy brows his eyes were sharp and perceptive. 'Is that so? Well, if you was to ask me, I'd say you was looking –'

'Yes, well, I wasn't asking you. And unless you intend to tell me I look the way I feel, which is in excellent health and spirits, I think we should change the subject.'

He raised his hands, palms out as if to fend her off. 'All right. Beg pardon, I'm sure.' He grinned. 'Here, I got a bit of

277

good news for you. The packet's ready to have her masts stepped and rigged.'

'Tom, that's wonderful! I certainly didn't expect – not yet anyway, especially as you're short-handed.'

The foreman hunched one shoulder, diffident and gratified at her genuine delight. 'Been working like buggery, they have, miss, begging your pardon. Look, I know you probably got a lot on your mind –'

She masked the sudden tight twist of fear behind a wry face. 'You could say so. My aunts and uncles are coming to dinner tonight.'

'They are? What, all of them?' His grimace matched hers. 'Well, you'll want to get on home soon as you done the pay. Best get on, then.' He gestured for her to precede him into the office. 'But what I was going to say: I expect you remember mister always had a bit of a celebration when a new ship's masts was stepped, and seeing how the men have worked so hard, I was thinking –'

'Of course,' Melissa broke in. Focused on the more immediate financial return from the wood, she had put the packet to the back of her mind. 'The tradition must certainly continue. Did you have a day in mind?'

Tom sucked in a breath through his teeth. 'Say the end of next week?'

'I'll send Gilbert down with baskets of food, a couple of barrels of ale, and a bottle or two of brandy for a special toast.'

Tom frowned. 'What do you mean, you'll send Gilbert down? You got to be here.'

'I don't know, Tom. I'm not sure it would be proper, with me still being in mourning, I mean.'

'You listen, my handsome. We're all mourning 'un. But the work have gone on just the same. And if it wasn't for all you been doing, getting they woods paying and all, we wouldn't have nothing to celebrate. Of course you got to come.'

'Well, I appreciate the invitation.' She smiled at him, pulled out the chair and seated herself on the creased, grubby cushion, and unfastened the purse. Above the crunch and clatter of boots she could hear male voices as the men came from the various sheds and outbuildings, from the slips and from inside the hull of the packet. As she read down through the names, checking the hours worked, her gaze lighted on Gabriel's name and her heart gave an extra beat so powerful it took her breath for a moment. Later tonight they would set sail for the other side of the Channel. Right now she must act as if he was just one more employee in Tregonning's boatyard.

Later, back in her bedroom, she realised that she could not simply disappear for two days. It would be too unfair on the servants. Sure she had come to harm, they would feel bound to inform her relations. Within hours, the whole neighbourhood would be ablaze with rumours.

That was precisely what she did not want, nor would Robert. His letter had stressed the importance of absolute secrecy. But there was one person she had no choice but to tell. Without whose help she would not be able to do what she had promised. Stepping out of her habit, she turned to her maid, who was at the closet selecting a dress.

'Sarah, leave that for a minute and come here.' Melissa sat on the edge of the bed and patted the coverlet. 'I want to tell you something. But first, I must ask you to swear a sacred oath that you will not breathe a word of what I tell you to a living soul. Will you do that?'

'Dear life, miss!' Sarah perched on the edge of the bed and smoothed her apron over her lap. 'Whatever is it?'

'First you must swear.'

'I swear on my mother's life. Not a word to a living soul,' Sarah said firmly.

Taking a deep breath, Melissa told her maid of Robert's letter, and how she and Gabriel were leaving that night to bring him back. Sarah's eyes grew enormous and her hands flew to her mouth.

'My dear soul! What if you get caught?'

Suppressing a pang of fear, Melissa waved her anxiety aside. 'The smugglers' boats make regular trips. Very few of them ever get caught.'

'But they're used to it. Still, I suppose Gabriel know what he's doing.' She clasped her hands to her chest. 'Ooh, miss, 'tis some romantic, you being the only one your sweetheart do trust to rescue him from his prison.'

'Oh, but I'm not –' Melissa began, then stopped as she realised the conclusion Sarah had leapt to – that Robert was the object of her affections – offered the perfect, if poignant, cover. For she would never care for Robert the way she cared for Gabriel. While Robert's rescue, and safe delivery of his information, were of great importance, without Gabriel to turn to she would never have attempted it. 'I'm not rescuing him from prison, just from a beach. Not half so dangerous.'

'Look at us! We haven't got time to sit around talking.' Sarah jumped to her feet. 'What time are you going?'

'As soon as the household is settled for the night.'

'What are you going to wear? Won't be easy climbing about on a boat in long skirts.'

'Oh Lord, I never thought.' Grabbing a robe, she pulled it around her. 'Come with me.'

Sarah was bewildered. 'Where we going? Here, you can't –'

'Hush.' Melissa opened the door, took a quick look both ways, then started along the passage. 'We're going to the attic.'

'Whatever for?' Sarah hurried along beside her.

'There are trunks full of my brothers' clothes up there. We should be able to find something that will fit me.'

'You're going to dress up like a man?' Sarah gasped.

'You just said I can't go in long skirts,' Melissa pointed out. 'You're right. I'll be far safer and much more comfortable in breeches.'

'Yes, but what if someone sees you? I don't like it. Truly I don't. 'Tisn't right nor proper.'

'If all goes well, no one *will* see me: only Gabriel and Robert, and they will understand the reason. So stop worrying.' If all goes well. Fear knotted her stomach.

Twenty minutes later, back in her bedroom, Melissa surveyed the clothes laid out on her bed. Rifling through the trunks they had found breeches, coats, waistcoats, shirts, neckcloths, and boots, and brought down several of everything in different sizes. Stripping to her underwear, Melissa began trying on each garment.

'As soon as my aunts and uncles have gone I shall retire to bed,' she said over her shoulder to Sarah, who held a well-cut frock coat of forest green superfine. 'You must tell Lobb and Mrs Betts that I have overstretched myself, and am running a slight fever. It is nothing to cause concern, but sufficient to keep me in bed for the next two days.'

She flung the coat away. 'It's too tight. Let me try that one, the dark blue.' She turned her back and slipped her arms into the sleeves while Sarah held it. 'I have left instructions that I am not to be disturbed. You alone are to attend me, and I desire nothing but hot water to wash with, and cool drinks. You must either drink them yourself, or pour them into the slop bucket. You may tell Mrs Betts I have no appetite, otherwise you will have to eat for me as well. Is everything clear?'

'Yes, miss.' Sarah surveyed her critically. 'That dark blue do look handsome. Here, try the grey breeches.'

Melissa surveyed herself in the long glass. As she turned, her hair swung forward over one shoulder and she grabbed it, meaning to toss it back. 'What shall I do with this?'

'Braid it up, shall I?' Stripping off the coat and breeches and setting them to one side, Melissa sat down on the padded velvet stool in front of her dressing-table. She gazed at her reflection for a moment, at the thick black, wavy tresses that tumbled over her breast almost to her waist. She thought of what might happen if they were sighted by another boat, or boarded. Her height, and male attire, aided her disguise as a man. Long hair, even braided around her head, would instantly betray her. Opening a drawer she took out a pair of scissors and handed them to her maid.

'Cut it off, Sarah.'

Backing away as if she had been offered a live snake, Sarah shook her head. 'Oh, miss, not your beautiful hair. I can't.'

Melissa looked at her through the mirror, and shrugged. 'If you can't then I'll have to do it myself. I'm sure to make a terrible mess. Then my aunts will want to know why I keep a maid who has so little idea of fashion –'

'All right, I'll do it, though it do grieve me something awful.' Sarah took the scissors and studied her mistress with a

281

frown. 'You sure now? 'Cos once it's off, I can't put it on again.'

'I'm sure.'

'Seeing you made up your mind, I can tell you this here new crop is all the rage. Not that I seen it myself, but Mrs Betts have got pictures in the ladies' magazine she do get from her sister. I must say it look handsome. I reckon it would suit you.'

'Then you'd better get a move on, Sarah, or my relations will be arriving before I'm ready.' Sarah picked up a comb, and Melissa closed her eyes against the sting of tears. It was necessary, and she wouldn't waste time regretting it. But she couldn't watch. She didn't look when Sarah told her she had finished cutting, and was just going down to fetch a pitcher of hot water.

'It will look even better when 'tis washed, miss. I won't be more than a minute.' True to her word, she was soon back with the pitcher in one hand and a small jug in the other. 'While I was waiting for the kettle, I beat the yolk of an egg with a pint of spring water and quarter of a pint of vinegar. Bring your curls up lovely, that will. Bend over the basin.'

'Now,' Sarah said, flicking the towel away after rubbing Melissa's head dry. 'I'll just put a comb through it and … There now. What do you think?'

Opening her eyes, Melissa stared at her new image. The short, bubbly curls gave her skull new definition. Feathered onto her forehead and in front of her ears, they made her cheekbones seem higher, her eyes larger. She swallowed.

'It's certainly – different. Thank you, Sarah, you've done a marvellous job.'

'You wait till your aunts see it. Be green with envy they will.'

'Oh my goodness! What's the time?' Melissa leapt up from the stool and, while she finished dressing, she gave Sarah more instructions.

'I shall need enough cold food for two people for two days, and some extra for the journey back as Robert will be with us. You know: bread, cheese, cold meat, pies, tarts, fresh fruit. If Mrs Betts asks, tell her it's for some poor folk in the village who've all been ill and unable to work. I'll give you my father's hip flask. I want you to fill it with brandy. You probably know better than I do where Mr Lobb keeps the kegs that Father didn't pay duty on. If you fill it from one of those, hopefully he won't notice. If there's any lemonade left, I'd really appreciate it if you could put some in a bottle for me.'

'You leave it to me, miss. I'll have it all ready, and no one the wiser.'

Hearing horses' hooves and the rumble of carriage wheels, Melissa slipped her feet into black and white kid slippers and adjusted the white plaited lace at the neck of her black silk gown. Then, taking a deep breath, she hurried out of the door Sarah was holding open for her, and flew downstairs.

Crossing the hall, Lobb glanced up, his normally wooden expression softening momentarily.

Self-consciously, Melissa raised one hand to her bare neck, still unused to her head feeling so light.

'May I say, miss,' the butler murmured as he passed her on his way to the front door, 'that you are looking particularly well tonight.'

'Thank you, Lobb. Just give me a moment.'

She hurried into the drawing room, and when he had seen her seated on one of the chairs near the fireplace, he opened the door. Listening to the sounds of her aunts alighting from the carriage, Melissa breathed slowly and deeply, bracing herself for the ordeal ahead.

She rose from her chair as Lobb announced her guests. Aunt Louisa was, as always, first to enter, swathed in black velvet over black silk. An elaborate turban of black velvet bound with a white bugle bandeau and three black-creped ostrich feathers sat behind a dense bunch of reddish curls at the front of her head. Aunt Sophie followed in black satin and lace. All her hair, except for a fringe of curls on her forehead and in front of her ears, was hidden by a chiffon bandeau decorated with twists of silk, a diamond pin, and several white ostrich plumes. Both kissed the air on either side of Melissa's checks and she responded automatically to their greetings.

'My dear –' Aunt Sophie beamed '– you have the new crop!

It is very becoming, and suits you well.'

'I am inclined to agree,' Aunt Louisa added before Melissa could murmur her thanks for the compliment. 'Perhaps this new effort with your appearance is a sign you have learnt your lesson at last. It is only to be hoped you have not left it too late.' Her gaze darted significantly toward James, who had just entered behind her husband and brother-in- law.

'Surely,' Melissa remonstrated quietly, 'it would not have been seemly for me to exhibit too great an interest upon a first meeting.' Leaving her aunt open-mouthed and speechless, she moved forward to greet her uncles with a curtsy, and offer James her hand.

He bowed over it. 'Dare I hope, Miss Tregonning –' he peeped from under his brows as he straightened, pressing her fingers '– that you are signalling a change of heart?'

Dropping a curtsy, Melissa withdrew her hand, masking her irritation with a demure smile. 'It is my earnest wish that the memories you take back to London will be pleasant ones. As for my heart, sir, that is as it ever was.' Let him make of that what he wished.

The table was a work of art: snowy damask; polished silver; glittering crystal that reflected the flames of the candelabra at either end, and bowls of cream and yellow roses releasing their delicate fragrance into the air. Gilbert served the first course, Lobb poured the wine, and Melissa breathed a sigh of relief as Aunt Louisa held forth on the effects of the cold among her acquaintance.

'My poor dear Charlotte is quite exhausted. Not a wink of sleep she had this past se'ennight.'

'I'm sorry to hear that,' Melissa sympathised. 'Was she very ill?'

'She wasn't ill at all,' Brinley Tregonning answered drily. 'It was her son.'

'Still, she must have been very worried. I imagine that sitting with him while –'

'Oh no,' Louisa interrupted. 'She could not risk infection. Her condition, you know. So she had to surrender him to the attentions of his nurse. A good enough girl in her way, but it's not the same as a mother's care. Poor Charlotte, she was beside herself with anxiety.'

Not trusting herself to comment, Melissa simply nodded in what she hoped was an understanding manner, and signalled Lobb to bring the second course.

Mrs Betts had excelled herself. Marcus and Brinley Tregonning were sufficiently impressed to remark upon the rich succulence of the duck, and announced the lobster salad to be the best they had tasted. Acknowledging their compliments and promising she would tell the cook of their pleasure, Melissa noted the tightening around Aunt Louisa's eyes and mouth and prepared herself for trouble.

'So –' Brinley looked up from his plate '– still no news from George?'

Melissa shook her head. 'Not yet. But I'm sure –'

'I do feel,' Marcus interrupted, 'that we have been somewhat remiss in leaving you to deal with so much by yourself.'

Melissa smiled and shook her head. 'Not at all. No blame can be attached to you. It was my idea. In fact, if you remember, I insisted upon it.' She ignored Aunt Louisa's snort.

'We thought –' Brinley took up the thread '– it would be best to allow you to find out for yourself.'

'Find out what?'

'That you are not as clever as you thought you were,' Louisa answered for him. 'And that headstrong wilfulness such as you have exhibited only leads to trouble.'

'Thank you, my dear,' Brinley said firmly, then turned to Melissa again. 'I imagine you must have discovered exactly how difficult and demanding it is to handle matters of business.'

Moistening her throat with a sip of wine, Melissa set the glass down with care and gave a thoughtful nod. 'I admit it has been time-consuming. I think that is because I lack my father's experience and quick brain. I cannot say it has been *difficult*.'

Aunt Sophie clasped her hands in admiration, while Louisa gasped aloud.

'Such immodesty is not at all becoming, Melissa. What

must James think? '

'While I have no desire to offend my cousin, his good opinion can be of no relevance when it concerns matters of which he is entirely ignorant.' Smiling sweetly, she glanced at each of them in turn, and felt a thrill of pure pleasure at the uncertainty on their faces.

Marcus cleared his throat. 'What about this tree felling? How do the trees reach the timber-yard? Are you paying for haulage?'

Melissa shook her head. 'No. When Mr Nankivell contracted to buy the wood it was part of the agreement that he would use his own wagons to move it.'

'Was it, by Jove?' Marcus exchanged a glance with his brother. 'How does the wood reach the wagons in the first place?'

Relief that she didn't have to admit to, or lie about, her own involvement allowed Melissa to relax a little. 'Since my father's hunters were sold, our groom has had more time, so he and the stable lad spend a few hours each day using two of the farm horses to haul the logs to a collection area where they are picked up by the wagons.'

'Sold the hunters?' Brinley began, but Melissa pretended not to hear him.

'In fact, Mr Rogers has informed me that the estate is showing a healthy profit.' Smiling, she picked up her knife and fork again. As she resumed her meal she noted the glance her uncles exchanged, and guessed they intended to adopt some of what they had heard on their own properties.

'What about the packet?' Brinley enquired.

She set down her cutlery once more, wanting to convey her willingness to answer all their questions. But the fact was that, despite the delicious array of food, she was finding it impossible to eat. Her stomach ached with tension, and each mouthful threatened to choke her.

'The men are making excellent progress. The ship is now fully planked, the decks have been laid, the gun ports cut, and the superstructure is in place. The steering gear, capstans, and deck fittings have been installed, and the masts will be stepped and rigged at the end of next week. After that has been done she'll be fitted out internally, the copper sheathing applied to the hull and ballast shipped. Then, once the hull has been painted and the decorative work done, she'll be ready for launching.' Melissa smiled. 'I have every expectation of my mother being home by then to perform the naming.'

As her two uncles and her Aunt Sophie concurred with this hope, Aunt Louisa signalled Lobb to refill her glass.

'I'm sure James must find such talk of limited interest. Let us change the subject. I must tell you, Melissa, about a party we attended last week. The new fashions are quite alarming. It is not enough that waistbands appear to have risen to the armpits, the dresses are made of such flimsy material that girls are going out in public wearing dresses that are little more than a chemise. It is quite shocking.'

Wondering why this subject should be of any more interest to James Chenoweth than the one so abruptly dispensed with, Melissa merely smiled politely. Taking another sip of her wine, she glanced at him over her glass and caught his expression as he hung on her aunt's words. Evidently she was mistaken.

As her aunt continued to give her opinion of the classic Greek look, Melissa's thoughts strayed to Gabriel and the voyage ahead.

# Chapter Twenty

'You got everything?' Sarah whispered as Melissa stepped out of the back door into the night.

'Yes.' Melissa hefted two baskets packed with food. 'Be sure you lock up as soon as I've gone.' Her coat and breeches were covered by a calf-length driving coat her brother George had left hanging on a peg near the back door.

'You take it,' Sarah had advised. 'Be glad of that you will, 'specially if it do come on to rain.' She had also covered her mistress's cropped curls with a man's soft-brimmed round hat. ''Tis always cold on the water.'

With Sarah's anxious warnings to take care ringing in her ears, Melissa quickly skirted the house. Walking on the grass at the edge of the drive to deaden the sound of her booted feet she made her way to the park, climbed over the fence, and hurried down to the footpath at the bottom.

Turning away from the yard and the village, she followed the path along the lower edge of two fields, then round the mouth of an old stone quarry that had taken a great bite out of the hillside.

Now her eyes had become accustomed to the darkness it was easier to make out the path winding between gorse, bramble bushes, and spiky blackthorn that snagged her coat as if to hold her back. The breeze had strengthened, and she could hear the slap of waves breaking on rocks sheltered by the overhanging cliff.

Above her, an inky sky was sprinkled with stars, and the moon played hide-and-seek behind fast-moving clouds. Her brother's top boots were a size too big and felt awkward, but they were far more suitable. Her own, shorter and laced up the front, would instantly betray her sex. She walked fast, anxious not to be late, knowing they must get away as soon as possible.

The dinner party had seemed endless. By the time it broke up, her nerves were stretched to breaking point. When the last goodbyes had been said and Lobb finally closed the door on the departing carriages, she had felt totally drained.

Waiting for her upstairs, having shrewdly guessed the state her mistress would be in, Sarah had helped her out of her dress, then made her sit down. Bathing her forehead and the back of her neck with lavender water, she had insisted Melissa swallow a small glass of brandy. Quarter of an hour later, much revived, Melissa was pulling on a pair of buckskin breeches.

The neckcloth seemed an added complication, and she was about to toss it aside when an image of Gabriel, his neck swathed in bandages, changed her mind. A length of muslin might prove useful and, easier to wear than to carry; it would be instantly accessible.

The path grew steeper and twisted as it wound down through thorny bushes to the inlet. With both hands full she could not steady herself and kept slipping on the loose earth and stones. Her footsteps sounded deafeningly loud, and beneath the two coats her shirt clung to hot, damp skin.

At last she reached the bottom and picked her way across the rocks toward the boat, held fast by ropes tied to trees that leant out over the water. She couldn't see Gabriel and assumed he must he stowing something in the sail locker in the bow. But as the moon reappeared, illuminating the inside of the boat, Melissa's mouth dried. He wasn't there.

She gazed round, frantic, and whispered his name as loudly as she dared.

'Here.' His voice came from behind her. She whirled round, almost losing her footing. 'I heard someone coming and thought it best to stay out of sight until I was sure ... I didn't recognise you in those clothes.'

'Did you expect me to turn up in a dinner gown and feathered headdress?' She was trembling from a combination of shock and anxiety, and reaction to both.

'No.' Taking the two baskets from her, he jumped down

into the boat. Her anger dissolved as fast as it had erupted, and she flushed. Pulling off the enveloping coat, she rolled it into a bundle and tossed it in after him. Then, grasping his extended hand, she leapt down onto the deck.

'I'm sorry.'

'There's no need to be. I understand perfectly. A difficult evening?'

She nodded, perilously close to tears, and swallowed hard. There was no time for weakness. She cleared her throat. 'What do you want me to do?'

His fingers tightened on hers, and she felt his strength flowing into her. 'Stay there for the moment.' He released her hand. 'I'm going to set the staysail and jib. They'll catch enough wind to get us under way. Then I'll come back and take the tiller while you release the mooring ropes.'

'How do I –?'

'Just pull the short end, the knot will come undone, then you coil the ropes inboard. Do you understand?'

Swallowing, Melissa nodded. A few minutes later, the boat was heading silently out into the creek. 'What shall I do now?' she croaked, her throat dry.

'Take the tiller while I hoist the mainsail.' As she caught her breath, steeling herself to remind him she hadn't sailed before, he continued, 'Just hold her as she is. Remember, you push the tiller away from the direction you want to go. Watch. See? The tide's still high so we don't have to worry about channels or mud banks.'

'Don't tell me,' Melissa groaned. 'There's already far too much I *do* have to worry about.'

Taking her hand he clamped it onto the tiller, his fingers warm and strong over hers. 'When the main goes up, the wind will take her and you'll feel her come alive.' She saw his teeth flash and realised he was smiling. How could he? 'You'll enjoy it, truly. See the headland over to the right? Keep the bow pointing to the left of that. All right?'

Teeth chattering, perspiration clammy on her back, Melissa nodded again. His hand was still holding hers to the tiller, and she dreaded the moment when he would remove it.

'Nervous?' he murmured.

She nodded jerkily, not daring to speak.

'After all you've accomplished in the past two months?' he mocked gently. 'Compared to all that, this is easy. Trust me.' Pressing her fingers lightly he let them go and crossed to the mainmast.

Melissa gripped the tiller as though her life depended upon it. Gabriel loosened the halyard and began hauling on the rope. Blocks squealed; the wooden rings holding the canvas to the mast rattled as the huge sail climbed higher and higher. Even though he had warned her, the boat's sudden surge forward as the wind filled the rectangular sail took her by surprise. She seized the tiller with both hands and peered so hard at the darker shape of the rocky headland that her eyes began to water.

'You all right there?' he called softly. 'If you are, I'll put up the gaff and jib topsails.'

'Yes.' It emerged as a squeak, and she felt an overwhelming urge to giggle as hysteria bubbled in her chest and rose in her throat. She could feel the wind pushing them like a giant hand, and he was putting up more sails.

The breeze snatched at her hat and instinctively she put up a hand to grab it. Pulling it off, she bent awkwardly and stuffed it behind one of the baskets. The tiller pressed against her hand. She grabbed it and pulled. The boat swung.

'Gently, Melissa.' His voice floated back to her.

How could he sound so calm? Biting her lip, she eased the helm up slowly and felt the boat respond. Suddenly, what he'd said made sense, and as she moved the tiller toward her, then away again, feeling the wind press harder on the sails, then more lightly, a smile spread across her face.

She loosened her desperate grip and the painful tension in her shoulders eased. A few minutes later, he was beside her once more. He released another rope to let the boom out a foot or so. As the boat heeled over a few degrees and picked up speed, Melissa lurched sideways, grabbed for a handhold, missed, and stumbled against him.

'I'm s-sorry.' His arm encircled her shoulders to hold her

291

steady while she regained her balance. She blessed the darkness, for her face was on fire. To be held thus was utterly improper, yet it was so comforting. She felt protected and safe.

'My fault, I should have warned you.' He sounded strained. 'The movement takes a bit of getting used to. But the wind is in our favour and we've made a good start. However, there's a long way to go and you've had a tiring day. It would be a good idea for you to get some sleep.'

'I couldn't possibly –'

'You must try.' There was an edge in his voice she didn't understand. Then it occurred to her that he too would need to sleep sometime. That meant her taking charge of the boat. Fear tingled unpleasantly through her limbs. She fought the sick feeling. Once they were far out to sea all she would need to focus on was keeping the boat pointing in the right direction.

'How do you know which way to go?' she blurted.

'I have a compass. I'll show you how to use it later. But now –'

'I know. I should sleep.'

'There are blankets beside the water cask. Wrap them and your coat around you.'

'Where should I –?'

'Try the sail locker. There isn't a lot of room, but you'll be shielded from the wind and spray.'

She looked round blankly. 'There isn't any spray.'

'Not yet. We're still in the Roads.'

Resolutely ignoring images of stormy seas she had watched from the solid safety of the land, she crawled into the cramped space under the half deck and curled up on the spare sails. The smell of wet wood, musty canvas, and seaweed was very strong. Pulling the blankets up, she buried her nose in them, certain she would never sleep.

Though the water hissing against the outside of the hull was only inches away, it was oddly soothing. The blankets smelled faintly of wood smoke and of the salves she had given Gabriel for his wounds. There was a hint of soap and the subtle male musk unique to him. She breathed in deeply, and her mind threw up random images of Gabriel as she had seen him during the past weeks. Her limbs relaxed, grew heavy, and she felt herself drift …

She woke with a start, not knowing where she was, felt panic squeeze her lungs. Then, as all her senses came alive, she heard the creak of timber and snap of canvas, smelled salt and seaweed, felt the dip and rise of the boat beneath her, it all came back with a rush. She sat up, and cracked her skull against the overhead decking. Her muffled cry won a terse "*Quiet!*" from Gabriel.

Pushing aside the blankets and coat, she crawled out of the sail locker and grabbed the boat's upper side. As she clung to it, trying to get her balance, the deck seemed to be sloping more steeply than she remembered. She looked toward the stern, the wind blowing in her face. Licking her lips, she tasted salt. Seeing Gabriel seated in the stern, she realised the dark blue of night had paled to grey. It was almost dawn. She had slept for hours.

Following his pointing finger, Melissa caught her breath. Though they were crossing the wide wake and the ship was already some distance away, it still appeared huge as it creamed through the swell, tiers of taut sails set at an angle on each of the three masts. Dropping to the deck boards, Melissa crawled to the stern, wedged herself in the upper corner beyond his feet, and hugged her knees.

'British warship,' he said softly, 'a two-decker, carrying between 64 and 80 guns. She's probably one of the Channel Squadron. Better if they don't notice us.'

Opening her mouth, Melissa shut it again, working out the answers for herself. Without any lines, nets or bait they could hardly say they were fishing. Nor would it be easy to explain why they were heading for the French coast with her aboard dressed as a man. Turning onto her knees, she started to crawl away.

'Are you all right?'

'I'm hungry,' she whispered over her shoulder. 'And thirsty. Do you want something to eat?'

'I'm starving,' he answered frankly.

They made a meal of bread and cheese, some slices of cold

chicken, and a raspberry tart. Melissa pulled the cork from the stone jar and held it up. 'Would you like some lemonade?'

'After you.' She took several mouthfuls. It was cold, sharp, and deliciously thirst-quenching. She lowered the jar reluctantly, but did not dare drink more. She felt up her sleeve for a handkerchief, realised she didn't have one, and started to pull out one end of the neckcloth to wipe the top.

'Don't concern yourself.' His voice, close to her ear, made her start. 'I could take no ill from you.'

'It seemed only polite.' She glanced up as she handed him the jar. 'Ridiculous, aren't I, in the circumstances.'

About to speak, he stopped and shook his head, then drank deeply before passing it back. When she had replaced the basket, she dipped one end of the neckcloth in a handful of fresh water from the cask and wiped her face and hands. Then, refreshed, she crawled back to the stern. After showing her how to use the compass, he stood up, adjusting his balance to the boat's rise and swoop.

'If you see anything that worries you, call me at once.'

As she nodded, he started toward the bow. Suddenly he stopped and half turned, but instead of looking at her, he scanned the horizon with narrowed eyes. 'By the way, so you may be comfortable, there is a canvas bucket under the seat.'

Despite her blush, she felt a great wave of gratitude. For though she had tried hard not to think about it, the slight discomfort she had noticed on waking had become a matter of increasing urgency, and embarrassment at the prospect of having to ask had increased in proportion to her need. She watched him crawl as far as he could beneath the half-deck. He pulled the blankets over him, leaving only his booted legs exposed.

She thought she heard him groan, and grew tense. But when he didn't move she dismissed it as the creaking of the boat and relaxed again. She waited a little while longer, and when his stillness convinced her he was asleep, she took advantage of the only privacy she was likely to have until she reached home once more.

She checked the compass, then sat back and watched the

eastern sky turn from oyster to pearl and then to primrose. Towering billows of cloud blown by the north-west wind changed from purple-grey to gold then flame as the sun rose in a burst of fiery light that turned the sky apricot, and the sea from black, to blood red, and finally to brass.

Watching the birth of the new day, Melissa shivered at the awesome spectacle, for this was an angry sky. Surrounded by a vast expanse of heaving water, every minute taking them further from land, the boat that had seemed large and strong now felt frighteningly small.

The colours drained away, leaving the sea pewter-coloured beneath sullen grey clouds. Hours passed. The boat ran on. The cloud thickened, dropping lower, and the breeze felt damp as it gathered strength. The swell broke into waves with tiny frills of foam appearing on the crests. Melissa's anxiety increased.

Just when she could bear it no longer, Gabriel woke and came to join her. Seeing him apparently unperturbed, her fear eased. They ate again. Then, at his suggestion, and only too glad to obey, for the strain of her lonely watch and the boat's constant motion were more exhausting than she had expected, she crawled into the sail locker to try and snatch a little more sleep.

When she woke it was late afternoon. She felt guilty at having slept for so long. But when she apologised, Gabriel brushed it aside, tense and disinclined to talk. Assuming they must be drawing close to the French coast, she accepted his silence, and did all she usefully could by preparing another light meal.

As daylight began to fade, she took the helm while Gabriel brought in the gaff and jib topsails. She could see on the horizon a faint dark line.

'Is that land?' He nodded, constantly scanning the ocean around them. Half an hour later, she sensed a new tautness in him.

'What is it?' she asked quietly.

'A boat. It would be better if you're not seen.'

Quickly, she scuttled forward to the sail locker, and sat in the nest of sails and blankets, hugging her knees, gazing toward the stern where Gabriel stood holding the tiller, deliberately visible.

The faint shout made her start. She couldn't catch the words, but guessed whoever was hailing them wanted to know the name of the boat. Cupping one hand to his mouth, Gabriel bellowed back.

After a few moments, another call floated across the water. This time Gabriel answered in more detail. It wasn't only his fluency in the Breton dialect that astonished her; he was acting a part, gesticulating as he shouted, waving one arm as he pretended irritation and self-mocking humour. She wished she knew what was happening.

As if reading her thoughts, Gabriel spoke quietly. 'The boat that hailed us is a Breton free-trader. I told him I'm out of Roscoff, lost my crew in a tavern brawl, and must reach Le Conquet before sunset. He's leading me in.'

Clenching her teeth to stop them chattering as fear made her shiver, Melissa could hear her heart pounding. The silence dragged on, and she couldn't bear it. It was bad enough not being able to see what was happening.

'Gabriel?' She kept her voice low, but his glance told her he had heard. 'Were you involved in – with the free-traders?' When he didn't answer, she hurried on. 'When you were at the house after your accident and you were delirious, you kept talking of smuggling. As you were speaking Breton I just wondered.'

'I have much to thank them for.'

'In what way?'

'Without their willingness to help me – at considerable risk to themselves – I would never have got back to Cornwall. Yes, you could say I am involved. I enjoy a glass of brandy as much as any gentleman who buys a keg knowing full well no duty has been paid on it. Hush now, it won't be long.'

To Melissa, hunched in the sail locker, it seemed like hours. The daylight had almost gone. Thick, low cloud meant there was no sunset.

She tensed as she heard a voice, faint on the gusty wind. But as Gabriel shouted thanks and God speed for a safe return home, she realised that they had reached the rendezvous.

'You can come out now.'

Stiff and cold, she crawled out, her heart beating faster as she moved to stand beside him. They had to find Robert and get away again as quickly as possible. The longer they remained, the greater the danger.

She took the helm, following Gabriel's whispered instructions as he dropped the jib then reefed the main and staysails. The boat slowed as they approached the inlet. Melissa's eyes ached as she strained to see through the gathering dusk. Then she caught a glimpse of something white, waving.

'Gabriel –'

'I see it.'

The gusty breeze made manoeuvring difficult and she concentrated fiercely. Gabriel dropped the mainsail, turned the boat and, reaching down, handed her an oar.

'Keep us off the rocks.'

It wasn't easy. They were in a channel between an island and the mainland, and the combination of wind and tidal currents added a new turbulence to the dark water. Sudden warmth and the taste of salt told her she had bitten her lip.

She heard the splash of footsteps in the shallows and saw Gabriel heave Robert in over the side where he collapsed, panting, on the deck boards.

Obeying the terse whispers, she dropped the oar inboard and pushed the tiller hard over while Gabriel hauled on the mainsheet. A few minutes later, the boat was speeding through the waves heading back out to sea.

Robert had pulled himself into a sitting position in the bottom of the boat, elbows resting on his bent knees, head bowed as he gasped for breath. He hadn't so much as glanced her way since his frantic scramble aboard.

Gabriel came back to take the helm. Standing beside him, Melissa hesitated, oddly reluctant to reveal her identity. Then Robert looked up.

'I'm more grateful than I can say. Will you not tell me your names, so I may know to whom I owe my freedom?'

Kneeling in front of him, Melissa smiled. 'My disguise must be better than I thought,' she said. 'Do you not know me, Robert?'

He stiffened as if turned to stone. Then, rearing back, he scrambled to his feet, clutching the rail.

'*Melissa*? What in the name of God do you think you're doing?'

Startled, she stood up, steadier on her feet than him, having had the long crossing to get used to the boat's movement. 'I'd have thought that was obvious. I came to –'

'I cannot believe you would be so foolhardy.'

'And I am astonished you should show so little gratitude,' she retorted, stung and angry.

'Your hair,' he said suddenly. 'What have you done to your hair?' It had the ring of accusation.

'You've been away too long, Robert. It's all the rage.' If he had not the wit to realise it had been a necessary sacrifice she certainly would not tell him. But the light retort cost her dearly.

'You were wrong to put yourself in such a position. I had assumed you would recruit someone from the yard or the village to come and fetch me.'

'That's exactly what I did. But we are short-handed at the yard; Gabriel couldn't come alone. So I volunteered. Who would you consider more trustworthy than me?'

Darting a glance at Gabriel, Robert took her arm, drawing her away. His voice vibrated with barely suppressed emotion.

'Have you no idea of the damage this will do to your reputation?'

She could not read his expression, for his face was just a paler blur in the darkness. 'Who will ever know, Robert? I will not tell anyone.'

'*I* certainly won't, you may be sure of that.' He lowered his voice, and drew her away still further. 'How do you know you can trust –?' He tipped his head. '

'Gabriel,' she supplied curtly.

'Gabriel, then.' He was impatient. 'How do you know he will remain silent?'

Taking a deep breath as she fought to control her rising

anger, Melissa pulled her arm free and moved back toward the stern, raising her voice so it was audible above the noise of wind and waves.

'I would trust Gabriel Ennis with my life. In fact, I did just that, to come and fetch you.'

Robert stepped closer, his shoulders raised, his posture tense. 'I am mindful of my debt to you, do not think otherwise, but I cannot pretend to admire what you have done. Nor, though they will be glad to see me safe, can I imagine my family will find your behaviour acceptable. Indeed, what of your own family? I cannot believe they gave their blessing to your actions.'

'Perhaps you have chosen to forget,' she said tightly, 'that it was you who swore me to secrecy.' She heard him gasp.

'You mean they have no idea where you are or what you are doing?' He raised one hand abruptly. 'You must forgive me, Melissa, but I find it impossible to discuss this further. The whole business – it is just too shocking.' Holding tight to the rail, he turned his back, leaving Melissa furious and mortified.

Gabriel leant down and murmured in her ear. 'Why don't you tell him about your father's death? It might help.'

'No.' She moved closer to him. 'It's not relevant. Nor will I use it to bid for sympathy.'

'Take the helm,' he said quietly. 'I'm going to put a couple of reefs in the mainsail. We're in for a rough trip back.' It took considerable willpower to mask the disgust he felt for Robert Bracey. It required even more to resist the urge to take Melissa in his arms and reassure her that her erstwhile friend's churlish response in no way diminished her valour.

Robert moved to the other side of the boat, apparently preferring the discomfort of flying spray from the bow wave to standing on the higher side with them.

'The wind's against us, so we'll have to beat back,' Gabriel told Melissa. 'I'm going to bring her about. When I give the word I want you to loose the staysail and jib sheets, then when she's on the other tack you haul in and make fast on the opposite side. All right?'

'Loose these then pull in those?'

'That's right. Ready?'

'Yes.'

'Now.' He loosed the mainsheet. Forward of him, Melissa released the other ropes. The boat came up into the eye of the wind. As the jib and staysail flapped, cracking the loose sheets like whips, Gabriel watched her dart to the other side and start hauling them in. The boom began its swing.

Robert moved away, intent on avoiding the young woman who had risked so much to rescue him. The huge mainsail caught the wind and filled.

Leaning against the tiller to hold the boat on her new course, Gabriel hauled in as fast as he could but the boom swung hard over and hit Robert, knocking him off his feet. He fell, hitting his head against one of the sturdy frames as the boat heeled and leapt forward on the new tack.

Gabriel belayed the mainsheet and Melissa turned, stumbling over Robert's feet.

'Come and take the helm,' Gabriel called. 'He'll be more comfortable in the sail locker.'

'What happened?' she asked as they passed. He could hear her teeth chattering.

'He got in the way of the boom.'

'Is he hurt?'

Crouching, Gabriel lifted the lieutenant's head, felt the lump, and the wetness.

'A bump and a small cut, nothing serious.'

A moment later, a neckcloth landed on the deck beside him. Soaking one end with water from the cask, he wrapped it round the lieutenant's head then dragged him to the sail locker. Turning him onto his side and throwing a blanket over him, Gabriel pulled out the driving coat and stood up. The first spots of rain dashed against his face as he made his way back to the stern.

'Here, stand up and put this on. The rain is starting.'

'What about you?'

'I'm used to it.'

'I'll share it with you. We're in this together.'

'Why don't you go forward? It might be a bit cramped but–'

'No thank you. I'd rather stay here. I prefer your company.'

It was like a knife in his heart. He forced a laugh. 'I don't think you need fear another scolding. When he comes round he'll have a headache. I doubt he'll feel much like talking.'

'I'd still prefer to stay here … That is if you don't mind?'

Her uncertainty tore at him. He wanted nothing more. If this was all there could ever be, then – 'I'm honoured, miss.'

'Don't, Gabriel, please. I don't want things between us to change just because –'

'Take the tiller, and give me the coat.' The rain had begun in earnest. He wedged himself in the corner and held it up for her. As she moved closer, still holding the tiller, his arm encircled her shoulders and he drew the coat around them both. He could feel her shivering against him.

'Listen, Lieutenant Bracey's reaction to your presence on this boat says far more about him than it does about you. But –'

'How could he? Doesn't he realise what we –'

'Hush. Please let me finish. It made me realise how isolated you have become from normal society, and how much I am to blame for that.'

'No! Without you –'

'Melissa, *please*.' He could not have devised a more exquisite torture than holding her close within the sheltering coat, inhaling her fragrance with every breath, her body warm against his. 'You may not like what I am saying, but you cannot deny the truth of it. When Lieutenant Bracey's escape becomes known, as it must, so too will my part in it, He will ensure I am given credit in order to hide your involvement.'

He could not tell her that the resulting interest in him, coming so soon after the gossip among the local men concerning the package of secret papers Janner Stevens was carrying, would increase the risk of his being recognised. A sudden thought struck him. Why had the papers Janner Stevens brought back been addressed to the Foreign Secretary in person?

He had assumed that, as Sir John had given him his assignment, he dealt with all such matters on Lord Grenville's behalf, to distance the Foreign Secretary from any embarrassment should an agent be caught and tortured into revealing that he was acting on behalf of the British Government.

'I believe what Robert cares most about,' Melissa said tightly, and Gabriel felt her slight shudder as she took a deep breath to steady her voice, 'is advancement in his career. Delivering his secret information will bring him to the attention of important people who will be able to help him gain patronage. I understand that.' She turned her head and her curls brushed his lips as she looked up.

'There is nothing wrong in being ambitious. I never wanted more from him than friendship. But it is plain to me that we do not understand one another at all. Not like you and I —'

'Don't,' he whispered. 'You must not. If I am recognised, not only will my own family be reminded of a painful scandal, they will also face the additional shame that I have been living under a different name and identity like some common criminal. That shame would reflect on you.'

'Gabriel, it doesn't matter. I rely on you. You have helped me with so much on the estate.'

'Hush,' he said gently. 'It does matter. Lieutenant Bracey will not wish me to remain in the area, knowing what I do. In fact, I expect him to make it impossible for me to do so. But you know enough now, and are strong enough, to manage by yourself until your brother's safe return.'

'Please, don't leave —'

'I must.' He tried to swallow the tightness in his throat. 'For both our sakes.'

She bent her head. Though she tried hard not to make a sound, he could feel her body jerk as she sobbed. His heart felt as if it was tearing. He lifted his face and the cold rain mingled with his tears.

# Chapter Twenty-one

Melissa was devastated. Though she might indirectly have done something useful for her country by helping Robert escape, it was her actions that had appalled him. Her actions that were the reason Gabriel had decided to leave.

She could not regret helping Robert if having done so would save lives. But she knew she would never marry him, or any man like him – which meant most men, for he was typical of his class and upbringing.

But nor could she tell Gabriel it was him she loved. She could not foist herself on to a man who had never said he loved her. Nor, even if he had, and were willing, could she bring him publicly into her life. He would never be accepted either by her family or by society.

Loving someone meant wanting what was best for them. If he could not stay on at the yard, could no longer be her friend and confidante, then she must keep silent, and let him go.

She wiped her eyes with her fingertips. She knew he was aware of her distress. She knew also that he would not mention it. She wondered if she should move away. But with Robert in the sail locker, where would she go? Besides, he did not appear to be anxious to put distance between them. If, when they reached Cornwall, they must part, then so be it. Until then she wanted to stay close and absorb the feel and smell of him. Memories would be her only comfort in the long, lonely days after he had gone.

She must have dozed, for the next thing she knew Gabriel was murmuring her ear.

'Wake up. It's time to go about again. I'd better take a look at Lieutenant Bracey. I'd have expected him to have regained consciousness by now.'

'Perhaps he did.' She sat up, flexing her shoulders, and stretching her legs out in front of her. The rain had stopped and the night was paling as dawn approached. 'He may have fallen asleep.'

As they worked together to bring the boat onto a new heading, Melissa's eyes filled and, with her back to Gabriel, she dashed the tears away, anxious that he shouldn't see. She had never used tears as a weapon or to get her own way. Even as a child she had recognised it as manipulative. She could not bear him to think that of her.

Agonised that he must leave her, feeling literally torn apart by her valiant efforts to hide her tears, he told her to take the helm. Putting the coat around her shoulders, he moved forward and crouched by the sail locker.

'Lieutenant Bracey? Are you all right?' He shook the blanketed shoulder lightly.

Robert gasped and reared up on one elbow, raising his free hand to his head as he muttered incoherently.

'Try to rest. You're on your way home. I'll fetch you some water.'

Robert's hand shot out and grabbed Gabriel's arm. 'Got to tell him. It's vital. Got to get back. Where am I?'

'You're safe and on your way back to Cornwall.' Janner Stevens had calmed him with those self-same words after his escape and transfer from the Breton boat, when he had woken suddenly and, for one heart-stopping moment, not known where he was. 'In a few hours you'll be able to pass on your information to Sir John.'

'Who? No! Lord Grenville.' Robert slumped down, clasping both hands to his head. 'Lord Grenville, no one else. Must tell Lord Grenville.'

Gabriel sat back on his heels, puzzled. The package Janner Stevens had brought back was for Lord Grenville. Now Lieutenant Bracey would speak only to Lord Grenville. Sir John had given the impression he was acting on Lord Grenville's behalf when sending him to Brittany. But what if he had been acting independently of the government?

What if Lord Grenville had no idea of what his aide had been doing?

Gabriel stiffened as his mind began to race. Sir John had sworn him to secrecy. No one but Sir John had known where he was going and his mission when he got there. Sir John was the only person who had known his true identity, and his assumed name. The truth hit him a hammer-blow: it was Sir John who had betrayed him.

Lunging forward, Gabriel grabbed the lieutenant's jacket, shaking him. 'Bracey! Wake up! Is Sir John Poldyce an agent for the French and a traitor his country? Is that what you have to tell Lord Grenville?'

'No ... Don't know ... What ...?' Robert groaned and lapsed into incoherent mumbling again.

Behind him Melissa cried out. 'What's happening, Gabriel? Is something wrong?'

Returning to the stern, he sat beside her and passed one hand over his face, trying to clear his mind. 'Is your family acquainted with Sir John Poldyce? '

'Not personally. My brother and his elder son were killed in the same battle. I understand his younger son died in a duel –'

'After,' Gabriel corrected absently, absorbed in trying to find answers.

'What?'

'It was after. He wasn't killed during the duel. He died some days later.'

'I didn't know that. Anyway, what about him?'

'One moment.' His thoughts racing, Gabriel laid his hand over hers where it rested on her lap.

He recalled his visit to Sir John. Had the baronet sent him to France expecting that he would swiftly be caught? But not only had he remained undetected, he had done what had been asked of him and obtained the information, sending it back with the free-traders. Too valuable to be ignored, it must have been passed on.

Who would have been given the credit? Had it been known that Lord Roland Stratton was the source of the intelligence, might it not have counted toward his rehabilitation?

Sir John had lost both his sons – the younger at the hands of a man who had not only lived, but had achieved the task he had been set despite immense difficulty and danger. Had he been unable to bear the thought of that man returning to England and once more picking up the threads of his life?

Loath to accept it, Gabriel knew he had his answer. It was Sir John who had betrayed him to the French. Had he also betrayed others? Or had Roland Stratton been the sole focus of his grief and hatred, and object of his revenge? The answer to that lay in the information Lieutenant Bracey would pass to the Foreign Secretary.

Gabriel turned to Melissa and, in the pearly light of the pre-dawn, saw her desperate anxiety. Seizing her hand, he raised it to his lips and watched her eyes widen.

'There is something I must tell you, many things.'

Her face reflected apprehension and dread, and the words tumbled out before she could stop them. 'Don't leave, Gabriel.'

'I won't. That is not unless you wish it.' He watched as shock dissolved into hope and delight.

'Of course I don't wish –'

'Wait. Hear me out.' He hesitated.

'What? What is it?' She studied his face, her own so open and vulnerable he had to drop his glance. He held her hand in both his own.

'You have trusted me with your worries and your confidences. Your friendship has been, and always will be, a precious gift greatly treasured. You know me as no one else has ever known me. It is my greatest wish that you will know me better still. Remember that in the days ahead.'

Melissa gazed at him. Between wild, windblown curls and dark beard stubble, beneath the black brows drawn close as he frowned, she met the piercing intensity of his gaze. Tiny shocks ran along her nerves and her heart skipped a beat.

'I don't understand.'

'I am not – what I appear to be. You know me as Gabriel Ennis. My full name – my real name – is Roland Gabriel Stratton. My father is the Marquis of Lansdowne.'

The shock took her breath away. As the boat pitched on the

306

waves, and she rocked with the motion, he put his arm around her and drew her close.

'*You* are Lord Stratton?'

He nodded.

'Your elder brother is the Earl of Roscarrock?'

He nodded again.

With one hand on the tiller and the other held fast in his, Melissa could only stare at him as she recalled the evening of the anniversary of Adrian's death and her parents' plea to her to give serious consideration to marrying.

In her head she heard again, with terrible clarity, her scathing condemnation of Lord Stratton's character: an opinion she repeated to her aunts. Despite the cold wind and spray her face burned, and she began to laugh.

Helpless and shaking, she buried her face against his shoulder, loving the feel of its warm, solid strength through his coarse shirt.

'I've said something amusing?'

'I'm sorry – it's just that my parents – and then my aunts –' She blushed, shaking her head. Then looked up at him again, suddenly serious.

'Naturally, I had heard about – what happened. I'm afraid I –'

'Drew the same conclusion as everyone else? That I fled rather than face the consequences of my actions? It suited Sir John Poldyce for everyone to think that.'

'Why? Because his son died, not you?'

'Possibly. But also because my apparent flight – upon which my father insisted – offered excellent cover for the secret task he had given me.'

'What secret task?'

'To visit the shipyards at Lorient and Brest and send back information about the ships under repair, and the new ones being built. This information, he told me, was of vital importance to the British Government.'

'That's why you were in France?'

He nodded. 'It took many months to obtain the information, but once I had sent it to Sir John I had served my purpose. It was then he had his revenge on me for the death of his son, betraying me to the French authorities.'

'Oh dear God.' Melissa's face reflected her horror. 'So that was why – the torture – your back – why you wanted to be alone.'

He looked away. 'I had nightmares. I was afraid I might say something, give myself away.'

'That's why you left the house so quickly after your accident?'

He nodded.

'How long have you known Sir John was responsible?'

'About ten minutes. I owe Lieutenant Bracey a debt of gratitude.' He felt her stiffen.

'I hardly think so. He has been remarkably sparing with his thanks.'

'But had he not asked you for help and had you not trusted me I still wouldn't know. Now at last I can assume my real identity once more.' He ran his forefinger lightly down her face. 'Though living as Gabriel Ennis has been a revelation. I cannot regret a moment of it.'

He pulled a face. 'I wonder what Tom will say. And Tansey, Billy, and the others. And Daisy Mitchell. That woman has a heart of gold. What of your family. How will they react do you think?'

As she pictured her aunts, Melissa dissolved into laughter. 'Oh heavens. I wish I could say they would be speechless, but I fear not. They were utterly convinced that my attitudes and behaviour had put me quite beyond the pale. That having been so foolish as to turn down possible suitors I should have welcomed with gratitude given my disadvantages, I would probably die an old maid and could blame no one but myself for that miserable fate. They found my reasons for refusing totally incomprehensible.'

'They would.'

'You understand, though, don't you?' She looked up at him.

'That you would not marry where you could not love? I understand very well. My own father thought me a great deal too fastidious.'

'Even your brother was suggested to me – oh, you will not have heard. He is to be married.'

'My brother is? To whom?'

'Grace Vyvyan.'

'Thank God.'

'You know her, then?'

'Probably, though I cannot call her to mind. It is enough that he is to be married. I hope with all my heart the happy couple produce an heir and a spare as soon as may be possible. But in any event I have no wish to return to Trerose. I have other plans: my own marriage for a start.'

Safe in the haven of his encircling arm, Melissa could at last allow her gaze to roam his beloved face. 'What qualities do you look for in a wife?'

He glanced at her, an upward quirk at one corner of his mouth. 'She must be tall. I have no desire to suffer the permanent backache that must result from constant bending. She must have a lively mind, and care nothing for public opinion –'

'Would you not find that – uncomfortable, in your position?'

'If you refer to my position in society, I can assure you, my dearest girl, that possession of a title permits behaviour which would be deemed totally unacceptable in anyone less fortunate. However, my father is a stickler for honour and duty, and rank carrying responsibility. I have to tell you that as a young man I made truly heroic efforts to ignore those principles.'

'Were you successful?'

'For a while. But such freedom exacts a heavy price. I had friends who thought it worth paying: I did not.' He paused, snagged for a moment by a thorn of memory. 'However, if you refer to my position as a husband, I can tell you to see my wife truly happy I would support her in whatever she wished to do.'

'What of your happiness?'

'That would be my happiness. Though naturally I hope she would take a genuine interest in those things that interest me.'

'Naturally. May I ask what those interests are?'

'Estate management, particularly of woodland. I spent some

time in Switzerland studying forestry. I hope you will permit me to tell you about it sometime. Also shipbuilding, and horses.'

'You are very specific in your requirements, my Lord.'

'Indeed, I cannot settle for less.'

Melissa's heart had begun to thud unevenly. 'Should you find such a woman, what would you say to her?'

His arm tightened. 'I should tell her that she is the woman for whom I have waited, the heart of my heart; that I am hers if she will have me; that I will love her always. I should tell her that a lifetime together will not be long enough, and that when we are very old, I hope to die first, for I could not envisage living without her.'

Scalding tears blurred Melissa's vision, transforming the rising sun into a ball of fragmented golden light. She swallowed hard.

'And then –' Gabriel bent his head so his lips were just above her ear, and despite the roar of the wind, the splash of the water against the hull, and the huskiness in his voice, every word was crystal clear. 'Then I would say Melissa Tregonning, would you do me the very great honour of becoming my wife?'

Looking into his eyes, Melissa pressed one hand to her chest to hold in the great swell of emotion. 'Oh Gabriel.' Her breath caught and the sound that emerged was half joyous laugh, half sob.

'Is that an acceptance? For God's sake, woman, put me out of my misery.'

'Yes.' She nodded. 'Oh yes. Please. Oh *Gabriel*.'

His lips were warm on hers and, as she kissed him back, her heart leapt as tenderness gave way to passion and they clung to one another.

A pain-filled groan brought them back to reality and they broke apart as Robert Bracey crawled out of the sail locker.

'Is there any water aboard?'

As Gabriel released her and she went to fetch food and water for them all, Melissa realised that everything was different now. She was no longer alone, and the future was filled with promise.

# Chapter Twenty-two

Left alone as the butler withdrew, Gabriel folded his length into a deep armchair and passed a hand across his face. It felt strange to be properly shaved and, instead of breeches and a coarse shirt, to be wearing fine, freshly laundered linen and beautifully tailored clothes. Would he ever take such luxuries for granted again? With a brief smile, he recognised that it was very probable.

The hours since their return to Cornwall had passed in a blur. After delivering Melissa safely back to the creek, he had taken Robert Bracey to Malpas. While the lieutenant's shocked and delighted family had fussed over their semi-conscious son, Gabriel had been able to slip away.

Returning the boat to its moorings and hurrying to the stable where Hocking, acting on Melissa's instructions, had Samson tacked up and waiting for him, Gabriel had ridden like the wind to Trerose.

It had taken a while to calm and reassure his anxious parents. At last he had been able to escape to his room where his valet waited with steaming water, soft towels, and a sharp razor. Having registered his opinion of the state of his master's appearance with a clicked tongue and pursed lips, Berryman remained tactfully silent as he went about his business.

Within an hour, Gabriel was ready to leave again. Refusing food and pausing only to swallow a cup of hot coffee, he strode swiftly out to the post-chaise awaiting him on the carriage drive.

Snatching what sleep he could between stops to change the horses, he had, on arriving in London, driven straight to Lord Grenville's town house. The butler had tried to deny him entry, claiming that His Lordship was dining out. But Gabriel knew politicians kept late hours in town. Polite but determined, he gave the butler his card and insisted Lord Grenville be informed that the matter was one of extreme urgency.

A very few minutes later the Foreign Secretary entered the room. Intelligent, upright, a man of strong principles, elected to parliament at the age of 23, his ability was evident from his rapid rise to his present position.

He came forward, his frown clearing as recognition took its place. 'Of course, Stratton.' He offered his hand and Gabriel shook it with relief.

'That business in Switzerland. A valuable service, as I recall.'

'I apologise for the intrusion.'

Gesturing Gabriel to a chair, the Foreign Secretary seated himself, his shrewd, steady gaze never leaving Gabriel's face.

'A matter of great importance?'

Ordering his thoughts, Gabriel related the events of the past year. Beginning with the instructions given to him by Sir John Poldyce, he gave a résumé of his activities and the route by which his information was sent back to England. He experienced à few moments' difficulty describing his arrest and subsequent imprisonment. The Foreign Secretary remained silent, calmly waiting for him to continue. After touching lightly on his escape and passage back to Cornwall, he concluded with the rescue of Robert Bracey.

'Sir, I fear Sir John Poldyce is no friend of this government or of Great Britain.'

The Foreign Secretary's gaze did not waver, but a shadow passed across his features. He inclined his head briefly. 'We owe you a debt of gratitude, Stratton.' He rose to his feet and Gabriel followed suit. 'You must be recompensed.'

'Sir, I seek no reward, except –'

'Except?'

'To clear my name. An official pardon.'

Grenville's eyebrow's rose. 'A pardon? For what?'

'Surely you must be aware that I was involved in a duel with Sir John's younger son?'

Lord Grenville nodded. 'Yes.' He waited, apparently expecting Gabriel to say more.

Gabriel didn't understand. If Lord Grenville knew about the duel, he must know the outcome. 'Sir, I give you my solemn oath I intended a flesh wound only. My aim was true and I caught him high in the shoulder. When I heard – I could not believe – I never expected …'

'Ah. I begin to see.' Grenville was quiet for a moment, his face taut with concentration. 'Stratton, the duel may have hastened young Poldyce's death, but it was not the cause.'

Gabriel stiffened. '*Not* –? But –'

'You have my word on it. The ball was easily removed and the wound was clean. However, the shock to his system – the young man was already in very poor health: a long period of heavy drinking plus other abuses which we need not go into. Had he been fit he would certainly not have died.'

Surprised to feel a sharp pang of sadness for whatever torment had driven Frederick Poldyce to such desperate lengths, Gabriel mentally reeled under the shattering realisation. 'Then – Sir John knew I was innocent.'

Had sending him to France, then betraying him been a spontaneous act of revenge by a proud man broken and half-crazed with grief? Or a brilliantly cunning move by a cold-blooded traitor aware of time running out and determined to cover his tracks? Gabriel did not envy the Foreign Secretary the task of unravelling the truth.

If only his father had not panicked, insisting he flee, this past year would have been very different. But had he not gone to France, he would not have been able to discover and send back information so important to the war effort.

Though he would not have suffered imprisonment and torture, nor, after his escape, would he have sought refuge in a shack in woods belonging to Francis Tregonning. He would not have worked at the boatyard, trusted and befriended by Tom, Walter, Billy, and the others. He would not have met Melissa, the love of his life.

'Lord Stratton –' the Foreign Secretary's face relaxed '– as you were not responsible for Lieutenant Frederick Poldyce's death no charges will ever be laid against you. You leave this room as you entered it, blameless. There is no mark against your name. As for your character, I would that England might find many such as you in her service. I must go now, but would you be good enough to call upon me again? I should like to discuss the possibility of your joining my staff.'

Gabriel bowed. 'You do me a great honour, sir. However, I beg you will excuse me. I am returning to Cornwall immediately.'

The two men walked toward the door. 'What will you do there?' Lord Grenville enquired.

Gabriel grinned. 'Sir, I am going to build ships.'

Three days later, Melissa was standing in the boatyard listening to Tom vent his anger and sadness at Gabriel's disappearance.

'I wondered if he'd been took ill, but I can't see it. Strong as a bull he was. No.' Tom sighed. 'I reckon he've just moved on. Never did let on where he come from. Nobody knew where he lived. Liked his privacy, he did. Well, why not? He didn't do no harm. Worked bleddy hard, I'll say that for 'un. If it hadn't of been for him, we'd have been right in the sh – bad trouble,' he corrected himself hastily. 'Look what he done with that wood? I tell you straight, miss. I never seen nothing like it. Maybe there was things in his past he didn't want spread around. Well, he wouldn't be the first. The men had taken to him too, which I got to say I never expected, what with him being an outsider and all.'

'You're absolutely right, Tom.' Melissa cleared her throat, fighting hard to keep a straight face.

Shaking his head and heaving another gusty sigh, Tom looked up at her. 'So then, miss. You come down for anything partic'lar? Only I can see you aren't dressed for working.'

'Actually, I have some good news I want to share with the men.'

His face brightened. 'Mr George coming home, is he?'

Melissa shook her head. 'No, but I have had a letter from him.'

It had arrived that morning, along with one from her Aunt

314

Lucy saying that her mother was making splendid progress. Reading between the lines, Melissa guessed that the two widowed sisters were enjoying each other's company, and neither wanted the visit to end.

'It was written before Father died. Anyway, the reason we hadn't heard from him for so long was that he'd been ill for several weeks with fever. But he's making a good recovery.'

'Well, now. That's good news all right. It make you think, mind. We'd have been in some stew if Gabe hadn't of turned up when he did. Don't bear thinking about, do it?'

'It certainly doesn't.' Her agreement was heartfelt.

'So if the good news isn't about your brother, what is it about?'

Melissa felt the glow of happiness spread from her toes to the roots of her hair. 'I'm to be married, Tom.'

'You are?' His momentary surprise was banished by a beaming smile. 'That's handsome, that is. Who's the lucky man, then?'

Hearing hooves on the road outside the gate, Melissa turned as a tall man rode into the yard on a glossy chestnut gelding. Swiftly dismounting, he tied the big hunter alongside Samson and strode forward, sweeping off his beaver hat. Dressed in cream breeches, highly polished topboots, and a superbly cut frock coat of pale blue, his jaw was smooth, his black hair cropped to short curls. The livid scar above his brow was already beginning to fade. Seizing her hand, he kissed it.

'My dear, forgive me if I am late.'

Melissa smiled at him, her heart swelling with joy and pride. 'You are not late, I was just telling Tom –'

'What the bleddy hell's all this then?' Tom glared up at Gabriel. 'Where you been? What are you doing dressed up like that? And you got no business making up to Miss Melissa like that. 'Tisn't proper.'

'Tom, it's all right. This is the man I'm going to marry.'

The foreman leant forward, worry deepening the creases in his weathered face. 'Listen, miss, you can't. I got nothing against 'un. You just heard me say he's a good chap and a hard worker, but it wouldn't be fitting.'

Melissa laid her gloved hand on his calloused one. 'Tom, you don't understand. This is Lord Roland Stratton, younger son of the Marquis of Lansdowne.'

Glancing at Gabriel then back to her, the foreman sniffed. 'I like a joke same as any man, but –'

Melissa's smile faded as she realised that her own pleasure and excitement had blinded her to the enormous adjustment she was expecting of the foreman. 'Tom, I'm so sorry. But I promise you it's not a joke. I wouldn't do such a cruel thing.'

'Will you excuse us, my dear?' Taking the foreman's arm, Gabriel steered him into the small office.

Realising after a moment's uncertainty that Gabriel would be able to explain better than she could the circumstances that had brought him here and the necessity for his disguise, Melissa walked to the carpenters' shop.

'Walter, Tansey, would you be kind enough to ask all the men to leave what they're doing for a few minutes and come up to the office. I have some good news to share with you.'

''Course, miss, right away.' Setting down his plane, Tansey knuckled his forehead then turned to his son. 'Go on then, you great lump. Get on down the slip. Joseph, you go to the paint store and the rope shed.'

With a smile of thanks, Melissa retraced her steps, and as there was still no sign of Tom or her betrothed, she went over to Gabriel's horse. As she blew gently into the animal's nostrils, he whickered softly, and bumped her cheek with a muzzle as soft as velvet. Samson swung his head round and snorted. Laughing, Melissa stroked them both while she waited.

As the men began to gather from all over the yard, Tom emerged, rubbing his neck and looking slightly dazed. Behind him, Gabriel smiled as he extended his hand toward her. Melissa heard the rustle of whispers as shock and curiosity followed hard on recognition.

'Dear life!' Tom sucked his teeth. 'I tell you, miss, I never heard the like of it. Some bleddy brave he is.' He gave a crack of laughter. 'Tell you what, I wouldn't mind being a fly on the wall when Jed Laity do find out who he tried to beat up. No disrespect, my Lord.'

Gabriel winced. 'He didn't try, Tom. He succeeded.'

'Only because you were still weak from being dragged through the woods when Captain bolted,' Melissa pointed out.

'Well, miss, if that's what he's like when he's weak, be a rare sight to see 'un strong. No offence, my Lord.'

'None taken, Tom.' He turned to Melissa. 'Ready, my love?'

After announcing her forthcoming marriage, and introducing Gabriel under his full name and title, Melissa handed over to him and stepped back, content to watch and listen as he held the men spellbound. He spoke lightly of the reasons for his disguise. But watching the men's faces, Melissa knew they recognised the reality underlying his deliberately unemotional explanation.

As he moved on and began talking of the yard's potential, and his ideas for expansion, subject, naturally, to Mr George Tregonning's agreement, the mood changed to one of eagerness.

Privately, Melissa and Gabriel had agreed once George knew who she was marrying, and that the estate would be expertly managed, it was virtually certain he would elect to remain in the navy.

Gabriel waved down the applause, whistles, and shouts. 'The demand for ships puts us, and I mean all of us here, in an excellent position to build this yard into something to rival any in Falmouth or Truro. I would remind you that I have first-hand experience of the tricks that go on, so if anyone feels he will not be happy working under my management, he's at liberty to seek employment elsewhere, and will be given a reference reflecting his performance.'

'That's you gone then, Tansey,' someone shouted.

Melissa looked at the tall, handsome figure of the man she adored. Just a few short weeks ago she had dreaded the thought of marriage, seeing it as a cage that would confine her.

Now, knowing herself loved, knowing she could trust Gabriel to care for the business as her father had tried so hard to do, the prospect of being wife to this man, bearing his children, set her trembling in joyful anticipation.

Gabriel finished speaking to loud applause. He turned and held out his hand. 'Time to go home.'

With the men's laughter ringing in her ears, her heart leaping as she met his gaze, Melissa went to him.